MW01012830

The Bunco Club

The Bunco Club

Karen DeWitt

Frame Masters, Ltd.
Matteson, Illinois 60443

The Bunco Club
Text copyright © 2013
Karen L. DeWitt
All Rights Reserved

This novel is a work of fiction. With the exception of historical figures all names, characters, businesses, places, events and incidents are either the products of the author's imagination or used in a fictitious manner. Any resemblance to actual persons, living or dead, or actual events is purely coincidental.

Cover by Karen DeWitt.

Published by Frame Masters, Ltd.
Matteson, Il 60443

ISBN-13:978-0615796680
ISBN-10:0615796680

Printed in the United States of America.

I truly have the best husband and son in the world.

To Bob and Rob with all my love.

Acknowledgements

I have been especially fortunate to have supportive friends and family help me with this book, so bear with me for a few moments, because this is where I get to thank them. I want to give a big shout out to my "Fab Four" who played a huge part prodding my first novel, *The Bunco Club*, out of my brain and into a readable format. My husband and son have endured my blather about this book for nearly a decade, and their input and ideas were invaluable. Therefore, I humbly thank the loves of my life, Bob Barber and Rob DeWitt-Barber for believing in me once again. My dear friend, author, and editing guru, Pat Van West, propelled me from a first-time writer into a committed author. The most excellent and patient proof-reader I could ever ask for, who never tired of re-reading my drafts and offering thoughtful ideas, my brother, Bob DeWitt.

Thanks to the many friends who enthusiastically read my manuscript, encouraged me, and/or patiently listened to my ramblings at one time or another: Jim Differding (along with numerous members of the Differding family), Jim Dickes, Sue Niendorf, Sandy Tedford, Liz Collins, Jenny Zoeterman, Sheryl Feminis, Faye Van Drunen. Alissa Kocer (and her friend Brian), Helen DeWitt, Joan Bauer, Roseann Feldmann, Carol Givens, Jaynel Gilmore, and Lynn Barber. My cousin, D. Patrick Raetzman, has spent decades researching our family's genealogy. I was excited by his discovery and wove it into my story.

And finally, I drew the inspiration for this book from my own Bunco Club. We are also a group of quilters who have shared our hopes and dreams and secrets while rolling the dice for over twenty years. Together our children grew, parents and loved ones passed, we have cried together and for one another, and occasionally even been annoy by each other, but one thing is certain—we set aside one evening every month to be among friends, enjoy too much food but never enough gossip, and toss the dice in the hopes of rolling a Bunco. Sandy Concialdi, Beverly Cooper, Liz Collins, Sandy Kowalski, Sharon Long, Faye Van Dunen, Sandy Tedford, and our substitute extraordinaire, Dorothy Persch—Long live our Bunco Club!

My love and thanks to all of you for your support and encouragement. If I have left anyone out, it's only due to a slippery memory, and not because I didn't value your time and input.

Author's Note

While Bunco is a simple no-skills dice game with few rules, there are many variations to the game. Some clubs add up points to determine a winner, while others keep track of wins and losses, and still others declare a victor by who rolled the most Bunco's. I've heard of clubs passing fuzzy dice between the players when someone throws a Bunco, or a Bunco roller wearing a crown until another member scores a Bunco. There are many Bunco clubs with 8 members and others with 12. Bunco has also become a popular fundraising event for schools and communities where literally hundreds of people play the game together.

My Bunco story may not include fuzzy dice or a favorite theme of your group, and I might reference a different way of keeping score than your club does, but please don't take offense. I wrote my book in the spirit of all Bunco Clubs no matter the rules. After all, the main point of Bunco is a fun night out with a group of good friends.

If anyone is interested in starting a Bunco Club, I encourage you to do so. Your life will surely be much richer.

AUGUST BUNCO - Lettie

Being an artist is a lonely business.
Thank goodness for the Bunco Club.

Chapter 1

"There's just no other way, I *have* to quit Bunco."

The odor of hair dye filled the small salon and caused Lettie's nose to sting, as she scrambled to think of an effective way to stop her friend from quitting their Bunco Club. All she could come up with was a lame cliché, "You've got to be kidding!"

With the rhythmic pat, pat, dab of the tint brush, Beth applied the last cold glop of auburn color to a section of hair near Lettie's scalp. "No, I'm not kidding. I just can't keep up." The chair hissed as Beth stepped on the foot pedal, and looking at the clock, she said, "Forty-five minutes."

"None of us are going to let you quit. We need you." Lettie's jeans squeaked as she slid off the leather seat and turned her back toward Beth. "Unhook this thing. I'm too damn hot." Beth unsnapped the mauve plastic cape and draped it over the basin of the shampoo bowl. "Besides, it's only once a month. Surely you can get out of the house one night a month. What does Tim say?"

"Tim doesn't know. By the time he's had a minute to realize I haven't been going to Bunco anymore, it'll be old news." Beth disappeared behind a corner and came back with a broom and a dustpan.

"Let me do that." Lettie plucked the broom from her friend's hand. The splayed brush dangled a mane of ringlets and curls as evidence of today's business. "You get ready for Rosa." She whisked brunette locks into blonde and gray hair, all the time maneuvering the fuzzy pile toward the trash. A jumble of bristle rollers remained on the counter from Beth's last client. They clung together in a solid mass, their spiky plastic hair grippers acting like Velcro. Lettie leaned on the yellow-handled broom, as she observed Beth tugging them apart with more force than necessary.

"What if we each brought an appetizer when it was your turn to host? I'm sure everyone would be on board to help." Whisking the fluffy mound onto the dustpan, Lettie flipped it into the trash. She tapped the dustpan on the edge of the bin and waited for a response, but Beth did not speak.

It had been Lettie's idea to form the Bunco Club many years ago when the eight women randomly met at a quilting retreat. Beth had shown resistance right away by saying she wasn't very good at playing games, and, besides, she had no idea how to play Bunco. Lettie reassured the group that Bunco was a 'no skills' dice game that took less than a minute to learn. "You have a partner and everyone takes turns rolling the dice. It's so easy it's almost embarrassing. Let's just try it, and then if you don't like it, you can quit." She had explained that they needed eight people, they'd play once a month, and they would take turns hosting. "That way you only get stuck hosting once every eight months. It's really just an excuse for getting together with friends, having fun, and going off our diets for the evening. We'll probably end up spending more time eating and talking, but we can also squeeze in a little hand stitching while we're together."

Beth remained unsure and asked what kinds of supplies were needed. That was the point when Marge jumped in, eager for everyone to commit. "I've subbed a few times for the group at work. It's a ton of fun. All we need are two tables—card tables will do. And enough chairs for all eight of us. We need three dice for each table." She slipped her miniature, ever-present notepad from her hip pocket, and with fingers flying leafed through pages of reminders, lists of suggestions, and random thoughts. Finally, securing an empty page, she sculpted a new list as she spoke. "I'll get the dice, enough pencils for all of us, and I'll make up a stack of scorecards." Drumming the tablet with the tip of the pen, she looked up at everyone and smiled. "Since Lettie volunteered for the first month, and if no one objects, I'll take the next." There was a slight pause while Marge flicked her eyes from woman to woman daring anyone to disagree. "So, we're all in." It was not a question. Beth snapped her gaping mouth shut, and Lettie remembered seeing her shoulders slump.

Tapping the dustpan to release the last bit of clinging hair, Lettie now realized that Beth had probably been struggling with a 'full plate' back then. She cocked her head to one side and forced her voice full of cheer, like a friendly greeter at a department store. "Hey, here's another idea, what if we just skip your turn for a rotation or two? No one would mind, and then you wouldn't have to host for a while. What do you think about that?"

Beth turned to look at Lettie. Unshed tears edged her eyes but did not slide past their rims, a reservoir of liquid sadness. Enveloping her distressed friend into a hug, Lettie guarded against smearing hair dye onto either of them. Over Beth's shoulder she spied the bristly hair rollers where they had been arranged like a fortress on the counter. Large rollers stood tall, protecting smaller ones in the center. The ingredients for the foul smelling perm were laid out alongside perm rods, roller picks, and a dispenser of mini-tissues ready for Rosa's appointment. Rosa, as usual, was late.

"Okay, there's more to this than you're telling me. Sit down. Let's talk." Beth sat under the hood of the propped up beehive hairdryer, while Lettie snagged two Tootsie Rolls from the candy dish. She handed one to Beth. "It's kind of chocolaty, so I'm sure there must be some healing qualities involved." Beth took the offering and smiled for the first time since Lettie had walked into her one-woman, at-home, basement-salon. They twirled the brown and white wrappers off the candy at the same time.

"Yeah, well, I'm afraid there isn't enough chocolate in the world to solve this one." Beth let a long puff of air escape her lungs. "I've thought of every possible angle, and there's just no way out. I simply don't have time anymore. It's the only solution." Popping the medicinal treat into her mouth with finality, she signaled 'discussion over' and twisted the wrapper into a tight wad.

Lettie shoved her hands into the pockets of her jeans and tried a new tack. "Look Beth, the eight of us have been together for seven years. We'd never find anyone to replace you. We don't *want* anyone to replace you. Talk to me. Let us help."

Beth stood and walked to the counter, her back to Lettie. She took one of the prickly rollers out of the center of the fortress and pointed to the void it left behind. "That's where I am. I'm stuck in the middle of a forest of sharp and painful spikes. Every day—all day long. There's nothing but thorns, problems to solve, and pain. I'm trapped, Lettie. I'm so damned trapped, and there's no way out. By quitting Bunco I can get rid of one little, annoying prick. One poke every month that reminds me how screwed up my life is." Beth slammed her palm on the counter, and the rollers jumped in place not daring to topple over, "I just can't take it anymore!" She covered her face with her hands, and a moan broke loose from deep in her throat.

"My dad needs so much help, it gets worse every day." Beth snapped a tissue from the box on the counter and held it to her eyes. Lettie remembered the last time she had seen George Munro was right after his second leg had been amputated from diabetes, and she was surprised when she realized that had been four long years ago. "The twins are getting older, and we always need to get them somewhere. Not to mention that Heather will be a senior in high school this fall, and we've got to get serious about her college search."

Guiding her to the beauty chair, Lettie's inexperienced foot fumbled with the pedal until the chair whooshed downward. "Sit." Lettie noticed it had been a while since Beth had taken the time to touch up her own head of 'blonde' hair, "Keep going."

"There's so much pressure. I go over to Dad's as soon as the kids get off to school in the morning. There's his shopping, groceries to put away, doctors to see, bills to be paid, and then I rush back here for appointments."

Lettie applied soothing pressure on Beth's back by tracing lazy figure eights with her palm. "What can I do?"

Retrieving a shredded tissue from her smock pocket, Beth swiped at her puffy eyes. "There's nothing anyone can do. I've thought it over, and in the big picture quitting Bunco is for the best. At least it's one thing I won't have to stress about."

"Beth, don't. I mean it, you'll regret it."

Lettie saw her friend's face plunge into a fresh wave of sadness. "Before you say anything else—and I know it's only one night a month—but Lettie, my house is a mess. It's a disaster, and I'm so damned ashamed." Beth swept her arm over the small salon. "This is the only room in my whole house that's clean. I thank God it has its own entrance. My kids can't have friends over. There's too much work; we just can't keep up."

In the past Lettie had noticed that Beth's house was a little more than simply cluttered, and she wondered, not for the first time, if Beth or Tim could have hoarding issues. Lettie would be hosting Bunco next week, and she never gave much thought to the condition of her home. She might fret over the 'perfect' menu, but being a single woman with no children, her house was usually just a dusting away from passing one of Marge's white-gloved tests. How sad for Beth to dread having her friends come to play a silly dice game once every eight months. Placing a hand on each of Beth's shoulders, Lettie softened her tone, "We can all help. We'll clean, look after George, whatever you need, but you're *not* quitting Bunco."

Beth slipped off the chair and walked toward the only window in the room. She stood again with her back to Lettie, arms folded over her chest, forehead resting on a pane of glass. "See those flowers? I planted them years ago when I was hopeful, but I don't remember how hopeful even feels anymore. They keep coming up year after year. Stupid things. Even with this damn drought and all that ugly crabgrass choking their roots, they keep holding on. Expecting someday I'll water them—mother them back to what they should be. But I won't. I don't have time. I want to go out there, yank them up by their sorry roots, and put them out of their misery." She paused, but Lettie knew she was not finished. "And my bird feeder—it's empty. It's *always* empty. I look at it every day, and it reminds me of what I can't get done."

Tilting her head all the way back, Beth looked toward the ceiling. Tears pooled in her blue eyes, and when she spun to face Lettie, they raced down her cheeks. "So I'm done with Bunco, and quilting, and anything else that requires my time. I surrender. I give up. I've been beaten."

The bell on the door of the salon tinkled a warning, and Lettie looked up expecting to see Rosa. Instead, Marge walked through the door with her notebook in hand, ready for the day's next challenge. At the sight of Marge, Beth released a feeble groan and sounded like a newborn pup attempting to stand.

"Hey, guys. I wanted to catch Lettie and Rosa to invite them to an impromptu guild meeting for the board members this afternoon." Marge (The Sarge, as the Bunco Club called her behind her back) was the newly elected president of The Legacy Quilt Guild and had a penchant for meetings. "I had hoped..." Marge looked from Beth to Lettie and then back to Beth, "What's going on? What's wrong?"

Before anyone had a chance to speak, the bell jingled on the salon door again. Juggling two lattes, her oversized purse, and a tote bag filled with quilting, Rosa fumbled her way through the door—rear-end first. A cold sweating drink wobbled in its cup-holder as she turned. "Sorry I'm late Beth, but I thought you might like an iced latte." Handing the overloaded tote bag to Marge as though she were an attendant, Rosa said, "Marge, what the hell are you doing here?" Surprise registered on her face when she stared at Beth—nose red, eyes swollen, "My God, Beth, you look like you've taken a beating!"

With Beth's story revealed, Marge made her exit promising to organize efforts to help take some stress out of their friend's overwhelming life. Beth's eyes remained red rimmed, and she occasionally sniffled while conversation floated between the women with the ease of familiarity. With Lettie's hair colored, cut and styled, Beth wound a section of Rosa's dark brown hair around a perm rod. The acrid smell of the caustic chemicals that coaxed Rosa's hair into her signature mass of wavy tendrils knifed through the small salon.

"Okay, I'm outta here." Lettie looked directly at Beth, "See you in three days. Bunco. My house."

Beth nodded, "For now, I'll be there."

"And Rosa, *try* not to be late." Lettie dropped a check for her cut-and-color on the counter and stole a peek in the mirror. "I love this new highlight, Beth. You're amazing." She swiveled her head from side to side and pivoted her chin down, eyes wide, as if critiquing a recently discovered Monet painting. "I'm going to head over to Marge's little board member's meeting at the library and tell her this is the last unannounced gathering I'll be attending. All I can say Rosa is that you're lucky you've got an excuse not to go."

"Yeah, sitting here with this crap stinking and stewing on my head sounds like a picnic compared to another of Marge's meetings."

Lettie surrounded her stylist in a goodbye hug, and Beth whispered, "Thank you for everything. I feel so much better after unloading my troubles on you."

Lettie squeezed her friend tighter, "We'll work it out together. That's what we're here for."

Chapter 2

Clouds of dust billowed behind Lettie's truck, as she drove down the unpaved access road that lead to Calico Meadows. Not for the first time did she marvel at the name her great-grandmother had given the farm almost a hundred and fifty years ago, when she had viewed the land for the first time from a covered wagon. Shades of greens, browns, and mustard yellows formed a patchwork of fields, and on a misty morning or a foggy evening, the haze reminded Lettie of the fluffy cotton batting she used in the middle of her quilts.

The surrounding farmland was no longer owned by her family, but driving through the towering corn and bouncing into ruts and over gravelly bumps gave Lettie a sense of belonging. The rows of corn were planted right up to the road, not an inch of fertile soil was ever wasted. During this time of year the stalks loomed so tall that even in her small truck it felt as if she was driving through a tunnel. Golden corn silk quivered high above her head, and deep green leaves rustled and trembled as her truck hurtled past. The heady aroma of earth and dampness combined caused her to think of her parents, and how, as a little girl, she would bounce around in the bed of her father's truck as they drove down this very road.

The red truck kicked up gravel, and it pinged off its underside as she burst beyond the tunnel of corn into a clearing. Up ahead, on a rare rise of earth, her home and studio came into sight. Heat waves hula-danced off the metal roofs and shimmied skyward. One final bump over a deep furrow that had developed during the last soupy rainstorm and Lettie passed her 1969 green Mustang convertible, the barn that housed her extensive studio, and pulled to a stop near the back door of her home. The afternoon lacked the heavy layer of atmospheric haze that typically prevailed in

Illinois during the summer, and she could see 40 miles to the north. The tips of Chicago's tall buildings were visible from this vantage point on her farm. Over the drone of late summer cicadas she heard a thin, faraway ripple of barking from the neighboring dog. The farm was nearly a mile away, but sound skimmed over the thick lush fields.

How she loved it here.

Having her hair colored today, dealing with Beth's unexpected confession to quit Bunco, and an unscheduled meeting with Marge had seriously cut into Lettie's studio time. Artists can tell when they've been away from their work for too long; it's like a blue-black storm cloud invading the brightness of their day.

Inside her farmhouse Lettie fumbled through the fridge until she found a plastic bag of leftover pizza. She tossed it into the basket that was left by the door to carry things back and forth to her studio. A slice of almond pound cake made its way into the container, she added a flashlight, and closed the lid.

Her farm dog lumbered toward her nuzzling for a scratch, as she made her way toward the barn that housed her studio. "Good boy. There's my Picasso." More and more gray crept into his black-as-coal-fur every day, calling to mind that her faithful German shepherd watchdog was aging. She set the basket on the grassy farmyard lawn and bent to wrap him in a hug. He smelled of pond water, hay, and unwashed dog fur. "What have you been up to?" Picasso was her faithful guard dog—too proud to ever go indoors except for the coldest winter nights, when he would reluctantly enter the garage through the doggy door and hunker down next to the front left tire of her Mustang.

Sunlight poured through the bank of southern facing windows that had been installed when Lettie renovated the old barn into her fiber art studio. After stowing her basket of provisions, she stood inside the studio door, hands on hips.

By simply walking into this massive space, Lettie was able to flip a switch in her brain and turn off the outer world. It was an isolated cocoon where her mind was free to plunge full force into its creative mode. Traditional looms of various sizes, golden wood gleaming, added a sculptural feel to the room. Colorful threads and yarns dangled throughout the studio dancing in a gentle draft as if to their own tune. Each loom displayed a different stage of a work-in-progress. Spools, shuttles, yarns, fibers, ribbons and strips of torn fabric were organized by a unique method of built-in shelving with baskets.

Clumps of colorful wool sat on a drying screen ready for inspection. They reminded Lettie of suspects in a police lineup—waiting for their true colors to be exposed. She squeeze-tested several tufts and determined they were dry enough to card. Carding is a soothing rhythmic job that she often did when she was tired. Later tonight would be the perfect time for carding her newly dyed wool.

22

Chapter 3

Late the next afternoon Lettie simply couldn't put off thinking about hosting Bunco for one more minute. The heavy wooden door on her studio barn squealed and bumped as she tugged it shut. In two days the other seven women from the Bunco Club would descend on her house, like a swat team ready for a night of food and fun. Picasso fell into step next to her. The old German shepherd turned playful when she tossed a twig for him to fetch. He pranced back to her with his own version of doggy-swagger and offered up the twig, hopeful to keep the game going. Shielding her eyes from the late afternoon sun, Lettie took a moment to gaze across the endless fields.

With a complaint from the hinge on the screen door, she entered her home. Picasso's claws clicked on the wooden boards. He found a comfortable spot next to a container of bright orange mums that lit up a corner of the porch. His eyes closed, and he snuffled into a contented position.

Complimenting tastes and smells in the kitchen gave Lettie almost as much pleasure as working with color and texture in her studio. The perfect Bunco menu for a hot summer evening took only half an hour to coax onto the 'blank canvas' of her legal pad. She fussed over ingredients, scribbled ideas, crossed appetizers off her list, and added others. By the time she had finished, the golden oak tabletop in her kitchen was littered with cookbooks open to savory favorites, tattered recipe cards stained from ingredients, and several printouts from Pinterest and Recipe.com.

Lettie chose her menu with the soaring temperatures in mind. High humidity was predicted with the promise that thermometers would reach in excess of 100 degrees. A heat advisory would be in effect, and Lettie didn't want to fire up her oven on a blistering hot day, when eight women were due to play a riotous game of Bunco at her house. With a zipping sound, she tore the final draft of her Bunco menu from the bright-yellow tablet and announced out loud, "Okay, girls. This should fill us up for the night." She placed her handwritten menu and itemized shopping list under the "I 'heart' quilting" magnet on her refrigerator.

MENU

BLT Dip with toast points
Egg Salad Spread on crackers
Fresh Fruit & Cheese   Cucumber Sandwiches
Chicken Salad on Croissant   Veggies and Dip
Pizza Dip (cold) w/ taco chips   Ham Roll-Ups
Pop - water – lemonade - wine

M & M's - chocolate covered raisins - mini Snickers
Popcorn

Barbs Ice Cream Sandwich Dessert*
Earl Grey Decaf
*recipe at back of book

Chapter 4

The back wheel of the grocery cart shimmied and thwacked, and Lettie had to pull hard to the right to keep the troublesome thing going straight. She wondered why she always managed to get the cart that pitched sideways down the aisle with a mind of its own. Wanting to double-check that she had all the items on her list, she jostled the cart to a quiet corner away from other shoppers, near the noodles, pastas, and sauces.

Lost in a world of food frenzy verification, a group of noisy teens pushed past her and gave her cart a hard bump. Lettie sensed the push was intentional. No one apologized. The girls giggled and covered their mouths with their hands, as the boys nudged and jabbed at each other. One boy twirled and hiked up his sagging pants, his eyes were as defiant as Lettie had ever seen them. Ricardo Mitchell—Rosa's youngest son, Ricky.

"Come on, Mitchell." A nameless baby thug reached out and yanked him back into the pack, like a possessive dog with a toy.

The knot of squirmy young people left behind a strong odor of cigarette smoke, and as they moved toward the end of the aisle, Lettie heard a noisy crash with the sharp clatter of glass breaking. Ricky Mitchell trailed his fist across a shelf of olives, pickles and relishes, leaving behind a dripping, oozy, dangerous mess on the floor. He turned to look at Lettie, smiled at her, and then took a few steps backwards before spinning around to catch up to the others.

She would wring his neck if she could catch up with him.

Ricky was her godson. A precious gift that her dear friend had trusted her with nearly fourteen years ago, and Lettie took the honor very seriously. Just as she had tip-toed through the obstacle course of broken jars and slippery vegetables, the horde of unruly teens burst through the exit door and ran away. Heading back to her abandoned grocery cart, Lettie spotted several dozen egg crates oozing glop and broken shells, a smashed watermelon in the frozen food section, and box after box of cereal sprinkled in front of the dairy case. Store employees bustled through the market trailing mops and pushing buckets of sudsy water on wheels. Other workers placed orange safety cones around gooey liquids that threatened to spread across the floor and become dangerous to customers.

Lettie went through the checkout lane in a mind-numbing daze. She was unable to process the contrast of the little boy she held so close to her heart with the vandal she had just locked eyes with in aisle three. As she hefted the final bag into the back of her Mustang, she knew she'd have to tell Rosa what she had witnessed. Ricky had become a fourteen-year-old handful. The child that was always in trouble and the trouble that Rosa *never* talked about. She had blinders on when it came to her youngest son. Since Rosa was so sensitive about Ricky, Lettie wouldn't embarrass her in front of the Bunco Club, yet she also felt it was not something to be discussed over the phone. By the time she turned onto the lane that led to her farmhouse, she had a simple plan. She would get Rosa to stay behind after Bunco and talk with her face-to-face. She felt peace return as the end-of-the-day sunlight sluiced through the fields transforming filaments of corn silk into a sea of glistening gold.

Chapter 5

A fierce heat wave had settled into the Illinois basin, and Lettie's air conditioner was having trouble keeping up with the extreme temperature and humidity. Her neck felt cooler as she pulled her shoulder length hair into a ponytail. The clock on her microwave flashed 6:30—only an hour before the Bunco Club would start to arrive fast and furious and hungry. The door on her trusty under-the-counter CD player hummed open, and she inserted the last disc of the audiobook she had been listening to. With a little luck, she could finish the mystery while she assembled the decadent ice cream dessert.

Sliding a thumbnail under the cold paper covering, she began to unwrap dozens of mini-ice cream sandwiches and assemble them inside a large glass cake pan. The overwhelming smell from the chocolate wafers compelled Lettie to gulp down one of the cold snacks. She sealed the deal by licking the wrapper clean. Over the layer of frozen treats she sculpted a heavy slab of Cool Whip followed by splashes and squirts of various toppings until it resembled a Jackson Pollock painting.

Making a mental checklist of her last-minute duties, Lettie spoke them out loud to help reinforce them in her mind. "Set up the card tables and chairs." A final spurt of caramel sputtered and sprayed from the nozzle, and Lettie shook the bottle to squeeze the last bit of golden brown onto the center layer of her cold creation.

"Sharpen pencils and get scratch paper. Fill the candy dishes."

More whipped topping was slathered across the surface, and with one fluid motion from her wrist, Lettie formed mini peaks of snowcapped sweetness. Artful swirls from a squeeze bottle of chocolate traced lacy trails over the mountains, and the whole concoction was generously sprinkled with salty chopped nuts. Voila! At least eight million calories per serving.

Juggling the sweet treat into the freezer Lettie reminded herself, "Light the candles. You *always* forget to light the candles." Her CD player clicked to a stop, and she realized she hadn't been paying attention to the audiobook. She sighed, "Oh well, tomorrow. When this is all behind me."

As Lettie wrung water from a yellow sponge and swiped it across the kitchen counter, she heard Nancy call, "Hallllooooo." The heavy door that stood as a barrier between the semi-cool inside and the intense heat outside was closed with a thud as Nancy let herself in.

Lettie flipped a dishtowel over her shoulder and snagged several M&M's from an open bag on her way to greet the first guest.

"I'm sorry I'm early, but my last kid didn't show. I figured by the time I would go all the way home and then drive out here, I'd be late." Nancy caught her outdated purse as it slipped off her shoulder and placed her quilting tote on the sofa. Lettie noted, not for the first time, that Nancy wore one of her traditional unbecoming and old-fashioned outfits—large, colorful, horizontal stripes on an over-sized baggy blouse that did nothing but highlight her extra weight. At thirty-eight years old, Nancy was the other 'never married' woman of the group. Her dishwater-gray/blonde hair was pulled into an unflattering ponytail at the nape of her neck and bound with a faded and frayed beige scrunchie. It was as though Nancy was trying to hide something behind enormous tops and unflattering outfits.

"I'm glad you're early." Lettie nodded in the direction of the kitchen as she popped a leg open on a card table. "Sit at the counter and keep me company while I finish setting up. I'm sure you could use a cold drink."

"I can help with something. What needs to be done?"

Balancing the table on end and flipping another leg out with a sharp snap, Lettie said, "Would you mind loading up those candy dishes? It doesn't matter what you put where, as long as there's at least one bowl of chocolate at each table." She set the table upright. "When you're done, could you light the candles?"

"Whatever you need." Nancy's gray eyes were magnified behind thick-rimmed glasses as she poured M&M's into a crystal candy dish. The colorful discs tinkled and bounced into the cut-glass bowl. Lettie snatched discreet glances at her long-time friend, as they chatted and worked. Unable to pinpoint exactly what was different about her, Lettie sensed a stiffness—no, a falseness, to Nancy's behavior. Overly cheerful with a touch of anxiety—edgy.

With tables, chairs and supplies in place, the next order of business was to attend to the feast. "Let's get the food set out. They should be here any minute." Lettie reached inside the fridge and produced a plate of croissants stuffed with chicken salad in one hand and a platter of fresh fruit with cheeses in the other. "Would you mind filling the ice bucket?"

Subtle scents of onion, bacon, and fresh fruits mingled and wafted through the kitchen, as Lettie brought forth the bounty she had prepared. "Ooo, is this the BLT dip?" Nancy asked. "I just love it!" She plunged a crisp toast triangle into the succulent blend of bacon and mayonnaise, wolfed it down, and reached for another.

Lettie heard the door thud again, and Helen and Nedra entered complaining about the heat. They deposited swollen tote bags and purses on the sofa next to Nancy's belongings. The bags bulged with quilts and projects in various stages of completion; ready for the traditional after-Bunco show-and-tell.

"Thank God you've got the air cranked. I'm about to combust!" Helen hugged Lettie, "What's on the menu? I'm starved." Helen was a hugger, and Nancy received the next embrace. "I really need a night out." She snatched a golden cracker, and with the quickness of a bricklayer spreading mortar, slathered it with Lettie's 'special' egg salad. She bit into it, shut her eyes, and purred approval.

"Before Marge gets here and accuses me of breaking one of her many Bunco rules by politicking…" Nedra put her hand up as if she were examining her red, manicured fingernails, "*I* spent the day touring the Obama home in Hyde Park. Michelle gave us the tour, and we had a short Q & A with her afterward."

"Holy cow, Nedra—that's so cool!" Nancy said with her mouth full.

"Screw Marge! It's not politicking *or* campaigning—it's work, and it's exciting for the rest of us to hear about it." Lettie had about an ounce of patience left for Marge.

"What was she like? Will you be writing the story for *Excel*?"

"Nah, I'm just researching and collecting facts for the magazine. An extra set of eyes—you know. But Michelle was cordial and very friendly. I was rather awestruck and still don't believe I was there." She nibbled the crunchy appetizer and delicately dabbed the corners of her lips with the edge of a napkin. "Someday I really would like to express my own voice at the magazine. But if I'm being completely honest, I don't think I'm ready yet—at least not with a story this big."

Marge entered Lettie's home and joined the women around the food, as she slipped her notepad into the back pocket of her jeans. "Ready for what?" she asked, but it was clear she didn't really want an answer as she kept talking. "Has anyone heard a weather forecast? It looks like a storm could be blowing in." Picking up one of the flaky croissants filled to bursting with chicken salad, she said, "I hope you didn't put as much mayo in here as you usually do, Lettie. You know how it makes my stomach upset." She slid the pizza dip closer to the taco chips and put the paper plates in front of the napkins. "Plates must come first," she said under her breath.

Nedra rolled her eyes, Helen shook her head, and Nancy, oblivious as always, just smiled. On her way to a western facing window, Lettie wove past Nedra and said so only she could hear, "God help me, I swear I'm going to rip her head off one of these days." Pushing aside a curtain to see a very distant bank of angry dark clouds mounting an attack on the perfect blue sky, Lettie thought perhaps she should turn on a radio or TV and monitor the weather.

The women filled their plates with mounds of veggies and fruits, towers of chips, and scoops of Lettie's homemade delicacies, Nedra asked, "What's up with Beth and her dad? Rosa told me she almost quit Bunco."

"She's pretty overloaded right now," Marge said.

The sound that came from the radio was nothing but noisy static and crackle. Pushing the 'off' button, Lettie said, "There are actually all kinds of ways we can help. Marge and I have visited George, so she can have a few minutes to herself. He told me he'd like to move to Heritage Manor, but that Beth isn't having it." She looked at Helen whose husband was the manager there, "I was thinking maybe you could set up a tour with Ben, he could show her around and answer any questions."

Helen bobbed her head, "I'll talk to Ben tonight about that."

The Sarge hauled her notebook from a pocket, flipped to a page flagged by a sticky-note, and made a check-mark. "Nancy, maybe you could have some input on what colleges Heather might look into. Beth told me she doesn't know where to start."

"Absolutely, and I can also visit George. Heck, maybe we can even go on a little field trip."

Within minutes Phree and Beth came through the door accompanied by a low rumble of thunder. Phree had a quilt draped over her arm, and Lettie remembered that she had completed the crazy quilt several years ago. "You guys aren't going to believe what happened last night." She flapped the quilt open, and right in the center of a delicate floral fabric was a huge burn mark. "I was using this as a summer table cloth, and I had a candle burning in a glass jar. Then pop! The jar broke, more like exploded, and in seconds the quilt was in flames."

"Thank God you caught it before it spread."

"It scared the crap out of me. I'm just happy I was in the room when it happened." Phree released the quilt to puddle on the floor and put her hands on her hips. "But what do I do with this stinky thing now? It smells awful, and it looks worse. Between the burn and the wax I think it's ruined—plain and simple."

Helen knelt on the floorboards of the farmhouse and examined the scorched quilt. Using her little finger to flick at the charred section and tattered edges of fabric, she stayed bent over the quilt, examining the fibers, deep in thought. Flipping to the back of the quilt, she checked to see if it had burned through. "How about appliquéing something over the burn? I'm thinking of a pattern we have at the Quilter's Closet that might do the trick."

"That's an excellent idea!" Phree said. "Do you really think we can save it?"

Helen refolded the quilt and hugged it to her middle. "I work tomorrow morning. Come by any time after 10:00. Can I take it with me? I'll have some ideas ready when you get there."

"Be my guest. It almost makes me sick to look at it like that."

The feeding frenzy was winding down, and it was no surprise that Rosa blew in late. "Sorry everyone. It was Ricky—long story. Let's get started. I can eat while we play." Lettie narrowed her eyes and scrutinized her best friend.

Could this be about what she had witnessed in the grocery store yesterday? "Oh, by the way, it really looks like a storm is headed this way. Anyone hear the forecast?" Rosa turned her back on Lettie, and went to the counter to pour an oversized glass of wine and load up a plate with food.

Following several moments of coaxing and prodding, Lettie managed to get the women seated. She took the last chair across from Rosa who was all big smiles and full of phony cheerfulness. As much as Lettie loved Rosa like the sister she never had, she knew those smiles were fake to the core. Raising her voice above the chit-chat and laughter, Lettie called out, "Someone ring the bell."

With the speed of a starving person placed in front of a free ham and cheese sandwich, Rosa snatched up the dice to claim the first roll at their table. The ivory colored cubes click-clacked against each other. "I'm warning everyone, I'm feeling lots of Buncos tonight." She tossed them in the center of the table—six, three, two.

Lettie teased her partner, "Rosa, don't forget we're looking for ones this time."

"Crap. Sorry Lettie."

Nancy swooped in for the next turn. Marge was her partner and scorekeeper for this round and had long ago announced that *she* would be the 'forever' scorekeeper no matter who was her partner. One, one, three. "Excellent," Marge said and totaled their points. "Keep it up." Nancy rolled until she had tallied an additional five points for her team. When no more ones appeared on the dice, she pushed the cubes in front of Lettie.

Lettie rubbed the dice between her palms and felt them slide from her hand. Six, four, one. "Way to go," Rosa said. "Shake those bones."

Screams and whoops came from the other table. Helen and Beth were high-fiving each other. Beth had thrown three ones, the first Bunco of the night. Game on!

Throughout the evening Lettie's antennae picked up that Nancy was quieter than usual, and because partners change after every round in Bunco, they were seated at the same table toward the end of the game. "So how's it going, Nancy? Anything new?" Lettie rolled, and the dice clicked out two sixes. She rolled again.

"Well, kind of." Two more sixes. Nancy kept tally of their score and urged her partner on, "Good one."

The dice spilled from Lettie's hand. "Well, kind of like what?"

"Like I got an interesting email from an old boyfriend."

Lettie stopped rolling. The whole table stared at her as if she had gone mad. The first rule of Bunco was that no one *ever, ever* slows the pace.

"Keep going," Phree and Nedra shouted at the same time.

"Well, we'll be discussing *this* over dessert." Lettie said. Thunder rumbled a long loud warning, and amid happy squeals from the head table the dice trickled into three sixes—the final Bunco of the night. And with that, the game was over.

The tea kettle whistled, and Nedra assisted Lettie by preparing two pots of Earl Grey decaf. With the aroma of hot tea steeping under cozies filling the kitchen, the women gathered around the frosty glass cake pan and stared at the chilled dessert as though it was topped with the Hope Diamond. Lettie cut generous portions of the cold treat so she wouldn't have the temptation of too many leftovers in the days ahead, and each woman claimed a plate heaped with the ice cream dessert. There followed a rare moment when no one spoke as they all savored their first taste. The heavy roar of thunder sounded directly above them, and Lettie heard the wind pick up.

"This is beyond excellent."

"Lettie, you outdid yourself."

"Why, thank you ladies." Lettie bowed her head slightly and then looked at Nancy. "So spill, Girlfriend. What's going on?" Rain pelted the window, and Lettie made a mental note that all the candles had burned out except one. The farmhouse often lost power during thunderstorms.

"As I said, I got this email." Nancy nudged her oversized glasses back onto the bridge of her nose and nibbled another forkful of dessert. A splotch of chocolate rested on her lower lip.

Rosa slapped the table with her palm. "Oh for God's sake, do we have to force it out of you?"

Nancy puffed out a resigned sigh. "His name is Michael. I dated him back in community college, and he emailed me last week. I haven't seen or heard from him in almost twenty years—when he dumped me."

Three women asked at the same time, "What did he say?"

"Oh, it was vague and polite. You know, 'How are you? What are you up to? What has your life been like for the last twenty years?' Those types of things. I wasn't sure what to do. After a few days, I got up my nerve and sent him an equally vague email thinking 'that would be that'. But then he sent me another, *and* he Facebooked me to be his friend." Nancy rested her elbows on the table and cradled her cheeks in the palms of her plump hands. Near tears she said, "I honestly don't know if I want him in my life. Back in college I used to think of him as The One, and I never found anyone else quite like him." She hung her head, "When Michael left me, I never wanted to be with another man as long as I lived. Yet, here I am thinking I should lose weight and entertaining thoughts about not only seeing this guy but fantasizing about taking it one step further."

Lettie smooshed her fork into the lone bit of dessert on her plate, "You know, it's natural to shut down when you've been hurt. But at some point you obviously got over him and moved on."

"Don't you think it could be kind of exciting to see him again?" Helen said and held up the teapot, "Anyone need a warm-up?"

Nancy slid her mug toward Helen. "As great as he seemed for the whole time we dated, he turned into a real horse's ass at the end. I'm not sure that I could ever trust him again. So the problem is what would be the point of even getting anything started?"

Nedra prodded Nancy, "In a nutshell, girl, tell us what happened in college."

"Well, we fell in love, and, by the way, he was so freaking hot back then. It sounds kind of silly now, but we were going to get married and live in a cabin in Colorado. He studied art and planned to do…I don't remember, jewelry or pottery or something hippie-ish. We'd have kids and live happily ever after. Then he started being a jerk and broke up with me." Nancy smiled, "How's that for the condensed version?"

Lightning imitated a strobe light, while thunder vibrated the glass in the windowpanes of the farmhouse. The overhead dining room light flickered, and eight pairs of eyes looked up as if expecting a secret message in Morse code. Marge rolled up her sleeves and huffed, and Lettie thought she looked ready to take on the thunderstorm, or Nancy's ex, or maybe both. Marge turned toward Nancy and offered her a sympathetic smile and a one-word command, "Continue."

"Well, what the heck should I do? Get revenge after twenty years and tell him to take a flying leap?"

"What do *you* want to do? What's your gut telling you?" Nedra, the thinnest of all the women was, as usual, plunging into her second helping of dessert.

"What do *I* want to do?" Nancy closed her eyes and puckered her lips as if she had never thought of this question.

When she opened her eyes she looked directly at Nedra. "I want to be eighteen years old again, thin, and madly in love. And this time I want it to all work out. I want to have the life we had planned together—and the babies we had hoped for..." Nancy shifted her eyes to study a microscopic scratch in Lettie's tabletop and ran her fingernail over the crevice until it clicked into place. She shook her head, and her glasses slid down her nose. "But there's no going back. I gambled on this guy once and I lost everything." Coaxing her glasses back into place she said, "Anyway, I'm actually pretty happy with where I am in life. Except, well you know, I always wanted a husband and family. Oh, damn it," she ripped her glasses off her face. "I get so damn lonely."

The storm raged outside, and something thumped against the farmhouse. Lettie pushed her chair back over the floorboards and stood, "I'm sorry Nancy, but I'm going to check my cell phone and make sure there isn't a tornado warning."

"That's a good idea. I'm done anyway." The lights flickered, and the room pitched into total darkness except for one flickering candle flame across the room. Several of the women launched into surprised little yelps and gasps.

"Everyone stay still," Lettie called over the groans. "I'll get some flashlights and more candles." Sporadic bursts of lightning bathed the rooms of the farmhouse with an eerie flashing glow. Lettie returned to the chattering women with a plastic tub of candle stubs and two flashlights.

Helen snagged a flashlight from Lettie, clicked the button on, and said, "Remember this?" She lit her face from under her chin, the shadow from her nose looked upside-down, and her cheeks shaded her eyes. Helen made her voice rumble low like the thunder outside. "I believe in Mary Worth. I believe in Mary Worth."

Rosa slapped Helen's arm, and the beam bounced off the walls and ceiling. "Cut it out! That always scared the crap out of me." Slowly the room filled with the yellowy blush of candlelight. A mixture of sulfur from the matches and the fruity blend from perfumed candles filled the muggy air.

"No one is going to be leaving for a while," Lettie said. "I'll use a match to light a gas burner on the stove and boil more water for tea. Nancy can finish her story."

The storm's fury unloaded directly overhead—a battle between the intense heat of the past several days and a cold front that was trying to force its presence into the Midwest. A mist of steam curled upward from the mugs of hot tea in front of the women. "What if he's matured after all these years and is no longer a horse's ass? Why'd he break up with you anyway?"

Nancy seemed a bit evasive, and her eyes darted around the room. "He met somebody else and took her to Colorado. I'm such an idiot." Nancy pressed a palm to her forehead.

"Why?—because you fell in love, or because you still feel like a fool after all these years?" Lettie had been through several relationships herself that hadn't worked out, and she knew from experience that some hurt more than others.

"No, because I always seem to pick jerks. I make bad choices in men."

"You're not the only one," Phree said. "Look at me. I married the biggest loser of them all. Gambling—affairs—no child support for years. What the heck was *I* thinking?" Several women nodded their heads in agreement. Phree's husband had left her close to penniless a few years back.

Nedra smiled at her troubled friend, "Trust yourself, Nancy. And remember, he'll have to go through the Bunco Club interrogation before we allow you to get serious with him."

All eyes went to Rosa. "What?" Rosa placed her hand over her heart and feigned innocence. "So I ask tough questions. Somebody has to do it."

Nancy took a long sip from her mug of cooling tea. "He married about four years after we broke up, and his wife died about six years ago. He has one son, about ten years old. He makes a good living as an artsy jeweler in Colorado and wants to move back here to be closer to his parents, so his son will have grandparents nearby." Retrieving a folded piece of paper from her pocket, she placed it in the center of the table—an offering to understanding friends. "Here's a copy of the email."

With the speed and stealth of a cat pawing at a mouse, Rosa claimed the missive as hers alone and announced, "I'll read it out loud."

"Maybe Nancy would rather you not do that." The Sarge scolded and, with a smug smile that Lettie wanted to rip from her goodie-two-shoe face, looked to Nancy for direction.

"Go ahead, Rosa."

Rosa straightened her shoulders in victory and read,

" 'Dear Nancy, I hope this letter finds you well.' "

"Sounds more like a business letter to me," Phree said. Nancy groaned, and Rosa continued.

> " 'I think of you often. As a matter of fact, I can't get my mind off you. It's taken me weeks to perfect this letter and a mountain of courage to hit the send button. I'm haunted by our past together, and the first thing I *have* to do is apologize and ask your forgiveness for what I put you through.' "

"So far, so good," remarked Beth as she curled her legs under her and grabbed a handful of chocolate covered raisins.

" 'There is no other way to say this, so I'll just get to the point. My son and I will be visiting my parents in Chicago around Thanksgiving or Christmas. I am hopeful that you might agree to see me. We plan to move back to the area next year when school gets out, so Nick can be near his grandparents. I miss Chicago, and I am looking forward to seeing you again.

It pains me how we parted, and that I left you with such a huge burden. Again, I ask your forgiveness and hope you will meet with me. I know this is probably just selfishness on my part. I don't want to hurt you again or bring up long-ago sadness. Please say yes. Perhaps it will be good for both of us.

Michael' "

Thunder rolled and Lettie knew without a doubt there was something Nancy was not telling them. But it was Rosa who blurted, "So what the hell is this big burden he left you with?"

Nancy shrugged, and her shoulders drooped. "Nothing really." Lettie thought Nancy appeared defeated.

Rosa wouldn't let up, "C'mon Nancy, we're not stupid." Lettie reached over and grabbed hold of Rosa's arm before she could say anymore. She shook her head to convey a 'don't do this' signal, and Rosa changed her approach. "Whenever you're ready, honey."

"I *have* thought that I'd like to lose about forty pounds before I see him—*if* I see him."

"And a makeover," Rosa blurted. "You'll need to do a makeover, too."

"It'll be fun," Nedra said, obviously attempting to reduce the blow of Rosa's harsh words.

"I'll diet with you," Phree offered. "I need to lose weight too, and it always helps to diet with someone else."

Beth stood so fast her chair wobbled on the back two legs before righting itself. She scooted behind Nancy and deftly removed the scrunchie from Nancy's mousy hair. "I've been trying to talk you into getting rid of this dull hair for years, and after tonight I refuse to take 'no' for an answer." She fanned out Nancy's straight-as-a-board, middle-of-the-back mane. "The next time you come in, we'll start experimenting with color and a flattering cut. I've got several ideas, but the first and most important is to get rid of these split ends."

"If you want," Lettie offered, "we can start a walking routine together. I go once a day to the high school and walk on the outdoor track. You can join me if you'd like. And after you lose those forty pounds, Nedra and I will take you clothes shopping."

"You're going to look just like you did back in college when we get done with you." Nedra smoothed a manicured hand over the sharp crease of her khaki slacks.

"What the heck, why *not* see him again? Show him what he's missed all those years," Helen said.

Beth stretched her arms, "I don't know about the rest of you, but I'm exhausted. Sounds like the worst of the storm has blown over, and since we can't do justice to show-and-tell without the lights, I think I'm going to head home. You gonna be okay here with no power, Lettie?"

"Yeah, I'm used to it. Sorry about show-and-tell everyone." Chairs scraped across the floor as the women rose.

"Hey, it's not your fault," Beth said. "We'll just have more show-and-tell for next time."

Phree sorted through the pile of bags on the sofa and asked Marge, "Is Bud still willing to help get those boxes and trunk down from my attic on Saturday?" She handed a purse to Nedra and a tote bag to Beth. "They're just too heavy for me to handle on my own."

"How does eleven o'clock sound?"

"Eleven is perfect." Phree continued to pass items to the women as they said their goodbyes and firmed up plans for helping Beth with visits to her father sometime over the next few weeks.

Lettie snapped the lid shut on the Bunco box of supplies. "Helen, hand this to Phree. I'm beyond happy not to have to see it for another eight months."

"Hot potato coming through!" Helen passed the gray plastic box to Phree.

"Crap. So, I get it next—lucky me. Everyone toss their money in already?"

A chorus of yeses peppered the room.

"Every time I get this box, I feel like that Edgar Alan Poe story about the *Tell Tale Heart.* I can just hear the thing going 'bum bump, bum bump, bum bump' in my closet over the next month. And the closer it gets to Bunco, the louder it beats."

The lights stuttered back to a blaze of brightness, and the air conditioner kicked on with a drone to begin cooling the stuffy room again. Lettie closed the door on the last woman to leave, but before she turned around remembered she hadn't talked to Rosa about Ricky.

SEPTEMBER BUNCO - Phree

Ya just never know.

Chapter 1

Lightning sparked off to the east, as the thunderstorm moved into Indiana leaving behind a steady splatter of rain. Phree tossed the Bunco box of supplies onto the passenger seat, turned the ignition key starting her ancient Honda with a rumble, and clicked the wipers to high speed. Her bangs dripped rainwater onto her already wet face. Following Helen's taillights down the long lane from Lettie's house, she wove her car around muddy furrows and splashed through rain filled ruts. Headlights from all the cars leaving the farmhouse bounced into the inky blackness and disappeared, an unrehearsed light-show produced by bounces and bumps. Phree thought it was just plain creepy driving down the middle of a cornfield, and not for the first time she wondered how Lettie could stand the isolation of living by herself on a farm in the freaking middle of nowhere. It would drive her absolutely crazy, but she had to admit that Lettie had a sweet thing going with her studio barn and all the other outbuildings.

At the intersection with the county highway, Phree made a right toward the town of Whitney. The car behind her also made a right. It must be Nancy. Phree tried to figure out what the deal was with Nancy. Why was she having such a hard time coming to terms with a 'long lost love'? She put herself in Nancy's position but kept coming up short. *I'm either missing something, or else Nancy's not giving us the whole story*. From her rearview mirror, Phree watched Nancy turn at the next intersection, heading toward her condo.

The tempo of the wipers swiping back and forth soothed Phree into a reflective mood. It was from firsthand experience that she knew how understanding and helpful this group of women could be. They had helped her through an ugly divorce from Gary—a.k.a. The Bastard. Just over four years ago Gary had admitted to cheating on her,and that his 'girlfriend' was pregnant. Phree had arrived at Bunco about half an hour late that night, and when she walked through Nedra's door, everyone was already grazing on the pre-Bunco feast. Rosa blurted, "Oh, my God, you look horrible! What happened?"

"What's wrong?" Beth led her to one of Nedra's ornate chairs. Phree had spent the past 48 hours sobbing, and while she had repeatedly splashed her face with cold water, and stopped crying for a grand total of fifteen minutes—she *did* look horrible.

Nedra set a glass of wine in front of Phree and placed a motherly kiss on her cheek, "Phree, dear—can we help?" A nice gesture, a kind word, and seven good friends; just what she needed to burst into a fresh wave of tears.

Grasping the arms of the antique English chair she gained a bit of control and, with puffy blue eyes, sputtered, "It's Gary. He's gotten someone pregnant!" Everyone gasped at the same time except Rosa, who shrieked, "That bastard!" Now, four years later, Phree was able to laugh at the outburst. She was always careful not to use the nickname around their daughter and only child. Even though it nearly killed her sometimes, Phree never bad-mouthed Gary in front of Emily. *What we don't do for our kids.*

The rain slowed to a sputter and spit, so Phree flicked the wipers to intermittent. She opened the car window to a cool rush of night air that was muggy from the rain but balmy and refreshing. Ahead in the darkness, utility lights flashed as an emergency crew worked to clear a fallen tree from the road. Phree shifted her car into park, as one of the men yanked a cord to coax a chainsaw into a whiny vibration. The metal teeth of the saw chewed into the tree trunk and spewed out a fountain of wooden chunks. Her car was the only one on the street, and a good looking policeman with an orange-tipped flashlight walked up to her and touched the brim of his police cap. "Evening, ma'am. We'll only keep you for a few minutes. Storm blew down a bunch of branches on Center Street, and we're clearing them up as quick as we can. Sorry for the delay."

"No problem. I'll just wait." *And gawk at you.* She relaxed her head on the headrest while watching the workers from across the dashboard of her car. The wipers occasionally swiped across the misty windshield, the chainsaw revved a pulsing rhythm of highs and lows, and the flashing yellow lights draped the scene in a mellow blush.

Phree picked at the thread of her previous thoughts and remembered how at that long ago Bunco, she was what could only be described as 'in a state of shock'. Nedra said, "I'm calling Brian," and arranged a meeting with her lawyer-brother for the next day. The Bastard's chin (with that stupid little 'soul patch' he had grown to impress what's-her-name) dropped to his chest when she walked into the courtroom with Brian, a 250 pound African-American former Notre Dame Football player. Her ex had been confident that he could bully her, but Nedra's brother had other plans, and Gary never knew what hit him until it was too late.

Brian had only charged her $1.00 for his services. "You and those other goofy white gals are Nedra's best friends, and if I can't help her best friends in their time of need, then what kind of brother am I?" He smiled, and his eyes softened to the deep color of tea that has been steeped too long. "Just to see her, I've got to squeeze in between quilting bees—whatever the hell *they* are—and Buncos."

She had no money. Nothing. Gary, the damn bastard, had gambled away their savings years ago, and she had only made excuses for his behavior. The one gift—and certainly without his knowledge—that Gary had given her was an in-depth understanding of computers. So she started selling things on eBay, and the first batch of items she made money on was everything that Gary had left behind. She began earning enough for her and Emily to get by, and then it happened—she discovered that she no longer gave a crap about her inconsiderate-selfish-poor-excuse of an ex-husband.

A wood chipper vibrated and buzzed with a grinding frenzy each time it was fed another sawed off section of the tree. The road was almost passable as the loud machine chewed the massive branch into small bits, and then spat them into the back of a truck. Phree thought the scene was similar to what Brian had done to The Bastard. The gorgeous cop tipped his cap as she drove past, "Careful now. Goodnight." Phree did not trust herself to answer, so she just smiled and checked for a wedding ring.

Chapter 2

Expecting Marge's husband to arrive any minute to help her with the boxes in the attic, Phree poured water into the coffeemaker. Twisting a hair-tie, she coaxed her dark frizzed-out hair into a ponytail. The aroma of fresh-brewed coffee blended with the heady scent of late summer humidity and drifted through Phree's bungalow. Bud wouldn't be there very long, but at least she could offer him a cup of coffee for his efforts. Emily would probably sleep several more hours. She might as well get her beauty rest with the start of her final year in high school a little over a week away.

Searching for her 'cheater' glasses, which never failed to elude her, Phree became excited at the thought of what she might find stashed in the boxes for her eBay store. This would be a major score of basically free goodies, yet it still remained a daunting task to sort, organize, photograph, and then list everything for sale. She hoped to find some nice serving dishes, tea cups with saucers, and, fingers crossed, some vintage clothing.

Her mother had never opened any of the boxes after she had packed them for Grandma when they had to admit her to a nursing home. The cardboard containers were stored in Mom's basement with the promise to 'go through them someday', and Phree had made that same promise when she moved them up to her attic ten years ago. The doorbell rang at the same time she spotted her missing glasses.

Bud, sporting his ever-present orange and blue Chicago Bears cap, greeted Phree with, "At your service."

She was surprised to see Terry, Rosa's husband, standing next to him, a grin on his unshaven face. "Rosa insisted I lend a hand, and believe me, I was more than glad to leave her arguing with Ricky over what supplies and new clothes he needs for his first year of high school." Terry shook his head, "I don't know who's more stubborn between those two."

"Come on in, guys. I really appreciate your help. Those boxes are big and way too heavy for me to handle alone, even with Emily's help." The two men followed Phree down a hallway, and she stopped at a set of retractable folding stairs that she had earlier pulled down from the attic. "The boxes are up there. I think there are about eight and a really big trunk."

Bud started up the stairs, "Where would you like us to put them?"

"I'd like them in the garage if you don't mind dragging them that far. That way I can spread out and organize piles of whatever is inside of them. Besides, they're probably musty and smelly from being in Mom's basement all those years."

Dust and filaments of cobwebs floated from the attic opening, as Bud and Terry jostled the boxes through the narrow space and down the wobbly stairs. When Terry scraped the trunk along the attic flooring a chunk of insulation snagged on a hinge and drifted down. Phree swatted it away.

"Sorry!" Terry grunted over his shoulder.

"No worries. I'll clean it up later."

Outside in the garage, with the trunk and boxes stowed away, Phree suggested they take a coffee break.

"Coffee sounds good, but I'd sure like to have a big glass of ice water first." A puff of dust burst from Bud's Bears cap as he thwacked it against the thigh of his jeans.

They were seated at Phree's kitchen table, having coffee and chatting about nothing in particular when the phone rang. Phree went to the wall phone, checked the caller ID, and groaned, "Oh crap, it's The Bastard." Hesitating only a second, she answered it. "Emily is still sleeping, but I can wake her if you need to talk with her." Phree started to pace around the kitchen with the receiver of the landline phone cradled between her ear and shoulder. She saw Bud raise his eyebrows in question to Terry. Terry shrugged at him, and she focused on what Gary was saying.

"Phreedom baby, I miss you and Em so much." She used to love it when he called her by the full, very odd name her hippie parents had stuck her with from their favorite Janis Joplin song. If he threw in her middle name of Aquarius, she'd just have to puke.

"And why is this *my* problem?" She loved having the upper hand with this idiot.

"Can't we get back together? Just the three of us—like old times?"

"You can't possibly think I'm that stupid can you? Or do you think it's that I'm desperate?" The curly cord was holding her to the confines of the kitchen within easy earshot of the two men, and after her last comment they looked pathetically uncomfortable. Bud tried to empty his coffee cup in one gulp, while he slid his chair back from the table. She held up her hand and then winked, to convey—don't leave, I'm really enjoying this.

"No, Gary. Not now or ever. We're perfectly happy the way we are."

Gary tried again but Phree cut him off, "I don't know how to make this any clearer. I don't want to see you, and I don't want to talk with you, unless it has something to do directly with our daughter."

"But, I'm not happy with Tiffany anymore. She's driving me crazy."

"Hey, like Rhett would say, 'Frankly, my dear, I don't give a damn.' "

"Come on, Phree. Can't I just come over and chat?"

Phree spun on her heal and her ponytail whipped across her cheek. "NO! DO NOT COME OVER HERE TO CHAT." She lowered her voice back to its normal range, took a cleansing breath, and with a calmness she didn't feel said,

"Now, I am saying good-bye, so hang up and go back to your pregnant wife and little boy."

Phree punctuated her final sentence by crashing the phone receiver into its holder, where it clattered back and forth like a pinball. She turned toward the embarrassed men, and said, "That went well." Tension left the room like a lid taken off of a pressure cooker, as all three of them began laughing.

Chapter 3

On Emily's first day back to school, Phree gave her a good send off with a healthy breakfast, new school clothes, and a kiss on the cheek. She *did* force the obligatory first-day-of-school-picture. Phree straightened Emily's collar and posed her in front of the same evergreen they had used as a backdrop since she had sent her daughter off to kindergarten. Emily cooperated by crossing her eyes and sticking out her tongue. "Mo-o-o-m, let's get this over with. Someone might see."

"Why are you so embarrassed? We're in our own backyard. No one can see us." Phree had to dig deep to remember how it felt to be seventeen and automatically humiliated by *anything* a parent did. "Come on. A nice smile for your nice Mom. That's it. Perfect." *This will be the last one.* "Okay, okay. Get going before I start crying."

"Oh, Mom, I'm just going to school, and besides," Emily called over her shoulder, as she walked toward the car, "if I don't hurry, I'll be late picking up the other girls." She faced Phree and took a few steps backwards while she jingled her car keys for effect.

"I know, Em. Get going." *And in one short year you'll be miles and miles away at some university. This will be a year of 'lasts'.*

Emily pulled the seatbelt over her body and locked it with a click. She took a quick peek in the rearview mirror and examined her teeth. Almost as an afterthought she said, "Love you, Mom."

"Love you, too, Emmy my gemmy." Emily made an effort at a weak smile and rolled her eyes. "Drive carefully and make sure everyone has their seat belts on." Holding onto the open window of the car for a few steps, Phree reluctantly let go as her daughter backed the car down the driveway.

Waving until the car rounded the corner, and she couldn't see it anymore, she went back inside, loaded the cereal bowls and juice glasses into the dishwasher, swiped a damp cloth over the table, and filled a large insulated mug with coffee.

The gears on the garage door rumbled open after Phree tapped the correct code into the keypad. As the door rose, the lopsided pile of boxes and the trunk came into view. Phree was eager to get started on this project.

It was a warm day, and a soft breeze brought some fresh air into the stuffy garage which smelled of grease and oil. With dust motes floating through rays of sunlight on the inside of the garage, Phree found a spot to set her coffee mug and randomly chose a box to open. The boxes had all been sealed shut with water-tape and were labeled 'Nellie's Stuff'. *Great description. Here goes nothing.*

Hours later, a stack of clothes inhabited one corner of the garage, and old-fashioned kitchenware took over the work bench. She had amassed a pile of crinkly fragile photos, most of which were stained with brown spots, that she 'sub-piled' into known (names on back) and unknown (no names). Several stacks of paperback books teetered next to a container of obsolete grocery store coupons. Pens and stubby pencils were tossed in the trash, and a heap of outdated medicine to be disposed of properly formed another pile. A vast collection of fabulous old fabric emerged, a horde of dated letters and other correspondence, and one box was half full of vintage shoes.

So far the biggest prize to surface from the confusion in the boxes was a pile of cotton feed sacks. Since most of the sacks were printed with a pattern, Phree knew they were likely from between 1920 and 1950. She was pleasantly surprised by about a dozen that appeared to be much older, and her limited knowledge led her to believe they might be from the turn of the 20th century. In addition she found some interesting dishes, several cool hat pins, a large canister of antique-looking buttons (which would require some research), two pitchers, several vases, and three gorgeous tea pots, one of which Phree thought she might keep for herself. She was especially intrigued by the fabric and thought surely it must be 1930's vintage. *Rosa, the queen of thirties fabric, will die.*

After Phree's stomach complained with several growls, she decided it was time to eat her low-cal, low-fat, low-everything, diet lunch. She *had* lost seven pounds in the week since Bunco, and even though five pounds surely must be nothing more than quick water weight, she still considered it progress.

Planning to check her email, eBay, Facebook, and Twitter accounts while eating lunch would help keep Phree out of the kitchen, where she might all too easily grab a handful of something fattening. Taking a large glass of water, some grapes, and an open-faced sandwich with only one tablespoon of peanut butter, she headed for the computer room. Clicking for a connection, she heard the familiar, "You've got mail." Two of her eBay auctions had ended—*and* with buyers. On top of it, she had gotten more money than she thought each item would fetch—*a good day.*

Chapter 4

Fall bees were swarming in the late afternoon sun and hunted for anything from juicy apples decaying on the ground to Phree's can of soda. Tired of swatting bees and worrying that one was lurking in her can, she was headed to the kitchen for a bottle of water, when Emily drove into the driveway. "Hey, Mom, what's up?"

"Still working on these boxes," Phree stretched her cramped arms over her head, bending from one side to the next. "I've gone through six already, but still have two more and that big trunk left. How'd your first day go?" She stood in front of a pile of empty cardboard boxes and, with a box-cutter, started slicing them into smaller pieces to be used as packing material for her eBay items.

"Really great. It felt good to be back and to *finally* be a senior. I saw a million kids that I haven't seen all summer, and this weekend is the first football game." Emily stepped closer to her mom and lowered her voice, as if someone might be listening, "You see Rosa, don't you?"

At the sound in Emily's voice, Phree stopped working and concentrated on her daughter. "Yeah, all the time. Why?"

"Well, something happened with Ricky today." Emily moved another step closer. "It was all over school. He got in trouble for fighting, and I mean big trouble. He's supposed to be either suspended or expelled from school. I'm not sure which one."

"Oh, my God!" Phree said, feeling behind her for the chair she had been using most of the day. "It's his first day in high school. Poor Rosa. What happened?"

"Well, I guess Ricky and some other guy were picking on a geeky freshman, and a senior came over to stop them. They argued for a while, and Ricky and Billy started to beat-up the senior. Mr. Johnson heard the commotion and rushed over. They got caught and suspended or something. You know how gossip is. There's a ton of different versions. All I can tell you is he wasn't in school for the rest of day."

"Dear Lord, I wonder if I should call Rosa. Maybe I'll check with Lettie first."

"Yeah, well, I gotta get back to school for swim practice. I forgot my goggles, and I just wanted to fill you in on Ricky." Emily turned to go into the house.

"Thanks, Emmy," Phree was having trouble focusing her thoughts on anything but Rosa. This was going to crush her friend. Ricky had truly been a sweet little boy and up until last year had gotten good grades in school. What the heck had gone wrong? Emily walked out the back door, cell phone in her hand, and goggles around her neck.

"What time will you be home for supper?"

"Probably not until 7:30. Our first meet is next Tuesday, and I'm feeling pretty rusty."

"OK, Emmy. Be safe."

"Mom, are you all right?"

"Yeah, I guess I'm just a little shocked about Ricky. Poor Rosa and Terry."

"Ricky's been acting crazy this summer. I saw him smoking last week with that group of creeps he hangs out with, and I probably shouldn't say this, but I don't think they were cigarettes. They had something in a little brown bag they were drinking and passing between them. It was probably just a soda, and they were trying to look like big-shots, but knowing Ricky and his loser friends, I suspect it could've been something a lot stronger." Emily bent and hugged her—a real rarity, and then started backing away toward her car, "but, I really gotta go."

"Yeah, get going, sweetie. I'll see you at supper. Love you." Phree shaded her eyes with her hand and watched her wonderful, precious, never-in-trouble-daughter drive away. *How lucky I am.*

She sat for a moment and let the bad news seep into her soul, until it became reality. Phree reached for the seventh box. Her train of thought about her boxes and piles and eBay had been shattered, like a broken mirror with fractured images of Ricky. Maybe she'd call it a day and start fresh tomorrow, maybe she'd phone Lettie, or maybe she'd go over to Rosa's house to see if she could help. But Rosa was so darn secretive about Ricky lately. Phree looked at the trunk and the last two boxes. She walked over to the garage door, pushed the button, and it lumbered shut. "Tomorrow is another day." *Thank you, Scarlett.*

Phree swatted at a bee as she made her way to the back door of her home. The sky was a brilliant turquoise with pink and peach splashes that would usually leave her weak with its beauty. Shrouded in sadness over the pain of a dear friend, she picked up the phone and called Lettie's cell.

Around 9:00 that evening Phree was folding laundry when her phone rang. Lettie said, "I just got home from Rosa's, and I'm exhausted. To start with they felt they needed a lawyer, so they called Brian."

"Oh, no. Is Rosa okay?"

"Here's the story," Lettie began. "Ricky was with that idiot, Billy Howard. It seems that Billy started picking on a freshman, and Ricky just stood by and watched. By the time the senior came to the rescue, Billy had gotten really worked up. Ricky claims he tried to separate them, but there are too many witnesses that discount his story. Apparently the senior protected his head with his hands and never even threw a punch. The witnesses all agree it was two against one." Lettie's tea kettle whistled, and Phree heard a splash of water filling a cup. Lettie paused, "The school's surveillance tape picked up the whole incident. It shows the kid curled on the floor, and Ricky kicking the crap out of the kid's head. It's actually a miracle the kid's not in a coma. He suffered a concussion and about 22 stitches. Sounds like he'll be in the hospital for several days."

"Oh my God, what the hell was he thinking? What did Brian say?" Phree sat on her sofa with a half-folded tee-shirt on her lap.

"Evidently the kid's parents are pressing charges of battery, and I don't blame them. Brian thinks that with the severity of the attack, maybe it's time for Ricky to see the inside of 'juvey' and what life is like for a thug. A few weeks or months in a place like that might give him a little perspective on life behind bars. He said there's an outside chance he could get Ricky's charges dropped, but suggested that Rosa and Terry make a unified decision which way they want to pursue this mess. Brian said it might be time for him to suffer some consequences for his actions, especially while he's still considered a juvenile. Rosa and Terry are going to sleep on it. Of course, Ricky is begging them not to send him to jail. It would be a clear case of tough love. Rosa cried most of the time I was there. I think she's scared for whatever choice they make."

"Wow, I can understand that."

"I haven't shared this with anyone, because I wanted to talk to Rosa first. But when I was doing my shopping for Bunco, I saw Ricky do some pretty destructive stuff at the grocery store." Lettie repeated the scene she had witnessed that day, and Phree shared the 'smoking/drinking' incident that Emily had told her about.

"I'd say they've got a big, life changing decision to make, and I wouldn't want to be in their shoes for anything." Lettie yawned, and, as usually happens, Phree yawned after her. "I need to get organized for an early morning meeting at a gallery, and then get myself to bed. I'm dead tired. It's been an emotional evening."

"Thanks for letting me know what's going on. I really appreciate it." Phree folded the last towel and restacked the folded laundry inside the basket.

"Well, we've got to stick together," Lettie yawned again, "and the sooner Rosa understands she's not alone in this, the better she'll be."

Chapter 5

As she slid into a fresh pair of jeans the next morning, Phree attempted to untangle the images of a dream-filled night from her head. Her dead Grandma was alive and walking around the garage, Rosa sat crying on the trunk with Emily telling her that Ricky was a bad kid, her neighbor showed up eating a sandwich, and asked if he could borrow her snow-blower. Thankfully, that was when Phree woke up, but it was so darn vivid it still lingered in her mind.

She coaxed a respectable breakfast of cereal, fruit, and juice into Emily, who finally pulled down the driveway with backpack, cell phone, seatbelt fastened, AND her swim goggles. The sky was an umbrella of September-blue, and the air held the heady hint of yeasty sweetness from crabapples fermenting on the ground. As much as Phree would have loved to play hooky, she headed to her garage with camera and coffee in hand. She would probably finish unloading the items this morning and start photographing some of the pieces for her eBay store.

Entering the code into the garage keypad, Phree stabbed the button for the door to open. It answered with a loud grinding of gears. As her half-Irish mom would have said, "The good fairies didn't come by last night and do your work, so you might as well get started." She lifted the humpbacked lid on the trunk and felt a rush of excitement.

Just enough of a novice history buff to know that the trunk might be valuable, she centered the trunk in the viewfinder of her digital camera and took five shots—one from each side and then the top. Opening the trunk, Phree shot the inside of the fabric covered lid, and then took a picture of the lift-out tray with its contents intact.

When she had finished sorting through the objects on the tray, a jumble of various items sat in front of her. The most interesting were five very old aprons that were in excellent condition. She was quite excited about the aprons, because she knew from experience they were extremely collectable and potentially worth a decent amount of money on eBay. Lifting out the empty tray, she examined the bottom and saw something written in pencil. She brought the tray out to the sunlight to study it closer. Eliza Jane Hicks, 1844 - 1917, and written underneath was the name Henrietta Hicks Snyder, March 2, 1870. Phree knew Henrietta was her great-grandma, and everyone called her by the nickname MeeMee. She remembered MeeMee as a very short, white-haired, old lady, who always wore a long apron and lived with Phree's grandparents. When Phree and her parents would visit, MeeMee would take Phree into her bedroom where she had a piece of cotton fabric already put into an embroidery hoop along with some colored threads waiting for Phree to do some 'fancy work' with her. Phree had completely forgotten about that until this very minute.

Her hand went to the primitive lettering and traced over it. Phree knew Henrietta had been born in Canada and, as a married woman, had homesteaded in Nebraska. She had lived in a soddy, and Phree's grandma was the oldest of MeeMee's eight children. Unfortunately, Phree had no further information about her own great-grandmother. What a shame she didn't know more than that speck of information. She guessed the trunk had belonged to Henrietta (MeeMee) and that Eliza Jane must be Henrietta's mother. That meant Eliza Jane was Phree's great-great-grandma. *Cool.*

She photographed the writing the best she could, and set the tray on a thick, protective tarp. Phree guessed the trunk to be at least 150 years old. *Do I sell it, or should I keep it? It's gotta be valuable, but now that I know who it once belonged to, it's like selling a family member.* She'd think about that later, after she found what else was in there. Standing over the full trunk, she took a deep breath and plunged in. She had hoped for vintage clothing, and she had just hit the mother lode. Most of what she found, she figured to be from about 1910 to 1930. Phree uncovered a small packet of letters, postcards, and pictures tied with a fragile pink ribbon that crumbled to the floor when she tried to unfasten it. She shuffled through the photos; dusty images of people she didn't know, all dressed in old-timey clothes, grim-faced, and proper. The enormity of what she held shook her core, like soundless waves from a sonic boom. These were most likely her recent ancestors.

When Phree got to the bottom of the trunk, she felt a sense of loss. All of this 'stuff' had belonged to her relatives and so many of them she never even knew. They had lived lives probably a lot like her own—some days happy, some days sad. They had loved and been loved, and now they were gone, and no one knew their stories or even their names—yet their blood flowed through her. Looking at the objects in front of her, she realized they must have meant something important to the people who had stowed them away for safekeeping.

Phree wished she could go back forty years and once again talk to the slightly hunched, elderly woman she had called MeeMee. She would ask her great-grandmother what her life had been like. She would ask her how and why she had gone from Canada to Nebraska, and she would ask MeeMee to tell stories about her joys and heartaches. Phree wanted to thank her great-grandmother for having the courage to homestead in a soddy on the lonely prairie, with eight little kids born one right after the other. She wanted MeeMee to know that she, Phree, had a good life and appreciated all the inconceivable sacrifices MeeMee had made in order for her descendants to have a better life. She sat back in her wicker chair and let the melancholy moment wash over her, as she stared at the trunk.

She sat and stared.

And stared.

And stared.

And then she saw it. She sat bolt upright.

She went closer to examine what she thought she saw. Yes, the *inside* bottom of the trunk rested about five or six inches higher than the *outside* bottom of the trunk. She reached down into the chest, and it smelled dank and musty like the remnants of decayed dreams. Using a light touch and all her senses on high alert, she cautiously felt around the perimeter of the bottom of the trunk. *Nothing*. Phree tried again—this time even slower and more gently. *There – there it was!* Nearly imperceptible to the touch and certainly to the eye, it felt like a little flap.

It took her only a nanosecond to make the decision to take the box cutter and slice into the fabric by the bump. She cut an 'L' shape to examine whether she truly found a flap or just a double thickness of fabric. Ah, yes, under the flap rested a hole just big enough for a finger. *This will either be the smartest thing I do or the dumbest.* She followed around the corner of the walls and the bottom of the trunk with the blade of the box cutter, freed the fabric, stuck her finger in the hole, and pulled.

She stared at two bundles, shrouded in fabric and approximately the same size. There was another smaller packet sitting in an incredibly old-looking wooden slat basket along with two more medium-sized parcels. She had no idea what she had found, but she knew if someone had taken this much trouble to hide it—it must be something important. Glancing at the false wooden bottom in her hand, she noticed more writing. Again, Phree went outside the garage into the sunlight. Fancifully carved was a name she had never heard of: Debra Soule.

Trying to calm herself, Phree picked up a cardboard box and placed the items inside. She wouldn't open them in the garage—they seemed too important. The basket turned out to be rather strong and in fairly good shape. It had two handles that swung up and met in the center. 'Hannah Brewster' was inscribed on the bottom in a very primitive fashion—possibly with the tip of a knife or some other sharp object. Underneath the name another carving became visible. It read 'ov Duxbury'.

Phree arranged newspapers on her kitchen table. The big bundles were heavy and felt like they might contain books; the others, she wasn't sure. The fabric around the objects had held up well—good sturdy linen, very old. She unwrapped the first large bundle end-over-end. The soft brown linen had protected its contents quite nicely, and it was indeed a book. She flipped over the book to examine the cover of what appeared to be a very old Bible. Phree's heart hammered, and her hands were shaking. Very, very carefully she opened the Bible. There were several loose sheets of paper filled with old fashioned handwriting that almost looked to be a different language. The words were so feathery she couldn't make them out. Phree smiled when she saw a few pressed flowers between the pages. *Some things never change.*

Being extremely careful to handle the vellum pages of the old Bible properly, she slowly worked her way to the family history. Her hands jerked away from the book as her eyes read what her mind could barely take in. The first person listed had the same last name as the inscription on the false bottom of the trunk: "George Soule, born 1594, England. Arrived at Plimoth 1620. Died January 18, 1678, Duxbury, Plimouth County. Married Mary Beckett 1624."

The rest of the writing became a blur to Phree as she fell into the nearest chair. "Good Lord, this guy came over on the Mayflower!"

She had to bend over and put her head between her knees. Her 'cheater' glasses slipped down her nose and clattered to the floor. Remembering her old Lamaze classes, Phree calmed herself with deep cleansing breaths. Still trembling, she avoided even looking at the Bible, unable to take in the extent of what sat resting on her kitchen table. She positioned her glasses back onto her nose and picked up the other large parcel. It was approximately the same size as the first bundle, and she had an exciting feeling that another Bible probably resided behind 'shroud number two'.

As she gently removed the linen wrapper another family Bible appeared, this one with much more wear but still in relatively good condition. Phree rested her hand on the Bible and whispered, "God, help me." As before, there were sheaves of paper tucked inside the cover (many more than the first Bible) and written in the same odd looking language but in a different, less flowery penmanship. She estimated there must be 50 to 60 pages.

This time Phree sat down in a chair as she flipped to the family section. The first line read: "William Brewster, born 24 January 1560, Scrooby, Nottinghamshire, England, arrived Plimoth, 1620, as pastr to the good peepl ov the Mayflower, died, 10 April 1644, Plimouth." Phree wasn't sure if she should laugh hysterically, cry, or throw-up.

An hour later, she sat staring at two family Bibles from passengers on board the Mayflower; three journals by the same person named in one of the Bibles-George Soule; a small handwritten booklet that looked to be a tattered diary; page after page of handwritten documents and letters; a dried up ink well; and Hannah Brewster's chore basket.

Holy crap!

The items had most likely belonged to her ancestors. Mayflower ancestors. That's Mayflower ancestors with an 's'—as in plural. Talk about the mother lode! Having no idea what in the world to do, she decided to call Brian to get his input.

A pleasant-sounding secretary answered, informing her that Mr. Barber had been called away to court and wouldn't be back to the office for another forty-five minutes or thereabouts. "Please have him call Phree Clarke as soon as he gets in. Tell him it's urgent that I speak with him today."

Phree spent the next hour at her computer Googling names from the two old Bibles and clicking any link that might help her get closer to solving the mystery that had been hidden in Grandma Nellie's trunk. She learned everything she didn't know, but should have known, about the Mayflower and her alleged ancestors. She intentionally stayed away from the kitchen where the overwhelming find now rested on her kitchen table. *Hmm, seems I've invented the Mayflower Diet.*

The ringing phone intruded on her Internet stupor of 1620 Plymouth, Massachusetts. "Phree?" Brian's deep voice boomed over the phone, "What's up? My receptionist said it's urgent."

"Brian, I am so happy to hear your voice," and with that she let out a pent up sob.

"God, is there something wrong? Is Emily okay? Are you okay?"

"No, I'm sorry, just a little stressed out." She bookmarked the last page she had googled and swiveled the chair away from the computer. "I guess you could say this is a good thing, but right now I find it staggering. Can you come over sometime today? I need your advice, and what I have, I probably shouldn't bring to the office."

"Well, you've really piqued my curiosity," Brian said. "I'm leaving here in about half an hour. Will that work for you?"

"I won't be going anywhere."

Phree greeted Brian at her front door. As he entered her home, he loosened his tie and slipped off his dark-blue suit coat. She ushered him into the kitchen and pointed toward the table. "I found this in my grandmother's trunk."

Five minutes later, Brian stared open-mouthed at what rested in front of him. "You found this staggering?" he questioned Phree. "'Staggering' I believe that was your exact term."

Thinking maybe she had overreacted, Phree felt her cheeks redden with embarrassment. "Yeah, I'm sorry to have bothered you. I just thought…"

"My dear, Phree," Brian said as he raked his hand through his hair, "if this stuff is authentic this is not just staggering—this is absolutely, unbelievably, crazy staggering! Tell me how in the hell this happened."

After repeating the whole story to him, she said, "So, what should I do?"

"We need a plan of attack," he stood and walked to the other side of the table, his eyes never leaving the items from the trunk. "My recommendation is first and foremost to think of your and Emily's safety. These may end up being some of the most important documents found in recent American history, and people would do anything to get their hands on them, or the person who found them, or her family." He looked at her, and she felt like she did in second grade when the teacher had caught her chewing her eraser. "I don't mean to be overly dramatic or scare you, but we must be extremely vigilant until these items are no longer in your possession."

Phree just bobbed her head, and tears sprang so quickly to her eyes she couldn't stop their flow. This had gone from a gift dropped in her lap to a huge burden in about two seconds. She set her glasses on the table, closed her eyes, and pinched the bridge of her nose.

"As senior partner, I have a rather large vault for documents and items that I deem important to my clients. We can store the items there until you make a decision on what you want done with them. This is a giant responsibility for you, and it will require you to make some hard decisions." Brian-the-lawyer unfastened his brief case and took out a legal tablet. He clicked open a pen and started to compile a list, and Phree right away thought of Marge. He continued with more suggestions and wrote as he talked. "We'll make a brief inventory of what's here and get the objects to the vault. Sunday afternoon no one is in the office, so we can take digital photos and make a more thorough inventory of everything. Perhaps I can find someone who would be discreet and could give us an idea of what the journals and those documents are all about. I'll put out some feelers, and see what happens. In the meantime, no one, and I mean NO ONE must know about this. Do you understand?"

The look in his dark-brown eyes told Phree he was dead serious, and it frightened her. But again, Phree just nodded.

Brian continued, "Especially Emily. Teenagers have a way of not being able to keep their mouths shut, and as much as we love Emily, she's still a teenager." Brian set down his legal pad and put his large dark hand over Phree's. "It's for her own good, and at this point, it's a burden she doesn't need to bear. I can tell that you can scarcely handle this, think of what it would do to her."

Phree whispered, "Okay."

"We need to get this out of here before she gets home. When do you expect her?"

Phree automatically looked at the clock—4:30. Could it really be only 4:30? Impossible. She had time traveled to 1620 Plymouth on the Mayflower and back in only four hours. "Emily has swim practice tonight and should be home about 7:30."

"Good, that will give us time to get this into an ordinary looking box and under lock and key. I am the only one with access to my vault. I'll drive you and the box over to the office, and you can witness me putting the articles into the vault. Then I will give you a notarized copy of said articles for your records. We will eventually need to move them to a more secure place, with around-the-clock security and surveillance, but my vault will do for now."

Phree stared at him. She found her mouth was hanging slightly open, and she snapped it closed.

"What?" he said.

"You're acting like such a lawyer."

"I damn well better be. If this stuff is the real deal, I'll soon be in possession of one of the greatest and probably most exciting finds this country has ever known about. And when word gets out, it's going to give 'duck and cover' a whole new meaning."

Phree looked at her little Midwest kitchen that she loved so much with a table full of trouble sitting in the middle of it. On her counter were two empty mugs of tea each with a label dangling from a string. The breeze from her overhead fan left the labels quivering ever so slightly—just how Phree's stomach felt. "I don't think I can afford 24/7 security, Brian."

"Dear Phree, when this is over, you'll be able to afford anything you want."

They each slipped on a pair of latex gloves to protect the valuable paper, as they started cataloguing the items. What Phree originally thought looked like a foreign language, was nothing more than fancy, frilly calligraphy apparently written in Old English. They took inventory and carefully counted the documents; eighty-three pages in all—twelve from the Soule Bible and the rest from the Brewster Bible. There was an in-depth diary from Mary Brewster (wife of the pastor) and three journals, all by G. Soule with one folded piece of paper in the first journal.

From her short hour of Internet surfing, Phree had learned that George Soule had come over on the Mayflower as teacher/tutor to the Edward Winslow family. The Brewster family Bible had belonged to William Brewster, the pastor on the Mayflower and at Plymouth. That explained the excessive wear on the book. She had also learned that there were no 'female' accounts from the Pilgrims first years at Plymouth and only two primary sources for the events occurring during the autumn of 1621 in Plimouth (Plymouth). Autumn of 1621 translated into the first Thanksgiving.

After closely looking at the family history section of one of the Bibles, she saw where George Soule's grandson had married William Brewster's granddaughter. Phree noticed how, after that point, the family section of both Bibles had carefully been kept up to date by the same handwriting. Of course, it changed with the generations, but Phree suspected that after the merge, both Bibles had stayed with one family. From there each generation had the responsibility to keep the list current. The records stopped with the birth of Henrietta Hicks on March 2, 1870. That would be her great-grandma, MeeMee.

Brian was inspecting one of G. Soule's three journals. With great care he unfolded a single sheet of paper that had been hidden inside the back cover. "They sure had good paper back then," he said. "No yellowing or falling apart at the folds."

"Rags," said Phree.

Brian shot her a questioning glance, "Pardon me?"

"Rags. They used pulverized fabric to make paper back then. It will virtually last forever—low pH. It's unlike our modern paper made from wood pulp which turns brown and brittle and has a lot of acid in it." The afternoon sun had worked its way to the kitchen window, where it streamed into the room. Phree rose to close the blinds and smiled at Brian, "I've learned a lot since I started eBaying."

Brian sucked in a long breath, puffed out his cheeks, and flopped back in his chair. Putting a hand on his forehead and resting his elbow on the edge of the table, he set the paper down with the reverence of a priest handling sacred hosts. "Holy Mother of…."

"What is it?"

"It seems that your thirteen-times-great-granddaddy left you a signed Mayflower Compact." Phree moved her lips to talk but no sound came from her mouth.

"This is too huge to comprehend, and I propose we not spend a lot of time right now trying to take this all in..." He squeezed Phree's hand, "I'm going to warn you that this will not have an overnight solution. It may take weeks or even months to have this authenticated and figure the best plan of attack for you and Emily. The timeline is difficult to guess because there are so many variables involved."

Emotionally drained, Phree nevertheless had supper on the table for Emily by 7:00 that evening. They chatted about school, Emily's girlfriends, and the latest gossip about Ricky. Emily took their plates to the sink and finally asked her mom, "So how did it go with the boxes? Find any good stuff?"

Phree felt like a cartoon character with the anvil dangling over her head. She was a horrible liar. Wringing out the dish cloth, she wiped their dinner crumbs off the table and onto her hand—the very table that just hours ago was full of treasure. "Oh, the usual. I'll probably sell most of it, but I plan on keeping a few things." She desperately wanted to share what she had found with her daughter, but remembered Brian's very stern, very lawyer-like warning.

"Cool!" Emily picked up her backpack and slung it over her shoulder. "Well, Mom, I've got a lot of homework tonight. All the teachers start the year with a bang. I'm gonna go to my room and study."

"Fine, Emmy. I'll finish up in the kitchen, and I'm going to head straight to bed and read for a while. Sorting through that stuff has made me really tired." Phree secretly thanked God that teenagers have about a seven second attention span for anyone but themselves.

Chapter 6

No one visited Phree in her dreams that night, but when morning came she sat straight up in bed, heart racing. *Yikes, will life ever be simple again?* She needed to put what happened the day before to the back of her mind. She had about ten eBay items that had come due yesterday, and she hadn't even looked at them. Emily's first swim meet would take place in less than a week, she had all that stuff in the garage, and, to top it off, she hosted Bunco in two weeks.

After Emily left for school, Phree spent the next four hours attending to her current eBay listings. She sent emails to the winners, prepared labels, and wrapped the items to be mailed. She still had about fifteen items coming due over the next few days and had decided not to put anything up for auction until after this Mayflower thing settled down. Maybe she'd just wait until after Bunco—but then again if Brian was correct about the value, her eBay days might just be over. The phone rang, and she heard Brian's voice when she answered it.

"Phree, I will be keeping my schedule as open as possible to concentrate on the 'loot'. Let's just call it that in case we slip in front of the wrong people. Anyone who knows you will automatically think we're talking about eBay."

Phree spun her office chair around, so she was not distracted by her computer screen. "Uh, Brian, I can't afford to keep you on an open schedule."

"Let me worry about my fee. Even if I take this case pro bono, I will get more publicity out of it than I could ever dream. I appreciate that you trust me and hope to do what is best for you as a client and a friend."

"Right now that means a lot to me."

"I've been toying with the idea of talking to Beth's husband, Tim. He does, after all, have a Doctorate in

American History and is the head of the history department at Sauk Trail Community College. He is also affiliated with the American history department at the University of Chicago. His being local is another bonus, and if he finds out the connection is to you, I assume he will use caution to protect the identity of his wife's good friend. I would, of course, do this without using your name. Any thoughts?"

"It sounds as good as anything to me," Phree told him. "Right now, I just want to go back to being Phree-the-divorced-eBayer."

"You can kiss that fantasy good-bye forever," Brian said. "I'll get a hold of Tim and see what he has to say. In the meantime, I'm looking for a safe place to keep the loot after we take inventory, photograph, and categorize everything. While I'm sure we can trust Tim, once we start calling in experts, it won't be long before the media learns what's going on and be camped out on my doorstep. I will field questions as to the identity of the owner, but it wouldn't take a genius to figure out that the mystery person lives in the Chicago area." Phree could hear Brian typing on a keyboard as they spoke. "With his permission, I'm going to suggest to Tim that we videotape his viewing. I can replay it for you, the owner-who-wishes-to-remain-anonymous, and if I have any need of it in the future, it can act as corroborating documentation."

"Sounds good to me."

"At least with Tim making the original connection, I won't be laughed off the phone when I mention I'm in possession of authentic Mayflower documents. Eventually, we will have to come up with a name for the loot. Something like the Clarke-Mayflower Acquisition…"

Before he could even finish his sentence, Phree shouted, "NO! I'm not putting that bastard's name on this. Even though Emily's in the lineage he's not, and I don't want his name connected with my ancestors. How about 'The

Soule/Brewster Discovery' or something like that. Besides, that will keep me more anonymous for the time being."

"I thought you might say something to that affect. I'll call you when I know anything from Tim."

Chapter 7

The inventory was completed on Sunday, and Phree had documentation of everything. It was a neat list, typed on a single piece of Barber and Greenberg stationery. Phree had made a copy with her printer and put the original in the little lock-box in her bedroom closet. She kept the copy in her jeans pocket and looked at it so much the folds were beginning to tear. Brian had moved the items from his office to a private location with security 24-7, and he invited Phree to his office to watch the video of Tim, and hear, first-hand, what he had to say.

The leather chair in the conference room felt soft and buttery, as Phree burrowed into its masculine scent. Brian had slid a DVD into a player, and it whirred as it sucked the plastic disc into its bowels. The flat screen TV on the wall went from video snow to an image of Brian and Tim looking into the camera. Brian pushed a button to pause the action and sat in the chair next to Phree, "You're going to enjoy this."

He started the recording with a remote control, and Brian was summarizing to Tim, in this very room, what was about to happen. Tim's eyes became unusually large when Brian explained what they would be doing.

Phree had to giggle at the reaction of her friend's husband, while Brian was assuring him it was not a hoax. Four unopened archival boxes sat on the conference table, and Brian gave Tim a brief description of how the items had been stored in a false bottom trunk; had probably come into this country through Canada for some reason; sat in a soddy for years; had unknowingly been handed down through the family with the chest, until his client ended up with them.

Brian handed Tim a photo of the trunk, and Tim noted that because of the humpback, it probably dated from the late

1790's or early 1800's. Tapping the photo Tim said, "There are no known trunks from the Mayflower. I suppose that through the years they were either destroyed or went back to Europe on subsequent voyages. Your information fits right in with what we already know about Soule," Tim looked into the camera. "He came over on the Mayflower as a teacher to Edward Winslow's children, and he was one of the signers of the Mayflower Compact. In the early 1640's, Soule, John Alden, and Captain Miles Standish laid out the first town, called Duxbury, which is located several miles from Plymouth. Shortly after, Soule moved there with his family, and he became the Deputy of Duxbury. Well, the long and the short of it is, years later when the Revolutionary War broke out, many of the Soule descendants would not fight against the Crown and went to Canada. From there, the trail went cold on numerous Soule families." Tim turned to Brian, "May I study the documents?"

"By all means, let's get started." Dangling two pairs of white cotton gloves Brian handed a pair to Tim. "I know there is a controversy about the effectiveness of these, but I'd rather err on the safe side for now." As they each slipped on a pair of the protective gloves, Brian added, "I'd like to start with what I feel might be the most astounding document in this collection." He picked up a small archival box and placed it between them. Lifting out a single piece of paper, he handed it to Tim. "I believe this to be another signed original of the Mayflower Compact, but this one appears to have the signatures of the women, as well as the men."

Tim gasped and sputtered so long Phree thought he might start to hyperventilate. She looked at Brian who was smiling as he said, "This is where it gets good."

"Dear, God!" said Tim. "This is incredible. I don't suppose you're at liberty to tell me *who* made this find?"

"I'm sorry, Tim, but at this juncture, I feel it is best for my client to remain anonymous. As a matter of fact, as soon as you are through with your preliminary viewing, these items will be going to a secure and guarded place." Brian paused and opened the other boxes for Tim's inspection. "In addition, I'm hoping you can give me some advice as to the next step to authenticate the articles. I would like to do that as soon as possible."

"Yes. Yes. I'll be able to help with that. I know some reliable and discreet sources for just that type of work. I can tell you these documents will fetch a pretty penny, that's for sure."

"So," Brian halted momentarily, "in your expert opinion, they appear at this time to be authentic?"

"Why, yes. I have almost no doubt. I can tell by several things, but to me the biggest clues are the handwriting and the wording—also the paper. Typical of the time and difficult to reproduce—not impossible, but difficult, and I'd say this is flawless. We wouldn't see flawless if this were a forgery. See here, where this word should have a double *s*, the *f*-shape is used. Also very common for the time were abbreviations such as *yt* for *that,* and *ye* for *the*. It appears as though the three Soule journals are rag content paper, both characteristic of the time and very durable. Parchment books were replaced by rag based papers sometime in the early 16th century. See this bit of brownish discoloration?" Tim pointed. "That's called foxing. Aside from a little foxing, these documents are all in extraordinary condition."

"That's wonderful news," Brian said. "Let's take a look at the other documents, and maybe you can give me an idea of what they are all about?"

Tim pointed to a pile of loose papers, "Well, just at a glance, I'd say the ones from the Brewster Bible look to be largely sermons or something of that nature. The three journals appear to be from Soule himself. It looks as though he started the first one back in England, continued it on the voyage, and kept them up throughout his life."

Tim picked up the tattered diary of Mary Brewster and waved a hand over the rest of the antiquities, "As priceless as this find is—and especially the Compact with all the adult passenger signatures..." he hesitated and then looked back at the diary. "I could be holding the real gem right here. We have nothing from a woman's viewpoint of the trials of the Pilgrims. Out of the eighteen women who made the voyage on the Mayflower, only five survived that first horrible winter. I'm not sure I can even verbalize how important this modest, little book will be to historians."

Brian remained silent, and then slowly nodded his head in understanding.

Up on the flat screen, Tim passed his hand over the treasures again. "These documents and journals will undoubtedly shed new light on the Pilgrims and their way of life. This is an invaluable find and will make for fascinating reading. Historians will be drooling to get a chance to study them."

"If you're interested, maybe we can work it so you can collaborate on the 'translation' of the pieces."

"Please keep me in mind. It would be a dream come true."

"You can count on it. And, Tim, I'll remind you again that this must be kept in the strictest confidence for the time being. I'm not ready to be bombarded by the media. So, I'm asking you to inform only those people that would be integral to authenticating these items."

"It's a powder keg to be sure," said Tim. "You have my word." He picked up Mary Brewster's diary and carefully opened it to the first page.

Sitting in a cozy leather chair in Brian's dark office, Phree felt tears flow down her face.

Chapter 8

Over the past week Phree had organized the piles in her garage into a priority selling order and put a few items for sale on eBay. She attended Emily's first swim meet and, as the mother of the team captain, even hosted the pasta party the night before. She dodged two calls from The Bastard and remained in touch by phone several times a day with Brian.

Bunco would be at her house next week, and she was more than ready to focus on her duties as this month's Bunco hostess. She would start with the prizes and slipped a tablet from under a stack of unopened mail. Writing BUNCO on top of the page she then noted: get movie gift certificates, popcorn, chocolate. Now, for the hard part—the perfect menu. Phree was probably one of the few women in the group who actually enjoyed hosting Bunco. Other than the Bunco Club she didn't have much of a social life, and she easily became engrossed in the planning.

Out of the blue, Phree had what she thought an ingenious and self-serving idea. Since she had been dieting steadily, and, as of today had lost a whopping twenty pounds from the Mayflower Diet, she would go off her regime for just one night and serve all of *her* favorite foods. *Brilliant. Simply brilliant.* Writing her menu list, going back and forth, adding ideas, scratching out others—she soon became lost in a savory delirium of throwing caution and her diet to the wind for one glorious night. After about an hour of non-stop food fantasy, she had her menu.

<u>BUNCO MENU</u>

Carmel Dip w/ Apples   Hot Pizza Dip
Fake 'Sliders'   Tomato Pie*   Sausage Roll-Ups

Mexican Fudge   Buddig Beef Ball
Veggies and Dip

Popcorn - M & M's
chocolate covered raisins - mini Snickers
Pop - Renee's Fake Sangria

Nearly as Good as Sex Pie
Earl Grey Decaf

*recipe at back of book

The phone rang, and as soon as Phree heard Brian's voice, her stomach knotted. "We're not going to be able to keep the lid on this thing for much longer. I've contacted some experts to authenticate the find, and word is bound to leak out and spread fast. I suggest you let me do the talking and run interference for as long as possible."

"How long can we hold out?"

"I know you'd like to remain anonymous, at least until most everything is sold. As we've discussed, it is unavoidable that, sooner or later, you will be identified. My suggestion is that, in order to keep control over the situation, *we* make the decision as to when to divulge your identity. We need to start thinking about your selling/donating options."

Phree white-knuckled the telephone receiver as she stretched the curly cord to its limit. She wanted to stand as far from the base as she could to avoid the temptation of hanging up on Brian. "What might those options be?"

"Well, top dollar would be to break it up into individual items. You know what that's like from your eBay experience. We'd put them up for auction somewhere like Christie's. Chances are some wealthy entrepreneur or oil tycoon will buy the whole thing, and that will be that. Or, possibly everything could end up in the Middle East and never be seen again, but you'd be unbelievably rich."

"I don't like that idea at all." Phree began to pace barefooted across the cool tiles of her kitchen floor. She focused on the simple pleasure of watching her toes as she walked, and somehow it calmed her. "I mean the part about the loot going to another country. I don't mind the unbelievably rich part."

"Good. I'd like to see it stay in this country, too. We can get the word out to wealthy private American citizens, and they could purchase it for their own personal collections, or perhaps donate it to a museum as a tax write off."

Phree sat in a kitchen chair and stared at her toes as she wiggled them up and down. "But what about the museums themselves? It might be naïve, but I think the items should be enjoyed by the American people. It's such an important part of our history, and these documents could unravel some of the misconceptions we've had about the Pilgrims and Plymouth. I don't really think of myself as a greedy person, but it would be nice to have some security, especially since I don't have any sort of pension." *Keep looking at your toes. You can get through this.* "I don't need top dollar to do that—just a nice chunk of money, along with the knowledge that I did right by my ancestors. That would make me happy."

"That would make me proud to know you and to be your attorney. Let's put out some feelers to the Newberry Library right here in Chicago. I know that's not specifically their thing, but it can't hurt to see what they say. Also, I think the Mayflower Society Museum and the Plymouth Plantation Museum will probably have some interest. I'm checking into Duxbury right now, they have a re-creation of the Soule home there."

"All good ideas." Phree paused. "I've been thinking, is there any way we can negotiate for the items to travel around the country to some of the larger cities? I think it would be great to have school children, and adults for that matter, see the stuff and understand these were real people and maybe appreciate what the Pilgrims went through." Wiggling her toes faster and faster, Phree felt liberated from her fears with the thought of all the good that could come from her discovery.

"This is going to be a major media blitz, and I'm going to start preparing for when the 'you-know-what' hits the fan. I'll try to hold out as long as possible, but someday real soon the news of this discovery is going to get out."

"Brian, I know this sounds dumb, but can you stall until after I have Bunco at my house next week?"

Phree heard a rumble come across the phone line as Brian laughed. "I'll do my best."

Chapter 9

In only two short days, Bunco would be at Phree's house, and she had spent much of her time spinning her wheels while accomplishing nothing. She had managed to make all of Emily's swim meets but had opted out of a sewing night with the Bunco girls at Nancy's condo. She had told Nancy that they'd be at an 'away' swim meet that night, and by the time she'd get home, get Emily settled down, and get some supper into both of them, it would be late, and she'd be too exhausted. Truth be told, Phree sat in her favorite chair—toes-up on the ottoman—by 6:30 that night.

Another fact that was probably going to bite her in the ass was that she hadn't sewn a stitch since the last Bunco and had nothing for show-and-tell. Rosa would probably pick up on this and wonder what Phree had been doing with her precious quilting time. Also, the whole Nancy/Michael thing had been simmering in the back of Phree's overloaded mind for the past few weeks, and she knew it had probably been discussed at sewing. She sensed there was more to Nancy's story, yet she truly had had no time in which to bounce her suspicions off any of the Bunco girls. Maybe she'd call one of them tomorrow and see if there was any news about the two star crossed lovers. …And then there was Ricky Mitchell.

The only good thing that had come from this madness so far showed itself every morning on Phree's scale. Her diet had been fast-tracked. Nothing like a little anxiety and nervous diarrhea to take the pounds off quickly. She had lost four more pounds this past week—over half way there in no time at all. Gotta love the Mayflower Diet.

With Bunco night closing in, the emails and Facebook messages from the Bunco Club started up with the pace of a sprinter who has the finish-line in sight.

"Can I bring anything?"

"Do you need any help?"

Helen left a message on Phree's voice mail, "I'm going to be about a half hour late. Ruby's school has their open house tonight, and I want to hang back and talk to her teacher privately for a few minutes."

And, of course, a group email from good old, always-in-control Sarge, reminding everyone that Phree had Bunco this week, and if anyone might be late or couldn't make it, to please call Phree and let her know so she could get a sub. Duh!

Standing in the produce section of the grocery store looking over her shopping list, she ran into Lettie, and they briefly went over the menu. "I just love that Tomato Pie," said Lettie. "My mouth will be watering until Thursday night—thanks a lot."

They shared a few other thoughts and discussed the update on Ricky. Rosa and Terry had decided not to push to get Ricky's charges dropped but to leave the decision in the hands of the judge. Their youngest son was schedule to do some time in juvenile detention starting tomorrow. Lettie told her that Rosa had broken down and was devastated, but Terry stayed firm that this might be just what Ricky needed. As they say, 'It will either make him or break him.'

"*That* should make Bunco interesting," said Phree, and at the same time thinking any Rosa/Ricky talk might take the spotlight away from her.

"You know how Rosa is, she'll probably just shut down and act like nothing is wrong. I really wish she'd open up and let us help her. Rosa and I are such good friends, but when it comes to personal problems, she just doesn't let *anyone* get too close."

"True." Phree examined the table of bright red tomatoes with the scrutiny of a librarian looking for the mistreatment of a book. One by one she turned the fruit upside down in her hand taking note of bruising or cracks.

Half of a dozen orbs passed inspection and made their way into the flimsy plastic bag. "You know how paranoid I am. I always thought Rosa intentionally kept me out of the loop, but I've come to realize she's built a pretty big wall around herself."

"Well put." Lettie grabbed a twist tie and handed it to Phree. "I'm glad the rest of us aren't so secretive with each other."

Phree faked a laugh, but inwardly cringed. *It's not really a secret, just private financial stuff—at least that's what I'll tell them when word gets out. Eye-yi-yi—how will I ever keep up this lie?*

Lettie started to turn her cart to leave, when Phree stopped her. "How was the bee at Nancy's the other night? Was there any news about her old boyfriend?"

"Oh my God! Wait till you hear this." Lettie grabbed Phree's arm. "After we all hinted that we thought she was holding out on us, she finally got around to adding another piece to this goofy puzzle. It still doesn't make sense and I'm more convinced than ever she's not telling us everything. That's certainly her prerogative..."

"Me, too!" Phree interrupted Lettie midsentence. "I'm so glad you said that. It's been bugging me ever since she told us about this guy. So what's the story now?" Phree felt so good to focus on someone else's problems, even if it was only for a few minutes.

"She claimed that Michael's uncle was a police officer, and he was shot and killed when he went to a domestic disturbance call. Several days later Michael broke off their relationship, and she never saw him again." Lettie shook her head, "If you ask me, none of this really adds up. Anyway, I've always had a hard time figuring out why Nancy never married or hooked up with anyone. She's really a caring person, and she would have been such a good wife and mother. We all know that's what she's always wanted. So, I just don't get it. But then again, I'm the last person that should be wondering why someone never married."

"Sometimes it's hard to meet the right person. I know all about mistakes in that area, but I know exactly what you mean. There seems to be such a void in her life."

"More like a sadness."

"Yeah, that's it—a sadness," Phree checked the date on a bag of mini carrots and placed them in her cart. "I wish we could help her."

"For that to happen she's going to have to tell us everything. We can't help her if we don't know what the heck happened."

Phree felt a pang of guilt as Lettie's statement hit home. "True," she pushed her cart toward the cucumbers. "I guess she's just not ready to share yet."

"For crying out loud, it's been twenty years. How long is she going to wait? If you ask me, we need to get that girl moving toward some kind of a resolution so maybe she can enjoy life."

"All we can do is encourage her to share the whole story with us, and we might have to accept that's just not going to happen."

Lettie looked at her watch. "Well, enough gossiping. I've got to get moving." Lettie hugged Phree and maneuvered toward the check-out line, as she cast a look over her shoulder. Just three of Lettie's long-legged strides had her halfway down the aisle. "Nice seeing you, and get that wrist warmed up for tomorrow night."

Back home Phree put her groceries away. She would clean her house today and do all of her food prep tomorrow. Her house had become cluttered and neglected over the past few weeks, so she rallied around a first-class vigorous cleaning which was just what she needed to make her feel back in control. Washing, polishing, scrubbing, and dusting gave her a true sense of accomplishment—the first in weeks.

Turning in a circle she surveyed her living room, dining room, and kitchen where everything gleamed with a delicious scent of pine and lemons.

With a clean house, calmness spread through her, like a warm quilt on a cold night. For the first time that day she thought of her Pilgrim roots, and it struck her that she would like to keep Hannah Brewster's very old, much worn chore basket and maybe even the inkwell. She said out loud, "At least I can hand something physical down to Emily from our ancestors."

Chapter 10

Waking to a clean house felt refreshing, and Phree was optimistic as she started her day of cooking for Bunco. Most of her menu could be prepared early with only a few dishes requiring last minute preparations. She set out several cream cheese bricks to soften to room temperature, and then baked the empty pie crust for the Tomato Pie, so it could cool and be ready to fill that evening. Phree browned the hamburger for the Fake 'Sliders' and when she added the dried onion soup mix to the sputtering beef, the aroma nearly made her dizzy. She knew she had gone a little overboard with the menu, but after dieting for the past month, she had an uber-food craving for salty, fat, and sweet. Working steadily over the next several hours she longed for the moment when the savory sausage that was swirled up inside of the light buttery crescent roll hit her tongue.

After finishing the food prep, Phree decided to get off her feet for a few minutes to check the computer for emails, eBay, and Facebook. Nothing substantial popped up on her in-box list except for a whiney email from The Bastard. She was about to delete the message, when a wicked thought crept into her mind, like a slow moving fog slipping through a cornfield. Pulling the email back onto the screen, she clicked on 'print' and made eight copies.

Phree's eyes skimmed over her living room. The card tables and chairs were positioned so the women could easily flow around them, like drivers in an obstacle course, as they jockeyed for food and chit-chat. Dice, bell, and pencils placed in the center of one of the tables, stood at the ready. She planned to present each woman with a copy of the 'special' scratch paper at the beginning of the game. The hot food had only ten minutes to go before coming out of the oven. Phree was as prepared as she could be for the Bunco Club.

The initial wave of guests started arriving. Lettie and Rosa rode together. "It smells fabulous in here." Rosa with her tote bag swelled to bursting, came through the door first. "I'm starving. I'm really glad you three dieters decided Bunco night should be exempt from the diet rule."

Phree pointed toward the table. "We've got at least a ton of non-diet food tonight, and there's more to come." Rosa instantly dug into the nearest bowl of chocolate covered raisins. "I've got to get some stuff out of the oven. Come on in and get started."

Their routine was a well-choreographed arrangement of tradition and personalities; a dance between good friends that needed no signals or leaders. Placing totes filled to overflowing with colorful show-and-tell projects in a corner or on a sofa, they'd head for the cold drinks. "Oooo, what's this?" Lettie swirled a long handled ladle in a punchbowl.

"Homemade virgin Sangria," Phree replied. "I just threw a bunch of stuff together and voila—there you go." In front of them rested a beautiful antique punchbowl, filled with ruby-red liquid and swimming with sparkling jewel tones of sliced oranges, lemons, limes, strawberries, grapes, and glittering chunks of ice.

As Lettie and Rosa filled punch cups, the door opened again. Nedra and Beth loaded down with tote bags, purses, and two folded quilts entered. They were chatting excitedly about something. "You've got to try this Sangria," Rosa told the newcomers. "It's to die for."

Beth got a funny look on her face and shook her head 'no.'

"It's unleaded," Phree called from the kitchen, balancing the sliders as she removed them from the oven. Beth never drank anything alcoholic, but no one knew why.

"Well, in that case, pour me one, will you Rosa?"

"Me too," said Nedra. "Marge and Nancy pulled in right behind us. Might as well line up another two cups. Where's Helen?"

Phree told the group that Helen would be about half an hour late because of Ruby's open house. "Helen was going to stay and talk to the teacher. I'm not sure, but I sense it has something to do with all the teasing that poor kid's been through."

"More like bullying if you ask me," Nancy said.

"I can't wait 'til she gets that quilting machine," Rosa said as she stacked several sausage roll-ups on her already full plate of food. "I've got a mound of quilt tops that need quilting, and I'm waiting for her to do them."

"So am I," Lettie added. "Man, she's got such a great talent for quilting. She'll probably be in such high demand, that she'll have a list of names so long she'll never get to *our* tops."

"*I* plan on getting my name on the list tonight." Rosa sounded proud of herself, as though she was announcing the birth of a child. "Whenever she gets that damn machine, *I'll* be her first customer." She pointed to her own chest and tapped it several times.

"Too late," Lettie grinned and licked caramel apple dip from her little finger, "I had her put me first on the list weeks ago."

Rosa shoulders sagged, as she visibly crumpled. "I can't believe it," she mock-slapped Lettie's arm, "I should have known you'd sneak under the radar."

"Hey, you two," The Sarge said. "Do you think you could each stop trying to be first at everything? This isn't a competition. We're supposed to enjoy quilting. There's no prize for being first." Rosa and Lettie joined forces as they glared at Marge with narrowed eyes and sent her the why-don't-you-mind-your-own-business look.

It became a balancing act as the seven women, plates wobbling and drinks sloshing, wove their way between the card tables and chairs to choose a seat. The door opened, and Helen crossed the threshold with the obligatory tote bag swollen full of projects.

"How was the conference?" Nancy asked relieving Helen of her tote.

"It wasn't exactly a conference. I just wanted to talk to Ruby's teacher for a few minutes after the open house. This is the grade I've been dreading. Her teacher is the mother of that little snit who teases Ruby the most. If mother is like daughter, I'm not expecting much compassion out of her."

"What'd she say?"

"At best I'd say she was annoyed. She told me if I wanted to talk about something specific to set up a meeting with her. So I said, 'How 'bout tomorrow, Bitch?'—but I left off the bitch part."

"Want me there? I often go to bat as an advocate for the kid or the family."

"Yeah, maybe. Let me think about it. She put me off until next week, so maybe we can come up with a plan by then. I don't want to piss her off too much. She's got a whole year to take it out on Ruby."

Helen reached for a plate, and Rosa sidled up next to her with an offering of a Slider and a syrupy request. "I need to talk to you about your long-arm schedule. Do you think you could squeeze in a few rushes for me?"

"For crying out loud Rosa, I don't even have the machine ordered yet."

"But Lettie's first." Rosa actually whined. "Can't you alternate us or something?"

Helen rolled her eyes and ignored Rosa. "Phree, this is the best meal I've had since we started our diets last month at Lettie's." Helen took another slice of Tomato Pie. "I'm so tired of small portions and no chocolate, I could scream."

"I must say, all three of you look like you've lost weight," Lettie looked from Helen, to Phree, to Nancy, but her eyes came back to rest on Phree.

"I've lost about nine pounds." Nancy pinched her faded jeans away from her hip to show the difference in her clothes. "But it looks to me like the weight has melted off Phree. She must know some kind of a secret."

Phree smiled and diverted her lying eyes to condensing the Sausage Roll-ups and Sliders onto one plate. "Thanks, Nancy. I've been working at it."

Beth was the one this time who asked the mandatory question about Ricky, but Rosa shut her out with, "He's doing fine. I'd rather not talk about it." Rosa had trumpeted her Dumbo trunk, and her child remained protected behind her bravado.

A little flustered by Rosa's curt reply, Beth turned the conversation to her father and filled in everyone on George's status. She thanked her friends again for helping with her dad, and Phree felt horribly guilty that she had not been over for a visit. "I've had a bad month, but I'll be by to see him soon." *Did that sound shallow and evasive? Yeah, probably.*

One by one the women wandered to the kitchen, threw their paper plates into the recycle bin, refilled their drinks, and returned to their places at the card tables—of course, talking all the way. Years ago it had been decided they would use only disposable plates, cups and utensils to make it easier on the hostess. "That's one for the Bunco bi-laws," they all agreed.

They were waiting for Phree to join them and antsy to start playing Bunco, when Rosa called out, "Hey Phree, we need some scratch paper."

"This should do the trick. Just use the back." Phree gave each woman a copy of The Bastard's email, and a general hoot went through the group. "I thought you could all appreciate this." Phree felt liberated as she laughed at her ex. "Can you believe him?"

After further comments about Gary's email, someone called out, "Let's get started!" The dice were rolled to determine the head table, and there was a chorus of groans from one table and applause from the other. The bell went to the 'head table', where Helen rang it immediately to start play.

By the third round, there were no Buncos thrown yet, and it looked like this would be a low scoring game. Then, Rosa started to hit them. Bunco after Bunco. At the end of the game, she had eight Buncos for the night and had tied the all-time high record. Screaming, high-fiving, and a general uproar followed. With each new Bunco thrown, the women got louder and more excited. Rosa even rolled a double Bunco, one right after the other, and her partner fanned Rosa's flushed face with her scorecard. "Open the door, I need fresh air," Rosa called out. "I think I'm having a hot flash on top of it!"

Phree was laughing so hard, she was afraid she was going to pee her pants as she heaved the door open for some cool air. A police officer stood there, hand poised, ready to knock. Phree let out a shriek and then gasped, "Oh, my God, what's wrong, is everything okay?"

"That's exactly what I need to find out from you," he said. "The station just got a call, and someone reported loud screams coming from this address. May I come in?"

Phree recognized the officer as the Hot Cop who stopped her car when the tree limbs were across the road last month. Opening the door wider for him she said, "Sure, come on in. Ladies, we have a guest," Phree sang out. "It seems that our screaming got out of control, and we were a little louder than usual tonight."

Marge looked mortified and was overly apologetic, "Oh, we are so sorry. Forgive us."

"But I just threw my eighth Bunco," said Rosa, "and it was a double!" Like he'd even know what that meant. "I'm going for the all-time record. This is important stuff, Officer, sir. Come on in. How 'bout a Slider?"

"No thank you, ma'am." *Not only hot, but polite, too.* I just need to check and make sure that no one is being killed in here."

"Well, I am," laughed Nancy. "Rosa Mitchell is killing us all, and it looks like I'm headed straight for a booby prize tonight!"

Hot Cop turned to Phree, "I'll just need your name and phone number for my report."

"You can have my phone number," Rosa yelled out. He blushed a deep red, while everyone other than Phree laughed.

"Sorry." Phree was truly embarrassed and felt her own cheeks flush, too. "You'll have to excuse us. Some of us don't get out much."

"I know you ladies are just having some good honest fun, but it'd probably be best to keep it down a little." He smiled, and Phree nearly swooned.

"Sure, I'm sorry. I feel pretty stupid. My teenager will never let me live this one down."

Rosa shouted from the living room, "Come back for dessert."

He turned and looked at Phree, as he tipped his cap, "I'd say you've got your work cut out for you keeping *this* group quiet."

Rosa won by a landslide and continued to be so wound up she could barely contain herself.

"Oh, Lordy, look at that pie," shouted Marge. "I'll pour the tea."

They settled into chatting, while they devoured dessert—all the dieters having seconds. Murmurs of "delicious" and "you really outdid yourself this time" could be heard.

"Nedra, did you get to work on the borders and binding of that wall-hanging?" asked Helen.

"All finished and ready to be hung." Nedra reached for her tote bag and unfolded a hand quilted vision of her backyard garden. "Ooo's" and "ahh's" filled the room, and everyone made it clear that Nedra should enter it in the next quilt show that their guild sponsored.

Rosa took the quilt from Nedra and stood with it stretched between her arms, as though it were hanging on a clothes line. "It is absolutely stunning. And, above all, you made up the pattern yourself."

"Anyone else have any show-and-tell?"

Tote bags were dragged across the floor, as other projects in various states of finish emerged. A half hour later, with show-and-tell finished, calendars were dug out from the bottom of purses, as they all agreed on a Bunco date for the following month. Nedra whimpered, when she realized she would be hosting next time. The women also penciled in their annual fall trip to the Amish village of Shipshewana, Indiana, in November.

Rosa turned to Phree, "You didn't have anything to show. Why not? Have you worked on that quilt with the burn mark yet?"

"I've been busy with getting Emily back to school and planning for Bunco. Besides, I had a lot of work to do with those boxes from the attic."

"Oh, yeah, Terry said there was a boatload of stuff."

"I guess you could say a boatload," Phree smiled at the secret pun.

"Nancy, you've been awfully quiet tonight. Do you have any news about Lover-boy?"

For the briefest of seconds, a rosy blush covered Nancy's cheeks and ran the length of her neck. Her eyes darted downward toward the table top, and when she looked up took a big deep breath and held it, then slowly let the breath out, and simply said, "We've emailed a few times."

"That's it?" Helen nearly shouted and then repeated Nancy's answer, " 'We've emailed a few times?' "

"What do you want me to say?"

"For starters," Nedra flung several questions at a rather defenseless Nancy, "does it appear to be going anywhere? How do you feel about it? ...About him? Are you looking forward to seeing him?"

Phree brought a fresh pot of tea into the room and went over to fill Nancy's cup first, "What are these emails all about—anything serious, or just a bunch of small talk?"

The Sarge, as usual, took over when she saw the horrified look on Nancy's face. "Give her some space, ladies. She doesn't have to tell us anything she doesn't want to. Just remember, Nancy, we're your friends, and we're here to help you in any way you need us."

Rosa gave Marge an I-could-just-smack-you look.

"I know," Nancy took a long sip of hot tea from her cup. "After all the years I swore that I hated him, I'm just having a hard time letting him back into my heart. One minute my gut is telling me to give it a chance, and the next minute I remind myself that my life has been fine without him."

"But has it really...been fine, that is?" Marge was trying to gently nudge Nancy, and Phree had to admit to herself that she was good at this kind of thing. "Have you forgiven him for breaking up with you?"

"Oh, yeah, I did that a long time ago."

"Then I'm confused." Lettie came right out and asked, "Is there something you're not telling us, Nancy? And what does his uncle being killed have to do with any of this?"

"Oh, it's such a long and complicated story. I don't think rehashing it will do any good."

"Keeping it all bottled-up inside is what's doing no good," Helen added her opinion to the mix, and Phree thought Nancy was beginning to squirm. "Have you discussed whatever it is with Michael?"

"NO!" Her shoulders slumped, and she whispered, "No. No we haven't."

Phree knew they had pushed enough, "When you're ready—we'll all be here for you."

Ashen faced, Nancy said, "Thank you."

Phree wasn't sure if Nancy had thanked her for the offer of help or for ending the cross-examination, but she took the cue and scooted her chair back, as she stood up and grabbed a handful of empty dessert plates.

"It's getting late," Marge said, "and most of us have work in the morning."

"We certainly do," Nancy said a little too quickly, and one-by-one all of the women rose to leave.

They were heading out the door when Marge said, "You dieters all look great, but, Phree, I don't know how you could have lost so much in one month. I'll have to get your secret."

"There really is no big secret. Just don't eat as much."

"That's easier said than done," Helen groaned, extended her stomach, and patted it.

"Ladies…" The Sarge let her voice trail off as she got everyone's attention. "We'll see everyone at Lettie's house for the bee in two weeks." She made a note on her calendar. "If you can't make it, please let her know in advance."

Lettie rolled her eyes behind Marge's back, and Phree had to look away before she started laughing. As the last woman left her home Phree closed the door. She clicked the lock and felt like her old self again. For the past 24 hours she hadn't given a single thought to Pilgrims or the Mayflower.

OCTOBER BUNCO – Nedra

Life has a way of getting your attention.

Chapter 1

Nedra was off schedule. Terribly, terribly off schedule. She estimated she was ten minutes late and for Nedra that was unheard of. Bunco had run long last night, and by the time she finally pulled the Egyptian cotton 1200 thread-count sheet over her weary body, her mind would not cooperate and turn off. She needed to get her rear in gear, or she'd miss the Metra train into Chicago. A chip in the *Seductively Pink* polish of her ring finger could be fixed on the train, and she would look up today's 'new word' on her phone. Ten minute delay—solved. *Seductively Pink,* smart phone, and blue-tooth were swept off the kitchen counter into her purse-of-the-day. She checked to make sure her train pass and sunglasses were in there as well. After tying the laces on her walking shoes, she grabbed the tote with her pretty and stylish red heels inside and left for work. She needed to be on the train platform in half an hour.

In her navy-blue business suit, Nedra boarded the Metra train out of Whitney—happy to find a window seat where she could snuggle into a corner and eventually close her eyes. It would be approximately 40 minutes to the end of the line in downtown Chicago, and if she played her cards right she could fix her chipped nail, find a new-word, and catch just a teensy little cat nap. She felt worn out—but what a fun night Bunco had been.

The over-large man next to her gave her a dirty look and a *tch* of the tongue after she opened *Seductively Pink,* and the stinging odor of nail polish polluted their small space on the train. Nedra ignored him. Within less than a minute, the cap was screwed back on, and she slid her very-cool-and-in-style sunglasses over her eyes. Nedra folded her arms over her chest with her bags between her body and the side of the train, their straps securely around her left arm. She called this the Vaulted Snooze Position (or VSP) and often used it when there was a chance she might doze off.

Intending to just rest for a few minutes, she would look up that new word as they got a little closer to the city. Burrowing into the corner as best she could on a rather grimy train seat and positioning herself as far away from Mr. Large as she could get, Nedra's thoughts turned to Nancy. She tried to make sense of her friend's love life and odd story. The familiar sounds of people talking in quiet tones, the gentle rocking of the train stopping and then starting again, and the doors whooshing open and closed were a train rider's lullaby. Before she knew it, she had joined about half the people on the Metra and started to doze.

What surely must have been only five minutes later, she jerked awake and looked around. They were stopped underground at Millennium Station—the end of the line. *My God, I slept so hard. Please don't tell me I've been drooling.* Rubbing her lips together, Nedra assured herself she remained drool-free. She hoisted her tote and purse and headed for the door of the train like everyone else. Once off the train a foot race ensued to her office. Thank God for walking shoes, but she wouldn't feel her appearance was complete until she arrived at work and slipped those cute little red heels onto her feet.

Nedra had worked at the magazine, *Excel Chicago,* for what felt like forever. After her husband, John, had been killed in a car accident fifteen years ago, she knew she needed to earn a salary to supplement the income from Social Security and the lump sum insurance she and the girls had received. Those sad days were a blur to her now, but the pain of losing her husband had never left. Thank God her younger brother, Brian, having just graduated from law school, helped guide her through the maze of pitfalls after such a tragedy.

Nedra had started working at *Excel* as a telephone receptionist just two months after John died; Allison had just turned four and Lizzie was eight. Nedra's pain and sadness never faded, and if it hadn't been for her daughters, she would have preferred to curl up and die. She made a conscious effort to 'put on a happy face' for her girls, and she discovered that her 'happy face' became contagious. While she never felt deliriously happy, Nedra could finally survive and get through her days without crying. Eventually, she got a stern hold on herself and began to take baby steps back into the world of the living. Her efforts paid off, especially with her daughters as they matured into young women.

She looked up in awe at the soaring skyscraper where *Excel* occupied three floors of office space. In the past fifteen years, she had gone from telephone receptionist to Executive Assistant to the Editor-in-Chief—not bad for a 50-year-old, widowed, African-American woman, with two children. Today she would assist Don, her boss, with the appropriate documentation and background history for a three part story on Chicago's Catholic High Schools. She needed to arrange interviews with several of the principals, deans, and athletic directors, and hoped for some input from students as well. Chicago loomed second place in the country with Catholic High Schools, and *Excel* wanted to expose all of the pros and cons of this phenomenon, especially the high number of successes with 'same sex schools'.

They had their work cut out for them.

Chapter 2

The outer office was full of chatty purposeful people. Nedra thought it resembled a beehive, which the writer in her quickly reprimanded for using such an overdone cliché. Storing her purse in the bottom drawer of her desk, she glided those red heels onto her feet and wiggled her *Seductively Pink* nailed toes. While snagging her laptop, she headed for Don's office, but remembered she did not have a new word for the day. *Damn.*

"Morning, Don. Ready to get started?"

Flipping through a tall stack of papers, Don was pulling out paperclips, removing file folders, and reorganizing the information into new piles. "Good morning, Nedra. Yeah, I'm really looking forward to working on this one. You know, I'm a little partial since my son went to Mount Carmel, and we loved the four years he spent there. I'd especially like to highlight their motto of 'Building Character for a Lifetime'. Mount Carmel is really the jewel-in-the-crown of the all-boys' schools here in Chicago. It's been around for over a hundred years." Don looked at Nedra and smiled, "Let's get some successful alums involved, and find out how their high school experience might have helped them." Nedra took notes on her laptop while Don kept up a steady stream of thoughts. "Once we nail down the Carmel story, let's move on to Brother Rice and Saint Rita. Those will be our three big powerhouse stories for boys. We can talk about..."

Nedra's assistant, Kathy, stuck her head in the door and said, "Sorry to interrupt, but I thought you might want to see this. It just came across the crawl on both CNN and Fox that they're about to go live with a story. It's something about some historical documents found here in Chicago. If it's interesting enough we might want to follow-up with an article."

Don said, "I got an email this morning saying there would be an announcement at the Newberry Library. It sounded rather vague, but I sent Tom over to cover it just in case."

They moved into the outer office where Kathy sat with her computer and three televisions—one tuned to Fox News, one to MSNBC, and another to CNN. Part of Kathy's job required her to monitor world events and clue Nedra and Don in on any breaking developments. Kathy sat at her desk, and Don stood behind her, arms folded, waiting for the local 'feed' to start, while Nedra half-leaned and half-sat on the side edge of Kathy's desk. Checking to see that her nail polish repair job was still intact, she looked up at the television just as the announcer said they were going live to Chicago. Nedra gasped as her brother Brian appeared on the screen.

"My God, Nedra, isn't that your brother?" Don said.

"Yeah, that's him." Nedra was surprised—no, she was shocked to see Brian on TV, the subject of a breaking news story. "What the heck is going on?" She didn't know how it had happened, but she now sat in Kathy's chair, and Kathy stood off to her side with a hand placed gently on her back.

Then Brian spoke, "I'll make a brief statement and open the floor to questions."

In his deepest, no-nonsense lawyer voice he stated, "My client, who wishes to remain anonymous, has come into possession of several rare and valuable books and documents. Included in this find are two family Bibles. One Bible belonging to George Soule, that's S O U L E, and one to William Brewster, B R E W S T E R. These two individuals arrived in this country in the fall of 1620 on…" Brian took a deep breath and paused. Nedra knew her brother was the king of dramatic pauses. He continued, "The Mayflower." Pandemonium shattered the quiet in the room, and Brian held up his hand for silence.

"Just for the record, we are calling this the Soule/Brewster Discovery." Brian spoke of details of the find, while both Don and Kathy scribbled notes. Nedra stared at her brother, a little in awe and a lot perplexed. After his descriptive list, the room filled with more convulsive gasping, along with waving hands and questions shouted at Brian. Once again, Brian held his hand up for silence. The crowd of journalists quieted, and Nedra began to get a little ticked off at her younger brother for not filling her in on this incredible news story.

"One final document of immense importance has been found." Again, a dramatic pause as Brian cleared his throat. No one dared to breathe, and the room fell eerily quiet. "We now have another copy of the Mayflower Compact. However, this Compact is signed by the women of the Mayflower, as well as the men." The room erupted into a frenzy as journalists, reporters, and cameramen all jockeyed for Brian's attention. In a cacophony of confusion, the most prominent question being shouted was, "WHO?"

For another half hour, Nedra, Don, and Kathy all watched as Brian fielded questions from reporters and journalists. He gave no information at all as to who the 'mystery' finder of such an extraordinary discovery could possibly be, or where they might be from. David, a new writer for the magazine, joined them at the bank of televisions. "Did you guys hear that? Right here in Chicago. How the heck does that happen?"

"That's what I'm about to find out." Nedra reached for a phone.

Chapter 3

After four long hours, Brian returned her call. Nedra hissed into the phone, "Brian, what the hell is going on?"

"So you've heard?" She could just see that shit-eating grin on his face.

"I'd have to live under a rock not to know about this! My God, Brian, I work for *Excel*," she groaned into the phone, and placed her head into her hand. "This place has been up for grabs since your little appearance on TV this morning, and everyone expects that I know something about it."

"How'd I look?" Again, shit-eating grin.

"You're an idiot, and you looked just fine. You know I want info, and I will disown you if you don't at least throw me a bone."

"Oh really, I hadn't guessed that was coming. I'll see what I can do. Let me get back to you." Long dramatic pause, but Nedra refused to play along and said nothing. "I'm pretty busy right now so this might take a while." He sighed—*he actually sighed*. "You know how it is for us Big Shot Lawyers."

Brian hung up before Nedra could say goodbye. *Big-shot-shit-eater of a lawyer brother, indeed!*

This time it only took about twenty minutes for Kathy to tell Nedra that her brother was on line two. She was tempted to tell Brian she was too busy to take his call, but snatched up the phone before she did anything out of simple sibling spite. She heard his voice come over the phone, smooth as melted chocolate.

"Here's the deal. My client is interested in remaining 100% anonymous until we have a done deal on the items, and they no longer belong to them." Right away Nedra picked up on his use of 'they' and 'them' to eliminate tipping his hand to the sex of the owner. "By the way things are popping around here, it won't be long until the objects are gone. At any rate, because you are my sister, I have been able to convince my client of your professionalism." Dramatic pause. She did not like the idea that he had to *convince* someone of her professionalism. "Also, I gave assurance that you will not disclose their identity until after the story breaks. Are you agreed to this so far?"

Her brother was pissing her off more every minute, but she said, "*I* agree to it, but if you're talking about an interview, I assume Don would do that himself. You'll have to get his word, but I suspect he'll also agree."

"No. Don will *not* do the interview. My client said that because you are my sister, and because you work at *Excel,* that you alone will do the one-and-only exclusive interview to be given. We will carefully set up a discreet location where the three of us will meet. You must write the article or story yourself. No one else."

"Are you crazy? What are we dealing with here some kind of nut-case? Is this person paranoid or something? They don't even know if I can write an article of this magnitude."

"No nut-case." Brian sounded so smug. "And I certainly wouldn't say that about your writing skills. You did two years at college as an English major, and you are the Executive 'whatever' at *Excel.* You're not a dummy, Nedra. You are more than capable of doing this. Now, go tell Don the good news. And Nedra—no photographer."

"I'm not so sure Don's going to think this is good news."

Nedra was wrong and Don was ecstatic. "This is unbelievable for *Excel.* We'll do a cover shoot of you and Brian—maybe even holding some of the treasure. Everyone in the country will want a copy. We'll have to double or triple our production." His wheels were turning faster than Nedra had ever seen, and she realized once again that this is the reason he's such a great editor.

He stopped for a moment, and put his hands on each of her shoulders. Narrowing his eyes, he said, "Nedra, I'm confident you can do this, but how do you feel about it?"

"I think I can handle it. Way back in college my dream was to be a writer of one kind or another…and…well, life got in the way." She felt a small, shaky grin break through the fear on her face. "I think I'd like to try."

Don's face reflected what Nedra could only describe as fatherly pride.

Events were moving fast, and timetables were roughed out on a dry-erase board. In only two short days Nedra would meet with the mystery person or people. Brian wouldn't give her a hint of what might happen. He just told her, "I'll pick you up Friday morning at 8:30, and take you where we need to go."

The media was having a field day, and was camped out with live coverage from Brian's office; all waiting for any tidbit of information they could pick up or contrive. Brian had released digital images of some of the items, and when the media got hold of the copy of the Compact, all hell broke loose. Don had decided it would be best not to disclose news of the impending interview until after Nedra met with the anonymous finder. No use asking for trouble.

It was finally time to go home, and Nedra felt utterly exhausted. Since the news of this Mayflower thing had broken this morning, she'd been going on pure adrenaline and she finally started to crash. Tomorrow would be a long day as Don, Kathy, and Nedra fine-tuned questions and facts for the interview. Brian said the amount of time for the interview would be open-ended, and Nedra thought that seemed odd for someone so secretive. Oh well, this whole thing was weird—weird, but incredibly exciting.

Back on the train heading home, Nedra tried closing her eyes to rest, but her mind raced ahead of itself. She went over the details of the interview in her head. This could be her big break—what she had hoped for so long. She had always wanted to be a journalist, and ultimately someday write novels, but after John died, she had given up on her dreams. She did not want to be hurt again by events over which she had no control. Yet this wonderful opportunity had fallen directly into her lap, and somehow she didn't feel afraid. She was beyond excited, yet felt peaceful and confident. Imagine, within hours she had gone from thinking she had been publicly drooling to clinching an important exclusive interview. Life sure has a way of getting your attention.

The train clicked over the tracks, the doors whooshed, and people talked in quiet, tired, end-of-the-day voices. After wriggling into the VSP, Nedra drifted off into a light doze.

Someone shook her arm. *What in the world…?*

"Um, Mrs. Lange." Through blinking eyes Nedra noticed one of the neighborhood boys who took the train into the city every day for high school. "I know this is your stop, same as mine. It looked like you might sleep through it."

"Thank you, Robbie. I believe I would have." As he turned to leave, she saw the Mount Carmel letter jacket. What was that Don had said today?—'Building Character for a Lifetime'. Hmm, maybe she could interview him for their story on Catholic schools.

The light pulsed red on Nedra's old school answering machine. She hit the button as she set down her purse and tote. Slipping off her walking shoes, she heard her brother, Mr. Cool, with the melted chocolate voice. "How you doing? Hang in there. This craziness will end soon. I'll see you Friday. Call if you need anything."

She'd order a pizza, and then take the polish off her nails. Maybe after that she'd finally take the time to find a new word.

Chapter 4

Friday morning Nedra began her day well before the alarm clock was set to ring. She showered, and sat at the kitchen table where she tried to get down a little toast with her tea. An old faded chenille robe protected her clothes from potential spills. She applied new polish to all of her nails (both fingers and toes) using her favorite color, *Glorious Red*. It made her feel confident to cope with whatever would happen at the interview later this morning. Ever so carefully, so as not to smudge her polish, Nedra reviewed the notes for the interview that Don and Kathy had helped her assemble the day before.

Kathy had turned into a fussy mother hen. "I've color coded everything for you. Warm-up questions are highlighted in yellow, background info on the Mayflower and Plymouth is in blue, and the really important questions in red." Kathy set the files on Nedra's desk, "Have you thought of what you'll wear?" They decided on a gray suit with matching straight skirt. Nedra would wear a single-strand of pearls, with a thin gold chain bracelet, and small diamond-studded earrings. She would make her fashion statement with a pair of kick-ass, leopard, peep-toe heels, with a hint, just a hint, of rhinestone. Professional, not imposing, yet evidence of style.

Nedra looked out her window, and saw Phree walking up her front steps. *What the heck is* she *doing here? I've got to get rid of her before Brian shows up. He'll kill me. Maybe I just won't answer the door.*

Phree knocked, and when Nedra snuck a quick look through the peep-hole, she saw Brian coming up the sidewalk behind Phree dressed in some kind of workout clothes. What was going on? He knew better than to dress like that for the interview. With Brian there, she'd *have* to open the door. But

Brian could help her tactfully get rid of Phree, and then they could still make it to the interview on time.

Flustered, Nedra opened the door and full of cheerfulness said, "Phree, what a surprise! And Brian, my goodness, what are you two doing here?" She blocked their entrance into her home, as though she hid a nuclear secret inside.

"May we come in?" Brian said, with a toothy grin.

With a smile to rival Brian's, Phree said, "I think a better question would be, 'Why isn't Nedra at work today?' "

"Well, I…well, um…that is, uh," Nedra stuttered and felt defeated, as she gave up her post and stepped aside for her guests to enter.

As she walked past, Phree said, "Wow, Nedra, you're sure all dolled up for someone who didn't go to work. Who are you trying to be with that nice dress and pretty string of pearls, June Cleaver?" Phree looked down at Nedra's shoes. "Cool shoes, Ned. Are those the ones you picked up when we went to that exclusive charity auction that *Excel* held in the spring?"

Nedra wanted the small talk to stop, and the blathering Phree to leave ASAP. She wanted Brian to *do* something, and gave him a wide-eyed get-her-out-of-here look.

Phree walked to the sofa, and sat down. "Nice day for a visit."

"Yes. Yes it is." Nedra was becoming anxious and looked from the grandfather clock to Brian. They needed to get going, and NOW. She frantically tried to figure out how she could get rid of Phree and still make it to the 'secret' interview on time.

Brian took her elbow, "Come. Sit down over here, Nedra." Leading his reluctant sister to a wingback chair, he sat next to Phree on the sofa.

Phree and Brian were smiling like they had some big private joke, and it was really beginning to piss her off. "Well

Phree, we've had our fun." Turning to his sister, he said, "Nedra, I'd like you to meet the owner of the Soule/Brewster Discovery."

"Is this supposed to be some kind of joke?" Nedra hissed through clenched teeth. "What are you two trying to pull off here? Brian, you know I've got important work I have to get to, and I think we need to get going right now, or we will be late…real late" She stood up, but Brian directed her back into the chair with a soft nudge to her back.

"It's true, Nedra," said Phree. "I found the stuff in the bottom of Grandma's old trunk that's been in my attic for years. I know it's a shock, but Brian and I decided it's important to keep my identity a secret for as long as possible."

Nedra just stared at the two of them. She simply could not find words.

"Please don't be mad at me for not telling you. What are you thinking?"

Nedra looked down at her *Glorious Red* nails on the ends of her primly folded hands and her kick-ass, peep-toe, faux leopard heels, and smiled at her worried friend. "I'm thinking that I'm slightly overdressed for this interview."

Three hours later sitting at her kitchen table, having changed into jeans and a sweatshirt, Nedra said to Phree, "This is the most remarkable story I've ever heard. You must have been out of your mind for the past month. I can understand completely why you didn't tell anyone, but I really wish all of us girls could have helped you cope with this. It would have made things so much easier for you."

Phree covered her face with her hands and shook her head, her hair swayed from side to side. "There have been so many times I wanted to tell all of you. I've been so scared, but at the same time I'm really thankful that Brian was here to help me." She took her hands away from her face, and somehow her eyes held the tears in check; a dam of emotion being held back by mere eyelids. "Now, with everything authenticated and bids coming in from museums, I feel a little better. Brian has made it perfectly clear to the media that everything is under lock and key, but I still fear that someone could hurt Emily to get their hands on the stuff or the money it will bring in. I can't wait until this is over, and it's all sold or donated."

"Oh, Phree, I can't even imagine what you've been through," Nedra pulled her friend into a hug, and Brian excused himself to let them do their 'women thing'. Phree needed to talk, and Nedra was a hell of a good listener.

About thirty minutes later, Brian entered the room carrying a brown shopping bag. He set it on the table, pulled out three sub sandwiches, a big bag of chips, and a pack of Pepsi. "Here we go, ladies. Let's have this high-end lunch and then get down to business, so we can figure out what is best to put into this article." He smiled at his sister, and she could read pride and softness in his eyes. Nedra smiled at him, and felt love for her shit-eating brother. She chided herself—*I'm going to have to stop calling him that.*

Chapter 5

Early the next morning, inside of *Excel's* conference room, Nedra related Phree's amazing story to Don and Kathy. Papers and printouts littered the dark mahogany table, as Nedra sat on the edge of a buttery leather chair showing copies of photos that Brian had given her. Phree had agreed that *Excel* (using Nedra as the writer) would release an early tidbit that a single woman, who belonged in the Mayflower lineage, had found the items. They had discussed all the 'pros and cons' of going public, and had all decided Phree would 'come out' for the *Excel* story.

Word spread rapidly that *Excel* had the exclusive, and Don wanted to fast-track the whole project. He pulled the graphics from the Catholic high school story off the current cover and arranged for a photo shoot of Brian, Nedra, and Phree. They would run a headline to the effect of "BROTHER & SISTER UNLOCK MYSTERY OF THE MAYFLOWER DISCOVERY—Exclusive interview by Nedra Lange." Don hoped the original trunk could be included in the shot, and he wanted all three of them to be holding what looked like original documents.

Nedra would interview both Phree and Brian. *Excel* would get a digital disc of all the documents and items, along with a modern English translation. Don would have his staff reporters do pieces on the Mayflower, the first Thanksgiving, George Soule, William and Mary Brewster, and anything else relating to the Pilgrims and Plymouth. And, on top of it, the timing was unbelievable—the October edition was already out, so this would be the November copy. Perfect!

If Nedra thought work challenged her before, she now faced the roller coaster ride of her life. It was one week to their deadline, and it would take every second to pull this off with competence and precision. Don wanted to wait until the last minute before going to press to include any final bids or sales that had occurred. There had already been an offer from someone in the Middle East willing to pay $30 million dollars for everything. When Brian said, "No," without even consulting his client, the anonymous buyer upped his offer another $10 million. Brian had explained the amount of money wasn't the issue, rather his client wanted the items to remain in this country. Nedra's heart had filled with pride for her friend Phree—not a lot of people would have turned down that kind of money for the principal of the thing.

Nedra had just put a sheaf of papers into a large white envelope and coded it for Don, when Kathy entered the office and stood stock-still. She gripped the door handle like a lifeline, eyes wide, mouth open but not speaking. She blinked at Nedra three times and squeaked, literally squeaked, "My God, Nedra. Oprah's on line four and she wants to talk to you!"

"Is this a joke?"

"No. I'm dead serious. She wants to talk to you." Squeak, squeak. "Hurry and answer before she hangs up!"

"Go get Don," Nedra commanded, as she reached for the phone. Kathy waved both of her hands in front of her face—flustered, unable to move. "Don't just stand there—go."

Two hours later, Nedra's head pounded so hard, she thought it might explode. She downed two Tylenol and prayed for strength, wisdom, and a pain-free cranium. She had acted so breezy and composed on the phone, "Oh, yes, my dear friend Oprah just called, and we chatted for a while." What in the world had she gotten into?

Oprah had explained to Nedra, that after being out of daily programming for several years, she had plans to air a "Giving Thanks" series of shows. Fourteen hour-long shows were scheduled to run two-a-week from mid-October leading up to Thanksgiving. Nedra had seen the recent commercial for the upcoming specials telling of Oprah's desire to share her life's most thankful moments along with those of others. The commercial hinted at stories of surviving "incurable" illness, parents and foster parents who went above and beyond, selfless caregivers, and extraordinary educators. By filming the shows at Harpo Studios, she would be revisiting the town where her professional journey began and thanking her fans and the people of Chicago.

Oprah proposed that Nedra and Brian come on her show within 72 hours after *Excel's* release of the story. This way they could feed off each other and not fight for 'top billing'. Nedra's confidence definitely wavered. One minute she felt at peace with the idea, and the next minute ready to hurl. Who did she think she was, anyway—going on Oprah's show?

Brian, Mr. Confidence Himself, had no problem. "Could be a hoot. If you get nervous, just let me do the talking."

"Do you think Phree will join us?"

"I think so. Part of the frenzy has been from everyone trying to figure out who the mystery person is. *Excel's* story and Oprah will both be the perfect venue for Phree to disclose her role in the discovery, and explain the items have either been sold or donated. I'm convinced the media circus will blow over fast, once everyone knows who she is."

Don entered the room, and they put Brian on speaker phone. Don told them he had just talked with Oprah's 'people', and he did not have a problem with all three of them going on her show after *Excel* hit the stands. The Oprah Show had agreed not to publicize their impending appearance so *Excel* could have that time to maximize their sales, and, at the same time, Oprah could hint of "special surprise guests". The timing would place the Mayflower story in the first or second show.

With all of these details swirling in the back of her head, Nedra excused herself. She would let Don, Brian, and

Oprah's people hash out the details. Right now she needed to write the best story of her life.

Chapter 6

Don had scheduled the photo shoot for Friday morning at 10:00, so Nedra arranged for an 8:30 limo pickup at Phree's house. Brian would meet them at the downtown studio, where the trunk had already been delivered. The three of them were to dress as they normally did for a day at work. Nedra and Brian wore business suits, and Phree provided the contrast in a pair of jeans with a comfortable dusty blue sweater. Phree was semi-perched, semi-leaning on one side of the trunk, Nedra on the other, with Brian standing behind. Phree had a 'fake' document in her hand, presumably the Compact. They all looked straight into the camera with large happy smiles. Back at the office Don was attempting to nail down the perfect eye-catching title.

The studio had strict instructions that the image be kept top-secret. After all, no one had any idea who the mystery person might be, and *Excel* wanted to keep the suspense at an all-time high. The magazine would come out on Tuesday of next week—the night after the Bunco Club got together at Lettie's to sew.

"We need to figure out how to break the news to the girls," Phree said in the limo on the ride home.

"I've got a rather fun idea."

Nedra went into her office on Saturday armed with stacks of information pertaining to the pilgrims and their lives. Kathy worked on the actual voyage itself, using the newly translated journals of George Soule and the sermons of William Brewster to provide insight and information. Don, as usual, undertook the daunting job of piecing the whole thing together to make a cohesive and interesting issue—one that no one in America could live without. Nedra was reminded how it seemed a little like piecing together a quilt.

The *Excel* team worked long into Saturday evening. Nedra had driven her car that day so she would not be at the mercy of a train schedule. By the time she reached home that night, her whole body ached. She went upstairs to draw a hot bath. Exhausted, but exhilarated at the same time, she knew they had knocked this one out of the park.

The next morning she slipped into comfortable jeans, a quilted sweatshirt-jacket she had made, and treated herself to one of those expensive lattes. Sitting at her patio table with a sheaf of papers, she began the task of editing. Fresh eyes would pick up mistakes easier than another proof-reading late last night. She felt so proud of this issue, she could just about burst. She knew her story was well written, the supporting articles by the staff were exceptional, and Don's editorial made her eyes tear up. He talked of the excitement of the past week, some of the moral issues that Phree had to deal with, the unique relationship between Phree, Brian, and Nedra, and finally, of his pride in Nedra as a writer and her unrelenting struggle of human perseverance. Snuggling the warm latte in her hand as the chill winds of October kicked up and played tag with the dry leaves in her backyard, Nedra closed her eyes and allowed herself to think of how proud John would have been of her.

Chapter 7

Nedra woke Monday morning in the same fashion she had for most of her working life—exactly one minute before the alarm was set to ring. Invigorated, she felt a confidence she hadn't acknowledged for a long time. This was D-Day, as in deadline. Ready or not, the story was going to print. She entered her office to find Kathy with a goofy smile on her face. "What's up?"

"Take a look on your desk. The proofs for the cover came in, and you guys look fabulous."

Picking up the proofs as she sat down, Nedra had to agree with Kathy. Staring back at her were two nicely dressed African-Americans, and a smiling happy-looking blonde-haired blue-eyed Phree. Don had been right to highlight the contrast between their office attire and the casual look of Phree. If the photo didn't get your eye, the headline sure would. Splashed across the top in red letters was: MAYFLOWER DISCOVERY REVEALED, and just underneath, in slightly smaller letters, EXCLUSIVE STORY BY OUR OWN NEDRA LANGE. *Our own Nedra Lange. Wow, that felt good!* Keeping her eyes on the cover, she picked up the phone.

"Phree, you are not going to believe how great this cover looks."

"Good, I was worried because you guys looked so professional, and I looked a little like someone fresh off the boat." Phree laughed at the ridiculous jibe.

The two friends discussed more aspects of the story, its upcoming release, and what they should wear to Oprah. They shared a good laugh about how The Bastard would take the news when he saw her on the cover of *Excel*, heard about her being on Oprah, and finally understood that she was a *very* wealthy woman. Finally they got around to tomorrow night's sew with the Bunco group. "I can't wait. They're going to have a freaking fit. This is going to be priceless."

The next evening couldn't get here fast enough for the two friends. They rode together to Lettie's house through fits of giggles. Phree experienced a sense of relief that her big secret was about to be revealed. They both knew what would hit them the minute they walked through the door, and Nedra had come prepared.

"Nedra tell us about this thing with Brian," Marge shouted. "We saw him on television last week."

"Oh, you mean that Mayflower thing?" Nedra played innocent.

"Yeah, of course," said Beth. "Tim is acting real weird about it. I think he wishes Brian would have let him see the stuff or something. I can't get a read on him. He's just not himself. Every time I bring it up, he grumbles something about how he just doesn't want to talk about it."

"I bet it just about killed Tim not to be able to get his hands on that stuff. So what does Brian say about it?" Nancy was eager for information, and Nedra noticed that she had lost more than a little bit of weight since the last time they were together.

"You know my brother. I haven't been able to get much out of him. He's pretty closed mouthed when it comes to attorney/client information."

After everyone had arrived, and the talk shifted away from Brian, Phree got up to use the bathroom. "Be right back." Nedra knew the plan. Phree would slip her cell phone from her pocket and call Brian.

About fifteen minutes later someone knocked at Lettie's door. "I'll get it." Phree had intentionally sat closest to the door, and when she opened it, Brian entered. There were 'hellos' and 'congratulations' shouted from everyone.

"Would you like to have a seat and something to eat or drink?" Lettie appeared a little confused but stayed in character as hostess.

"Please don't tell me this is about my son," Rosa moaned, and Nedra saw terror flash across her friend's face.

Everyone collectively held their breath until Brian said, "No, it's not about Ricky."

"Is something going on, Brian, or did you just stop by to sew with us?" Beth joked.

With one of his massive arms, Brian pulled Phree to his side, and she put her hand on his enormous chest. "Phree and I have something to tell all of you." *Lawyer voice, shit-eating grin—he's got them right where we wants them.*

"Dear God in heaven, are you two dating or something?" Rosa shouted.

Phree bent over double with laughter, and Brian's grin just got bigger—if that was possible. Always the diplomat, Brian said, "Well, as much as I love Phree, and all of you for that matter—no, we're not going out."

"Maybe I can help." Nedra reached into her tote and pulled out eight copies of tomorrow's release of *Excel Chicago*, and handed one to each of the women.

"Holy good God Almighty," said Helen, as she melted back into her chair.

As the women each realized it was Phree, Nedra, and Brian on *Excel's* cover, it was prissy Marge who further shocked the group when she said, "What the fuck is going on?"

Everyone flipped through the magazine to find the page where the story started, and in a calm but somewhat bossy voice Nancy said, "All three of you sit down. You've got some 'splaining to do!"

"Not quite yet," said Nedra, and she handed each woman a ticket for Friday's Oprah Show. "Now Brian—start 'splaining."

The group of women sat in astonished disbelief as they listened to the three conspirators recount the exciting story.

After the basics were covered, and everyone had most of their questions answered, Brian excused himself so the women could continue without him. He had enjoyed watching them all go from shock to more shock, and when the Oprah tickets came out, utter joy. He finally understood why Nedra loved these women so much—they were the sisters she never had. First bound by quilting, then by Bunco, some by motherhood, and finally connected with each other by a cherished friendship that crossed all boundaries. As he walked out the door, he looked back to see his dark-skinned sister throw her head back with laughter among all of her light-skinned sisters. The rest of the world could take a lesson from these eight women.

Chapter 8

Nedra got off the train as she always did at Millennium Station. She walked past the newsstand, and there they were—five rows of *Excel Chicago* with her face on the cover smiling back. People were pushing and reaching to get a copy. The hype surely must have achieved a new high for *Excel* sales. She continued on, and heard someone shout, "Hey, I think that's her! Nedra Lange is that you?" A fraction of a second hesitation gave her away, and she immediately found herself surrounded by people wanting her autograph.

Nedra smiled and signed her name, and at the same time wished she could be anywhere but here. She wanted to crawl into a hole, or become invisible, or jump back on the train and go home to the suburbs. There were about a half dozen people crowding around her. Some people wanted the magazine cover signed, others the story page, still others wanted her to sign both.

Nedra was as polite as she could be until a rather plump African-American Metra Policewoman came over, and with a full blown Chicago attitude, pointedly asked, "What. Is. Going. On. Here?"

Breathless, someone answered, "It's Nedra Lange, from the Mayflower."

The policewoman said, "Honey, if she's from the Mayflower, then I'm Christopher Columbus. Now let this poor woman get to work, and you all do the same. Move along! Let's go! We've all got a long day of work ahead of us."

Nedra turned to her and mouthed, "Thank you."

"No problem, honey. But I suggest you get to work as quick as you can."

A raw nor'easter was whipping off Lake Michigan as Nedra approached the *Excel* building. About a half block away she stopped when she saw people gathered around the revolving doors. *How am I ever going to get in there?* Frankie from the mailroom approached her—he made Brian look small. "Don sent me down here to look for you. Come on." He grabbed her elbow, and she was sure her walking shoes hadn't touched the ground until she was safely inside the elevator. Only slightly disheveled, she thanked Frankie for his help.

"No problem. I used to be an offensive lineman in college. If I could run interference for my running-back through those slabs of meat on the field, getting you though that crowd was a piece o' cake."

With a shaky hand and *Magnificent Magenta* nails, Nedra adjusted her hair. Both Don and Brian had warned her she might be sought after for a while, but they had assured her it would blow over very quickly. Nedra remained confident that by next week no one would even remember her, and her 'fifteen minutes of fame' would be over. But in the meantime her 'fifteen minutes' appeared to be stretching into another long day. In her office she glided into a pretty, yet serious, pair of navy heels with a nicely embellished golden buckle.

Resting on her desk were several notes from Kathy. Fox, CNN, and MSNBC, as well as the six local news channels, all wanted to do brief segments with her. Nedra would have to be a magician, but she knew this would generate sales for *Excel,* and that also translated into being especially good for her.

The offices at *Excel* were fairly buzzing and humming with excitement, and once again the beehive cliché really hit home. There were phone calls to juggle, interviews to schedule, photo-ops, and even offers of book deals. Sales were off the charts, and Don couldn't have been happier. Nedra thought surly his cheeks must be hurting from grinning all day. By the end of the day she had repeated her story so many times, that she didn't know what she had said to whom.

Nedra knew that Phree was to spend the next few days at Brian's office, where they would hammer out the final details of the sales and donations. At this point, the Soule Bible was going back to Plymouth, Massachusetts, to be on display in or near the re-creation of the Soule family home. The Brewster Bible and handwritten sermons were donated to the Smithsonian by an anonymous buyer, and would be on display with Mary Brewster's precious diary. Brian had just put the finishing touches on the agreement for the three Soule journals to stay together and be part of the permanent display at the Mayflower House Museum. This seemed particularly fitting, since the house itself was built by the great-grandson of Edward Winslow, and George Soule came over as tutor to Edward Winslow's children. The 'Complete Compact' as it had been dubbed, would head off to the Pilgrim Hall Museum in Plymouth, where it would be on display for about a year. It would then tour major U.S. cities for approximately two years before returning to its permanent home at Plymouth. Things were wrapping up nicely, and Phree had told Nedra she was pleased with her decisions.

By Thursday afternoon Nedra turned her back on the quieting hubbub, and decided she needed a little downtime to prepare for the Oprah Show the next morning. Oprah's limo would pick them up Friday at 6:00 a.m. to make sure they were there and settled for the 9:00 start. At this time, the audience had no idea who the surprise guests might be, but then again none of them cared—after all they were going to see Oprah.

Chapter 9

As the sun rose over Lake Michigan and pooled its reflection in the calm waters, the sleek limo sped into Chicago. Brian remained composed, while Nedra and Phree were both nervous and excited. Nedra checked her nails about every three minutes, until Phree shouted, "For-crying-out-loud-STOP-THAT! You haven't done anything to chip your fricking nails—they're fine."

Brian smiled at them, and under his breath said, "Just like two sisters."

Forty-five minutes later they were pulling up to Harpo Studios where Oprah had taped the bulk of her shows over the years. They were ushered into the guest area of the studio, also known as the Green Room, and briefed on the order of what would happen. Oprah would give a little introduction, with the cover of *Excel* shown on a large screen behind the seating area. She would introduce Nedra and Brian first, get a little background on them and their connection to the Soule/Brewster Discovery, and then bring out Phree. They were told that Oprah had questions and comments prepared, and they simply needed to answer them. *Easy for them to say.* Nedra hoped she could get the cotton out of her mouth in time to sound coherent.

Word came back to the Green Room that their group had arrived in the audience. As time neared for the taping to start, Nedra and Brian were led to the spot where they would come onstage. Before leaving the Green Room, Nedra and Phree hugged for a long moment, clinging to each other for dear life. "Good luck," Phree said. "Save me a spot."

"Right next to me." As Nedra walked away, the two women stretched their arms out until they had to let go of each other's hand.

Standing behind stage, Nedra had a death-grip on Brian's arm and held on as though it were a lifeline. They could hear the crowd cheering and applauding, while Oprah said with enthusiasm, "It's good to be back in Chicago!" After the adoration died down, she continued, "I want to thank you for joining me for the second show in our "Giving Thanks" series, where we are sharing journeys that have something to do with thankful situations. Last week this country was astounded by the announcement of a discovery relating directly to the Mayflower and the Pilgrim's lives at Plymouth. The initial statement gave us no indication of who had found the items, or where and how. This past Wednesday the magazine, *Excel Chicago*, featured an exclusive interview with the 'mystery' person written by Nedra Lange—who just happens to be the sister of Brian Barber, the lawyer who broke the news to us." Oprah smiled, cocked her head to the side and said, "Are you following me?" The audience chuckled. "Today we're going to get to the bottom of this mystery, because we have Nedra Lange from *Excel*, and Brian Barber attorney for Phree Clarke, here with us today." The audience applauded as Nedra and Brian walked out and shook hands with a smiling Oprah. "Welcome."

For about five minutes Oprah questioned them on various aspects of the discovery. She noted again that they were brother and sister, and prodded them for a little background on their lives. Oprah told the audience that on the surface it seemed a natural progression that Brian, being the lawyer, should involve his sister, the journalist, as the person to get the 'big' exclusive written interview. Oprah then said, "But this story has an interesting backdrop to it, and we have a little surprise for you. Phree Clarke has agreed to join us today for her one-and-only television interview. Along with Nedra and Brian, she will explain how this incredible event happened. Please welcome, Phree Clarke." The studio audience rose to their feet applauding Phree. She walked out and shook Oprah's hand and then hugged Nedra and Brian.

Oprah warmed things up by saying, "I LOVE your name. I know what it's like to have an unusual name, but I must say there is quite a tie-in with your name, Phreedom spelled with a P-H, and the whole Pilgrim thing. How did your parents give you such an unusual, yet fitting name? Do you think they knew about your Mayflower ancestors, yet chose to keep it a secret?"

For more than thirty minutes Oprah prodded with appropriate questions to keep the interview flowing and on track. Photos of the discovery flashed on the screen behind them; one showing the false bottom trunk. They all speculated why the Compact that the women signed had been stored away, while the other one held the prominent role as the 'official' version. They recounted the scene where Brian and Phree walked in on an unsuspecting Nedra and announced Phree to be the mystery person.

Oprah sat far back in her cushy chair, crossed her arms, and in her Oprah-ish way said, "Now, tell me. How'd a white girl come to be such good friends with these two black people?" The audience laughed and nodded, while applauding.

Phree and Nedra gave a brief description of that first quilt camp over seven years ago when they had met. Nedra said, "A group of us got along so well at camp, that one of the women suggested we start a Bunco group so we could continue to get together once a month." Nedra looked at Phree, "I have to admit at first I felt a little anxious about hanging out with seven white women, but I thought I could always quit if I didn't like it. I kind of felt like they were holding out a hand to me, and I thought if I didn't accept—well, how will things ever chance on a larger platform?"

"Don't let any of this fool you," Brian said. "I've seen these women in action for seven years, and they're all as close as sisters. If one needs help, the other seven are there before she puts the phone down."

Oprah said, "I truly admire all of you getting along so well, and you're absolutely right—breaking down barriers on an individual basis will lead to it working on a larger platform. After all, that's what it's all about. But for those of us that don't have a clue," Oprah raised her eyebrows and questioned, "tell us...what exactly is quilt camp and Bunco?"

Phree smiled and offered Oprah a short description of camp, and then went on to explain, "Bunco is really great fun. It's a no-skills dice game where we get together once a month. Each month a different woman hosts at her home."

"That way," Nedra added, "you only have to host once every eight months. It's really a lot of fun. But, the best part is knowing you've got a date on the calendar to be with good friends, and that you're going to eat, gossip, and play a little Bunco."

"Just out of curiosity, how many people in our audience play Bunco?" Oprah asked. She seemed genuinely shocked when over half the women raised their hands. "Well, I might just join your group sometime and see what this is all about.

"Okay, getting back to our story here," said Oprah, "I understand, Phree, you could have been *very* rich right now. Why did you settle for less money than you could have gotten?"

Phree explained, with Brian's help, what her reasons were for not taking top dollar, and they assured Oprah that Phree would not be going to the poorhouse anytime soon. Phree ended by saying, "I just want to go to sleep at night knowing my ancestors would be proud of me."

"And I'm sure they are. Thank you for giving me this opportunity to meet all of you and learn more about this amazing story, that so beautifully fits our 'Giving Thanks' theme." Turning to a camera on her left she reminded the viewers of the date for her next show. The red tally light turned off over the lens, signifying that the camera was no longer live—and it was over.

Oprah once again thanked her three guests. As she shook their hands, she looked down at Nedra's feet, "By the way, *very* cool shoes." And The Queen of Talk was whisked away.

Chapter 10

It turned out to be a sun-filled fall weekend as colorful leaves fell from trees and raced each other to earth. For the next few days, Nedra used her caller ID and the peep-hole on her door to screen unwanted well-wishers and nosey-types. After she had taken George Munro to church and out to a late breakfast on Sunday morning, Nedra took advantage of the cool crisp autumn air and sat on her patio. Curled on a lounge chair, she reflected over the past month. It had been a wonderful whirlwind, and she wouldn't have traded the experience for anything. She marveled at the chain of events over the years that had brought her to this point in her life, and how changing just *one* of those events would have taken her on a different path. It started with John's sudden death, and her working as a receptionist at *Excel Chicago*. Nedra remembered frequenting the local quilt store where Helen worked, and how Helen encouraged her—no, practically dragged her to that first quilt camp where the Bunco Club got its start. Brian had it right—the other women had become the sisters she never had and so badly needed. She thought back even farther and realized that if her grandma hadn't taught her to quilt, she probably never would have been interested in the first place, never met Phree, and never had this opportunity.

A large flock of cooing Sandhill Cranes caught her attention, as they dipped and glided high overhead, like a group of synchronized parachutists. Breaking her train of thought, Nedra shaded her eyes with her hand and watched them circle, until they disappeared off to the south. She would thoroughly enjoy these few days off, which Don insisted she have.

Walking through the remnants of her little vegetable garden, she noted there were carrots waiting to be pulled and a few green peppers clinging to withered plants. She began to think about the menu for Bunco night. Nedra had sorely neglected her gardening this past month and felt a pang of regret. Retrieving her garden tools out of the shed, she donned a pair of work gloves to protect her *Perfectly Rose* nails and labored for the rest of the morning in her flower beds and vegetable garden. Other than quilting, nothing could bring her an inner peace more quickly than working in her gardens. The Bunco girls always teased that she was the African-American version of Martha Stewart, and she had to agree that it was a nickname she had unquestionably earned. Spotting a beautiful purple mum, Nedra thought it would be cheerful in her mother's vase that she kept next to her kitchen sink. While she raked away the leaves that had accumulated and pruned back her perennials, she mulled over the menu for Bunco and came up with a simple approach to a crisp autumnal feast. *Okay, maybe I do sound just a little like Martha Stewart.*

Back in her kitchen, Nedra wrote out the menu. Stuffed Green Pepper Soup would taste good on cool fall night. She'd serve two types of homemade bread with jams that she had preserved earlier in the summer along with mounds of whipped butter. Spring greens would combine to make a sweet and tangy salad to complement the soup, and, of course, she'd have the obligatory Bunco night Pizza Dip heated in the oven and served with tortilla chips. There would be a few other minor munchies included such as veggies and dip, and her own personal favorite Oyster Cracker Blend. Chocolaty squares of brownies and a fresh strawberry pie heaped with mountains of whipped cream would be a simple, yet tasty dessert. *There…menu done.*

Bunco Club Menu

Sweet and Tangy Salad
Stuffed Green Pepper Soup*
Pizza Dip w/chips   Veggies & Dip

homemade breads with homemade jams
Oyster Cracker Blend

Popcorn - M & M's
chocolate covered raisins - mini Snickers

Liz's Strawberry Pie
Brownies
Earl Grey Decaf

*recipe at back of book

Now for her least favorite part—the prizes. Nedra decided to get gift cards from The Quilter's Closet where Helen worked and give a fat quarter (a quilting term for a specific size of fabric) for each of the four booby prizes. She'd call the shop on Monday, put the order on her credit card, and Helen could bring everything to Bunco on Tuesday night. *That was easy.* Nedra planned to get her grocery shopping done on Monday and start some early preparations in the afternoon. Meanwhile, she had a clean house, menu planned, a manicure with new color, and some time on her hands. It was the perfect occasion to do a little quilting.

She took several clear plastic bins off the shelf and peered inside at the unfinished projects, or UFO's as most quilters call them. An idea came to Nedra to make a quilt telling the story of Phree's Mayflower discovery and her own involvement. She thought maybe the two of them could work up a pattern together and each make a Mayflower quilt. *I'll run it past everyone at Bunco, and see what they think. They'll probably have some good suggestions.*

In the meantime she decided to work on a quilt she would surprise her daughter with for Christmas. The kit had been in her stash for several months. She started by unfolding and then pressing the fabric free of wrinkles. Her iron puffed steam as she breathed in the scent of new cotton material being heated and misted. Measuring and cutting the fabric was repetitive and soothing, like wipers on a windshield. Before she knew it, two and a half hours had gone by, and Nedra's stomach began to growl. Taking a sandwich to the kitchen table, she opened up her Kindle Fire where she checked emails and Facebook. Phree had sent a message telling Nedra not to worry about scratch paper—she'd provide it on Bunco night. *Must be a doozie from The Bastard.*

When she turned off the bedside lamp that night and crawled under her covers, a bright moon lit up the chilled darkness. She was looking forward to another peaceful night, and would sleep until her body signaled her to wake up in the morning. With a slight breeze off the near prairie, Nedra fell asleep designing the Mayflower quilt in her head.

Chapter 11

There would not be an over-abundance of day-before prep work that needed to get done—mostly cleaning and chopping vegetables, making the Pizza Dip, and the Oyster Cracker Blend. The Stuffed Green Pepper Soup would be ready to serve on time, and she planned for the savory loaf of bread to come out of the machine just as the women arrived for the pre-Bunco feast. A golden loaf of French bread would be made in the early afternoon, so it could cool and have a crisp, chewy crust. Nedra would cook a double batch of soup and have enough to freeze in individual servings for quick meals after work.

Her favorite gardening basket hung just inside her back door, with a pair of work gloves folded over its handle. She followed a cobblestone path to her garden, where she picked several remaining bright-emerald green peppers. Plucking about a half dozen plump orange carrots from the loose earth and brushing dry soil from them, she rested the long tubers beside the peppers in her basket. There was a decent sized pumpkin clinging to a swirling vine, and she envisioned how she would cut off the top, gut it, and then fill it with fresh cut flowers from her flowerbed to use as a colorful centerpiece. As an afterthought she'd bake up some salted pumpkin seeds to set out as a treat. She remembered how her little girls had loved crunching on the salty snack. Adding the pumpkin to her basket filled it to overflowing, so she went back inside the house and tightly fastened the door behind her. It would be a cold evening, indeed, with a chilled wind coming off Lake Michigan.

Nedra sliced and cut piles of crisp green peppers, pungent with a fresh yet earthy garden scent, and then bagged the chopped emerald cubes to keep them fresh. She knew the Pizza Dip by heart, and had it completely assembled and stored in the fridge within twenty minutes. Late in the day tomorrow, she would slice the top off the pumpkin in a zigzag fashion, fill it with beautiful fall flowers, and nestle the orange orb on a bed of colorful fall leaves.

In one of her two china cabinets, Nedra located the antique soup tureen that had been her mother's. It would contrast beautifully with a contemporary candle-scape, that was highlighted by the plump orange pumpkin-vase slightly raised in the center. She chose eight intentionally mismatched china cups and their saucers for tea with dessert. Polished silver dessert forks and teaspoons, as well as silver tongs to use with sugar cubes, were retrieved from protective cloth bags with drawstrings. Nedra was most definitely in her element, as she enjoyed fussing over placemats and vintage candy dishes. An antique quilt that she had found at a flea market became a stunning tablecloth, and its holes and imperfections were covered with strategically placed serving dishes and baskets. By the time her table was dressed, Nedra was exhausted but serene and happy.

Tuesday morning arrived and brought a raw cold rain with a gray cloud-covered sky. Only ten degrees colder, and the rain would be snow. Nedra hoped that wouldn't happen for at least a few more weeks. A cozy fire in her living room fireplace would be perfect tonight. Carefully measuring the ingredients for the crusty French bread, she started the bread machine mixing the dough. Since she had made good progress the day before and was ahead of schedule, she prepared a fresh cup of steaming creamy coffee and set off to her sewing room. After three more blocks of the quilt had been pieced, the house smelled of yeasty, freshly baked bread.

At 7:00, Nedra had just ladled the soup into the fanciful tureen, when the door opened, and the Bunco Club started to arrive. As the women entered, they complained about the weather, but the soft crackling fire and smell of freshly baked bread changed everyone's mood. Each woman spooned generous portions of the flavorful soup into bowls accompanied by thick slices of tasty bread that was slathered with butter. Sitting around the dining table, they complimented Nedra on what an original table setting and flower arrangement she had designed.

Someone questioned Rosa about Ricky, and Nedra noticed 'the wall' went up. "Fine, he's just fine," was Rosa's standard curt reply.

"Rosa, if there's anything we can do…" said Beth.

"No," Rosa cut her off with a clipped tone. "There's nothing. He'll be fine."

An uncomfortable moment followed until Nedra asked, "More soup anyone?" And talk turned to quilting.

Helen said, "I'm dying to show everyone this great new Block-of-the-Month that just came out." She dug into her bag and retrieved a pattern. "It's going to be available in January, but Sandy said I could bring this copy to show you guys tonight." Sandy owned The Quilter's Closet where Helen worked. "She's limited to making 60 kits by the manufacturer so I wanted all of us to see it early. If anyone likes it, I'll sign you up."

The women fawned over the design, and they all decided to take part. "If one of us has it, we've all got to have it." Rosa seemed to be rebounding from the Ricky questions and suggested, "Why don't we start with show-and-tell tonight instead of waiting till after dessert?"

"Good idea," Beth said and reached for her bag. "I'm hoping that Lettie can help me with this crocheted afghan I'm struggling with. I just don't get how to do one of the stitches." Beth had recently started crocheting. "You're the yarn queen around here, Lettie. What am I doing wrong?" They put their heads together and discussed the troubling stitch.

Marge showed two pillows she had finished which would match a quilt she made her daughter for Christmas. Nedra and Phree talked about the 'Mayflower Quilt' and asked for suggestions and input. Helen discussed the new line of fabric that would match the B-O-T-M (block of the month) pattern she had brought, and updated the group that she was getting closer to placing the order for her long-arm quilting machine. She hoped to order it before Christmas and have it delivered after the holidays. Individual discussions about quilting led to talk about kids, holiday plans, their annual Shipshewana field trip in November, and the usual question for this time of year, who-was-stuck-cooking-for-Thanksgiving. Nearly an hour later, The Sarge suggested they stop talking and get down to playing Bunco.

While the women each found a seat at one of the card tables, Phree passed out this month's version of scratch paper. Each of the eight women read aloud a different email from The Bastard, with each letter begging Phree to get back together with him.

"Now that he thinks I'm loaded—I can do no wrong," she laughed. "Funny thing is about two years ago I would have jumped at his offer. But I've had three years of no arguing, no dirty clothes lying around, and the toilet seat is always right where I leave it—DOWN. No thanks. I am so done with him."

Rosa teased, "I bet you wouldn't mind that cute cop leaving your toilet seat up once in a while." They all laughed, but Phree turned a bright red and ducked her head into her shoulder.

"Do I detect that maybe he already has?" Nancy asked.

"Well, you never know."

"Okay, spill." Rosa crossed her arms over her chest. "This game is not starting until we know everything." Phree looked at Nedra, eyes pleading for help. Rosa badgered both of them. "Oh sure, looks like the two of you have more secrets."

Nedra put up her hand for everyone to stop talking. *Nice nails. No chips.* "We were going to get around to this discussion at dessert but since some of you just can't wait—go ahead Phree tell them."

Another fifteen minutes went by as Phree explained how Brian had called the police department the day before the Mayflower story broke. He asked the police to keep an extra watchful eye on both Phree and Nedra's homes until the Mayflower event blew over.

"Of course," said Nedra, "we noticed Lieutenant Hayden—Bill—making the rounds of Phree's house fairly regular. And the long and the short of it is..."

"I invited him in for tea," Phree smiled and actually glowed. "What can I say, I was lonely and scared. I couldn't talk to anyone but Nedra and Brian, and they were always at work." She kept smiling.

"They've dated twice," Nedra added.

"Get out!" As everyone peppered Phree with questions she tried to finish the story.

"Well, we didn't really go out. They weren't technically dates. I couldn't go anywhere for the first few days after our pictures were on the cover of *Excel*. And then we were on Oprah which doesn't exactly put you on the sidelines. I had him over for a movie, and Emily and the two of us played Scrabble one night."

Rosa crossed both hands tight over her mouth and sucked in air, "You lucky dog—he's gorgeous!"

"Right now, we're just friends. You know, getting to know each other." But Nedra noticed that Phree couldn't stop grinning. "He's also recently divorced himself, about a year and a half."

"And just in case you're wondering," added Nedra, "he's 45."

"Holy crap," said Rosa. "Just when you think you know someone. And by the way," she turned to look Nancy straight in the eye. "Any movement between you and Michael-the-Jeweler?"

"Well, funny you should ask. You'll all be happy to know that I've agreed to see Michael when he comes back here for the holidays."

"That *is* progress for the slow boat," said Helen. "Anything else?"

"Yeah, there is. We've talked on the phone a few times, and I'm beginning to think that maybe this whole thing isn't such a bad idea after all. I think I might even kind of like him." Nedra watched, as Nancy blushed a dark red. "At least I remember *why* I liked him in the first place."

"If I didn't know any better, I'd say Nancy Walsh almost looks happy."

"Let's play," Nancy said. "We'll have to spend the night here if we don't get going."

Nedra added a bundle of logs to the fire, and the bell rang to start the round. She felt sure that Nancy was still holding back both her feelings and her story. She also noticed that smile on her face seemed a little forced and just might be ready to melt into sadness.

By 11:45 calendars flipped between pages as they determined the date for next month's Bunco. Since Thanksgiving and their annual trek to Shipshewana were both looming at the end of the month, they planned Bunco for the week before Thanksgiving. As the women gathered up their tote bags and jackets to leave, Nedra handed the Bunco box to Rosa, and said, "It's all yours honey, and I'm sure glad this month is over for more reasons than one."

NOVEMBER BUNCO – Rosa

Just waking up scares the hell out of me.

Chapter 1

Shortly after midnight Rosa maneuvered her vehicle down the Mitchell's driveway and into the left side of their detached two-car garage. She had toyed with phoning Nedra earlier in the day to tell her she didn't feel well and would have to skip Bunco that evening. Ricky had only four days left in juvenile detention. It would have been so much easier to stay home and hide from the pity and concern she saw reflected in her friend's eyes. Every day was a struggle to swat away the darkness that hovered just above her head, like a suffocating layer of pale-green algae choking the life from a summer pond. Terry had insisted she should go to Bunco and enjoy the evening with her friends. Against all of her protests, her husband had coaxed her into an evening out as planned.

The night was so quiet that Rosa heard the click as the motion detector caught her movement and spread a buttery glow over the patio. She hitched a wayward outdoor chair and dragged it toward the glass topped table where it belonged. The metal legs of the chair scraped along the bumpy paver-brick and made a grating sound far too loud for this time of night, but Rosa didn't care.

When she last visited Ricky in juvey, he had refused to see her. Rather than spend time with his mother, Ricky had preferred to stay in the company of boys whose parents hadn't bothered to show up. Like a surfer she rode a wave of loss and disbelief, crashing into shore again and again while roiling with a fury of anger and rage. She worked to keep her feelings hidden from everyone, except when she snarled and spit accusations at her husband. Rosa had struggled to mend her family life back together, but a gaping hole was left in her heart where love had seeped away.

The emptiness in Rosa's spirit truly alarmed her. Empty like when the boys were little, and they would take a big spoon to scrape out the seeds and gloppy orange filaments from their Halloween pumpkins before they carved them with scary faces. All of her hopes for Ricky had been torn from her and replaced with sadness. At this moment—this very low moment—she could see no positive future for her son.

Rosa stopped at a large urn, which only months ago had been alive with vibrant annuals of red, white, and blue—the color theme for the Mitchell's container gardens this past summer. She remembered how showy the flowers had grown in such a short time, and she allowed herself to think about Mother's Day weekend. All four family members had worked together on the planting project. Every year Rosa's Mother's Day gift translated into the boys and Terry schlepping in the garden at her command—whatever help she wanted *and* with no complaining. She ran her leather gloved finger along the edge of the urn, which now held the dry withered remains of faded summer splendor. Rosa made a mental note that they needed to get the outdoor area ready for winter.

Sliding her key into the lock of the French door, Rosa did not hear the familiar sound or feel of the latch clicking open. Odd—the door *should* have been locked. She gave a tentative push with her gloved hand and created an opening just big enough to see indoors to the family room and kitchen area. The colorful flickering glow from the television told her Terry was most likely still awake. The Pizza Depot had closed almost two hours ago, and when her husband came home he usually unwound by watching either sports or cable news. Rosa had hoped he'd be in bed by now. She wasn't sure she wanted to see him any more than she had wanted to see her friends tonight. Terry had been the one that stood firm about sending Ricky to juvey, and, at this point, Rosa was still angry with the decision and far from convinced it had been the right thing to do.

The hinges on the door squawked like a yard full of starlings as Rosa opened it wide and crossed the threshold. From this vantage she could see Terry lying on his back, asleep on the couch. Her husband's neck was bent backward on a pillow with his head tipped upside down. Snoring lightly, his mouth was wide open, and she could see his tongue and lower teeth. Rosa tilted her head and looked at him, as she took off her coat and scarf. How strange he looked, bent and tortured and ugly—just like she felt.

Reaching behind her, she closed the door with a loud slam that shook the room. Picture frames on the adjoining wall clattered and then bounced to a lopsided standstill. Terry did not move. A suspicion she had ignored all evening ran the length of her spine, and chilled her more than the frosty night air.

Stepping into the room, Rosa's eyes trailed down Terry's arm, as it dangled off the sofa. His hand rested on the blah-beige carpet next to a half-dozen empty beer cans and a drained bottle of whiskey. *Not again.* She stared at Terry, and her body slid to the floor under the weight of her grief, like a chocolate Easter bunny melting on a hot stove. As she pooled on the carpet, silent heaving sobs bubbled from her midsection and escaped through her mouth. Along with Ricky being in juvey, the economy had tanked, and The Pizza Depot was producing about half the income it had only a year ago. The Mitchell family had taken one devastating blow after another, and Terry had reacted to the sequence of overwhelming problems by drinking. *Am I to lose everything?*

Rosa hugged her legs and rested her chin on her knees. She watched her husband's chest rise and fall. A trail of drunken drool meandered down his chin. When her heart wasn't empty and numb, it was filled with anger and despair. Terry and Rosa had been wildly in love when they first married. They had started the restaurant so they could work side-by-side and never be apart. Together they had made two beautiful baby boys, and, at that point, Rosa had felt her life was near perfect.

Somewhere between then and now something had gone terribly wrong for them. She understood why his drinking had escalated—she really, really understood—but that didn't mean she didn't feel betrayed. In the past year their life together had been strained through a sieve, and the lumps that remained were giant hunks of frightening problems.

Unfolding a well-used flannel quilt, she pulled herself into an overstuffed chair. The warm protection the quilt provided spread over her, as she coiled her body like a cat in a basket. Her head rested on the massive arm of the chair, legs folded on the ottoman and drawn close to her body. Logic and common sense returned to her bruised mind and anguished heart. *I* will *pull this family together…we* will *survive.* A vision of Scarlett O'Hara with her fist wrapped around a scrawny carrot flashed through her mind, but she was too tired, and the situation too serious to find any humor in the comparison.

Rosa dozed in fits and starts, and sometime in the middle of the night she got up to pee. Terry was still asleep on the sofa, but curled on his side, facing out toward the room. His arms were folded tight against his chest, knees pulled toward his belly—as if he were cold. Rosa took the flannel quilt that was still warm from her body and covered his legs. While it nearly made her nauseous to show him any kindness, Rosa took these simple steps to help let go of the anger and bitterness she felt was consuming her. With Ricky only days from coming home, Terry *had* to get his act together and his drinking under control. She would force the issue if needed.

Using the remote control, Rosa clicked off the muted TV, switched off all the lights except for a small lamp on the desk, turned down the thermostat on the furnace, and climbed the stairs to her bedroom. When Terry had sobered up they would discuss a plan together and then begin the daunting task of rebuilding their family.

Chapter 2

Along with being royally pissed off at her husband and worried sick about Ricky, a bad case of menopausal night sweats had also kept Rosa awake long into the night. Sometime after five in the morning, with the help of a window cracked open, and the overhead fan switched to the 'high' setting, she was able to string together a few respectable hours of sleep. She had gone through a wild ride of emotions, with anger being the underlying and recurring theme, topped off with a heaping portion of doubt and self-pity. Not a good combination for moving forward.

Still damp from the sweats, Rosa's hair was stuck to her cheek, and the sheets beneath her had a sour smell. Terry had not come to bed last night, and there was a teeny part of her that was glad he hadn't witnessed his wife swimming in a puddle of sweat, like a marathon runner after a race. Straining to hear any sounds from downstairs, Rosa knew she could wait him out by pretending to be asleep. Lifting a blind slat ever so slightly, she checked for his truck in the driveway. *Good, he's gone.* She didn't want to see or talk with him until he was well on the other side of his hangover.

Stripping her bed, Rosa tugged at the fitted sheet. The final corner on the opposite side of the mattress would not let loose. With a frustrated yank that could have easily ripped a discount store sheet in two, Rosa's lavish Ralph Lauren designer sheets finally lost the struggle and popped free. She stuffed the bitter smelling nightgown along with the bed sheets into the washer, eyeballed a splash of detergent, twisted the dial with an angry spin, and snapped the washing machine lid shut.

Their son was sitting in juvenile detention with a bunch of really, really bad kids, because her husband thought "tough love" was the right answer. True, Rosa reminded herself, that she had eventually agreed to the plan, and they had made the decision together, but it was just so much easier to put the blame on Terry than take any responsibility for their son's current address. Then something Brian had said came back to her, something she had ignored and didn't want to admit—that Ricky was ultimately the one who was responsible for his actions. Not Rosa, and not Terry.

Chapter 3

"I get it!" Lettie raised her voice in frustration. "But, Rosa, you've *got* to stop being so pissed off. It doesn't help anything." Reaching across the kitchen table, Lettie laid her hand on Rosa's arm. In a softer voice, she added, "Rosa, you've got to let it go."

Rosa felt her shoulders droop. The tension she'd been carrying in her back since she drove out to Lettie's farmhouse over an hour ago released itself, like she'd been lounging in a hot tub. She hung her head, covered her eyes with her hands, and that was finally when the tears started. Lettie came around behind her chair and wrapped Rosa in her arms. Resting her cheek on Rosa's head, she rocked her best and dearest friend gently and repeated in a low soothing voice, "Let it all out, honey. Go ahead, and get it out."

"Oh, Lettie, I feel like such a horrible mother."

"Rosa, you are *not* a horrible mother. Ricky is the one who made some really bad, really stupid decisions." Lettie sat next to her friend, snapped several tissues from the box, and handed them to Rosa. "You've been holding this in, and trying to hide it for a long time. I know you so well. Your eyes betray that phony smile you force, and, for the record, it's way too fake."

When Rosa had left her house that morning, she didn't know where to go or what to do. She only knew she desperately needed to get her head on straight, and be able to talk—keyword, *talk,* to her husband. Not yell at him, accuse, or nag, but talk calmly and rationally with him. She found herself at a Starbucks buying her usual latte, and after she had paid, she apologized as she added another coffee drink to her order. She arrived at Lettie's carrying a decaf-vente-mocha-latte with extra-whip as an offering for the one person who would stop whatever she was doing to help her.

Rosa brushed at her eyes with the tissue. "I don't know where to start. Honestly, Lettie, I'm crazy scared."

Lettie crossed the room to her kitchen counter and retrieved a small wooden slat basket filled with blank index cards of various sizes. "You know I'm a visual person and an obsessive list maker to boot," she said, as she also reached for a spiral notebook of lined paper and a block of yellow sticky-notes. "I need to write things down, or draw them out on different size cards, where I can move them around until I get a good fit. I think of it as my mobile problem solver." She handed a tablet to Rosa. "Here, you can take notes on this."

"What are all those for?" Rosa pointed at Lettie's handful of various colored roller-ball type pens.

"These," Lettie said with flair, as she swooshed one through the air, "are for color-coding your problems, my dear. And red is, you guessed it, for your most pressing issues." Lettie sent a dark chocolate Hershey's Bliss sliding across the table to Rosa. "And this is for what ails ya."

Rosa felt a smile on her lips, and *not* one of those forced smiles like Lettie had accused her of earlier. Just for that brief moment she allowed herself the luxury of letting someone take over her troubles. Sharing with a friend was, indeed, the medicine she needed.

"Okay, this is how I see it, and I'm going to use a disclaimer here. These are just the *opinions* of your friend. Take it or leave it. Your choice and no hard feelings." Lettie took two index cards and said, "One for Ricky, and one for Terry." She wrote a name at the top of each card, and then gave Rosa a hard look. Without taking her eyes off her friend, she reached for another card. "…And one for Rosa."

Their lattes were empty long before the puzzle of problems was pieced together. Rosa fanned out a handful of "to do" index cards, and her shoulders sagged with the daunting realization of what she needed to accomplish. "I've really got my work cut out for me."

"I don't pretend this will be easy," Lettie told her. "But you know I'll help in any way I can."

"I just don't know if I can do this." Rosa waved the stack of cards back and forth. "It all seems so hopeless."

"It's just because you're overwhelmed. We've *got* to make it work." Lettie smiled at her friend. "You can do it, Rosa. You're one of the strongest—or should I say the most stubborn, bullheaded people I know."

"I prefer strongest, please." She tapped the index cards on the table to straighten them into a neat pile and snapped several cards off the top of the stack. Sighing, she said, "This is what's scheduled for today."

"Remember, it gets easier as the pile gets smaller."

After leaving Lettie's, Rosa fortified herself with yet more caffeine in the form of another latte from the drive through. Her first order of business was to confront—no, Lettie would not like that—was to *talk* to Terry. She drove to The Pizza Depot where Terry's truck was the only vehicle in the lot. The restaurant would not open for another four hours, and she hoped that would be enough time for them to take the first step on the path to restoring their life.

She used her key to unlock the elaborately carved wooden door of The Pizza Depot. Even though smoking in restaurants had been banned years ago, the slight scent of stale cigarettes could still be detected as Rosa stepped inside. It took her eyes a moment to adjust to the dark entryway, and in those seconds she feared she would find Terry slumped in a booth with a bottle of whiskey.

"Hello? Who's there?" Terry called from the direction of the kitchen. He rounded the corner clutching a dripping mop in his hand and stopped dead in his tracks when he saw Rosa. "Oh," was barely audible, and Rosa thought he sounded disappointed that it was her. Was her husband hoping it was someone else? He stood the mop in a corner where it would not slide to the floor and folded his arms over his middle.

Rosa wanted to turn around and leave. She wanted to lash out, and scream at him. She wanted to be sarcastic and say, *Is that anyway to greet your wife?* Or *What's that supposed to mean?* Or even, *What's up asshole?* But instead she took a very deep breath, waited just a beat to calm herself, and said, "You got a minute?"

"Not really. Why?"

"I thought maybe we could talk."

Terry snorted and pulled on the brim of his Depot baseball cap—a gesture that Rosa knew meant he was nervous. "Yeah, I'm sure that's what you want to do—talk. More like you want to bitch at me for kicking back and having a few drinks last night."

Rosa had been here for less than a minute and was already frustrated. She was also beginning to get angry, "You know you're really starting to piss me off. What's with the attitude? Could you be any more belligerent? Come on Terry, you know as well as I do that we're in deep trouble on so many levels, it isn't even funny. Ricky comes home in three days, and we've *got* to get our shit together if we want any chance of saving our family."

"Oh, I get it—it's all my fault that we're having problems!"

"Did I say that? Did you hear me accuse you of anything?" Rosa was so furious, she was shaking. "Okay, let's take a deep breath and start over…"

"YOU take a deep breath! I don't have time for this crap." He yanked the mop handle toward him, and water sprayed from the braided ends as he swabbed at the floor.

"Terry, I know what you're doing. You're trying to make me so angry that I walk out of here and leave you alone, but I'm not going to do that. No matter how mad you are, we *need* to talk. We're running out of time for figuring out how to help Ricky. It'll go so much better if we could discuss this together." She headed for a booth in the dining room, "Let's sit in here where it's more comfortable." She didn't look behind her to see if he was following, but she heard the handle of the mop strike against the wall and knew he was behind her. Rosa was not going to bring up his drinking right away, but Terry didn't know that. She hoped he would calm down and open up about his feelings toward their son.

Unbuttoning her coat, Rosa placed it next to her on the seat of the booth to indicate that she was not planning to leave any time soon. Terry slid in across from her and drummed his fingers on the table top. "Say what you have to say. I don't have all day."

"Oh, for God's sake Terry, can you spare the crap and have an honest conversation with me?"

He squeezed his eyes closed, and his shoulders wilted in defeat. Rosa knew he wasn't really a bad-ass and wouldn't be able keep up this act for long. She just had to make sure she didn't blow-up at him in the meantime, or all communication would come to a stop. "We've got a number of things we need to discuss, but the most pressing is Ricky. He can't come home to us while we're like this. We *must* have a united front, or he'll find our weakness and use it against us." Rosa waited for a moment, and her husband made no attempt to respond. She spread her hands out in front of her, "Do you have *any* thoughts or ideas?"

"Other than I'm a total failure and a lousy husband and father? No, I have no thoughts besides that. That's all I can think about."

Rosa was stunned. She never for a moment thought of him as being a lousy husband or father. They had had ups and downs in their marriage, certainly many as of late, but she still loved and trusted him. She stammered, "No...but..." She knit her brows, perplexed by what he had said. Was he serious or just throwing himself a pity-party after his latest slip-up with drinking? "Terry, come on, that's just not true. You've been a great husband and father, and the boys and I both love you." She swept her arm out to encompass the rest of The Depot. "You built this place into a successful business. You're far from a failure."

Terry looked down into his lap and shook his head. When he looked up at her, his eyes were dark and sad. "To start with *we* built this place. And in case you haven't noticed—and you *should* have since you do the books, but we are making half of what we did since the economy went south. We're bleeding money, and I don't know how to fix it."

"But Terry," she reached over and took his hand, "the good news is we've been savers all these years, and we've still got a decent rainy-day nest egg sitting in our business account. We can float by for a while if need be. What happened to the business after the economy tanked is *not* your fault, but it *is* our new reality." Rosa felt that her husband was losing a bit of the attitude he had when she first walked in. "We can do this. Neither of us has ever been afraid of hard work."

"Okay, so what do we do about it?"

"We put our heads together and figure out how we can implement some new marketing ideas to help The Depot. It's probably going to take some tough changes, but I know we can figure it out. We just haven't wanted to face what's been going on both here and at home, and it's only been getting worse on both fronts. I've been so tied up with Ricky, I know I haven't been carrying my weight around here for a while." Rosa reached across the table to the shiny dispenser for a paper napkin and blotted at her eyes before tears fell. "I've left it all up to you, and I'm sorry for that." She wanted him to understand that he was not the only one responsible for neglecting to take action when business had dropped off. She also didn't want to push him into a corner, where he'd become defensive by the time she brought up his drinking.

"Do you really think we can get this place back on track?" He massaged his forehead with his fingertips. "This all just sucks, and I feel so damn helpless."

"I know, but it truly isn't hopeless. We just *have* to work on this together." Rosa was the behind-the-scenes half of the team. She did the books, payroll, inventory, ordering and other jobs essential to keeping a business running. She had been able to do most of her work from their home office, so she could stay around the house with a flexible schedule while the kids were little. "I think it might help if I moved my office back to The Depot. I'd be better able to get a hands-on feel for what needs to be done to improve our bottom line, and I could be home when Ricky gets out of school at 3:30."

Nodding his head Terry said, "I'd really like that. I think it's a good start and would help to take some pressure off. We always worked well together."

"I don't know, but maybe we could think of offering lunches here at The Depot. How about serving individual pizzas and a really good salad with breadsticks?"

"Maybe I could come up with a unique recipe for pizza soup."

"I *love* that idea! Wow, pizza soup—that could be a big draw during the cold months. What if I did something like approach some of the local offices for catering lunches or meetings? I know some of the private grade schools have pizza day once a week for the kids, and I could put together a proposal for the schools that don't already have a plan in place. Maybe with all of the concern over healthy eating for kids, we could promote salad and a pizza slice."

Terry smiled for the first time, and Rosa could literally see a touch of excitement in his eyes. He added, "What about supplying pizza slices for football and basketball home games at the high school? Or the Snack Shack at the Swim Center in the summer? You've always had a knack for sales, Rosa, and I know you could make some of these ideas work."

"I admit that I miss not being here and working together. We've both been so isolated in the last few years—like parallel work instead of parallel play. If we could only recapture half of the excitement that we felt planning the business when we first opened The Depot—it would be like a much needed shot of adrenaline for both of us." Rosa's cell phone rang in her purse, but she didn't reach for it. Whoever it was could leave a voice mail or call her back.

"How about we start tomorrow clearing out the old office?" After Rosa moved her office to the Mitchell's home, the empty room at The Depot became a black-hole for storage and junk. "I think we could get it emptied in a couple of days," Terry said, "and then over the weekend I could paint it."

The Depot phone rang, but they ignored it. Terry typically didn't answer the phone unless they were open for business, and, since Rosa was here, he knew it wasn't her. "I think that actually sounds like fun. Do you have a tape measure? I'd like to get some measurements and figure out what I can use from home. I'd rather not buy anything new if we can help it."

"I haven't felt this hopeful in ages," Terry said, as Rosa's cell rang again.

Trying to remain positive before she lowered the boom about his drinking, Rosa said, "I love these ideas. We can make this work, Terry. I know we can." It felt good to smile for a change and really mean it. Smile and feel hopeful—Rosa wondered how long it would last. "Maybe we could think of the business as though it's our third child, and the recession is forcing us to figure out how to help it grow in a whole new direction."

When Terry nodded agreement, Rosa took a long deep breath and silently prayed for help. She looked directly into her husband's eyes, and said, "Terry, we have to talk about your drinking."

At that instant their heads both swiveled to the front of the building as they heard the door to The Depot open. Rosa remembered she hadn't relocked the heavy wooden door after she came in nearly an hour ago. Terry started to rise, just as a male voice boomed, "Hello? Terry? Rosa?"

Rosa's hand flew to her throat when she saw Brian round the corner. "Brian, you scared the crap out of us!" She was smiling and breathless, but her smile faded instantly as she noticed he was not smiling back. The lightness and hope she had felt in her heart only moments before tumbled to her stomach with a thud. "My God, what is it?" she whispered.

"I've been trying to reach you two." And then Brian said the two words Rosa didn't want to hear. "It's Ricky."

Chapter 4

Rosa sat shaking in the passenger seat of Brian's car, while Terry followed them to juvenile detention in his truck. She put their conversation on speaker phone with Terry's cell, so he could hear every word Brian was saying. The problem was that at this point Brian didn't have much information himself. After repeated calls to the Mitchell home went unanswered, a social worker at juvenile detention had called Ricky's lawyer of record. There had been a rather extensive disturbance, or, as Brian said, "Probably two gangs going at it," and Ricky, along with several other boys, had been collateral damage. He had taken a shank to the left forearm and also had a possible broken leg. By the time the guards had things under control, Ricky had a wound that needed immediate attention at the in-house infirmary, not to mention a fracture that needed x-rays and setting, along with a possible concussion.

"I don't understand, how could this happen?" Rosa was panicked and wanted answers. As ridiculous as it sounded, she said, "I thought he would be watched over and somewhat safe in there."

While driving as fast as he could without tempting the police to stop him, Brian placed a hand on her arm, "He's going to be okay, Rosa. They assured me it was a slight gash on his forearm, and that he will probably need several stitches to close it up. Try to stay calm. As soon as we arrive, we'll get answers to all our questions."

"Just a year ago he was an A student and on the eighth grade basketball team. What happened Brian? He was always such a good little boy until last summer. What did I do wrong?" And there it was—mother guilt. She started sobbing. "Our family has splintered so badly these past few months, that I don't even recognize it. Did you know that the last time I went to visit Ricky, he refused to see me?"

"I can't even begin to imagine how much that must hurt. I wish you'd have told me. I could have looked into what might be troubling him."

They pulled into a space in the main parking lot, and Rosa had the door open before Brian stopped the car. Terry jumped out of his truck and grabbed Rosa's hand as they hurried toward the entrance, wisps of breath trailed behind them in the cold autumn air. Rosa felt her husband's strength surge through her, like the charge from a jolt into a dead car battery.

Wiping her mind clean of Ricky in trouble, she forced herself to think of the child she loved and nurtured. Brightness sparked in her son's eyes with his infectious dazzling smile, which always made her weak in the knees and had fused her heart to his forever. Visions of "untroubled Ricky" vanished as they reached the main entrance. She had successfully blocked out the building before her, It was designed to look like something other than what it really was.

Terry opened the door, and she felt his hand on the small of her back. The reality of where she stood and why she was there crashed into her. Brian talked to a receptionist-guard who sat behind thick plexi-glass which had been frosted with scratches in places. A large steel door sat opposite the one they had just entered. An uneven row of orange and green plastic chairs lined another wall, as handbills and posters tacked to a ragged and crooked cork board fluttered from an overhead fan.

And then there was the smell. Rosa could never quite put her finger on exactly what it was, but it was definitely unpleasant and unique to this place. A touch of sweat, disinfectant, and urine combined with the odor of unwashed bodies, barely masked the overpowering scent of terror and panic. It was a smell she would not be able to wash off herself, or out of her mind, for days.

The guard was speaking with Brian through a hole in the plexi-glass, and Brian set a sheaf of papers into a metal tray. The guard retrieved the papers and started thumbing through them making red check marks at certain places. He finally inked up a large hand-stamper, and pounding the top sheet with it, left an imprint of a red box where he further scribbled information. Looking at Brian and pointing to the row of chairs, he said, "Okay, sit over there. Someone will be with you in a while."

Rosa refused to sit. After twenty minutes of pacing the postage-stamp size room, she melted into one of the orange molded chairs. Her heart was weighed down by panic and grief at the thought of seeing her son again—how sad was that? Aware that Brian and Terry were talking, she could not concentrate or focus on anything they were saying. She closed her eyes and breathed slow and deep. Remembering the old Lamaze techniques she had used when the boys were born, she visualized pure air going into her lungs and anxiety being forcibly expelled.

The big steel door opened and in a flat disinterested voice, a guard said, "Mitchell?"

They all stood at once, and Brian spoke while he thrust his hand toward the guard. "Brian Barber. I'm Ricardo Mitchell's lawyer, and these are his parents."

After what seemed like a lot of double-talk from Brian, they were finally going to be able to see Ricky. Coats, gloves, scarves, cell phones, her purse, and other personal items were not allowed past a certain point and were stored in a coin operated locker. They were then lead to a curtained off area inside the infirmary.

Ricky lie on a narrow cot, his eyes hooded and glassy. They didn't speak to each other, but Rosa reached for his hand. At her touch he mouthed 'Mom' and then murmured, "I'm sorry." A small bubble of saliva formed at the corner of his mouth—his eyes rolled back and then closed. They had been told he was heavily sedated. Terry placed his hand on her shoulder and gave it a light squeeze. She didn't take her eyes from her son's face as she bent to kiss his forehead. Like all mothers, she knew the scent of her child, and while his scent now mingled with fear, she nonetheless filled her lungs and breathed him in. Over the next few hours she would ride the peace of that scent and closeness like a hawk spiraling on a current of wind.

She caught Terry's eye and nodded at their son's hand. She didn't trust herself to speak, in case he was aware behind those closed eyes. In very small letters only about ¼ inch high F U C K was spelled out down his thumb. Rosa hoped it was drawn on with a pen, but her gut told her it was a tattoo—permanent and ugly—forever a reminder of the past several weeks. Husband and Wife looked at each other, and both shook their heads ever so slightly. This would not be a battle they would fight today, and Rosa wondered if this was the reason Ricky hadn't wanted to see her the last time she was here.

Brian had left them momentarily to find out what would happen next. In a low voice he told them, "They will most likely keep Ricky here at the infirmary until he leaves the facility in three more days. With that broken leg and a damaged arm, he's not going to be able to use crutches. He'll need a wheelchair for a while, and they won't allow that in general holding." Brian looked at his watch and told them, "We've only got a few more minutes, and they're going to insist we leave." He patted Rosa's back. "We'll talk about this more when we get out of here. It's going to be okay, Rosa."

She would always remember this day as the lowest point in her life. It had started so hopeful that morning as she sat with Lettie and sorted through her problems while sensibly organizing them and making promising plans. That was followed by a reasonable discussion with her husband about their lives and their future. And then she had visited her youngest son in a correctional facility, at its infirmary, where he had just received 31 stitches for a shank wound in some sort of a gang fight. She was reasonably sure that five years ago she didn't even know what the word shank had meant.

Chapter 5

Rosa sat straight up in bed—blinking and straining to hear. Next to her Terry was on his stomach, where deep regular breaths told her he was sleeping soundly. She waited and listened, wondering if she had really heard Ricky, or if she had been dreaming. Her heart thudded in her chest, and she could hear the blood rushing in her ears. The voice had been so clear as if he was right outside their room and called out with a touch of panic in his voice, "Mom." That one word had disrupted a rare blissful sleep, but she needed to see for herself that he was alright. When her heart slowed, she quietly glided from beneath the covers and slid her feet into her slippers.

Her son had been home for just two weeks, but Rosa could tell he was fragile and broken—no more Mr. Tough-Guy. On the way to the stairs, she passed his 'old' bedroom, the one he had occupied since he was a baby. If all went as planned, he would get out of the wheelchair in another week, and shortly after that be able to maneuver the stairs. In the meantime, they had set up a temporary bedroom for him in what used to be Rosa's office on the main level.

The day after the brawl at juvey and, with Lettie's help, Rosa had boxed up her at-home-office. When they bought their home, the room was referred to as a den or fourth bedroom. She sent all of the dated files, office furniture, and miscellaneous items to The Depot, where Terry had single-handedly, and just as quickly, emptied the room that had been the storage catch-all. The paint job for Rosa's new office would have to wait. She kept only what she needed at home to pay bills and payroll. For the next month or two, she would conduct her business from the dining room table.

They moved Ricky's bed downstairs to the emptied office space and set up an ancient box-sized television. A card table would give him a surface for his computer, and his wheelchair was able to snug underneath. Without ever saying it, both Terry and Rosa knew this was *not* the time for her to transition to her new office at The Depot while leaving Ricky home alone all day.

No movement came from under the covers as Rosa leaned on the door jam and listened for Ricky's breathing. Not for the first time she thought, *We've got to get him back on track.* He had been responding well to most of the suggestions that Terry and she had laid out for his future. As difficult as it was to admit, being in the middle of a gang fight might have been the best thing that could have happened to her son. He had confessed to being scared to death, and that he *never* wanted to go back there again. For Rosa it was the slender thread of hope she needed to get through these difficult days. The next morning they would sit at the now cluttered card table and discuss his future in high school.

"I think I'll just go back to Whitney High. I really don't want to go somewhere new." Ricky was surprised when the next morning Rosa told him there were two options for going back to school. Neither of them would take him close to the group of kids he had befriended the past summer. He pounded his fist on the flimsy table top, and the pens danced a jig. "This sucks."

Rosa held her breath and pressed her lips into a thin line, "Yeah, well, too bad. A lot of things suck around here."

Ricky folded his arms over his chest, "So, what do you have planned?"

She wanted to say, *What I have planned is for you to behave better. What I have planned is for you to have a future outside of prison. What I have planned is for you to stop being a tough-guy-smart-ass.* Instead she set two printouts in front of him and kept it simple, so she wouldn't explode, "We need to choose one of these schools."

He flicked the papers away, "Fuck, I'm not going to either of those." He glared at his mother.

She stood, palms flat on the table and bent to within a foot of his face, "I have told you not to use that word in front of me, and YES, YOU WILL GO TO ONE OF THESE SCHOOLS." She sat back down in her folding chair—moments from tears. Why had she ever told Terry she wanted to do this without him?

Ricky picked up one of the stapled information sheets and said, "So what is this, a place for bad kids?"

She tried to sugar-coat, "Not really bad kids, but kids that got off on the wrong foot." Ricky looked at her and snorted. He wasn't buying it. "Well, some of the kids might have gotten into trouble, but this school has a really good record for getting them back on track."

"Shit, this is a Catholic school. I'm not going there."

"Language, please." Terry and she had spent hours studying online information and making phone calls to potential schools. "So simply because it's a Catholic school you don't want to go there?"

"You probably have to go to mass every day and act holy."

"No, to both of those. So if that's your only objection, I suggest you be a little more open-minded, and give me some credit." They were Catholics in name only, in other words ChrEasters; they went to mass on Christmas and Easter.

"Do I get to choose or have you and Dad already decided?"

At this point Rosa didn't care where he went, as long as it wasn't back to Whitney High. "Dad and I have narrowed it down to these two choices." They had used success record as their number one criterion, then cost, and transportation. They were also hoping for a day school rather than a boarding school but had kept all options open. "And I was hoping we could have a discussion today, instead of fighting over the whole thing."

"What do you think?"

He was scared, Rosa reminded herself. That's why he's being so belligerent. He's just afraid. "I like either of them, but I think this one," she picked up the Catholic school packet. The school counselor had met with Rosa and Terry and explained how they use sports and school clubs as an outlet for frustration, anxiety, and aggression. By the time they were done with practice, games, meetings, and homework, there was literally no time and often no energy left for most of them to get into trouble. On top of that, the boys immediately felt a sense of pride belonging to a team and also proud of their individual accomplishments. And that was way better than belonging to a gang. "They have a lot of after school clubs and a really strong sports program."

"In case you haven't noticed, I'm still in a wheelchair."

Smart ass. "Trust me, I'm aware of that. But you *will* heal, and there are sports that don't require running—like swimming and water polo. And don't forget there are lots of clubs."

"That sounds gay."

"Come on, Ricky, that's just not necessary." She figured at this point he was just trying to piss her off. "Fine. Then go to the other one. I really don't care, but by next week you legally have to be registered in high school, and you're *not* going back to Whitney."

"If it's really my decision, I'll go here." He slid the all-boys Catholic school printout toward her.

Rosa felt bruised, as though she had just gone three rounds in a boxing match. "Good. I'll make the call."

By the fourth day of delivering Ricky to the Metra station to take the commuter train into Chicago to attend his new high school, Rosa popped her head out of the cloud of despair that had surrounded her. She discovered that autumn was in full swing. Sunlight accentuated the brilliant red and mustard colored leaves that still held tight to their trees. How good she felt when a crisp, cool fall breeze washed over Rosa, cleansing her of old fears and bringing her new hope for her youngest child. The good weather continued, with mild and sunny days full of the wonderful aroma of damp leaves on earthy soil. Rosa thought it was ironic that everything outdoors screamed of dying this time of year, yet for the first time in several months, she had the hope of spring in her heart. Ricky was doing well at school, and the early morning rush-to-the-train was going better than Rosa had ever expected.

Terry had asked her if she would stop by The Depot after she dropped Ricky at the train station, and, as she pulled in to the parking lot, a cold November rain began to fall. Running toward the door, it felt as though little needles were being hammered into her skin, and she hoped it was not a bad omen.

"Hey, babe. How ya doing? Did everything go okay with Ricky this morning?" Terry kissed her cheek.

"Actually, it went really well. He told me he wanted to join the art club, if you can believe it. And then he said he'd like to try out for the swim team, but isn't sure he can with his leg, as he would say, "fucked up". I'm almost afraid to breathe, thinking this is all going to tumble down on our heads again." She took off her coat, and rain drops sprayed the entryway floor. "It's pretty crappy out there. What's up?"

"Come this way."

He led her to her 'new' office, and smiled proudly as he opened the door. "Ta-da."

Rosa's hands flew to her mouth as she gasped, "When? How?" The walls were a beautiful and cheery buttery yellow. They had picked out the color along with some much needed and upgraded office equipment and supplies weeks ago. They had agreed that their first priority was to get Ricky settled in school. She didn't let her husband answer, "I can't believe you got all this done so fast. It's really very nice, Terry. You did a great job. Thanks."

Terry reached for her hand, "It's good to have you back on board."

Chapter 6

"It's kind of weird how couples who have been together for years just know when the other person has reached a limit," Rosa told Lettie, as she fingered an especially delicate beige-on-beige batik fabric. Lettie had asked Rosa to join her some morning for shopping and "girl time" at the Quilter's Closet. They chose a time when they knew Helen would be working. "I mean last month when I got home from Bunco, he was in a drunken stupor. I was so pissed off, I seriously was thinking of asking him to move out until he could get his act together. Then the next day when we had our big talk, all I got out of my mouth was, "We have to talk about your drinking." That was when Brian interrupted us to give us the news about Ricky." Rosa slid the bolt of fabric from the shelf and cradled it in her arms like a baby. "I swear he has not had a drink since that night, and I never had to say another word."

"I'd say count your blessings." Lettie thrust a fat-quarter at Rosa, "Look at this one, I think it's new."

"I don't know if I should say something like, "I'm glad you're not drinking anymore," or if I should just shut-up about it. I think he knows he had pushed it too far, and you know how men are—they don't like discussing issues anyway."

"That's certainly true. Maybe you guys have enough on your plate, and you should just let it lie as long as he keeps it under control."

"That's exactly what I was thinking *and* hoping you would say." Rosa felt someone tap her on the shoulder. "Nancy. I'm surprised to see you here in the middle of the day."

Nancy held up four spools of thread. "I had a little time between clients and zoomed over here for some variegated thread that I needed." She looked at the bolt Rosa held in her arms, "Wow, that's really nice fabric. So, what's up with you guys? Anything going on?"

"Well to start with, you look great." Rosa looked her up and down, taking in a new self-confident-Nancy that she had never seen before. "Falling in love must be agreeing with you. Isn't that a new coat? And how the heck much weight have you lost anyway?"

Nancy pulled her shoulders back and raised her chin, "Thanks. I'm down about twenty-five pounds with only ten more to go. My clothes are hanging off me, but I don't want to buy too much new stuff until I reach my goal."

"That's probably a good idea, but a little bit of new clothes here and there helps you to dig deep and keep dieting."

Lettie popped her head over the row of fabrics, "So, when does Lover-boy get here?"

"I'm not sure when they'll move back here permanently, but the plan is definite that Michael and Nick will be back for the holidays." Nancy scrunched up her eyebrows and took a deep breath. "I've got to be honest, the closer it gets the more nervous *I* get. I keep thinking that maybe it's a sign that I'm not ready to see him."

"Now, Nancy, I thought we were past that." Rosa wanted to keep her friend feeling positive. "It's just nerves. Take a breath, honey. As my mom would say, 'It'll all come out in the wash.' " Rosa eyed her up and down again saying, "And, you *do* look fabulous."

"Thanks, Rosa. I never get tired of hearing that."

"My God, how could I not have noticed?" Lettie said, "You're not wearing your glasses."

"Holy crap, your eyes are a different color, too," Rosa squeezed her hand. "You look hot, girlfriend."

Nancy shrugged and looked rather embarrassed. She admitted that she had gotten contacts with a slight blue tint, "I really like them."

"You claim not to know whether or not you want to see this guy, but c'mon, Nancy, admit it—you're excited about the whole thing. What's next, back to blonde hair?"

"Maybe." Nancy became coy and cute, something Rosa had never seen her do. "You'll just have to wait and see."

"Well, I vote that you cover up that gray before he gets here," Lettie added.

Helen finished with her customer and motioned them all to the cutting table. "Wow, Nancy, Miss Hot Stuff! Even with that big winter coat I can tell you've lost weight, and your eyes look beautiful." Putting a bolt of fabric on the cart to be re-shelved, she asked, "It's weird to see you all in here at the same time. Anything up?"

"Lettie needed girl-time, and I needed away-from-Ricky-time."

Holding up the spools again, Nancy said, "I just needed some variegated thread, and I wanted to ask you how things are going with Ruby?"

"The usual—not well. I wish I could help her, but everything I do just seems to make things worse for her. I know she's hurting, and there doesn't seem to be a darn thing I can do to stop the teasing and name calling. It really sucks."

"Kids can be so cruel," Rosa said, and she wondered how many times her own son had tormented the different looking kids in his class.

Helen unwound a bolt that Lettie handed her and smoothed it for cutting, as she changed the subject, "So how's the Rickster doing?"

"I'd love nothing more than to say everything is fabulous, but honestly it's a day-by-day struggle with him. One minute I'm hopeful, and the next I'm waiting for the other shoe to drop, and thinking he'll be back in juvey before the year's out. He's like Jekyll and Hyde sometimes." Rosa shrugged, "It's difficult."

"You've had to make some hard choices in the last few months," Nancy told Rosa. "I'm proud of how you've handled the situation."

"This truly has been one of the most confusing and devastating things I've ever been through." Her hand smoothed the bolt of fabric in her arm. "I mean here's your kid, who you love more than anything in the world, and suddenly he's acting like the kid you'd never let him hang out with." She looked up at her friends. "I felt guilty because I was ashamed of him." Someone holding three bolts of fabric stepped in the cutting line behind Rosa. "Go ahead," Rosa told her. "I'm not ready yet."

The three friends stepped aside, while Helen questioned the quilter about the amount of fabric she needed. Nancy told Rosa and Lettie she had to get back to the clinic for her next client, but before she left her friends, she said to Rosa, "So you've got the Bunco box. Have you even had time to think about Bunco at all?"

"Not really, and I've only got four days before the big night, so I guess I better get crackin'."

"Don't worry about us. Just throw out a bag of chips and some chocolate, and we'll be happy." Nancy smiled, and once again Rosa thought how pretty she was looking.

"Speak for yourself, Walsh." Lettie teased. "I'm expecting a full-blown spread of food as usual."

"I wouldn't dare do anything less," Rosa said. "The Sarge might kick me out of Bunco if I don't measure up."

"So very true. Okay, gotta go." And Nancy turned toward the checkout register with her four spools of variegated thread.

Rosa set the bolts of fabric on the cutting board, "Half yard of each—as if my stash isn't big enough."

Helen began to rotary cut and then folded the half-yard pieces of fabric. "It's probably a good thing we're not having a sewing bee this month. Between Bunco, Thanksgiving, and our road trip to the Amish in Shipshewana, we'll be lucky to fit it all in."

"I can't believe the holidays are right around the corner." A pattern that Rosa had never seen before caught her eye, and she added it to her pile of fabric. "Do you know who has Christmas Bunco this year?"

"I think it's Sarge," Lettie said.

"Good, that'll be right up her alley. We all know how much she loves planning and decorating for the holidays." They chatted a little longer until another customer stood at the cutting table with several bolts of homespun. Picking up their stacks of fabric, Rosa and Lettie headed to the cash register, as Helen turned her attention to the next customer.

Back in Lettie's red truck she told Rosa, "If you want, why don't we discuss the Bunco menu. It might take some pressure off. And really Rosa, please, I can make some of the food if it would help you out."

"Helping with the menu would really be key. I can't seem to wrap my mind around Bunco right now at all." Rosa snagged her purse and rummaged to find paper and pen. By the time Lettie pulled into the Mitchell's driveway, the Bunco menu was written in stone. "E-mail me that Pinterest Pumpkin Bar recipe you were telling me about," Rosa told her. "If I could get it today, I'd like to get my shopping done as soon as I can."

"I'll go right home and send it off." Lettie flipped the end of her one-of-a-kind scarf creation over her shoulder. "Good luck with everything, Rosa, and call me if you need anything. I mean it."

NOVEMBER MENU FOR BUNCO CLUB

Artichoke Dip   Rumaki   Buddig Beef Ball
Pizza Dip* w/chips   Veggies & Dip
Little Smokie Links   Wheat Beer Bread with Herb Dip

Variety of snack crackers

Hot Apple Cider, Pop, Water
Wine Wine and more Wine
Popcorn - M & M's
chocolate covered raisins - mini Snickers

Lois's Chocolate Pie
Pumpkin Bars
Earl Grey Decaf - Wine(s)

*recipe at back of book

Rosa would work on her shopping list later, as well as clean the house. But this afternoon before Ricky got home, she planned a little artistic getaway. By creating pretty quilted envelopes she would present the Bunco prize money with flare. They would be fashioned from fabric and fancy scrapbook paper. A variety of colored ribbons could be used to close the flaps on the envelopes—each containing the appropriate amount of money for the first through fourth place winners. Rosa made an assembly line. Bits of paper and snips of fabric cluttered the oak floor as she cut, sliced and sewed. A little Heat 'n Bond here, a dab of double-stick tape there, and her envelopes were pretty yet whimsical—and best of all finished and ready for Bunco night. In addition she made five small drawstring pouches; four for the booby prizes and one for the most Buncos. She felt rejuvenated after spending time in her sewing and craft room and thought the quilted novelties would add a warm touch to giving cold cash for the Bunco prizes.

Terry phoned as she was stowing away the last of the supplies. He was short-handed at work. Two of the wait staff hadn't shown up. "I'll be right there," she told him.

It had been a while since Rosa had worked a wait-shift at The Pizza Depot. She fell into bed exhausted at 1:30 in the morning. Her feet tingled and *not* in a good way. When she awoke the next morning groggy with what felt like a head full of dandelion fluff, she headed straight for the Keurig. Ricky had unbelievably started his homework with no nagging, and they sat in their own little 'morning worlds' at the kitchen table. Rosa, in her pink chenille robe, thumbed through the Saturday newspaper looking at grocery ads. A 'So Many Quilts, So Little Time' mug of steaming dark coffee with a bowl of oatmeal at her side.

When Rosa finished her shopping list, she started to rummage through her cabinets making sure she had enough paper plates and plastic cups. Terry slipped up behind Rosa and put his arms around her, kissing her on the top of her head. "What can I do to help my favorite waitress get ready for Bunco night?"

She loved the feel of his arms around her, and she nestled into him. "How do you feel about light cleaning? If you could do the bathrooms and wash the kitchen floor, that would help me a lot." This wasn't exactly a romantic discussion, but with two kids and 24 years later, it was real life.

"You got it." Terry turned his bride to face him for a longer kiss.

By the time Rosa got back from the store, Terry had just left for work. He had exceeded her 'wish list' and had nearly the whole house clean. His note read: "All that's left is vacuuming, and Ricky promised to take care of that. See you tonight. Love, T."

By Monday afternoon, Rosa found herself well on her way to being prepared for tomorrow night's Bunco Club. She had made the creamy chocolate pie first to allow it to freeze thoroughly, and tomorrow she would pile it high with whipped cream and then shave chocolate curls onto the stiffened fluff. She assembled several of the appetizers that could be refrigerated overnight to let the flavors meld into a savory taste sensation. Veggies were cleaned, cut, and put into zipper bags to stay fresh. When she started the dishwasher, it gurgled into high-gear just as she was leaving to pick up Ricky at the train station.

By the end of the next day, Rosa would be passing the Bunco box of supplies on to the next hostess and not seeing it for eight long months. Then she would start implementing their new plans for getting more business at The Depot.

Chapter 7

Coats, scarves, and gloves were peeled off as the women of the Bunco club arrived at Rosa's. Orange slices stabbed with whole cloves bobbed in the hot apple cider. It was a huge hit on a very cold night. Plates towered with food, as the chatter went from quilting to books to kids. Rosa snagged four more rumaki, while Beth slathered wheat crackers with her third helping of artichoke dip. Rosa brought the group up to speed about Ricky.

Lettie, arms over her head, bracelets tinkling called out, "Everyone, quiet please." She held her hands out one-by-one toward Nancy, Phree, and Helen. "I think we need to congratulate some people on their weight loss." She started clapping, and the other women joined in. Marge put her fingers to her lips and did a splendid wolf-whistle followed by a long loud trill. *So un-Sarge like*, Rosa thought.

After a few simple calculations it was determined that Nancy had lost the most weight. "I have a hair appointment next week with Beth. So you can all say 'goodbye' to mousy-gray me and 'hello' to my new highlight and lowlight blonde and blue-eyed self." Nancy beamed.

"Any news on the Lover-boy front?"

"Michael emailed me today with the dates he'll be back here for Christmas, and we actually have an 'official' time we're getting together to see each other." Nancy held up her paper plate for Marge as she collected the empty plates and used forks from the women who had finished eating. "I'm both excited and a nervous wreck thinking about seeing him again. It's one thing to email and occasionally phone each other, but to see him in the flesh after all this time…"

"Oooo, listen to you, in the *flesh*." Rosa made her lips into an exaggerated pucker on the oooo, "I guess we know what you're thinking about?"

"Get your mind out of the gutter, Mitchell," Lettie told her, as she popped another tortilla chip loaded with pizza dip into her mouth.

Rosa turned her voice fake-sugary sweet, "Nancy, dear, you know we're all dying to meet him."

"Why don't you bring him to the Christmas Bunco?" Nedra curled her legs under her on the couch and grabbed a handful of chocolate covered raisins.

Rosa sucked in a sharp breath, and her eyes got wide, "Yes, excellent idea! I'm surprised I didn't think of that myself. Then we can get a feel for what kind of person he is…"

Helen fisted her hand, stuck her thumb out and jerked her fist at Rosa, "She means interrogate him. Watch out for her Nancy."

"True. I may have a few prepared questions." Rosa started clearing the table of appetizers and gave Nancy her most innocent smile, as she picked the last rumaki off the plate and ate it. "But I promise to be gentle."

"We've all seen you question the unsuspecting," Beth made air quotation marks with her fingers when she said question, "and it's anything but gentle. But Nancy, I *do* think it's a good idea if you invite him to the Christmas Bunco."

"I'm not so sure it's *that* good of an idea," Nancy drained her cup of apple cider—buying time, obviously uncomfortable. "But I'll think about it. I'd really like to have you all meet Michael, but I think I'll see how our little reunion goes first. After all these years and everything that has happened, I'm still shocked that he's back in my life."

Scooping a bowlful of popcorn, Lettie said, "Why are you so hesitant to see him again? There must be more to your story."

"It was such a long time ago. It's not like talking about it could change anything." Nancy crossed her arms over her chest as though she was attempting to hold in her story.

"It might change how you feel about yourself." Rosa came over and sat on the footstool directly across from Nancy and took her hands, "Nancy, love, you don't have to tell us anything you don't want to. After what I've been through with Ricky, I, of all people, understand the safety of hiding behind a wall." Rosa gently squeezed Nancy's hands, "But, I can also tell you how liberating it feels to share a burden with people you can trust."

Nancy's smile was thin and wobbly, like a crayon line drawn by a first-grader. "I assure you this is going to be a doozie."

"Go ahead, honey," said Nedra, "that's what we're here for."

Rosa let go of Nancy's hands and leaned back on the footstool.

"First of all, I know I told you what a jerk Michael was when we broke up. I have to admit that's not entirely true. We were both outside our—oh, I guess you could call it our maturity zone." Nancy lowered her eyes and studied her folded hands like they were the Holy Grail. "Believe me, I can only tell this story because I *think* I have finally put all the pieces together after many years of agonizing over what happened. Michael and I were twenty years old and in our last semester at a community college. We were both going to be heading off to a four-year college in the fall, and we were arranging to go to the same university. I wanted to work with children in some capacity, and he was a very talented artist. You all know that moment…the excitement of realizing your whole life looms in front of you. One night, well…" She struggled with her next words, "we got a little too, you know—intimate. Okay, so we had sex."

Helen, the youngest in the group, smiled. "I think most of us can empathize with that. Twenty years old—raging hormones—we get the picture."

"I know it probably sounds way old-fashioned by today's standards, but we really were trying to wait before we had sex. Anyway, it was one time—once. And, sure enough, you guessed it—I got pregnant."

Everyone stared at Nancy. For once Rosa didn't speak, but was reprogramming her brain—Nancy was thirty-eight years old, never married, no children—she deleted the 'no children' part.

"I was about six weeks pregnant when I figured it out and took one of those pregnancy tests. Back then you had to wait until you had missed a period to test for pregnancy. I told Michael the results, and right away he wanted to get married." More reprogramming—this time, maybe Michael is not such a horse's ass. "I was in shock and didn't know what to do. You know how my mom is—so concerned with her friends and what they think. I just knew my parents would disown me. I'd never be able to finish school, I was too young to be a mother, my whole life was ahead of me—you all know the drill. I started to buy into the 'it's my body, my choice' thing. It would be so convenient to just have it go away. After all, we were being told over and over that it's only tissue—nothing more." Rosa noticed Marge squirm ever so slightly. She had made it known that she was pro-life but had also never been preachy about her views. Nancy locked eyes with her. "I'm sorry Marge. I was twenty years old and scared. Today I'd have a whole different attitude."

Marge smiled at Nancy. "Oh, sweetie, it's not for me to judge. I understand how hard this must have been for you."

Rosa thought and not for the first time—*I wonder why Marge irritates me so much? She's got a good heart and really is not all that bad.*

"Well, the long and the short of it is, with Michael's support, I decided to keep the baby and not have an abortion. We scraped our money together and went out for a fancy celebration. A let's-figure-out-what-to-do-and-how-to-tell-the-parents-dinner." She paused, and her eyes scanned the room resting on each of the women for a beat. "Within six hours, I entered the hospital with acute food poisoning. They pumped me full of antibiotics and fluids, but I was so violently ill that I lost my baby." Nancy looked down at her hands again. When she looked up a tear left one of her pretty new blue eyes and tracked down her cheek. "They told me it was a girl. My daughter was growing inside of me once. One baby was all I would ever have. And I lost her."

Rosa got up from the footstool, went to her kitchen, and brought back a box of tissue. She passed it around the room. Each woman snapped several squares from the box and started dabbing at eyes or swiping noses. Marge sat next to Nancy on the sofa, put an arm around her shoulder, and pulled her into a motherly hug. She said very softly into Nancy's hair, "Your baby is with God. Have peace with that knowledge."

"I do." Nancy wiped at her nose. "Now, I finally do."

"Oh, Nancy, we're all so sorry." Beth knelt at her friend's feet and took one of her hands. "You must have been in so much pain."

"The next day, Michael's policeman uncle was shot and killed while doing a domestic disturbance call. I think the double disaster was just more than he could deal with at that age. I never saw him after that."

Marge held Nancy tight and spoke as though it was only the two of them in the room. "What was her name? What did you call your baby girl?"

Rosa wanted to slap a hand over Marge's mouth and drag her away. *I can't believe she is being so insensitive, and that only two minutes ago I actually thought she had a good heart.* Rosa was surprised when Nancy smiled, and her tear-filled eyes sparkled with what could only be pride, as she was finally able to share her baby's name. "I named her Skylar, and I call her Sky for short. I like to think of her up in the sky—up in heaven." Nancy lowered her head and picked at a thread on her sweater. "Maybe she's watching over me and has forgiven me."

Marge tightened her mother-hug. "I like that so much. I'm sure she's watching out for you. I have no doubt she feels there is nothing to forgive."

"I calculated her birthday the best I could and every October 12th, I have a little remembrance for her. Wherever she is—if she *is* somewhere—I want her to know I love her very much and will never forget her. I never got to experience full blown motherhood, but somehow I feel so lucky to have had my daughter for the short time that I did. I only wish that I could have held her just one time."

Again, Marge was the one with the soothing words, "There's no doubt about it, Nancy—you are a mother with a true mother's love. Don't ever shortchange yourself in that department." Marge released Nancy from the hug but held on to her hand. "So what happened to Michael?"

"After I got out of the hospital and physically recovered it was nearly graduation. We just kind of drifted apart, and, as I said, we never saw each other again. In all fairness, his family was suffering from the shock of his uncle being killed, and I did nothing to try to get back together with him either. Now, being nearly twenty years older and looking back, I think we were just in over our heads and didn't have a clue what to do. I had missed so much of my last semester that I had to repeat it, and that meant I wouldn't get my degree in time to transfer." Nancy grabbed another tissue and dried her nose. "Michael moved on to the University of Colorado at Boulder, and I stayed behind to finish my AA. Several years later my mom told me she heard he had married."

Marge gently questioned, "Did your parents ever find out about Skylar?" Rosa cringed at Marge's question and how she boldly used the baby's name.

"I don't think so. I begged the hospital not to tell them. After all, I was twenty and considered an adult, but it *was* before all the HIPPA laws. Mom and Dad thought the whole episode was only about a very bad case of food poisoning. If they ever knew, it would be just like them to pretend it didn't happen and never approach me about it. Back then I just couldn't bear the thought of them finding out I had been pregnant."

"So you went on to get your degree and have been helping children for years. I'm proud of you for hanging in there and doing that." Rosa and several of the women nodded their agreement with Marge.

"After all this happened, I never wanted to get involved with anyone ever again. I blamed everyone, but mostly I blamed myself. I used to think that if I hadn't even *thought* about an abortion, none of it would have happened. For a long time, I felt like I was being punished." Nancy shredded the tissues in her hand. "At the very least, I finally have the peace of mind knowing I didn't really cause my baby's death. It took me a long time to get to that place."

"It takes an awful long time to get around that much pain and sort out the confusion." The Sarge was in 'the zone' and knew just what to say. "I don't say 'over' it, because you can never get 'over' something like that. But you *can* move forward and, with time, detour 'around' life's diversions and sadness."

At this point Rosa was downright stunned by Marge.

"I know you're right, Marge. I shut every possible male relationship out of my life for the past twenty years. I guess if I'm being honest, that put me in a position where I could never get pregnant and be hurt again. I'm sorry to say, that sometimes I look back and wish I would have taken the risk—but I can't change that now. If there's one thing I've learned from this, it would be that you can't change the past so don't even try."

"Amen to that," Marge said. "You can shred and burn evidence of your past that you don't like, move to a different town, even change your name. You can trick yourself into thinking, 'If I never speak of it, it didn't happen.' Get rid of it—cover it up. But at the end of the day, when you put your feet up and close your eyes to go to sleep—it's right back where it happened—in your past. As fast as you can run, it will always outrun you. So, the only thing that's left is to accept it and move on."

Seven pairs of eyes stared at Marge—many with gaping mouths attached. It was obvious that *something* monumental had happened in Marge's life that she never discussed. Phree leaned forward, elbows on knees, "Well, this sure explains your reluctance to see Michael again."

"One minute it feels like it's the right thing to do. You know, tie up some very loose ends, or as they say nowadays, get some closure. The next minute I'm filled with utter panic. I mean, for God's sake, we had sex once, and I get pregnant." Nancy shrugged her shoulders, "I often wonder what our lives together would have been like—if I would have had more children. My life would be so different than it is today."

Rosa stood and put her hands on her hips, "I say that it's time you find out. You owe it to yourself and Michael to see what you can salvage from that long-ago relationship."

Everyone collectively agreed. Heads bobbed, and 'yes' and 'good idea' could be heard.

Nancy smiled, "Well, one thing's for sure—I feel better having told all of you what happened. I've never, *ever* told anyone. It's a huge step for me to have shared all this."

Nedra unfolded her legs from under her. "Nancy, you have nothing to be ashamed of. We're all fumbling through life every day. Most of the time we're just flyin' by the seat of our pants."

Nancy stood and said, "Enough of discussing my past. Let's get started."

"Good idea," Nedra said. "And someone get these chocolate raisins away from me before there aren't any left." The women made their way to the card tables. Marge and Helen went down the long hallway to take turns in the bathroom, while Beth and Phree each gave Nancy a quick hug. Rosa went around the tables splashing refills of clear white wine into tall stemmed goblets or offering other beverages to the non-wine drinkers.

Taking the last open seat at the table across from Lettie, Rosa reached over, grabbed the dice, and shook them. "Let's go."

Phree rang the bell to start the action.

On the first roll of the game, Helen threw a Bunco. Beth, her partner, let out a shriek as they 'high-fived' each other. Play continued for several more minutes, while their team racked up additional points.

As they were switching partners, Beth announced, "Helen's going to be the hot one tonight."

"I get her next," yelled Rosa. She pushed her way toward the table, hip-bumping Nancy out of the way in order to be Helen's partner.

"Ladies. Ladies." Marge called out. "Let's remember ourselves."

"Oh, Marge, shut-up and have some fun for a change." Rosa picked up a gold-wrapped chocolate kiss and threw it at her.

"I'll show you fun." Marge lobbed three foil kisses across the room, where they bounced onto Rosa's table—two of them skidding onto her lap.

"Let's remember ourselves," Rosa imitated Marge perfectly, as she dodged a dozen incoming candies from other women joining in on the aerial assault.

One piece splashed squarely into Nedra's wine glass, and Beth clasped her hand to her mouth, eyes wide, "Sorry Ned."

Tilting her glass, Nedra used her perfectly manicured fingernail to capture the wayward goodie from the bottom of the goblet. After shaking a few clear droplets onto a napkin, she unwrapped the foil and popped the chocolate into her mouth. "Wine and chocolate—what a perfect combination."

"Okay, enough! Let's keep this game going so I can be the big winner tonight." Rosa peeled the covering off the nearest chocolate, and it disappeared between her lips. Someone rang the bell, and both dice and women started chattering.

When the game ended, the women double-checked their scores, and arranged the scorecards from first place to last. "Do you believe I never threw another Bunco all night and ended up with a booby prize?" Helen slipped her scorecard into the last slot.

Rosa set a wicker basket in the center of the table that contained the fancy envelopes and bags she had made. "Now don't get too excited, girls. With all the crap going on around here, I didn't have time to run around looking for trinkets. So, I decided to give money for tonight's prizes."

"Nothing wrong with money."

"I'd say those bags and folders look like the real prizes to me."

"These holders are gorgeous. I think I'm going to steal this idea for Christmas gifts," Lettie said.

Helen picked up a money folder and turned it over examining the construction. "You could make these with a masculine or sports theme for guys or kids. Baby fabric would work great for money and gift cards for new parents." Rosa handed each winner her appropriate prize, and Beth asked to see the pattern.

"I kind of made it up as I went, but I can show you how I did it."

Rosa cut the pie and slipped a generous wedge of creamy chocolate sweetness onto eight plates, then added a slice of pumpkin bar to each.

Marge poured hot cups of Earl Grey decaf from a tea pot that was shaped like a black and white cow. Tea emptied into the cups from the cow's mouth. "After all the chocolate we eat in a night, it sure is a good thing we drink decaffeinated tea."

During show-and-tell, Helen pulled out a large brown mailing envelope sprinkled with colorful stamps. "You're not going to believe this. I got this the other day from Ben's mother." She pulled out a folded section of blue cloth, and several small pieces of fabric in various colors and shapes fell to the floor. "Ben's grandmother, who's been dead for eighteen years, started this quilt-top a long time ago and never finished it. My mother-in-law found it the other day stuck in the back of a closet." Helen billowed the quilt top in front of her, like a breeze had caught it on a clothes line. Phree grabbed at a corner and held it up to help Helen show the whole piece.

"Oh, my God, that's beautiful." Beth got on her knees examining the tiny stitches of the dated appliqué of dogwood blossoms. "These stitches are so small and perfect—they're invisible. Helen, what a treasure this is."

"This note was inside." Helen reached into the brown envelope and took out a folded piece of paper. " 'I thought you might like this. Grandma Libby started it a long time ago but never finished it. If you don't want it, just toss it.' " Helen flopped her arms at her side. "Toss it—can you imagine. Just knowing that Ben's grandma had worked on this quilt makes it special. The rest of the pieces are cut out. It's all vintage fabric, and they just need to be appliquéd." She fanned out the colorful fabric again, "Of course, I'll finish it."

The women packed away their show-and-tell and agreed on a date for the Holiday Bunco. Marge would be the lucky one to host this year's big event. "Just give me a head count about a week before, and I'll get back to everyone with how many tables and chairs we'll need. When we get together for the Shipshewana trip, we can talk about food for Bunco."

Rosa sidled up next to Nancy and encouraged her to bring Michael, "You too, Phree. Bring that cute cop with you next month. Talk about eye candy."

Seven women sorted through the pile of coats, scarves, and purses until they had retrieved their own items. Hugs and Happy Thanksgiving wishes were given to each other, along with good luck wishes for the women who had to cook that day. Phree said, "Thanksgiving will have a whole new meaning for me this year."

"Just think of those Pilgrims with those big belt buckles," Rosa handed Helen her tote bag, "and be happy you don't have to wear one."

"Hey, be careful, you're talking about my stylin' relatives there."

"See everyone bright and early for Shipshewana." Lettie flung one of her newly knit scarves around her neck. Every shade of green was represented in the hand-dyed yarns. Large loopy areas were softened with pale tones of various blues and peach, and ribbons added the perfect unexpected contrast in both color and texture.

"You know I don't do mornings, although I am getting a little better now that Ricky catches the train. But we'll still have to stop for coffee on the way, if you don't want me to fall asleep at the wheel."

Marge picked up the Bunco box before Rosa could hand it to her, and said, "I'll bring homemade chocolate chip cookies as usual, and we'll pick up doughnuts when we get coffee. Everyone remember to bring a salty snack."

All was well with the Bunco Club. The Sarge was in control.

DECEMBER BUNCO - Marge

Whatever you do, you need courage.
Ralph Waldo Emerson

Chapter 1

Marge felt a panic of big-mouth-remorse, as she left Rosa's house. She chided herself for always needing to be so damned helpful, but quickly wiggled off the hook by reminding herself, *That's who I am, but did I say too much?* The familiarity from years of backpedalling, while weaving lies into the story of her life, actually calmed her into a mental safe haven. Through thick winter gloves, Marge fumbled for the cold door handle on Helen's mini-van. "Get the heat going as fast as you can," she bossed. "I'm about frozen just walking to the car."

Puffs of steamy breath fogged the inside of the windows, as Helen turned the defroster on full blast. "We'll have to let the car warm up for a few minutes before we can leave." Helen's teeth chattered while half-moon shapes appeared at the base of the windshield and then slowly grew larger. "It seems awful early to be this cold. I heard a weatherman talking today, and he said this could be the coldest winter in twenty years."

Gloved hands made a muffled shooshing sound, as Marge rubbed them together. "Great, it's not even Thanksgiving yet."

"Are you cooking this year?" Helen put the car in gear and pulled away from the curb.

"Yeah, I always do. My two sisters and their families are coming here Wednesday. I have Thanksgiving at our house, and my youngest sister, Laura, hosts New Year's. Jill does Christmas. It works out nice that way. No one gets stuck hosting more than one of the holidays."

"That sounds like a good idea, as long as everyone gets along."

"Oh, we tolerate each other. How about you?"

"Ben's brother, wife, and kids are coming down from Wisconsin on Wednesday afternoon and spending two nights. They'll go home sometime Friday. My sister-in-law helps me with the cooking on Thursday, while the men entertain the kids. I think we have the better part of the deal. Us girls get to spend the day together messing around in the kitchen without kids underfoot." Helen reached over and turned the defroster down and the heater up. "We all get along pretty well, and our kids are close in age, so that helps."

"Sounds like a plan."

"So, what did you think about Nancy's baby bombshell?"

Marge exhaled a long steamy breath that left a frosty spot on the inside of the windshield. "Sorry about that," she said and hesitated for a moment. "Oh, I don't know, Helen. All I can say is after what we found out tonight, my heart just hurts for Nancy."

"Yeah, you're not kidding. What a night. By the way, you did a great job helping her. How was it you knew just what to say? I never could have been as confident as you were."

Marge knew Helen was fishing for information, more like gossip, and so she simply looked straight ahead and said, "I guess being a nurse helps." Helen let it go, but Marge sensed she hadn't convinced her friend of anything. They remained silent until they pulled up in front of Marge's home.

"Well, here we are. Have a great holiday, Marge. See you on the Saturday after Thanksgiving—bright and early."

Grabbing her purse, Bunco box, and overstuffed tote bag, Marge said, "You have a good holiday, too." Then before closing the door she smiled and added, "Don't eat too much turkey." She only had to stay composed for a few short steps to reach her door. By helping her friend, she had emotionally relived the worst time in her life—the terrible time from which she could never run fast enough.

Bud sat in his favorite chair watching television, or rather he *had been* watching television. Marge's husband appeared to be in a deep sleep, stockinged feet crossed at the ankles resting on the ottoman, remote control for the television forgotten on his flannel shirt—slowly rising and falling in time with his breathing. He stirred as Marge opened the front door, and a blast of cold air followed her inside. "Hey, there," Bud yawned and swiped a hand across his mouth, as he leaned on his arm to sit up straighter. "How were the gals tonight?"

"Bunco was fun as usual, but poor Nancy opened up to us about something that happened to her years ago." Marge paused as she took off her gloves and unbuttoned her winter coat. "She told us that back in college she had been pregnant, unmarried, and then lost her baby." When she looked up at Bud, he looked worried. "I'm okay."

"Was it hard for you? I mean to be there and not respond?" Bud patted the ottoman for her to sit.

"Well, that might be a problem. I think I may have seemed a little too familiar with the situation." Bud moved his feet so Marge could sit on the ottoman, and her fingers started nervously combing through the fringe on her one-of-a-kind 'Lettie' scarf. "I just couldn't help myself. I *knew* what she had been through, and how she felt when she lost that baby. My God Bud, she's never told anyone—not even her parents. Poor Nancy, she seemed to want to get it out in the open."

Marge stopped the intense organization of the fringe and looked around with panicky eyes, "Where are the kids?"

"Val's in bed asleep, and Zach's playing cards at Jim's. It's okay. Go on."

Marge's shoulders wilted, and her head drooped forward. "Bud, I've got such mixed feelings. At the time I just wanted to help her, and now I'm almost sorry."

"I've told you a million times, that you don't have to apologize for what happened." He reached out and stilled the fringe-combing by holding one of her cold hands between both of his large calloused palms and rubbing warmth into it. "If you want to keep what happened a secret forever, that's all right with me. But if you want to tell the world, I have no problem with that either."

"I sometimes wish I could open up about it, and tell anyone who would listen. It all happened so long ago, and I just don't know how the kids would take it. That's what scares me the most."

"The *kids,*" Bud said, as he tilted his head and raised his eyebrows, "are nearly adults. Val is a senior in high school, and Zach is in his second year of college. Now, turn around."

"Why?"

"Just do it." Bud gripped her shoulders and angled her to face away from him. Marge swung her legs to the other side of the ottoman, back stiffening as she became aware that she was no longer in control. Bud's strong hands started to smooth the tension out of her back and continued to knead the knots, as though he had just completed an advanced course in massage therapy. They said nothing, but soon Marge began to relax and let out a few low growls as the pressure increased and the tension eased. When he stopped, he put his arms around her and tenderly pulled her well massaged back into his chest. "Maybe it's time to stop hiding and have some peace, Marge."

"But how do I do that?" Marge snugged the back of her head into the crook of her husband's neck and relaxed. "Not to sound too much like a pathetic martyr, but I've always thought my lot in life was to suffer silently."

"To start with, we could tell the kids." While Marge liked that he said *we,* at the mere mention of this horrible idea she sat bolt upright and spun around to look at him. As she sputtered, or to be more exact tried to sputter, Bud placed a finger over her surprised lips. He looked her straight in the eyes, and whispered, "Margie, honey, why don't we try to find him?"

Marge swatted at his hand and then placed her other hand over her mouth. As she stood and stepped away from him, her scarf pooled to the floor. With her arms wrapped protectively around her rib cage, she whirled on Bud as she inhaled a sob.

"Come on, Margie. This is enough for one night." Bud stood and put his arms around his wife, "Sleep on it, sweetheart." With a kiss to the top of her head, he added, "Always remember that I'm right beside you."

Chapter 2

It was just like Bud to give her space to sort things out, but after a week, Marge still had no idea what to do. To be honest, she'd been sorting out this dilemma since she was sixteen, and her way of coping was to hide what had happened. She was beginning to think that maybe she wanted to take the next step—but what *was* the next step, and did she really need to consider taking it? She thought she might have a heart-to-heart talk with her sisters when they were at her house for Thanksgiving. No one knew her background better than they did. After all, they had lived it and suffered it right along with her.

Marge let the approaching Thanksgiving holiday be her excuse for putting the quandary out of her mind and doing nothing. But as she set out snacks while waiting for her youngest sister to arrive, she sensed she was facing one of life's crossroads. Do nothing and be sorry she had let the situation paralyze most of her life, or be pro-active and possibly live with regrets she couldn't even imagine at this point. But then there was that glimmer. The far-off hope she never allowed herself to enjoy. That someday she would finally have a relationship with her son, along with the support and love of her family.

It was late afternoon, and Marge expected her sister Laura would be the first to arrive. She would drive in from the north side of Chicago, where she had a public relations job with the Chicago Cubs Baseball team. Laura loved her career, and she also loved sports, and while Laura would be some guy's dream-come-true, she had never married. Middle sister, Jill, would show up later in the evening with her husband Jack and their three kids (ages six through twelve) and most likely be more than a little disheveled. Jack and Jill O'Donnell were used to people guffawing over their names, and Jill always told them, "It could be worse, I'm just thankful our last name's not Hill."

Their family ritual was firmly rooted. After a simple dinner of sub-sandwiches and chips, the men would collect all the kids in the family room, where they would watch their traditional Thanksgiving DVD, *Planes, Trains, and Automobiles*. The three sisters would happily hole-up in the kitchen under the pretext of getting things ready for the next day's festivities. They would take advantage of the opportunity to reconnect as sisters without too much interference from kids and spouses. Marge thought that might be the perfect time to finally get their input.

Not only was Laura on time, but she was decked out like a walking billboard. Sporting a stylish and slimming Cubs outerwear vest, with a Cubs tote dangling from her arm, she held a thermal coffee mug imprinted with the Cubs logo. The latest Cubs baseball cap topped her mass of dark curls, yet still managed to show off a Cubbie-blue streak of hair tipped in edgy bright red. Marge knew Laura's cell phone had a Cubs protective case, and suspected her sister would be wearing Cubs underwear if there was such a thing.

Jill had been keeping Marge updated with her family's delayed progress due to the heavy traffic. As expected, travel around O'Hare Airport was slow going, but holiday congestion seemed worse in general due to snow falling on Chicago's north side. "I'm glad I left home when I did," Laura said. "I stayed just ahead of the snow AND the traffic."

Laura's phone pealed a kitschy version of "Take Me out to the Ball Game." "It's a text from Jill. She says they're about 20 minutes out and starving."

"That's just about perfect timing. Tell her Bud and the kids will be here with the food in about half an hour." Marge's husband and two children had gone to pick up the sub-sandwiches along with a large bag of ice. The two sisters chatted, while they set out a stack of paper plates along with napkins, condiments, and several baskets of potato chips. Laura opened a box of plastic ware that made a synthetic tinkling sound as they chimed off the oak table top. She scooped them into piles of knives, forks, and spoons.

With muffled sounds of car doors closing, loud voices, and much laughter, Marge could hear the group approaching before the door even opened. Family streamed inside carrying suitcases, sleeping bags with pillows, and covered dishes of food. Her children each toted a bag of ice, and Bud brought in a box full of subs. Jessica, the youngest O'Donnell, squealed her way around the others, dropping her pillow and teddy bear onto a chair, she slammed into Marge hugging her around the legs and squeezing tight. "Aunt Marge, I missed you so much!"

Marge hugged back. "I missed you too, baby girl." This was one of the best moments of the year for Marge—her whole family coming together for a festive and thankful holiday. It was her own private reality check, and reminded her that she had much for which to be grateful.

After hellos and more hugs, the hungry extended family crowded together around the dining room table. Tomorrow morning Bud would put the two leaves in the table and expand it to comfortably seat everyone, but tonight's meal was always informal and cozy. Non-stop chatter and laughs filled the room, as the family reconnected. They ate like they hadn't seen food in a week, and finished off their subs like a school of hungry piranhas.

Val wiggled to a stand from her crowded place at the table, cleared her throat to get everyone's attention, and with much flair mimicked Steve Martin's character in *Planes, Trains and Automobiles*. "'You're like a Chatty Cathy Doll, but you pull your own string!'" She yanked at an imaginary string connected to her chest, "'Awk, awk, awk!'"

Jill's children shrieked, and Jessica started off toward the family room while jumping up and down—ponytails bouncing along the sides of her head. Clearly unable to control her excitement after the long car ride, she shouted, "Let's get started! Can we Uncle Bud? Can we—now?"

Zach grabbed her hand and stopped the leaping by reciting, "'Here's an idea, when you tell a story have a point. It makes it so much …'" He left off the last part of the quote.

Jessica threw her arms in the air and then jammed her hands on her hips yelling, "'…more interesting for the listener!'" Ignoring the comments and howls of approval for her performance, Jessica pulled with force on Zach's arm. "Come on, everyone. I can't wait!"

Marge felt deeply happy as she watched the two generations being bound together with a festive thread of laughter and applause, making yet another stitch in the fabric of their family quilt. Shooing the group off to the family room, she rolled up the sleeves of her handmade quilted sweatshirt, "You guys all go ahead. We'll clean up here."

Val elbowed her way through the family members, "I dibs the big chair!"

"No fair," Jimmy chased after her, "you had it last year."

"So what, I dibs-ed it first." Bud gave the NFL referee signal for taunting.

"You can share," Marge called after the arguing cousins.

Jack turned to the three sisters, and Marge noticed for the first time he was balding. "Wish us luck! Maybe we should draw names for twenty minutes each in the coveted 'big chair'. Come on Bud. Duty calls."

Kissing Marge on the cheek, Bud said, "We'll be back in about an hour to make popcorn and take an intermission." Then he clapped his hand on Jack's back and they headed for the family room. "Last call for a potty break," Bud shouted above the shrieks and rough-housing.

The women stepped into the kitchen and settled into retro red-and-white vinyl and chrome chairs. Empty mugs were in front of them, and a kettle of water was set to boil on the stove. "Better them than us." With a groan, Jill lowered herself onto one of the 50s style chairs.

"Whew," Marge said, "What a whirlwind!" She reached into a cabinet, and brought out a foil covered plate she had hidden there the day before. Setting it on the table, she poured the boiling water into a decorative tea pot. "Anyone prefer wine or a cold beer?"

"I'll take a beer," Laura said.

"Nah, I'm good with a hot cup of tea," Jill said. "To me this is the best part of Thanksgiving, when just the three of us get to be alone for a while and talk it up." She leaned back into her chair in a comfortable slouch.

"Me, too." Marge lifted the foil wrapper from a plate of homemade chocolate chip cookies, and the aroma blossomed into the room. "Dig in, girls, before the hungry hordes come back."

Jill started with three cookies and had already eaten one, as Laura daintily snapped a cookie in half and rested it on a napkin in front of her. They talked for a while about jobs and kids, and, because of Laura, professional sports. After about thirty minutes of idle chit-chat, two more beers for Laura, and a fresh pot of tea, Marge lowered her voice and picking up the other half of Laura's cookie said, "I need to talk to you guys about something."

"Ooo Margie, this sounds serious." Jill and Laura still called their big sister Margie.

"Well, it is—rather." Marge put an elbow on the table and rested her chin in her palm, "It's about, you know, what happened when I was sixteen."

"Oh, Margie." Laura lowered her voice, "What's going on?"

"Something came up last week, and I helped a friend who went through a similar situation over twenty years ago—only she miscarried. It just stirred something in me, and I'm feeling haunted." She took a sip of tea, and when she replaced the mug on the table said, "Bud not only thinks it might be time to tell the kids, he even suggested we might try to find him."

"Holy crap, Marge. How do *you* feel about that?" Laura broke off a piece of cookie and popped it into her mouth.

"That's just it, I don't know. I'm so paralyzed by it, that I can't make a decision. I guess having the truth buried has become safe for me. All I can say is it's beginning to feel wrong to keep this a secret from the kids. I mean, think about it, when is the right time to tell Zach and Val that they have a half-brother somewhere?"

A gasp came from the dining room doorway, and all three sisters snapped their attention in that direction. Marge's daughter Val stood before them, face draining of color and eyes wide, hands gripping the door frame. She tilted her head ever so slightly and questioned in a whisper, "Mom?"

Marge stood, hands palms down on the table, and a sleeve of her quilted sweatshirt slipped down to her wrist.

"Mom? What did you just say?" Val backed out of the kitchen, as though she could erase what she had heard simply by rewinding her footsteps.

"Val. I…uh. Sweetie, I…um." Marge was thrown off balance by the pain on her daughter's face. She felt dizzy and struggled for words, but none came. *This is it. This is happening right now. My daughter knows. She heard the secret I've hidden for years.*

Jill took charge. She pushed back her chair and told her niece in a firm, no-nonsense voice, "Val, come sit over here." Val did not move, nor did she take her eyes off her mother. "Margie, luv, sit back down." Jill gently guided Marge back into her chair. Marge's eyes never left her daughter. Laura sat stock still. The only thing moving was her eyes, as they darted around the room like a cornered animal.

"Aunt Jill, what's going on?"

"Please, Val, come over here, and sit down."

Val moved slow, feet shuffling, zombielike. The fashion forward young woman that Val had become suddenly looked small and very, very afraid. "I don't get it. What the hell? Is this some kind of joke?" She made her way to the chair next to her mother, and Jill pushed the chair under her.

"I need to use the bathroom," Laura said and started to rise.

Jill caught her arm with a firm grip and stopped her sister, "Not now. Marge needs us." Laura lowered herself and put her face in her hands.

"Tell her Jill, she needs to know the truth." Marge's voice was thin.

Jill sat next to Marge and rubbed her sister's back. She looked at Val. "Your mom had an extremely hard life growing up. I know you've heard stories about how crazy Grandma and Grandpa were."

Val nodded and looked so damned scared that Marge interrupted, "No excuses, Jill. Just tell her what happened."

Jill drew in a ragged breath and then slowly let it out. "Your mom fell in love at sixteen and got pregnant. Our parents sent her away to have the baby all alone. She had a little boy, and gave him up for adoption."

Except for Laura's darting eyes and a flickering flame from a candle on the counter, all motion in the room had stopped. It was as though they were posing for a photo back in the old days, where no one dared move or it would ruin the picture. Marge's heart counted every second by pounding louder and louder with each beat. She finally looked at her daughter and saw such raw pain that her heart nearly broke for this child she loved so much. *She feels betrayed.* Marge needed to do something, but couldn't.

"I don't get it. Why didn't you tell me? Why keep this from me...from us...or does Zach already know? Oh my God!" Her hands flew to her cheeks, "Does Daddy know?"

As Rosa would say, it's time to put on your big girl panties. "Val, I never meant to hurt you. I'm really sorry you had to find out this way." Val started to bite her thumb nail, a habit from when she was little and afraid—when the world seemed too big and scary. Marge hadn't seen her do that in several years, and the action piled on more guilt. *Look what I've done to her. She'll never trust me again.* Marge took her daughter's hand and removed the thumbnail from her mouth. She brought the back of Val's hand to her lips, where she brushed a kiss on it. Setting her daughter's hand back on the table, Marge continued to hold it.

"I did what I thought best. I only meant to keep it from you when you were little, but the time never seemed right to tell you. It was my burden, and one you didn't need to carry." Marge could feel tears pooling in her eyes and was unsuccessful to stop their free-fall down her cheeks.

"I...I...don't know what to say." Val brushed her bangs back with her free hand, and Marge noticed some color coming back to her daughter's cheeks. "I'm confused, Mom. I'm not mad that it happened. I'm just shocked, and a little pissed that you never told me...us. I just need to...need a second to grasp it, I think." Val placed the back of her mother's hand up to her own cheek. "Didn't you trust me? It's just a lot to take in, and I feel so bad for you. It must have sucked."

That's a fucking understatement. But Marge said, "It did, honey. It sucked big time."

"Do you know where he is? What's his name? Who's his father? What about Dad and Zach?"

"I don't know anything about him. I saw him when he was born. Against the rules, a *very* kind nurse placed him in my arms for about a minute, and when she left the room with him I never saw him again." Sensing an acute case of sibling rivalry brewing, Marge said, "Zach doesn't have any ..."

"For crying out loud, Val, what's taking so long? Where's the popcorn?" With the energy of a hungry boy and the body of an adult male, Zach propelled himself into the kitchen. Marge's son had the requisite hair style of a male college student—it stopped at his shoulders where the ends were forced into the slightest flip. He took in the scene in front of him. "What in the...? What's going on in here?"

Laura shot up from her seat, "You can sit here, Zach." She patted his shoulder as she walked past him and finally escaped the uncomfortable drama.

Jill repeated the story to Zach, and this time Marge was the one who was shocked. "Mom, I suspected something like this for a couple of years."

"How?"

"I needed my birth certificate for some paperwork when I was a senior in high school—for some college application or something. You and Dad weren't home, but I knew the place you guys keep important papers. I'm sorry Mom, I really wasn't snooping, it just happened. I found an envelope and looked inside." Marge nodded. She knew exactly what he had found. "You named him David."

"My beloved. His unofficial name. The name I called him the only time I ever saw him."

"He turned 39 last September," said Zach. "September $8^{th.}$ A guy doesn't forget his brother's birthday."

Marge nodded, and Val swiped at a tear that was threatening to fall. "Did you ever try to find him, Mom?"

"No. I was so young when it happened and by the time I became old enough to do anything, I figured he was well established in his own life with the parents who raised him. I wasn't part of his life, and I didn't want to do anything that might upset him."

"I can tell you it was the hardest thing your mom ever had to do, but she did it in the best interest of her baby," Jill said. "It was a difficult and unselfish thing for a sixteen-year-old to do."

"I bet we could find him with all the information on the internet. There must be tons of stuff for adoptive kids and moms. Maybe he's been looking for you." The mascara that had trailed down Val's cheeks became part of her smile. It reminded Marge of an abstract painting.

"I just don't want to interfere in his life." Now that her kids knew about her firstborn, Marge felt a prickle of excitement that was rapidly followed by a sense of dread.

"Slow down, Val, Mom needs to think about this." Zach told his sister. "Besides, it's not going to be as easy as you think. You watch too much TV."

"Shut up, dickhead. Go in the other room if you don't want to help. I was thinking that if he's 39, he's probably married with kids. Mom, you could be a grandma. I could be an aunt!"

"And I could be Uncle Dickhead." Zach mocked his sister's enthusiasm.

This made Marge chuckle and helped ground her to reality. "Okay, you two, enough posturing. I guess it can't hurt to look, Val, but I'm not promising anything." However, Margareta Miller Russell knew she'd move heaven and earth for a chance to see her son again.

Val stuck her thumbnail in her mouth and bit down, a loud snap filled the room, "Mom, does Dad know?"

"Of course, Stupid," Zach said. Marge started to object to the 'stupid' reference, but stopped. This was not the time for that battle. "Mom and Dad are like the perfect parents. They're each other's best friends. Of course he knows." But Zach looked toward his mother for reassurance.

"Yes, Dad knows."

"So, can I look for him, Mom? It will be cool to have another brother."

"We have to remember he may not want to be found, so we shouldn't get our hopes up too high. We have to respect *his* wishes first, *and* it's really important not to make up fantasy scenarios in our heads. If you can remember those things…yes, Val, you can find David for me."

"So what can you tell me about his birth?" Val swung around and snatched a small tablet from the counter, the kind Marge usually kept in her back pocket. "Where was he born? Any details you can remember could be helpful." She poised a pen over the tablet waiting for her mother's response.

"Val, let your mom sleep on this for a night or two."

"It's okay, Jill. I've had 39 years to think about this, and I'm ready to stop running."

"So what was the deal with the baby's father? Maybe something there could blow this wide open."

"What did I tell you?" Zach said, "Miss CSI here is ready to 'blow the cold case wide open'."

Ignoring her squabbling children, Marge said, "He was eighteen when I got pregnant, and six months later a bullet took his life in Vietnam. He never knew I had gotten pregnant." She hesitated and looked directly from Zach to Val. "Jerome Wittson, my baby's father, was black."

Chapter 3

On the Saturday after Thanksgiving, the sun was not yet up when Marge tugged her fashionable and sensible winter boots over her double-socked feet. Her clothes were well layered, as all the women's would be. The Amish town of Shipshewana was surrounded by Indiana corn fields. There was nothing to block the freezing wind that blew over the Midwest prairie, as the Bunco friends would scurry from one shop to the next. Not wanting to leave anything behind that they might need for the long day ahead, Marge made checkmarks on her notepad as she took stock of her surroundings.

Making the short drive to Helen's house, Marge allowed herself the luxury of reliving the events from the other day that she now thought of as the 'big reveal'. Overall, her children had taken the news quite well. Initially Val was upset at being 'lied to', but Zach had told her to 'shut up and stop thinking about yourself so much'. Marge had occasionally found Val bent over her laptop, and assumed her daughter had started the search for her half-brother. While this both terrified and delighted Marge, she supposed it could take years before they ever connected with David. *If* they could find him at all.

Red coat unbuttoned and flapping, Helen bolted from her front door before Marge had the car parked, singing, "Shipshewana Here We Come" to the tune of "California Here We Come". Shutting the car door, Helen let out a breathless, "Yes. Finally!" as she flopped the back of her head onto the headrest. "Oh, Marge, do I ever need this trip after a house full of people these last few days. With the kids out of school and their cousins gone home, they'll be fighting and complaining all day. I almost feel sorry for my poor husband." She puffed air out of her mouth and made a motorboat sound, as Marge backed out of the driveway.

"Thank God the weather warmed up. It's supposed to be in the mid-forties today. How was your Thanksgiving?"

"Oh, just fine. We had a quiet one." *Liar.* "How was yours?"

"Noisy and long, but we had fun. I'm so happy we're not supposed to get snow today. I checked online for weather in the Indiana Snow Belt, and it looks clear. Remember that year we ended up spending the night there, because it snowed so hard once we got to Shipshe?" Marge thought maybe Helen might have already had one too many coffees. "I'm hoping to find a few Christmas gifts today for some hard-to-buy-for people. What are you looking for?" Helen finally took a breath and looked over at Marge, "Anything special?"

If she only knew what I'm looking for. "Well, I need some backing for two quilts that I'm making for Christmas presents, and, of course, our must-have bacon." Marge stopped at a red light. "I need some scrapbooking supplies, too. I'm hoping to get Val's four years of high school done by graduation." Marge turned down Rosa's street. "Looks like Nedra and Nancy just beat us."

Nedra opened the car door and waved. She reached back into the car and pulled out a tote bag spilling over with snacks. Nancy popped the trunk open to expose a large cooler, and they each took a handle and heaved it to the ground.

As Marge and Helen got out of the car, Nancy said, "It's so damn early, but man am I pumped for this."

Rosa backed her van out of the garage and stopped it at the end of the driveway. "Here come the other three," she announced opening the driver's door. As they all loaded the van with essentials, Beth said she needed to use the bathroom one last time.

"Good idea," Lettie said. "Me too."

"God, I'm dying for some coffee," Rosa moaned. "You know I don't do early o'clock very well."

"If anyone needs gloves, I brought along a few emergency pairs," Marge said.

As though they were grade school children with assigned seats, the women piled into the van and claimed their usual spots. Lettie always sat up front with Rosa because she got car sick so easily. Nedra, Beth, and Marge were in the middle, with Helen, Phree, and Nancy in the way-back.

"I brought some Christmas CDs," Phree said and handed them to Beth. "Pass these up to Lettie, will you?"

"Oh, I love this one." Tapping Lettie on the shoulder with the corner of the CD said, "Put this one in first."

Rosa looked in the rearview mirror. "Everybody buckled in and ready for take-off?"

With her notebook in hand, Marge jotted down the current mileage from the odometer, so she could calculate the MSPM (money spent per minute). She then compiled coffee orders with the speed of an experienced waitress.

As they pulled away from the coffee shop, eight cups of various sizes and flavors of coffee fueled their excitement another notch higher. With Anne Murray singing Christmas songs in the background, and at least three separate conversations going at any given time, the Bunco group eased onto Interstate 80, and cruised into the sunrise and northeast Indiana.

Chapter 4

After eating a hearty Amish breakfast at the Blue Gate Restaurant, the women followed their yearly shopping routine by heading to Yoder's Department Store. The small community of Shipshewana had a population of just over 500 people, and Marge swore they all must quilt. Rosa pulled into Yoder's just after 10:00, and the women exited the van to the clip-clop sound of horses pulling Amish buggies. The two cultures co-existed with each other and after spending time here, Marge often felt that she had taken a day-trip in a time machine. Yoder's had an extensive fabric department, and everyone exited the van with shopping lists in hand. They were barely able to contain their excitement, that soon they would be browsing through thousands of bolts of fabric. "Who will be the winner today?" The 'winner' meant the one who spent the most money.

"As usual, I'm sure I'll be in contention," said Rosa.

"I think we've all got a crack at it this year," Nancy laughed.

The friends descended on the fabric department, like snow melt crashing down a waterfall and then settling into a pool. Phree pointed toward a colorful display of quilts hanging in the long entrance of the department store. Amish men and women kept to themselves in their 'plain' clothes, while they spoke their unique Indiana dialect of Pennsylvania Dutch. A young Amish mother held the hands of her two small daughters. All three wore drab colored dresses with the traditional head covering, kapp, of the Amish women. The little girls, blonde hair in braids, stared at the cluster of women that walked by smiling at them. It was obvious that each group was equally curious about the other, but nothing beyond a few shy smiles and this chance crossing-of-paths would ever materialize.

When they entered the fabric department, the eight friends split up and went their separate way. They would probably spend at least an hour here, and their paths would cross many times in the store, as they needed second opinions and shared nice-looking fabrics. Rosa quickly had several bolts of fabric in her arms, and desperately looked for a cart to pile on more.

The day progressed quickly as they went from shop to shop, and they made it a point to get to the Meat Market before it got too crowded. They purchased an abundant amount of their much-loved bacon, a bounty of jams and jellies, and at least a ton of homemade Amish cheeses.

"Ever notice how food works its way into everything we do?" asked Lettie, as they pulled up to the bulk food store. Here they found food in tubs and plastic bags priced ridiculously low compared to costs back home. They chose tubs of sesame and poppy seeds for general use in cooking; dehydrated celery, chopped onions, and bay leaves along with other spices for making soups; and mounds of snack crackers and chocolate—all of which they would split and share. Even their favorite tea was sold in bulk, as well as any type of flour you could imagine. The van quickly became full of shopping treasures, and after each stop packages needed to be rearranged to fit in the new purchases.

It was nearing time for the stores to close, and an exhausted Lettie offered to go to the Blue Gate Restaurant to put their name on the waiting list for dinner. "I'll go with," said an equally tired Marge. "I need to make a pit stop anyway." After telling the hostess, 'Mitchell, party of eight,' Lettie found an Amish made oak bench, and after visiting the restroom, Marge plopped down next to her

"I'm pooped," Marge said. Shifting a package to an empty place beside her, she asked, "How long did they say?"

"About twenty minutes. Can you believe it was only this morning when we left home? It feels like days ago."

"I know. I also can't believe I'm hungry again."

Beth and Nedra wandered in and found seats near Marge and Lettie. "Rosa is doing her customary last minute panic shopping," said Beth. "The last time I saw her, she had headed back to the bakery to get more English Muffin Bread for Terry."

"Good old Rosa," Lettie smiled. "I bet she wins as usual."

Marge's cell phone rang, and while digging through her purse to find it, she said, "Hmpf, I wonder who this could be?" The other women continued talking among themselves. As Marge answered the phone, Nancy, Helen, and Phree walked over to the crowded bench and talked about the last shop they had visited.

Marge clicked on her phone. "Hello?"

"Mom," Val's voice came across the miles. "Mom, I didn't know if I should call you while you were with your friends, but I couldn't wait." Val's voice sounded full of excitement. "Mom, I found him!"

Marge couldn't take a full breath, as her lungs felt constricted from the weight of what Val had said.

"Mom—did I lose you? Hello?"

"No, I'm here, honey. What exactly did you find?"

"Mom, it's so cool. I not only found him, but we've already emailed each other…and guess what? I talked with him on the phone!"

Marge closed her eyes and whispered, "Oh, my God."

She felt someone shaking her arm and saying, "Marge, is everything okay?" But she simply could not speak. She was not prepared. It was all too fast. Something had been set into motion that was too big to contain, and she, Marge, had lost control.

"Mom? Mom, are you there? Are you okay? I'm sorry. I shouldn't have called you. I'm just so excited. Mom, I'm sorry." Val started to cry which awoke the mother in Marge, and that power alone broke through decades of guilt and sorrow and hiding.

Marge managed a weak response, "No, Val. No, I'm glad you called, sweetie."

"Oh, Mom. I'm so sorry. Zach was right. I should have waited. I'm so stupid to tell you like this when you're so far away."

Rosa had just walked up to the bewildered group and knit her eyebrows in confusion. Marge, once again, recalled Rosa's typical response in the face of any crisis—*Time to put on those big girl panties*. "It's okay, Val. I'm with friends. Is there anything else? What did he say? What's his name?"

Val was sniffling and blew her nose. "I was right, Mom. His parents have passed away, and he *was* an only child. He's been looking for you for over ten years. He's a professor at Indiana University in Bloomington and teaches math. His name is Jacob Gordon. Doctor Jacob Gordon, but it's the PhD kind, not the MD kind. He got married four years ago to this real pretty girl named Niesha, who teaches art—drawing I think, at the same university, and guess what, Mom? She's pregnant. You're going to be a grandma!"

It started with a single tear, but Marge finally let go of 39 years of pent-up sadness. She felt as though she could actually see the weight of the sadness leave her. The other girls watched as Marge's eyes followed an invisible object upward, while tears spilled down her cheeks. Lettie put an arm around Marge, and Phree knelt at her feet patting Marge's leg. Nedra rummaged through her purse and came up with a small packet of tissues. She took one out for Marge and handed the packet around to the circle of friends.

"Are you there, Mom? Are you all right?"

"Yes, sweetie, I'm here. I'm a little shocked, but I'm okay." Marge closed her eyes for a beat. "What else?"

"Well, we talked for about half-an-hour, and I told him all about our family. I said you were a great mom, and I told him how much you've always loved him. I told him you never stopped thinking of him and hoped someday he would want to meet you. Is that okay, Mom? Did I say the right stuff?"

"It sounds like you handled it very well." And then—the questions she had wanted answered for over three decades, "Did he say he had a good life? Is he happy? Was he loved?"

"His parents were great, and he said he was very happy. But like I said, they were older and passed away within three months of each other. His wife's parents are still alive, and she has three sisters, so at least he has all of them as family. She grew up right here in Chicago, and he grew up in Texas. I think he said Houston. They met in college, but I don't remember which one." Marge was watching her friends, confusion and concern showed on their faces. Lettie still had a strong arm around her and was patting her shoulder. "He would like to meet us and have all of us meet his wife. She's only about three months pregnant, and their baby is due in June, or maybe he said July. It's a boy—they already know."

"That's wonderful," Marge whispered. Her tears would not stop, and for the first time she didn't want them to.

"Here's the best part, but it's really weird. Guess what name they have picked out for him?" But Val didn't wait for Marge to guess. "David. They're going to call him David. Can you believe it? They had no way of knowing that's what you called Jacob all these years. Isn't that cool?" Val was just like the Energizer Bunny—she just kept on going and going. "I told him that's what *you* called *him* all these years, and he thought it was an amazing coincidence, too. He emailed me a picture of him and Niesha. He's really handsome, *and* he's my new brother!"

At that Marge finally laughed. "I can't wait to see the picture."

"You don't have to. I sent it to your cell phone. Their picture is on your phone right now."

"Oh, my God. I don't know how to get to it."

"Ask Rosa or Phree, one of them will know how to do it."

"Okay, that's a good idea. Do I have to hang up to do that?"

"Yeah, you probably should. I can't wait till you get home Mom, so we can talk about all this."

"Is Dad okay? Does he know you found him?"

"Mom, he's fine. He even talked to Jacob for a few minutes. He's happy for you and all of us. I'm going to let you go so you can look at the picture. I love you, Mom. This has really been one of the most exciting days of my life."

"Mine, too, and one of the happiest. Thank you, honey, I love you."

As she clicked off the phone, over the loud speaker they heard, "Mitchell, table of eight."

Looking at her bewildered friends, always-in-control-Marge swiped at her face full of tears and her runny nose, and croaked, "Let's get seated, and I'll tell you all about it." Grabbing packages and shopping bags, the eight women followed the hostess to a large round booth in the corner. Marge slid in first so she could be front and center to tell her tale.

Chapter 5

"What's this all about, Marge? Are you okay?" Helen snagged a package of breadsticks from a basket in the center of the table and passed the basket to her right.

"It's a very, very long story, but, yes, I'm doing fine. I'm just a little shocked that's all." Marge was still holding tight to her cell phone. "Do any of you know how to get a picture to come up on this thing?"

"Easy as pie. All these phones are different," Phree tapped the screen, "but at the same time, they're basically alike. There." She looked at the image. "Who's that?"

Marge took the phone from her and literally gasped when she looked at the photo of the smiling African-American couple. Jacob appeared so handsome, and his wife looked beautiful. Marge didn't take her eyes from the screen as she said, "This is my firstborn child, Jacob Gordon, and his beautiful wife Niesha. They are about to have a baby, and I'm going to be a grandma sometime in June or July." At that moment, an explosion in the room would have gone unnoticed by the eight women sitting at the booth in the corner.

Stunned into silence, and then all talking at once, the cell phone was passed from woman to woman, as they commented and asked questions. Marge started her story, and only stopped for everyone to order their meals. The more she talked, the more strengthened she felt from the comments of her friends. True, they were surprised at first. But after hearing Marge's story, they had nothing but encouragement and respect for the decisions she'd been forced to make at the age of sixteen.

"What I want to know," said Phree waving a French fry in front of her face, "is how you got from that point in your life to now? It seems like most people in that type of situation keep spiraling downward." She took a bite of the fry. "There you were at sixteen, no real parental help, and two younger sisters looking up to you. How did you *ever* get to college?"

"I know this probably sounds overly dramatic, but about a week after I delivered David, eh, Jacob, I read something—one simple statement—but it changed the course of my life. I can quote it word for word today. 'You are what your parents make you, but it's your fault if you stay that way.' I realized the second I read it, that my destiny was in my own hands and in my own choices." Marge tore off a small corner of a roll, and put it in her mouth. "Up to that point, my parents had shaped me and my life, but after that point—*I* would be in control. I had always wanted to go to college, but my dad had pounded it into my head that 'girls don't need to go to college.' I think it was his way of not having to pay for my sisters and me to get an education. That way they'd have more money for booze."

"I never knew that your parents were so screwed up, and yet you've overcome so much," said Helen. "You could be an inspiration for a lot of people."

"Now I get why in the hell you have to be in control all the time," Rosa said. "Of course I mean that only in a good way."

"I know, Rosa. My young life had been dictated by irrational parents."

"It's no wonder you crave order," said Nancy. "It's perfectly understandable."

Marge was surprised she was so transparent, "My God, is it *that* obvious?" Between head shaking, shoulder shrugging, crooked smiles, and a loud, "Duh!" from both Beth and Rosa, she realized her attempt to hide her controlling personality had not been very successful.

"I've been afraid of my past for years," Marge told them, "but I am so ready to say goodbye to all that guilt. I want to meet Jacob, but I don't want to intrude on his life. I suspect I'm going to have to walk a real fine line."

"What would you think if we made a baby quilt for them?" asked Nedra. "We could have a quilting bee, and I'm sure we could get it done in a day."

"I think that's a great idea." Helen reached for a small bag at her feet, pulled out several patterns, and held one up. "I just bought this today for a baby quilt I need to make. It would work well as a fast group project."

"I don't want them to think I'm pushing myself on them." Marge felt her old friend Panic encroaching on her new friend Peace.

"Who wouldn't want a handmade quilt for their first child? It would be given with love from Grandma's friends." Rosa crossed her arms over her chest signifying 'end of story'.

Marge raised her eyebrows. "We have to remember that I'm the birth mother. The people who raised him and cared for him are the people who deserve the title of Grandparents. I plan on taking all my cues from Jacob and his wife as to how much they want me in their lives. Just knowing he is alive and had a good life has been an answer to my prayers."

"That's probably wise," Beth said, "but surely a gift given from your friends will show love and support, not interference."

The waitress came back and asked if anyone wanted pie. Even though Marge really wanted to get going, she went along with the group and ordered a half slice of Coconut Cream Pie. She would be home soon enough to face reality.

The ride home from Shipshewana was generally much more sedate than the morning drive out. One or two of the group usually dozed off, while the others quietly chatted and even did some hand stitching with the aid of an overhead light. Marge opted for putting her head back on the headrest and pretending to sleep. She had a lot to think about. Halfway home she remembered they had never discussed the Christmas Bunco Bash she would host in two weeks. They had planned on talking about the menu and other details during dinner tonight, but obviously more important things had taken precedent.

Marge licked her lips, opened her eyes, and sat up straighter. "I just realized we never talked about the holiday Bunco plans."

"Marge," Lettie said kindly, "if you aren't up for it, I volunteer to fill in for you."

"So could I." Phree raised her hand like a school child.

"Me, too," said Nedra.

Marge felt moved by their willingness to help her. "That's really nice and I appreciate it, but, you know me, I think it's best if I keep to my schedule. Besides, my family really looks forward to this evening."

The women began to go over details of who was coming, and who would bring what as far as the tables and chairs were concerned. They discussed how much money everyone should pay to play and what the prize breakdown should be. And finally, they did what they love almost as much as quilting—they discussed the food they would serve. Because this was a bring-whoever-you-want Bunco, it was always well attended. Since Marge was this year's hostess, she would be responsible for the desserts, two appetizers, and the paper and plastic products that would be used for eating. Rosa and Terry traditionally supplied several pizzas along with a heaping pile of bread sticks, and the other women each brought two appetizers of their choice. In the end, Marge had been able to get her mind off her new-found-son for a while, as they made their holiday plans.

Nearing the Illinois border, Marge announced, "If no one minds, I think I'd like to skip show-and-tell tonight. I want to get home before it's too late so I can talk with Bud and the kids."

Of course everyone understood Marge's needs, and Beth offered to drive Helen home so she could participate in the traditional shopping re-hash. As the van was being emptied of colorful bags, stacks of boxes, bakery goods, and mounds of fabric, Marge did her best to pick through the items to retrieve her purchases. "I'm sure I must have left *something* behind. Let me know if anything turns up unclaimed."

"If we find anything," Helen said, "I'll bring it by your house around 10:30 tomorrow morning on our way to church." After words of encouragement, many hugs and final goodbyes, Marge finally found herself in her car—alone—heading toward the refuge of her home and family.

Chapter 6

A pot of tea rested in the middle of the kitchen table, and Marge set out some of the cookies she had purchased earlier in the day at an Amish bakery. The photo of Jacob and Niesha filled the screen of Val's laptop, as the Mitchell family discussed the emails and phone calls. Marge noticed that several times Bud's eyes pooled with unshed tears, and she was reminded of what a dear tender man he was.

"I could tell that Jacob is excited about talking to you tomorrow," Val said. "I told him you were with a group of friends shopping in Shipshewana, and he said his wife goes there once in a while, too."

Marge told Val again how impressed she had been at the way she handled the phone conversation with Jacob. "You did a great job, sweetie. I'm proud of you."

"I can't wait to meet him. Do you think it will be soon?"

"I don't know, babe, we have to be sensitive toward his needs. Let's see how the phone call goes tomorrow, and try not to have too many expectations." Val had told her several times that he would call around eleven in the morning. Stifling another yawn, Marge said, "I'd better get to bed if I want to be able to put together any kind of a coherent sentence when he calls." Marge rose and turned to her family. "I want to thank you all for being so kind to both Jacob and me. I was so awfully young and did a stupid thing, and both Jacob and I have paid an enormous price over the past 39 years. I'm happy to have finally found him, but I'm sorry for the hurt it may have caused any of you."

"Aw come on, Mom. You haven't caused us any problems," Zach said. "It's actually kind of cool to think of having an older brother out there."

Marge stood and kissed Zach on the top of his head. "Thanks, honey." She kept her hand on his back as she bent over her daughter and kissed her cheek. Her eyes connected with Bud's across the table and held them. She tried to non-verbally communicate 'I love you'.

Chapter 7

From bed Marge stared into the night until the cold gray light of morning snuck between a chink in the unclosed curtains. She had kept her panic under control by maintaining steady breathing, but sleep could not sweet-talk her into letting go of thoughts about Jacob Gordon. Fear and guilt, her old companions, haunted her for one last night. Somewhere around 7:00 Bud rose, and, with the practiced stealth of a cat, he dressed and left the room.

Hot water exploded from the showerhead, washing away any residual travel grunge from Marge's weary body and at the same time calming her fearful spirits. This would be the day she had waited over 39 years to face. She would accept whatever happened and weave it into her being. Marge dressed in jeans and a quilted sweatshirt, towel dried her hair, and headed downstairs to await the phone call.

Bud sat at the table with the Sunday paper open in front of him and a Chicago Bears mug filled with dark roast. "Hey, there." She walked up behind him, slipped her arms around his shoulders, and kissed his balding head. "You are the most caring man alive."

"No, I'm just the smartest. I picked you."

"I've always felt that for some reason I don't deserve your kindness. But I'd like to believe that if the tables were turned, I could be as compassionate and forgiving as you."

"You would be, and as a matter of fact, you are."

Marge poured a cup of coffee from the thermos carafe and added cream. "Well, I admit to being pretty nervous about this phone call. I'm afraid I won't know what to say or maybe say the wrong thing altogether."

"Just be yourself, and think of this as a new start—a fresh canvas. There is no right or wrong at this point." They sat in silence, reading the Sunday paper, and waiting for the phone to ring in case Jacob called early. Marge got up and rinsed off some dishes in the sink, and then put them in the dishwasher. She wiped down the stovetop and the front of the fridge, and finally brought the remote phone to the table.

Val shuffled into the kitchen in her slippers, rubbing her eyes. "Hi, Guys," she managed to get out between yawns. "I'm hungry."

"Pancakes or French Toast?" Marge asked.

"Pancakes would be great. Did you hear anything yet?"

"Not yet." Marge opened a cabinet reaching for a large measuring cup. She set the over-sized griddle across two burners on the stove and soon had the first batch of Sunday-morning-pancakes ready to flip.

Zach leaned against the doorway and raked his hand through his hair. "Pancakes? Count me in."

Bud talked with the kids about the team that would, hopefully, be losing to the Bears today, and Marge questioned them about their plans. The doorbell rang and Marge said, "Oh, shoot, that's probably Helen. She said she'd stop by around 10:30 to drop off anything I left in Rosa's van." The clock read 10:45, but Marge knew Helen usually ran late.

Bud stood. "I'll get it."

Marge lifted the cooked pancakes to a warm plate and poured new ones onto the griddle. The batter sizzled as it hit the hot surface. "Get yourselves some juice," she told the kids.

Behind her Bud clear his throat. "Marge."

"Oh, hey, Helen—be with you in a minute," Marge called over her shoulder. "I haven't had a chance to go through my stuff yet. I was pretty exhausted last night."

Bud placed a hand on her shoulder. "Marge, it's not Helen." Before Marge could turn around, Val dropped the glass she was holding for orange juice.

"Honey, are you okay? Be careful of that glass. You're just wearing those thin slippers." Flipping the last pancake off the griddle and onto the plate, Marge turned toward Bud and said, "Who is..."

There he stood. Right in front of her. Her Jacob—a handsome grown man. The kitchen became unfocused as Marge saw nothing in the room but her firstborn son. They locked eyes, both sets the same steel blue color. Zach reached over and grabbed the plate of pancakes that threatened to slide from his mother's hand. Her eyes filled with tears, and she allowed them to fall, releasing her pain and cleansing her guilt. And then there was nothing but joy. Marge let out three sobs, each one louder than the last. "Jacob. Can I—can I hold you?"

"I had hoped you'd want to." They held each and both cried, but Marge was nearly uncontrollable. She knew she needed to get a grip, or she might scare him away.

"I'm sorry." She pulled away but noticed he hadn't let go of her hand. "Val thought you were calling or I would have..." she stammered as she smoothed her hair with an unsteady hand. "I would have looked a little more put together instead of standing here making pancakes for the kids." In the seconds it took her to say that sentence, Marge saw herself through his eyes—a middle aged, 'full-figured' women, with a thick mass of nearly pure-white hair pulled back into a pony tail, wearing mom-jeans with a sweatshirt, and not a drop of make-up.

"You have no idea how wonderful you look right now. I've wanted to meet you my whole life—to see what you were really like, and to meet the rest of your family. I can see you must be every bit the great mother that Val told me about yesterday." He looked over and smiled at his half-sister, "You must be Val." He reached out a large hand to shake hers, but instead Val embraced him in a quick hug. The newly introduced siblings stood close, each with an arm around the other, and Val looked small standing next to the towering height of Jacob.

Val motioned to Zach. "This is my brother…um, *our* brother, Zach."

"Hey, man." A fist bump was exchanged, and Zach reached in for a man-hug with a shoulder thump.

Jacob turned and held out a hand to the smiling woman who stepped into the circle of his new family. "And this is my lovely wife Niesha, who is expecting our first child. Niesha this is…"

"Marge. Please, just call me Marge." Niesha reminded Marge of a combination of Lettie and Nedra. She had the creative aura of Lettie, sporting clothes that shouldn't typically be worn together, but looked fabulous on her. A wrist full of dangling bracelets, and, what Val would surely describe as 'way cool hair', made her artsy and hip. It was clear she had the poise and confidence that Nedra also claimed which made for a warm first impression. Marge understood that women were the 'gatekeepers' of the home, and when Niesha reached in for a hug, she was relieved to instantly feel a mutual connection.

"I'm sorry if we shocked you by showing up unannounced," Niesha said. "We were at my parent's condo in Chicago for Thanksgiving. After Jacob talked with Val yesterday, he got the idea of stopping to meet you on our way back to Bloomington."

"To be honest, I wasn't sure I could do this until I actually pushed the button on the doorbell. I think I stood out there at least five minutes before I had the courage to ring the silly thing."

Bud suggested they go into the living room and sit down before Marge toppled over. His attempt at a little humor helped to relieve some tension in the room. Jacob and Niesha sat on the love seat, and Marge sat on the end of the couch closest to them. "Can I get anyone something to drink? Coffee? Water?" Bud put his hands out palm up, "How about some pancakes?" The awkwardness eased when smiles brightened the room like sunshine coming from behind a cloud.

"I'd like some water," Niesha said and absently rubbed her not-yet swollen belly.

"When are you due?" Marge asked.

"July tenth," Niesha continued to smile. "I'm hoping to be able to finish spring semester. We already know it's a boy and have picked out the name David. It means beloved."

"Yes, it does," said Marge softly. "That's a lovely name for a little boy."

Jacob again said, "I'm sorry to have burst in like this. I can tell it upset you."

"Oh, no. Not at all. I've imagined this day for a long time." *I've got to get them talking and have them feel comfortable, or they'll never want to come back.* "Val tells me you're both professors."

That halted the awkwardness as the young couple started talking about teaching and their future. "Niesha plans to quit work for a while when the baby's born, and I've recently interviewed for a position at the University of Chicago's Math Department. With the baby coming, we'd like to be closer to her parents and sisters. Being at U of C would also be an excellent career move." If he got the position, they would move to Chicago after spring semester ended at Indiana University, and Jacob would start teaching at U of C in the fall. "I feel there is a rather good chance of securing the post."

"That's absolutely fabulous. I'm so proud of both of you, and I'm sure your parents would be as well, Jacob." Marge paused a beat before asking, "Can you tell me about them?"

"I always knew I was adopted for as long as I can remember. Mom explained how it took a brave person to know when she was unable to raise a child and to entrust her baby to someone else. She made me understand that my birth mother must have loved me very much. They truly were wonderful people."

"It's wonderful to know you were loved and happy. I wish I could have known your mother."

"I do have to tell you one funny thing." Marge was already in love with Jacob's smile, and she was surprised when she realized that after all these years she saw Jerome in his grin. "My parents never knew your name or my father's name. They just knew I was, as they said back then, 'mixed race'. Until yesterday, I had no idea if you were the black or the white one." Jacob became serious, "Is there anything you'd be willing to share with me about my birth father?"

Marge told him everything she knew and ended with, "Since he never knew about you, there would be no way his family knew either. I heard his parents moved away from here back in the eighties, but I don't know where. Since Jerome passed away, I suspect it might bring them some peace to learn about you."

Jacob took care to answer all of Marge's questions, sharing interesting stories and anecdotes about his years growing up. When a long empty pause hung in the room, Jacob took the lead. "It's getting late, we should start heading back toward Bloomington. It's a long drive, and we need to make frequent potty stops." He smiled toward his wife.

"Thank you for so graciously welcoming us into your family," Niesha said.

"We wouldn't have it any other way," Bud told them. "It has been our long awaited pleasure." Knowing the surprise visit was nearing an end, Marge's eyes must have filled with panic as Bud added, "I hope this is the first of many more visits. You are both always welcome here, and please know that if we can ever do anything for either of you, all you have to do is tell us."

Val, who had been unusually quiet, spoke, "Now that we've met, I would really like to stay in touch. Would that be okay with both of you?" She looked so sincere it was almost heartbreaking. "I'd like you to think of me as your sister. I could even help when the baby comes...if you need a sitter sometime."

"I would like that, truly I would. After all, you'll be David's Aunt Val." He turned to Marge. "If you wouldn't object, Marge, I'd like to stay in touch with you as well."

Marge could feel her heart literally fill to overflowing with joy, and as hard as she tried not to, tears formed again in her eyes. Her voice came out in a thin whisper. "Yes, I'd like nothing more." There were additional hugs and handshakes, and at the door one final hug between Marge and her son. She took his face in both her hands and softly said, "I wish things could have been different. I have always loved you—every minute of every day."

"I can tell you did." He took one of her hands and kissed the palm. "Let's make this our new start. You will soon have a grandson to love. I hope our visit brings you peace."

Jacob and Niesha walked down the sidewalk to their car, settled in, and drove off. Marge kept her eyes on the head of the person sitting in the driver's seat, until a left turn claimed the vehicle from her sight. He was gone—again. But she *did* have peace, and at this moment that was all she could have hoped for. Val approached her first with a hug, then Zach, and finally Bud. With a weak smile and through tumbling tears, she thanked them again for their support.

"He seems like a great guy. It was really cool that you finally got to meet him." Zach slipped his cell phone out of his pocket and checked the time.

"Thanks honey. It seems hard to believe that after all these years I finally met him. But don't I remember that you were supposed to meet some people at the campus library at noon?"

"Yeah, we're doing a group presentation for biology, and I guess I'm kind of late."

Val said. "Jenny's supposed to pick me up soon. We're going to do some Christmas shopping. Is that okay? I can stay home, if you need me."

"Both of you have things to do, and we need to get back to the 'real world' anyway. I have housework to do and then get ready for work tomorrow. It's been a long, busy weekend." Marge was, in fact, happy that both of her children had plans, and that she could have some time alone to let the events of the past 24 hours wash over her and sink in. In fact, the routine of cleaning up the breakfast dishes, taking the overflowing trash bags to the cans in the backyard, replenishing the bird feeders for the hungry outdoor birds, and sweeping the kitchen floor would allow Marge to regain a sense of control.

With the kids gone, Bud said, "The game has a three o'clock start today. You up for a little football?" The Russell family was avid Chicago Bears fans. Marge and Bud's first date had been to a Bears game over twenty-five years ago.

"That sounds near perfect to me."

Marge usually worked on hand sewing, spread out on the love seat or big chair, while they watched the game—but not today. At 3:00 sharp, she and Bud were sitting side-by-side on the sofa, ready for kick-off. She rested her head on Bud's shoulder and felt reassured by his closeness. Not even quilting could pull her away from her wonderful husband and a Bears game on this cold November afternoon.

Chapter 8

The next two weeks became a fast-paced blur of activities for the Russell family. Marge and Jacob continued to keep in touch, mostly through emails and an occasional phone call. They planned an informal family get-together between Christmas and New Year's, when Jacob and Niesha would come to the Russell home for a casual visit and dinner. Marge had, of course, updated her Bunco group with the news of Jacob's surprise visit, and she felt a little more confident about all of them making a quilt for the baby.

Fully focused on Saturday night and the holiday Bunco, she fingered down her 'To Do List' and crossed off chores as she finished them. The Russell's had a large, finished basement with high ceilings and plenty of room for the extended Bunco holiday group. Marge continued to fuss and rummage around in the basement, until it looked perfect for the big event. Little white twinkle-lights illuminated three twig-trees, and hundreds of sparkling lights were tastefully hung in a snowflake design on the ceiling. The lights gave the space a warm dreamy glow. She would set out multiple baskets of fresh cinnamon-apple potpourri Saturday afternoon, and the scent would waft throughout the area. Covering a long table in the middle of the room with an Irish Chain quilt that she had pieced in fabrics of red, green, and white, Marge placed an assortment of candles onto mirrored tiles and positioned them on top of the quilt. 'Organized Marge' was as balanced and reliable as a metronome, her rhythm ticking along to a steady beat, until the room was dressed up and ready for a night of Bunco.

Sitting in the midst of the holiday splendor with her ubiquitous tablet and pen, Marge started flipping through cookbooks and handwritten recipes. She'd already decided to make more than two appetizers. Rosa would bring her much-loved Rumaki, and, as silly as it sounded, no one could match Helen's Specialty Popcorn. Stopping at a recipe called Stuffed Mushroom Caps she wrote it on her list—she would make several different varieties. Everyone especially loved her meatballs, and with the large crowd she'd need to make at least a triple batch. Liver Sausage Pate, another holiday favorite, was simple to make, and everyone loved it. She would serve the pate with mini-rounds of rye bread.

Because men would be joining them for Bunco, she wrote down some typical 'guy' food—sliced sausage, cheese cubes with crackers, and chip and dip. Of course the females would all need their favorite Bunco chocolate standbys—chocolate covered raisins, M&M's, mini-Snickers, Jr. Mints, and a big bowl of Sno-Caps would all be the perfect complement to Helen's salty popcorn. Marge would supply several cartons of eggnog, along with cans of whipped cream to spray over the thick, creamy beverage. A sprinkle of nutmeg would add the finishing touch to the holiday drink. She would set out a number of filled ice buckets, along with numerous carafes of tea and coffee, and a tub full of chilled water bottles. Some of the men would bring beer, and Rosa always brought several bottles of wine and some champagne for a holiday toast.

Dessert was always tricky with a large crowd. She chose to make double batches of three different kinds of Christmas cookies, and she thought a minty-flavored Candy Cane Pie might add the perfect touch. She could use the good old assembly-line method and crank out four or five pies—or maybe she'd simply order them from the local bakery. The choice seemed like a no-brainer, so she made a note on her tablet to call the bakery. Marge would, however, make three homemade Red Devil's Food Cakes from her mom's very old, much loved recipe. That should do it. Cookies, pies, cakes—traditional Christmas sweets. Marge was happiest when she was in control, and at the moment Marge felt *exceptionally* happy.

Holiday Bunco

*Stuffed Mushrooms   Meat Balls**

Liver Sausage Pate

Sliced Sausage, Cheese Cubes, Crackers

Chip & Dip

*****

Pecan Butter Balls   Old Fashioned Oatmeal Raisin Cookies

Magic Bars   Candy Cane Pie

Mom's Red Devils Food Cake   Microwave Fudge

***

Tea   Bottled Water   Ice

**recipe at back of book*

Chapter 9

The hallway was dark as Marge pulled the bedroom door closed behind her. It whispered a muffled click. By the time she reached the kitchen and turned on the overhead lights, she felt certain she hadn't woken any of the family. It took her eyes a moment to adjust to the brightness, and she flipped the switch on her coffeemaker.

Today's priority was to bake dozens and dozens of Christmas cookies. Several pounds of butter lined the counter, where they were allowed to reach room temperature overnight. The evening before, Marge had pre-chopped pounds of walnuts and pecans, bagged them, and stored them in the fridge alongside three cartons of fresh eggs. Several five pound bags of sugar and flour rounded out the bulk of the supplies she'd use in her Sunday baking spree. The Bears game started at 6:00 this evening, and her goal was to be finished baking cookies, and sitting next to Bud at kickoff. She would be exhausted by tonight, but her holiday cookies would be finished. As she began to work, she thought she might send a pretty package of homemade cookies to Jacob and Niesha.

Starting with the ultimate melt-in-your-mouth favorite, Pecan Butter Balls, she decided to make a triple batch. These would be the most labor intensive, so tackling them first was a smart move. Only four ingredients went into the actual cookie dough, and after they were baked, but still hot, they were rolled in confectioner's sugar and then set on a rack to cool. She mixed the dough in the largest bowl her stationary mixer would accommodate and spent the next hour meticulously rolling the cookie dough into little round balls. The kids each woke up during this step, and Val squealed like a little girl when she realized her favorite cookie was being made.

After a loud open-mouthed yawn, and with his eyes desperately wanting to claim sleep again, Zach grabbed a cup of coffee, and announced he was heading to the shower. Val passed him on her way into the kitchen and said, "Morning, Dickhead."

" 'Sup ugly?"

"Alright you two, let's not start out like this." Marge chuckled inside, but didn't want the sibling rivalry to get out of hand this early in the day.

"Hey, she started it—and besides she *is* ugly."

"Yeah, and you're a dickhead, Dickhead."

Marge groaned. "Come on you two. Zach, get in the shower, and Val, fix yourself some cereal." Without further comment, Zach shuffled out of the kitchen.

While her daughter ate breakfast, Val chatted with Marge. "So, who's all coming next week?" she asked with her mouth full.

Marge went through the guest list, happy for someone to talk to while performing the boring job of rolling the cookie dough into petite orbs. "Rosa and Terry will bring Alex and Ricky."

"Alex is pretty cute, but Ricky is kind of creepy." Val wasn't shy about sharing thoughts with her mother. "Go on," Val said, taking a drink of juice.

As Marge continued rolling cookie dough between her palms, she went down the list of expected guests, and Val kept up a verbal tally. "And here are the best parts. Both Phree and Nancy are bringing boyfriends."

"Get out! You're kidding. Aren't they kind of old for that?"

"I think I'll *not* tell them you said that."

"What about Jacob and Niesha? Do you think they'd like to come?" Val sounded hopeful.

Marge placed the final ball of dough onto a cookie sheet and looked at Val, "Oh, honey, I think it's a bit too early in our relationship to involve them with such a large group of people they don't know. It's a really thoughtful suggestion, but I'd hate to have them feel awkward." She rinsed her hands under warm water to get off sticky bits of dough. "Maybe by next year we'll all be more familiar, and I'm hopeful at that point it could work out for them to join us."

"That's probably best." Val took her cereal bowl to the sink, rinsed it, and then put it in the dishwasher. "Anyway, I want to get some more Christmas shopping done today. Any ideas for Dad?" Mother and Daughter discussed Christmas gifts, as Marge slipped three loaded cookie sheets into the oven, and lined up ingredients for the next batch.

Hours later, with a spotless kitchen, and the cookies stored in plastic tubs in the chilly attic closet, Marge relaxed next to Bud on the sofa. They had ordered carry-out, and little white containers of Chinese food rested in the center of their coffee table along with a bottle of wine and a sampling of freshly baked Christmas cookies. Marge took a heaping plate of Beef Fried Rice and settled back to enjoy the game.

"Hang in there, honey, it'll be over within a week," Bud chuckled, "and then you can pass that damned Bunco box on to the next person."

Chapter 10

A light snow started falling an hour before the Bunco Christmas Party was scheduled to start. Forecast to be a wispy covering of three to four inches, travel would be no big deal for experienced Chicagoans. The snow blanketed the Russell's front lawn and made the outdoor twinkle-lights sparkle more than usual. Feeling a little frazzled, Marge still found herself right on schedule, as she loaded the compact disc player with Christmas music and their favorite Bunco CD. Three years ago Helen had given each woman a CD she had burned of all their favorite tunes—the ones that made the group spontaneously burst into song whenever they heard them.

Extra tables and chairs had been delivered earlier, mostly by dutiful husbands or older children, and Marge had everything in place and ready to go. She was just lighting the candles when she heard the doorbell ring, and she walked over and hit the play button on the CD player. The old-time crooning voice of Bing Crosby singing "White Christmas" filled the room, and she turned the volume from ear-splitting to able-to-hold-a-conversation. Marge had put her daughter in charge of 'door duty' tonight, and she heard a bubbly Val welcome Beth and her family. Val's job included welcoming the guests and relieving them of their outerwear. Zach was to escort people down the stairs, and help them carry any precious food bundles. Bud would fill in where needed.

Marge had just greeted the Stevenson's with a hug, when she heard another family arrive. Taking two stairs at a time, Zach raced back up to perform his task again. The routine repeated itself for the next twenty minutes, until all the guests were present. After arranging covered dishes on the festive table, everyone started heaping plates full of food and chatting like they hadn't seen each other in years. Marge had decorated a small square box, and cut a rectangular hole in the top. Everyone eventually got around to dropping their required $5.00 per person into the box to be divvied up as prize money.

The high school and college kids mingled amiably in one corner—laughing and talking with one another, while the adults were more interested in the food and conversation. Marge couldn't help noticing that Ricky slouched in a chair, dangling a leg over the arm, with what could only be described as a scowl on his face. He obviously didn't want to be here.

Rosa had Phree and her friend, Officer Hottie, cornered by the eggnog. Marge nudged Nedra, and together they walked over to where the three of them stood. Rosa had just said, "So, tell me about…" when Marge grasped Rosa's elbow and gave it a tight squeeze.

"We need you over here, Rosa," and firmly walked her away from Lieutenant Hayden. When they were out of earshot, she added, "Cut it out, you're going to frighten him away."

"What?" Rosa mocked innocence, "I'm just being friendly."

"Friendly my foot," said Nedra. "It's more like an interrogation."

"Okay, okay." Rosa held up both hands and pushed out her lower lip. "I promise not to even talk to him. Will that make everyone happy?"

"Yes!" they chorused at the same time.

"And that promise goes for Nancy and Michael as well. We're all happy she brought him, so don't go scaring him either. Our radar is up, and we all have our eyes on you tonight. We're all sworn to intervene if you get in either of their faces."

"Aye-aye!" Rosa saluted. "But look at her. You've got to admit that Nancy has never looked this happy."

The heads of the three friends leaned in together, as though they were discussing government secrets, and Nedra added, "He sure is a looker. He must have been gorgeous back in college."

"I nearly fell over when Nancy walked down the stairs," Marge said. "I truly didn't even recognize her. I don't know what Beth had to do to get her to change her color and style, but, WOW, is all I can say. And her outfit is incredible, Ned. You're a freaking miracle worker."

"Once I got her going, she didn't want to stop. She's got a closetful of new outfits with shoes and purses to match. I may have created a clothes-aholic."

Rosa waggled her eyebrows and smiled. "I'd like to know details of how they are getting along," she made quotation marks with her fingers. "If ya know what I mean."

"Oh for God's sake, Rosa. This is why we have to keep you away from them."

"I'm serious. Just look at the way they are together. Doesn't it show? They're both practically glowing."

Michael had whispered something in Nancy's ear, and she had placed her hand over her mouth and giggled. With a wide smile on his face, he looked up just in time to see the three women gawking at them. He winked.

"Oh, crap. We've been caught," said Marge.

Rosa, on the other hand, gave him the thumbs-up sign.

"Mitchell, you're shameless," Nedra told her, as she grabbed Rosa's arm, and spun her around. "It's time we mind our own business, and leave them alone," Nedra linked arms with Rosa, and escorted her toward the food table. Nothing could get Rosa's mind off of gossip faster than a little Rumaki and a glass of wine.

Marge thought some damage control was in order so she crossed the room toward Nancy and Michael who were sharing a plate of food. On the way she snagged Bud and Terry to follow her. She introduced the men to Michael, and

Terry said, "We're one step ahead of you, Marge. We've already met him."

"He's going to join us at The Depot Monday night for the Bears game." It had become tradition that whenever the Bears played Monday Night Football, all the 'Bunco men' met at The Pizza Depot to watch on the big screen. It worked out perfectly, because the restaurant was closed on Mondays, so the guys had the run of the place.

"Even though I've lived in Colorado for a long time, I never could shake my allegiance to the Bears and the Cubs," Michael told them.

"Oh no, did I hear a Cubs fan?" Beth asked, as she passed by with a fresh supply of meat balls on her plate. Beth was a die-hard Chicago White Sox fan, along with Rosa. The rest of the women were all staunch Cubs fans—except for Helen who came from California and didn't care at all about sports. You simply couldn't live in Chicago your whole life and not have an opinion on the Cubs and Sox.

Brian called out, "Go Cubbies!" While Rosa put her hands on her hips and glared at him.

"Okay, okay, let's not turn this ugly," Lettie said. "How about we round up the kids, and get started playing Bunco?"

"Did everyone have enough food?" Marge asked. There were groans as several people reached down, patted their tummies, and nodded their heads. Marge noticed the kids had disappeared. When she heard the heavy thumping of bass coming from the family room, knew they had gone upstairs to listen to their own music and to take a break from the 'rents—as in pa*rents*. Ricky, however, had already come back downstairs and sat slumped in the chair again, clearly impressed with his own 'too cool' persona. Marge wasn't sure if she felt worse for Rosa or Ricky.

When everyone finally had taken a seat, she gave a brief run-down of how to play Bunco for those who had never played, and also as a reminder for those who only played once a year. The head table was decided upon, and how the 'winners' and 'losers' would rotate among the eight tables.

Hand poised over the brass bell, Lettie rang it, and play began. Dice clicked and chatter started, and it wasn't long before someone threw the first Bunco. Shouts were heard as Alex and Val high-fived each other—game on. More hoots from high rollers were accompanied by groans from others not so lucky. Michael and Officer Hottie, the two newbies, each had the deer-caught-in-the-headlights look. But three rounds later, as partners, Michael threw a Bunco, and they hooted and high-fived each other like they'd been playing Bunco for years. The game continued as Christmas carols droned on in the background.

With this many people playing, they always did a potty break at the half-way point. Drinks were refreshed, and there was more nibbling on whatever goodies remained on the food table. The CD player changed to the Bunco Favorites CD, and when the first horns blasted out the opening of "Respect" by Aretha Franklin, Marge cranked the volume. Several of the women let go with their best rendition. Some held fake microphones, while others wiggled their way together and sang side by side. Onlookers clapped and sang along to the rock classic.

Marge kept a watchful eye on Ricky, hopeful to see some sort of a normal response, but there was none. With arms folded over his chest and wearing a disgusted frown, it was obvious he was not enjoying himself nor was he even trying. Rosa had not wanted to bring him, but the other women had encouraged her.

Halfway through the song the group gradually stopped singing until everyone had dropped off. "Okay, that's it—NO MORE SINGING!" Brian pleaded.

"We promise to be good," Beth said.

"We don't care if you're good, just don't sing anymore."

This caused laughter, but Rosa stuck her tongue out at Brian, and said, "Where's my pretend microphone? Has anyone seen it?"

"That's real mature, Mom." Ricky groaned, and under his breath Marge heard him add, "Idiot."

Phree got everyone's attention by flicking the lights. "Let's start playing again," she shouted above the din. After returning to their seats, the bell sounded, and they were off and rolling for the second half. More squeals and moans punctuated the room, as the different generations got in the spirit and fun of the game, and caught up in the competitiveness and excitement.

With the game finished and scores tallied, Brian had come in at first place. Amid all the congratulations, he said, "In the spirit of holiday giving, I propose we take the money collected tonight and donate it to a charity. I think it could be the start of a nice tradition for the group." Everyone applauded and cheered the idea, even the young people.

"Any ideas who we should give it to?" Rosa asked.

"Well, actually I *do*." He looked directly at Beth, and smiled, "I thought maybe this year it could go to research for the American Diabetes Association. If my calculations are correct, we should have collected $160.00 tonight, and I plan on adding another $100.00 to the total."

Beth's hand flew to her face and covered her mouth. Her eyes instantly filled with tears. Tim put his arm around his wife's waist and said, "Thank you. That's very kind."

"I'll match your $100.00," said Bud.

"Me, too," called others, and additional cash was deposited into the pretty decorated box in the middle of the table.

While everyone was donating money to ADA, Marge and Lettie arranged the desserts and made several pots of tea and coffee. The younger crowd took their treats and went back upstairs. Marge noted that Ricky was no longer downstairs and was hopeful he was making an attempt to fit in.

During dessert Phree stood and announced, "I've got a little surprise for the Bunco gals." She smiled as she reached into a tote bag, pulled out a miniature chest, and set it on the table. In front of them sat a tiny imitation of the chest in which Phree had found the Mayflower items. Everyone looked at the chest, then to Phree, and back to the chest again. "Well, someone open it," Phree commanded.

Rosa reached for the tiny replica. She looked around the room, and everyone looked puzzled except for Phree. "Go ahead, open it."

Rosa unfastened the clasp on the chest and took out eight travel brochures for Las Vegas. "What the heck is this?"

Phree glowed. "We're going to Vegas! All eight of us!" There were gasps and sputters, and Phree finally explained, "I wanted to have a little fun with some of the money from the Mayflower discovery. Emily and I are going to travel to Plymouth and Duxbury next summer to see, first hand, where our ancestors landed. We want to know more about them and how they lived." Her smile spread across her face. "Then I got this big idea—wouldn't it be fun if we could all go somewhere? You know, all eight of us together. What could be more fun than Vegas?" She put her hands out, palms up, and shrugged her shoulders.

"But when?" Nedra stammered.

"I know everyone must be thinking about work, and kids, and being able to get away for a while, but I thought we could put our heads together and determine a date that suits all of us. We only need to find three or four days that work for everyone, and then I'll buy the tickets and reserve a couple of rooms. Maybe we could go over a long weekend, or spring break, or even summer—whatever suits everyone best."

"Phree, this is so generous, thank you!" Helen, followed by the other women, went over to Phree and hugged her.

"Our very own most excellent field trip."

"What a blast!"

"I can't wait!"

"I've always wanted to go to Vegas."

Nancy reached over and smacked Brian's shoulder when he said, "Look out, Elvis, you've got competition."

The night wore down, but the Bunco women could have gone on for many more hours. Marge brought the decorated box with the cash to where Brian stood, and handed it to him. "I'm putting you in charge of this, sir."

He lifted the decorated lid, looked inside, and then back at Marge. She knew by the expression on his face that something was wrong. She accepted the box back, but didn't even need to look inside. She knew the money was gone, and so was Ricky.

The news of the missing cash spread through the space like watching a slow motion sports replay—hoping for a different outcome, but knowing it's not going to happen. When Rosa heard the news her eyes darted the room for her son, and Marge could tell the second she knew. She slumped against Terry and said, "Just kill me now."

After it was determined that the Russell's were missing two iPods and a Kindle Fire, Brian urged the ladies to check their purses. Several hundred dollars of cash, a few cell phones, and three credit cards had also disappeared. Once the preliminary shock wore off, Marge and Lettie sat with Rosa, Terry, and their older son, Alex, offering comfort where none would help. The others pitched in with clean-up duty, until the worst of the mess was under control. Brian stepped up to the Mitchell's, hands in pants pockets, and rocked back and forth. "I've notified the police that Ricky is missing, but I haven't told them about the money or other items. Let's sleep on this tonight and figure out what to do tomorrow. I'm hopeful, in the meantime, he'll show up and have some sort of good explanation."

"Brian, we both know there is no good explanation for what he did," Rosa said. "All I can do is hope he doesn't get hurt and that he comes home in one piece, so I can kill him." Rosa wiped her nose, and her red eyes trailed tears. "This is our life now, and it really sucks."

Terry rubbed his wife's back. "You ready to leave, babe? Maybe we should take off, in case Ricky goes home."

"That's probably a good idea," Brian said. "Would you like me to come with?"

"No," Terry said. "I have a feeling tomorrow's going to be a long day, and at least one of us should be well rested."

"Call me if you need me anytime tonight."

"That goes for all of us," Marge said. The Mitchell's stood to leave, "Just head home, Rosa. I'll pack up your things and bring them over tomorrow sometime." Marge held her friend by the shoulders. "This will pass, Rosa. It may take more time than you'd like, but it *will* pass."

"I'm just always so sad, Marge. Tonight was the first fun I've allowed myself to enjoy, and I feel like the good old Mitchell's ruined everything. We'll pay back the money tomorrow."

"Let's get Ricky back first and worry about the money later." Marge brushed aside an errant section of Rosa's bangs. "Hang in there Rosa. We're all here if you need us."

Zach came over with their coats, and Rosa leaned in to Marge for a final hug. "Merry Christmas, my dear friend," she choked out in a whisper.

"Merry Christmas, Rosa, and may peace be with you."

JANUARY BUNCO - Helen

Inside beauty sometimes needs a little help from outside pretty.

Chapter 1

"I *HATE* HIM!" On the word 'hate' Helen's daughter slammed the car door so hard the snow that had accumulated on the car's windows slid off in a mini-avalanche to the ground.

"Ruby, what? Who?" Just moments before Helen held onto her husband, Ben's, elbow and watched their step on the snowy sidewalk. They had been chatting about what a fun evening it had been, until Ricky disappeared with the prize money.

Ruby's head wagged from side to side with attitude, like Helen had seen women use on the Maury Show when they were trying to convey more confidence than they felt. "Ricky Asshole Mitchell that's who."

"Ruby, your mouth. Please." Helen couldn't figure out why her daughter was so angry with Ricky's little stunt, and she couldn't wait for Ben to finish scraping, brushing and shoveling snow to help with Miss Potty Mouth.

"Remember Ruby, he said he doesn't want to be called Ricky anymore," six-year-old Brad told his sister.

"Yeah, well he can kiss my ass if he thinks I'm ever going to talk to him again." Ruby folded her arms over her chest and muttered, "What a douche."

"Ruby! Enough! What is going on? Are you upset because Ricky stole the Bunco money and other stuff tonight?"

Ruby snorted and Brad whined, "Mo-om," in two syllables—a sure sign he was tired, "he wants to be called Cardo."

"Shut up dipshit." Ruby whacked her brother's upper arm which sent Brad into a howling flop that would have gotten him to the foul line in an NBA game.

"Brad, stop yelling, she barely touched you. Ruby leave him alone, he's tired. And stop the bad language in front of your brother."

"I AM NOT TIRRRED!" wailed Brad. "It's her fault. And besides she always says those bad languages when you're not around."

"What the heck is going on here? We walked into Marge's like the Cleaver family and walked out like the Osborne's." Brad had quieted to a snuffley whimper, and Ruby stared out the window watching her father help Lettie scrape off her red truck.

In a little voice Brad said, "He was mean to her."

...And with that, Helen knew exactly what had happened.

Chapter 2

When her daughter was born, Helen knew she was absolutely the most beautiful baby girl in the world. Blue eyes, like most babies, with nearly translucent Irish skin, perfectly formed little baby body—not a flaw to be found and bald as a cue ball. Helen envisioned this little newborn growing up to be the envy of all the girls with an endless amount of boys from which to choose. She would have the charmed social life that Helen never had as a rather scrawny and extremely shy little girl. Helen would have a second chance at the social echelon of girlhood, as she watched her daughter become oh-so-popular yet still maintain her core values of sweetness and purity—*sigh*. In high school she'd be a cheerleader *and* homecoming queen, while in her spare time she would surely do volunteer work with the hospital and help underprivileged children.

"I want to name her Ruby—after my Grandma. It's my middle name, and I've always loved it." Helen looked up at Ben from the hospital bed, as she held her daughter for the first time in their little family circle. She knew she could have told Ben she wanted to name their baby Bertha or Godzilla or Moonshine, and at that moment he would have agreed.

He smiled and nodded at her. With happy tears threatening to fall, he placed a hand on his daughter's bare head, and Ben whispered for the first time, "I love you, Ruby."

Her baby's beautiful new name would be the worst unintentional error Helen ever made.

Chapter 3

Once Ben got in the car, the ride home form Marge's party was quiet. Brad fell asleep in a matter of minutes, and Helen could hear him slurping and sucking his thumb. Ruby continued to stare out the window, but through the eyes-in-the-back-of-her head, Helen detected her daughter occasionally swiping at tears. Unfairly annoyed that Ben was oblivious to what went on while he was out of the car working on snow removal, she wouldn't be able to share what had happened until after the kids were in bed. Helen was just plain worried for her daughter and, as always, guilty.

In the Delaney's kitchen Ben held a half-sleeping Brad, while Helen freed first one arm from his coat and then the other. She bent down to hug him and kissed the top of his blonde head. Her little boy even smelled tired if that was possible. Whispering into his hair she said, "Daddy will take you upstairs and help you get ready for bed. Don't forget to brush your teeth, little man."

"Can't *you* come up and read to me?"

"Not tonight, babe. Dad will tuck you in and read to you. I need your sister to help me with something. Get right to sleep. You've got a big play day tomorrow at Bobby's house."

Ben hoisted his son to his shoulder. "Come on, bud. Say goodnight to Mommy."

"G'night Mommy." Brad was having trouble staying awake. "I love you."

Helen threw him a kiss as Ben started toward the stairs, "Love you too, sweetie."

Turning to Ruby who had been 'holding up the door frame' as her mother would have said, Helen pointed to a chair at the kitchen table. "Sit."

"I'm tired. I wanna go to bed, too."

"No way. Sit down and tell me what that scum-sucking little bastard said to you."

Ruby eyes grew wide, which was the reaction Helen had been going for. Faking a disgusted demeanor, Ruby said, "Mother, your mouth."

Mom and Daughter sat across from each other at the kitchen table. Helen reached over the trompe l'oeil she had skillfully painted of a double wedding ring quilt and took hold of one of Ruby's hands. The moment Helen gave the slightest squeeze, tears formed in Ruby's already red rimmed eyes. "Mom, it's the same old story. Red hair and freckles and my name is Ruby. I hate it so much. On top of it I'm smart. I'm taller than everyone in my class…even the boys. I'm ugly, and everyone teases me. They all hate me. I hate me."

It wasn't the first time that Helen wished she hadn't named her daughter Ruby. Her little bald cue ball of a daughter had started sprouting bright red hair within six months, and by the time she was four years old had a face and body full of freckles. Turns out that Helen's mother's Uncle Marty from Ireland had a dome full of red hair and was known as the Beacon of Trim, County Meath. They had been over this ground hundreds of times, and each time Helen felt her child's hurt so deeply that she could never be impatient with her. "To start with, you aren't ugly."

"You *have* to say that. You're my mom. It doesn't count."

Helen put her hand up to stop Ruby. "No one's opinion counts more than your mother's. Trust me on this, honey, one day you will be the woman that other women envy, and someday you will even love your name."

"Don't tell me some bullshit about being beautiful inside Mom. That's just another way of saying I'm ugly on the outside." Ruby reached for the tissue box behind her on the counter. "I hate my hair. I hate my name. I hate school and everyone in it. And I *really REALLY* hate Ricky Mitchell."

"So what did that little prick say to you?" Helen didn't use this kind of language in front of her kids. But if a little cussing got her daughter's attention, and at the same time gave the impression she was majorly ticked off at Ricky and had Ruby's back in this, then she'd gladly cuss up a storm.

"I was having fun with Val and Emily. They're way older than me, but they're real nice. They're seniors this year and they were talking about going to college and guys and stuff. We were listening to music, and some other kids were hanging out on the other side of the room. Even though I'm just an eighth grader, they both asked me if I knew what I wanted to be, and if I wanted to go to college someday. It was really cool and fun. Val even said I could visit her wherever it is that she decides to go, and Emily did too. I mean they were talking to me like there wasn't anything wrong with me."

Helen's heart soared and was grateful for the kindness of her friends' children, but then quickly took a nosedive at Ruby's description of herself. "Ruby…honey…there's nothing wrong with you."

"Yeah. Right. Anyway, we were upstairs in the family room, and Ricky walked in behind me. He smacked me in the head and said 'Yuck, I hope that ginger shit of yours doesn't rub off on me.' Val told him to get lost. Then he said…" Ruby put her head in her hands and started sobbing.

Helen got up and went around the table where she sat down next to her precious daughter and pulled her into her arms. She smoothed Ruby's red hair and deposited kisses on the offensive tresses while cooing and purring her mother's love into her daughter's aura.

When Ruby was cried out, she stayed curled in the safety of her mother's embrace and hidden from the embarrassment of eye contact. "He said that the reason there is so many years between me and Brad is because Dad and you couldn't stand to look at me and never wanted to have another monster kid. He said you guys said that you were so happy when Brad was born normal, and that you had planned to send me away but couldn't afford it."

Helen was angry enough to have done bodily damage to Ricky Mitchell had he been in the room just then. "Oh my God, Ruby. Tell me you didn't believe that asshole not even for one second!" When she didn't get an answer, Helen took Ruby's chin in her hand and tipped her head back, so Mother and Daughter could look eye-to-eye. "It is absolutely 100% not true."

"Then why *is* there so much time between Brad and me?"

"Oh, baby, you know I had you when I was pretty young—I had just turned twenty. Dad and I tried all those years to get pregnant again, and then finally Brad came along. That's all it is. Nothing sinister. Just eight years of waiting and hoping to be blessed with another wonderful baby." Helen wiped a tear from Ruby's cheek. "As much as I love Brad and can't imagine life without him—well, had he never come along I still knew I was the luckiest mom in the world to have gotten you." Placing a light kiss on Ruby's red nose she prodded for more information. "Is there anything else?"

"He calls me Ruby-Pubes. I *hate* him, Mom. I was so embarrassed."

"Did anyone say anything while this was going on?" Helen was beginning to seethe with the thought of all those kids doing nothing to help while laughing at her daughter's expense.

"Oh, yeah—everyone did. Emily said he was nothing but a bully and to shut up. And Val called him a dickhead and told him to get the fuck out of our faces. In the end, his older brother, Alex, pushed him real hard out of the room. He shouted at him to go back downstairs and if he ever heard him do that again, he'd be sorry. Then Alex came over by me and apologized for his ignorant thug brother. By then I was so embarrassed, I just wanted to die."

Still stroking Ruby's hair Helen said, "Honey, I'm so, so sorry. I wish there was something I could do to make this meanness stop. Do you want me to talk to Rosa?"

"NO!" Ruby shouted, "That would just make it worse. Who knows if he'll ever show up again anyway? He could be anywhere with all that money."

Helen knew just how far a little less than $500.00 would *not* get someone, but at nearly fourteen years old Ruby was young enough to think it was a small fortune. If Ruby thought Ricky Mitchell was out of the picture for a while, that might be just the relief she needed for the moment. "Why don't we get some sleep and talk about what we can do tomorrow."

Chapter 4

Both the house land-line and her cell phone kept ringing. Each time Helen checked the caller ID and saw it was Rosa, she let it go to voice mail. She didn't want to talk to her, or hear the latest about her delinquent little bully-thief, or discuss how hard it was being a mother. She was so furious at Ricky, that it had sloshed over into her feelings toward her friend. Like those champagne glass pyramids, her anger flowed into the next flute and the next and the next. She flat-out did *not* want to talk to Rosa Mitchell this morning.

When Helen had finally gotten to bed last night, she talked with Ben in hushed voices so as not to let Ruby hear. At one point she had to restrain her husband from getting out of bed and heading to the Mitchell's at 1:00 a.m. "Settle down, Ben, it won't do any good, Ricky's probably not even there. And even though I'm mad as hell at all of them, to be honest, they've got a mountain of their own crap to deal with right now. If they're lucky enough to be asleep, let them have some peace."

Helen floated a few ideas past her husband and after discovering Ben had a few of his own, they came up with a game plan. Both realized that with all the bullying their daughter had been forced to endure socially, she was facing a fork in the path of her life. They wanted to see her choose the path that would make her a stronger person and not journey down the one of self-loathing, until she found solace in drugs or cutting or, even worse, suicide.

Helen got Brad off for his play-day at Bobby's and spent the next two hours and several cups of coffee at her computer Googling everything she could find about bullies, being bullied, and parents of bullied children. She searched private high schools in the area and had just hung up the phone from talking to Beth when Ruby came downstairs.

Rubbing her eyes, which Helen noticed were rather blood-shot this morning, she walked right over to her mother and slid into her arms. "I love you, Mom. Thanks for helping me last night."

"I love you too, Ruby, and I will always be there to help you with anything anytime you need me." She linked her arm with Ruby's and said, "Now, favorite daughter—how about some breakfast?"

While Ruby was enjoying a special treat of blueberry studded pancakes, Helen cleaned up the kitchen and loaded the dishwasher. "Now remember you are sworn to secrecy. If your brother finds out that I made you pancakes today, while I served him oatmeal this morning, he'll make both of our lives miserable."

"He won't find out from me." Ruby smiled and licked her empty plate for effect.

"Give me that. The last of the evidence needs to get in the dishwasher, so I can start it up." Helen set the plate in a slot on the top rack, closed the door, and pushed the 'on' button. Folding the dish towel that had been draped over her shoulder, she sat down across from Ruby.

"So," she took a big breath, "do you have any suggestions or thoughts about what can be done to help you?" The phone rang, and Ruby jumped to get it. "Don't pick that up. Let it go to voicemail."

Ruby sat down but cocked her head to the side. "Mom, that's the third time it's rang since I started eating breakfast. Who is it?"

"It doesn't matter. Probably just a telemarketer, and I'm *not* in the mood."

"Whatever."

"Well, any ideas?"

"I can tell you what I *don't* want to do. I don't want to go to high school next year with all the kids that have tortured me since kindergarten."

"That's understandable."

"It is? I mean, you get it?"

"Of course I do Ruby. So does Dad. We both want you to be happy and be in an environment where you can enjoy school. Do you have any ideas what we can do about it?" Ben and Helen had already come up with a list of ideas that might help their daughter, but Helen wanted to get Ruby's input first. There easily could be something they missed or didn't 'get' as Ruby had put it, and Helen was surprised when the first thing Ruby suggested was a school they had never thought of.

"Well, I don't know how these schools work or how you even get into them, but I was thinking maybe something farther away could get me out of this mess." Ruby did not make eye contact with her mother, as she dabbed at a drop of syrup on the tabletop with her finger and stuck it into her mouth. "There's this place called IMSA. It means Illinois Math and Science Academy, and I might like to look into that. The bad part is that it's way out in Aurora, and I think I'd have to stay there during the week."

Helen tried not to look or sound shocked, but she felt like Mr. Math, Albert Einstein himself, just made a house call from the grave and punched her in the stomach. She forced a smile, "What a great idea. I hadn't thought of IMSA." The truth was she'd never *heard* of IMSA. "I'm sure we can find out the details and procedure for going there." Visualizing packing up her fourteen-year-old daughter to attend high school two hours away (and that was in good traffic) she said, "It sounds like you had other ideas too." *Please God, let there be closer solutions.*

"Yeah, there's Providence. It's a Catholic school about a half hour away. Val has a friend who went there and they really liked it. It would be nice to get a fresh start and maybe have some girlfriends. I was hoping that because it was a

Catholic school maybe they wouldn't tolerate bullying so much."

"All good points." *Half hour away…I can live with half hour away.*

"I know there are entrance exams and stuff, and I know there's tuition to these places. Maybe it will be too expensive. I don't know, Mom, they were just ideas."

"What about Marian?" *Oh, that's right, Marian is in our backyard. That would be way too easy.*

"I thought about that, but I think it's too close to everyone that teases me. Some of the kids are going there from my class, and besides, I've heard it's real cliquish."

"Again, all good points, honey."

The phone rang, but this time neither of them moved. Four rings and it went to voicemail. With the thought of Ruby going away to stay on campus somewhere for high school, Helen found herself in major Mommy-Panic mode. *Get a grip. You HAVE to do what is best for your child. Think of Ruby and not of yourself.* Helen stood and went to the stove, her back to Ruby. With shaky hands she picked up the empty tea kettle, "I'm going to make a cup of tea, would you like some?" Turning to the sink she filled the kettle with water.

"Sure, Mom."

"I have another idea." Back at the stove Helen turned the knob, and the electric element clicked several times to light the gas. "We could talk to Beth, and see if she has any suggestions for highlights or toning down the red in your hair."

"Seriously?" Ruby's jaw fell open. "I've wanted to do that since fifth grade. You always said I had to wait until I was at least a junior in high school."

"Well, I've reevaluated the situation. Next week is Christmas—we'll try for an appointment the day after. My treat."

The doorbell rang, and Ruby jumped up. "I'll get it." But first she threw her arms around her mother. "Thanks, Mom. I love you." As she ran to the door, still in her pajamas, she called over her shoulder, "Do you think Beth can fit me in?"

Ruby didn't see the smile on Helen's face or hear her say in a low voice, "I've already made the appointment."

As Helen set down the red Christmas mugs decked out with green holly, she looked up to enjoy the happiness on Ruby's face again as she entered the room. "Who was it?"

Ruby didn't answer. She walked into the kitchen with her arms crossed over her chest, smile gone, and the excitement that was in her eyes only a moment ago had disappeared. "I'm going up to take a shower," she grumped. When her daughter left the doorway to go upstairs, Rosa appeared.

"Why didn't you answer your phone?"

"Why should I?"

"What the hell are you talking about, Helen? I thought we were friends."

Shrugging Helen said, "What do you want?"

"What do I want? I want to talk to you, that's what I want. Oh, and by the way, thanks for asking, but Ricky is still missing."

"Is there a point to all this, Rosa?"

"You're damned right there's a point. My kid is missing, otherwise I would have dragged his sorry ass over here to apologize to your daughter and plead for her forgiveness. All I can do now is express regret over the way my son behaved. I don't know what's wrong with him or how the hell to fix it." Tears fell steadily down Rosa's cheeks but she continued. "Alex told me everything last night, and it made me sick and ashamed. Helen, I am begging you not to hold what Ricky did against me. I don't want to lose our friendship, and I am devastated and beyond angry with what he did to Ruby. I'm asking your permission to speak with her and express how sorry I am."

Before Helen could say a word, Ruby stepped into the kitchen. She clearly had not gone upstairs to shower since she was still dressed in her pajamas, and she had obviously heard every word that Rosa said. Helen stiffened—what would her daughter do? She desperately wanted to interrupt and suggest Ruby be graceful in this situation—more graceful than Helen herself had been a few minutes ago, but she needed to let it play out. Ruby's reaction would tell her just what kind of woman her daughter was heading to be.

Standing before Rosa, Ruby towered over her mother's long-time friend by a good head and a half. The moment seemed frozen as both women waited for young Ruby to react. After a glance toward her mother, Ruby focused on Rosa. "I want to be mad at you, but I can't." Rosa let out a long slow breath, and Helen realized she was doing the same. "I won't lie and say it doesn't matter or didn't hurt, because it did. I also can't see my mom losing a good friend because of something someone else did to me. The two of you will have to put this behind you and move on. If I can do that, both of you should be able to also." For once Rosa didn't say anything, but she reached for Ruby's hand and held it in her own. "I'm still mad at Ricky, and hope I never see him again." Ruby filled her lungs with air. "That's the best I can do right now."

"That's more than I had hoped for," Rosa whispered and rubbed Ruby's arm with her free hand. "Thank you, sweetheart."

Ruby turned to go upstairs. "I need to get that shower now."

But Rosa pulled Ruby into a hug. "I want you to know something." It was clear Rosa was struggling to speak. "Dear, sweet, Ruby, this is true and sincere. I want you to know that with my whole heart, I honestly wish I had a daughter exactly like you."

Chapter 5

Steam filled the bathroom. As Helen stepped out of the shower, she cracked the door an inch to let some of the churning mist rush into the much cooler bedroom. Swiping at the fogged mirror with the corner of her towel, she actually felt happy to be scheduled for work this morning along with the next two evenings. She would have to compartmentalize what had happened to Ruby and her long talk to Rosa the day before, in order to get through her shifts at the Quilter's Closet. The truth was that the shop would probably be so busy with last minute purchases made by quilters frantically trying to finish their holiday projects, that Helen would never have time to dwell on her personal life. Toweling off her hair, she applied a large dab of gel and finger-scruffed it through her short do. Once air dried, her hair would sport its signature spiky-punk style. At that point, clipping in a blue streak of hair would reinforce her artsy look. Helen found it ironic that she was taking extra steps to have people notice her hair, while her daughter would soon have chemicals applied to her head in the hope that people would *not* notice her hair.

One leg slipped easily into her jeans, and when the telephone rang, she tried to quickly slide the other foot into the pants. Her toe caught on the crotch, causing Helen to lunge at the phone and knock both the handset and herself to the floor. The receiver skittered under the bed, and Helen pulled on the curly cord reeling it in like a fisherman with a prized catch. Not having time to look at the caller ID, she said a breathless and questioning, "Hello?"

"Helen?"

It was her husband, and she started laughing. "I'm such a clutz, Ben. I knocked the whole phone off the nightstand." She intentionally left out the part about the ungraceful swan dive and her one-legged-toe-stuck-in-the-crotch dance.

"Are you okay? It sounded awful on this end."

"Yeppers. Just feeling kind of stupid." She sat on the floor in her bra with her jeans bunched around her ankles. Her upper arm was throbbing and already starting to bruise from where she hit it on the corner of the table.

"I just wanted to let you know that it's confirmed—Marge's son will pick up Ruby and Brad around 11:00. The Heritage holiday party starts after lunch, but Zach needs to set up his band and equipment. I figured the kids could either help Zach or stay busy visiting with the residents."

"Sounds good to me." It was tradition that the Delaney children helped their father at many of the Heritage Manor parties and picnics. They often balked at going, but once they were there, they usually came through like troopers. "I've got to leave here in about a half hour, but I'll make sure Ruby is awake before I go. She can wake Brad and get him moving at the right time." With the phone wedged between her ear and shoulder and her jeans still tangling her feet, Helen pushed herself up and sat on the bed. Standing to pull up her jeans, she said, "Smart move getting Zach to pick them up."

"Yeah, I suspect once Ruby finds out they're not only riding with Zach but helping him set up his band, she might finally be happy that her father manages a retirement home."

"She'll be out of her hormonal teenage mind." Helen threaded her sweater over her head, slipping the receiver off her ear and back on so fast she never missed a word. "Hey, I gotta get going, but I keep forgetting to ask where Beth's dad is on the list of new residents?"

"I think he's pretty close to the top of the list." Helen heard the muffled sounds of a keyboard as Ben typed something on the computer. "Here it is. He's actually at the top of the list, so he'll be called next." Helen knew Ben politely meant that when someone passed away, George

Munro would be offered their vacant apartment. "Has Beth been asking?"

"No. Just my own nosiness that's all."

"You…nosy?" Ben laughed, "Hardly seems possible. Hey, how about I bring home pizza and maybe some of those breadsticks we like for dinner tonight? The kids will have earned a treat, and you'll probably be exhausted from a mad rush at work all day."

"Right now, that sounds near perfect to me."

Chapter 6

Generous amounts of balsam scented potpourri strategically placed throughout the Quilter's Closet wafted through the entire sales area. Realistic looking pine boughs were woven with colorful Christmas lights that flickered on and off around the window frames, and oversized red bows festooned the corners and center of each of the six large panes. Sandy, the store owner, was arranging a platter of holiday cookies and candies near the checkout counter. "Ready for the onslaught, Helen?" With only three days until Christmas Eve, they were expecting it to be rather crazy, and Sandy had implemented extended hours with all of the shifts fully manned. "T-minus five minutes and counting till opening."

"Copy that," Helen said as she slipped off her coat and headed for the employee break room, where there were hooks for hanging outerwear and purses. "You need anything from back here?"

"Yeah, thanks. Could you bring up some register tape? I think number two is about out." That would be the closest thing to a one-on-one talk that Helen would have the whole day with her boss, until ten hours later when the OPEN sign on the door was turned over and finally read CLOSED.

Both women were bone tired, but Helen stayed to help Sandy reconcile the daily receipts and deposit. Setting a green zippered bag with the bank's logo and a plate of cookies on the counter between them, Sandy said, "I held out a little goodie bag for us from this morning. I figured we could use some sugar right about now." At least two dozen cookies and candies sat on a red paper plate, and when Sandy unzipped the bag, the scent of chocolates and sweets about knocked Helen over. "Also, Mrs. Elvery brought this box of candy for the staff. She really appreciated how we all helped her with her first quilt last summer." Sandy reached behind her and turned off the iPod dock. "As much as I love Christmas music, I've heard about six hours too much today."

Helen puffed out her cheeks. "Thank you—so have I." Pulling a stool up to the counter and enjoying the silence, Helen opened the cash register. "Good call on the goodie bag. Do you believe we were so busy that I never even got one cookie all day? They must have been gone an hour after we opened."

"Oh, they were." Sandy closed her eyes and popped a whole green Spritz cookie, in the shape of a wreath, into her mouth. "I refilled that platter five more times."

"What I love is how many men we had in here today."

"I know—it had to be a record. Our customers will be very happy when they get those gift cards for merchandise and classes that their husbands purchased. Men are always so uncomfortable in our shop, but they're so thankful to be able to pick up an easy gift the last minute." Sandy handed a stack of checks to Helen, "Can you verify the checks and cash, and I'll work on the credit and debit card receipts?"

Helen had just placed an entire piece of fudge into her mouth, so she nodded, "Mmhmm."

"Oh, I almost forgot," Sandy reached for a small pile of notes next to the register. She pulled out an index card that had names and phone numbers listed and set it down by the stack of checks Helen was adding. "I had three more women today wanting to be put on your long-arm quilting list."

While wanting to say, *Oh, crap, I'm scared out of my mind just thinking about that machine,* instead she simply said, "Great, thanks Sandy."

"Are you still on target to have that beauty delivered the first week of January?"

"As far as I know it's a big thumbs up and all systems go." *A big thumbs up and all systems go? Where did that come from? I don't talk like that.*

Sandy's head swiveled to look at her employee through narrowed eyes. "Feeling a little nervous?"

"Actually, I'm scared to death. What seemed like such a great idea months ago is almost reality. I don't know if I can work that monstrosity, or if I'll even like long-arm quilting for other people. What if…"

Sandy held up her hand, "Like my Momma used to say 'someone's tired'. You'll do just fine, Helen. You've worked on a smaller model for years when you helped Janice during her busy season. You're talented and creative, and I've *never* known you to *ever* make any kind of visual error. I know you'll catch on quickly to the bigger machine and be fine."

"You're probably right." Helen wrapped a strip of adding tape around the checks and neatly set the cash on top. "It's just that as you get closer to grasping a life-long dream, it becomes almost scarier than never having it come true at all." She slid the stack of money toward Sandy. "I wonder why that is?"

Chapter 7

There is a peacefulness that is unmatched in the early morning stillness of the day after Christmas. Quiet reigns, and the house is at rest, as it matches the steady breathing of the sleeping children within. Mothers everywhere feel a sense of smug happiness at pulling off a successful family Christmas, and the giddy bliss of knowing the next one is a full year away.

Helen tightened the sash of her new light-blue plaid flannel robe, as she slid her feet into her day-old Christmas slippers. It would take weeks to mold the footwear into the butter-soft comfortable fit that she loved. Heading toward a much needed cup of coffee, she closed Ruby's and then Brad's bedroom doors. There were several hours before Ruby's salon appointment, and Helen was craving some calming alone time—time where she could restructure her home after the chaos of a successful holiday, by doing some much needed damage control before the kids woke up.

Tip-toeing around toys, boxes, and discarded ribbons, Helen switched on the lights of the Christmas tree. The room filled with the soft glow of lazy flashing lights. Picking her way through the debris, Helen headed to the kitchen for that mug of coffee. She had purchased a Keuring coffee maker for Ben for Christmas and was thrilled to have a no-muss, no-fuss cup of coffee in front of her within minutes.

Walking back into her living room with the aroma of coffee trailing behind, the magic of soft sparkly lights, and quiet that was almost as rare as the prospect of nowhere to be for hours, she said out loud, "What the hell." From under a pile of holiday rubble, Helen unearthed the new quilt book her husband had given her and then picked her way toward her favorite chair. Amid the wreckage and aftermath of a successful Christmas day, Helen propped up her feet, sipped on her coffee, and read her new quilt book as her children slept peacefully upstairs. Cleaning could wait.

By the time she had downed her second cup of coffee, Helen heard the toilet flush upstairs, and she could tell by the sounds that Ruby was awake. The shower started along with music, and Helen knew her daughter was testing out her new wireless-shower-thingy for her iPod. It wouldn't be long before her son was awake. After attempting to prolong the magical day as long as he could, Brad had fallen asleep on the couch around midnight. Helen closed her book but took a moment to smooth her hand over its cover. It had been a glorious morning—a beautiful book, tranquil moments with a hot mug of coffee, wearing a new robe and slippers, blinking Christmas lights, and children safely asleep upstairs. She sighed...*let the day begin.*

Ruby's salon appointment was at 1:00. After much discussion with Beth over the past week, Helen had agreed to simply drop her daughter off and let her have the experience without Mom breathing down her neck. They had figured out Helen's comfort zone, and together they had set parameters for color and highlighting. Beth also suggested a nice arch to Ruby's eyebrows and possibly a little mascara to darken Ruby's light lashes. When Helen balked at the mascara, Beth had put a hand on her arm and said, "Mom, you can't just give someone a cake for their birthday—you've got to put a *little* frosting on it, too. She's going into high school next year, let me show her how to apply eye makeup correctly along with a little lip gloss, and she won't look like a circus clown when she tries to do it behind your back."

Deep down Helen knew Beth was right, but she felt her little girl was suddenly disappearing before her eyes. Pulling into Beth's driveway Helen put on her best happy-mom-face and said to Ruby, "Good luck honey. I can't wait to see how it looks. Just call me when you're ready to come home."

Ruby looked stunned. "Aren't you coming in?"

"I thought it would be best if you and Beth discussed what you want and what would look good. I trust both of you to figure it out, and I thought it would be fun to be surprised." *Happy-mom-face, happy-mom-face, don't fail me now.*

"Are you mad at me for doing this? I feel horrible."

Oh crap, this is not going the way it's supposed to. "Not at all. I thought you might like some space, that's all."

"Mom, I want space when I'm listening to music or talking on the phone, NOT when I'm making big decisions. Please? I need your help. I'm kind of scared."

Helen put the car in park. "Come on Brad, let's get your sister settled, and then we'll get a snack."

"Thanks, Mom." Ruby's whole body relaxed. "You're the best."

The bell on the door tinkled a thin welcome, and Beth looked up from her appointment book. Helen noticed the look of surprise on her face as she registered that Ruby was not alone. Trying to convey through wide eyes and a slight shake of her head that this was not her idea, Helen said, "Hi Beth. Big day here. Brad and I won't stay long. We just came to help Ruby settle in."

Ruby, innocent of the unsaid conversation passing between the two friends said, "I'm so excited, but I wanted my mom to help us with the color choices."

"Absolutely, that's a very good idea."

Helen rummaged through a stack of children's books in a basket and handed a couple to Brad. "Sit over hear, sweetie. I won't be long." Brad was far more fascinated by the big hair dryer hovering over his head than the books in his lap, but at least he was quiet.

Beth had Ruby sit in the beauty chair, where she instantly started running her fingers through the problematic red tresses. "I've been thinking about this since your mom made the appointment, and I have some colors picked out that I feel would complement your skin tones." She had several sample charts with small tufts of gradations of colored hair setting on the counter at her station. Beth went through a number of options that she had earmarked with little sticky arrows, and talked to Ruby about ease or difficulty of upkeep and age appropriate coloring. "I've got lots of ideas for a youthful yet sophisticated style, too."

As hard as it was, Helen kept her mouth shut, unless she was directly asked for an opinion. It only took about ten minutes, and Ruby had decided on a toner that would change her hair to a soft light brown. Beth suggested some highlights to 'make it sing,' as she put it. Helen was ready to gather Brad and leave, when Ruby asked if she could use the washroom before they got started.

As soon as the bathroom door closed, Beth whispered close to Helen, "I didn't want to say anything in front of Ruby, but I heard from Rosa this morning. Ricky called her yesterday for Christmas, but he wouldn't say where he was or when he might come home. She said at this point she's happy just to know that he's okay and still alive, but I honestly think she's barely holding it together."

There was a muffled sound of the toilet flushing. "Thanks for sharing. I know she's embarrassed to update me. It's gotta be hell for her." The bathroom door opened and Helen said in a louder voice, "Okay, just call me when you're done." To Ruby she said, "Have fun, honey. Can't wait."

Hand on the doorknob, smile on her face, Helen took a big breath and pulled the door of the salon open. It had been a little over three hours since she had left the shop. The bell announced her presence. She took in the heady combination of sweet smelling sprays and prickly chemicals, along with the slightly balmy sensation that seems to be the signature of all salons. She didn't see her daughter and immediately furled her eyebrows in confusion. *Where was Ruby? Had something gone wrong?* She focused on Beth who was approaching her, with a big smile on her face.

"Sit over here, Mom" Beth fussed. "I think you're going to be happy." Helen slipped her coat off as she sat—her turn in the big dryer chair. "Okay, Ruby. Come on out."

Helen gasped and slumped back into the chair, hands at her cheeks. She croaked out, "Oh," on a puff of air.

Beth placed her hand on her friend's shoulder, "Isn't she beautiful?"

Standing and moving slowly toward her daughter she stammered, "Oh, my God! You're…you're…you look so…so grown up." Unable to take her hands from her cheeks she circled around her smiling little girl. "The color…the style…it's perfect."

Ruby said, "Check out my eyebrows, Mom."

One of Helen's hands flew to her mouth. "I never thought eyebrows could be so important, but they look fabulous. YOU look fabulous." She spun to look at Beth who was smiling as though she just finished painting the Mona Lisa. "Beth, you did a great job. Thank you for all of your help."

"I *LOVE* it, Mom." Ruby turned her head from side to side, and the strategically placed highlights looked like threads of delicate gold spun through warm flowing medium brown hair. The way Beth had cut the new style accentuated cheek bones that Helen didn't even know her daughter possessed. But the biggest surprise, and quite a bonus, was that Ruby's freckles seemed much less obvious. Could something as simple as a color change do that? "I feel so pretty!" Ruby hugged herself like a little girl.

Helen had waited a long time to hear her daughter say those words. She realized that with all the talk about being beautiful inside, for the first time Helen thought that just maybe the inside beauty sometimes needed a little help from the outside pretty in order to shine through. "Let's go home and show Dad."

Chapter 8

As successful as Ruby's make-over had been, Helen was still a protective mom. She realized her daughter would have to face going back to school with potentially a whole new set of taunts from the bullies. She had kept these fears to herself. In the days that followed the salon experience, several of her Bunco friends stopped by to see the 'new' Ruby. Helen watched as her daughter's confidence rose when Marge brought Val, and then Phree visited with Emily. The women had sealed the deal with high praise in the form of jaw dropping ahhhs and girly squeals. Emily asked if Ruby would like to go clothes shopping with her the next day, "I've always wanted a sister, especially one I could go shopping with."

Helen was anxious as she helped her daughter get ready to head off to the first day of school after her winter break. The big moment was finally here, and Ruby would be walking into school and down the halls in a matter of minutes. It would take only one smart-ass hurtful attack for the glow that her daughter had lived with this past week to hurtle her back into a devastating dark place. As Ruby was leaving to catch the bus, Helen had to be very careful how she phrased the next few sentences.

"You look fabulous, honey."

"Thanks Mom. I can't wait to get to school, and I never thought I'd ever say that." Ruby was arranging a new scarf around her neck—one that Emily and she had picked up on their shopping trip.

"Look Ruby, you know there might be..."

"I know, Mom, there might still be jerks at schools that are going to tease me no matter what, but I just don't care anymore. *I* feel pretty, and that's all that matters. They can all go to hell."

"Oh…well said. You're absolutely right." Helen walked over to Ruby and gave her a hug, "Have a good day, babe."

Ruby bent down to kiss her mother, "Thanks, Mom, and thanks for caring. I Love you."

It would be seven—eight hours tops before Helen knew what happened to her daughter at school today. *Can a mother hold her breath that long? Sure – no problem.*

By the time the bus picked up Brad in the front of their home, it was starting to snow. The flakes were large and heavy, full of moisture and falling fast. *This could be a big one. …But first the Keurig awaits.*

Fortified with an extra-bold espresso, Helen walked through the door that led to the garage. Even though Ben had finished putting up the drywall and painting last November, it still looked odd to see their three-and-a-half car garage partitioned off with barely enough space for two cars. Walking around her mini-van and through the space where Ben's car usually sat, she opened the door to her quilting studio. With all the holidays, the kids' winter break, extra time at work for both her and Ben, Helen had scarcely had time to do more than toss several bags of purchased supplies into the space.

Flipping one of the switches just inside the door, overhead fluorescent lights flickered as the room brightened. Helen only had today to accomplish a ton of work in preparation for the delivery of her new long-arm quilting machine. Most quilters personified their machines by giving them a name, and Lily Marie was scheduled to arrive around 10:00 a.m. tomorrow.

The desk, in what would represent her office area, was repurposed from an old nightstand, a short filing cabinet, and was topped off by a slightly chipped and half-priced piece of countertop from a big-box store. They had purchased and assembled three units of deep sturdy industrial chrome shelving to help with organizing everything from incoming and outgoing orders, to large cones of colored threads, and various sizes and types of batting. Helen had hired Marge's husband, Bud, to fit the room with its own fuse box, plentiful waist-high outlets, and spectacular overhead spot lights above where Lily Marie would be installed. She had the option, for an additional charge, that the company would set up the machine upon delivery. That seemed like a no-brainer to Helen, so by tomorrow evening, Lily Marie would be ready to go.

Helen thought she might throw-up.

Setting her coffee on her desktop, she allowed the peacefulness of the silent clean space to wash over her, cleansing away some of her uncertainties. Her first order of business was to make sure that ample room existed for the men to work and set up the quilting machine. Opening the many bags of supplies, she organized and shelved the new materials with equipment she had arranged earlier. Helen flattened empty boxes and stacked them inside the garage for recycling. Finally, she opened a large cardboard box that held dozens of colored cones of thread. She had devised and built a system within the industrial shelving to house the large cones, and she was pleased to find her design was both useful and successful.

Helen had kept a watchful eye not only on the clock, but on the weather outside the large window of her studio. It was nearing 3:00 and her children would soon be home. She sent another silent prayer for Ruby's strength and happiness, as she swept the faux wood floor. All was ready to welcome Lily Marie tomorrow morning. Now she needed to figure out something for dinner, and how she could get the kids to help with the removal of about six inches of deep wet snow. Reluctantly, she left her haven, but told herself that tomorrow at this time her long awaited treasure would be in place.

"Mom you won't believe what happened!" Ruby carried in wet snow that dripped off her coat, falling to puddle just inside the back door. Her cheeks were red, and Helen didn't know if it was from the cold and snow or something else. "Amanda, that bitchy cheerleader who's always hated me, you know the one, she started teasing me at lunch like, 'We all know you just covered up your ugly and it's still there ginger girl' and Cory, the really tall popular guy who's the captain of the basketball team slapped his hands flat on the table and got right in her face and told her to shut-up and leave me alone!" Snow melt along with ice crystals sprinkled from Ruby's gloves, as she snapped off one and then the other. "No one said another mean thing to me all day! Isn't that awesome?"

Helen was all too aware that solving one problem can often be the beginning of another. "Yeah, awesome, sweety." She slipped on her happy-mom-smile. "I'm glad you had a good day for a change." *And who the hell is this Cory guy?*

"Well, what do you think Mom? I mean why would he do that?"

"Maybe Cory is tired of bitchy cheerleaders, too."

Chapter 9

"Excited?" Ben took a final swig from his morning coffee. He set the large paper cup under the spout of the new coffee maker, pushing the button to make one for the road.

"I can't believe it's finally going to be here today. I'm excited and nervous all at once. But mostly I'm really scared."

"You'll do fine." Ben picked up the two ends of his tie, raised his chin, and within seconds flipped and tucked his Christmas present from Brad into a perfect half-Windsor. "Just remember, Helen, you went up to Michigan and did a weekend of classes on how to operate the thing. Once it's together, you should be able to jump right in and get started making tons of money." Ben slipped on his sport coat and then his winter topcoat. He smiled at his wife, kissing her cheek.

"Thanks, I guess I just needed to hear that."

"You know," Ben said as he held Helen's shoulders, "I really am very proud of you. You've worked hard, and planned a long time for this. There's no doubt in my mind you'll be successful." Picking up his keys from the corner of the counter where he always left them, he said, "Call me when it's here and set up. Okay?"

Getting the kids out the door went smoothly, especially with Ruby. After yesterday's lunchroom standoff between the cheerleader-bully and the boy-hero, she was eager to get back to school. Helen made a mental note that if she had a dollar for every time her daughter had said the name Cory since yesterday after school, she would be a rich woman.

As much as Helen wanted to go into her quilting studio and putter around, she didn't even remotely want to miss the delivery truck when it arrived. She opted to sit at the kitchen table with a fresh espresso and work on her menu list for Bunco. She was a little distracted at first by day-dreaming of Lily Marie, but she finally settled into the repetitive job of looking up recipes, checking her pantry for ingredients, and making a grocery list.

The main course would be hot sandwiches. Shredded beef in the crock pot would cook all day and be melt-in-your-mouth delicious. She'd top it off with homemade mac and cheese—perfect Midwest winter comfort food. She would serve them with fresh yeasty whole-wheat rolls, strong enough to hold a liberal portion of beef with a generous ladle of au jus. Very easy. Now, for another side dish and a few appetizers—she thought a cold fruit salad would complement the beef sandwiches nicely, and help chase away the beginnings of cabin fever that everyone was feeling. By the time Helen heard the low rumble of a truck around 9:30, her menu was set in stone.

Lily Marie had arrived!

BUNCO CLUB MENU

Shredded Beef with Rolls   Mac and Cheese
24-Hour Fruit Salad   Hot Pizza Dip w/ chips
Jo's Fantabulous Taco Dip   Veggies & Dip
Homemade Caramel Corn

Pop Water Wine
Popcorn - M & M's - chocolate covered raisins
Sno-Caps

Scones with Clotted Cream*
Chocolate chip Scones
*recipe at back of book

The workers took about four hours to unpack, assemble, and install the machine. Helen had gotten used to seeing her sewing studio almost empty, and the quilting machine seemed to swallow the whole room. The deliverymen left and took with them the empty boxes and crates. Suddenly she was alone—face to face with her long-time dream.

Helen stood before Lily Marie and was filled with awe. She was surprised when she started to cry. They were not uncontrollable sobs, and not from sadness, or joy, or fear, but from the remarkable satisfaction of realizing a dream, and the journey on which it had taken her. She allowed herself a few moments to wallow in her emotions, and then she called Ben to share the final step with her husband and best friend.

Chapter 10

Since Helen's part-time job at the Quilter's Closet had turned into full-time during the weeks before Christmas, her boss had agreed to give her star employee two weeks off to familiarize herself with her new quilting machine. After spending the past several days getting to know Lily Marie's strengths and quirks by experimenting on batting between plain muslin, Helen was feeling more confident and in control with her new undertaking. She was hopeful that within a month she could start taking orders from her friends. She would propose giving them a discount, with the understanding that they'd be her 'learning curve'.

Ruby's life at school had leveled out with only a handful of mean guys teasing her, but she had assured Helen that those were the jerks that harassed anyone not in their little gangster-group. Cory had dropped off the radar when Ruby found out he had a girlfriend, who just happened to have red hair, and went to a junior high in the next town over.

It was time to face the fact that Helen was hosting Bunco tomorrow night. With plans to prepare most of the food today, she would be in good shape for tomorrow. Since both the pizza dip and taco dip required sliced green onions and black olives, she worked until she had piles of both on the cutting board in front of her. Then she diced fresh plum tomatoes for the pizza dip. After assembling the two appetizers and putting them in the fridge, she put a check mark by each one on her hand-written menu.

Cucumbers, carrots, celery, and broccoli didn't escape Helen's sharp knife as she prepped, sliced, chopped, and bagged them to stay fresh. Cutting the broccoli florets off the large stalk, she sprayed a stream of water over them in a colander, and then cut them into small bite-sized pieces. To keep everything as fresh as possible, she would combine the ingredients for the Broccoli Salad tomorrow afternoon and top it off with a pound of crisp and savory Shipshewana bacon. The stacked bags of multi-colored fresh vegetables reminded her of the vibrant cones of thread in her studio as she placed them in her refrigerator.

Brad would be home in a matter of minutes. She planned to continue with more prep work, while he sat at the kitchen table, and ate a snack. After dinner she'd put up her feet and relax with the family. Maybe they'd play cards, or a board game, or just watch a movie. But the best news was that after tomorrow, the Bunco supply box would be someone else's problem.

The outside temperature on the digital thermometer in the Delaney kitchen read a very cold -10 degrees at 7 in the morning, and it was forecast to get colder throughout the day. Only her children's eyes showed between scarves and hoods by the time they opened the door to go outside. Ruby protested the 'mummy look' as she called it, but Helen insisted she keep every stitch in place. "You're going to thank me about halfway to the street," she told a grousing Ruby. Holding the door open just long enough, Helen heard their feet crunch on the crusty cold snow. Each of her children ran toward the sound of their bus that was hidden behind a clouded veil of exhaust. Her own breath came out in bursts of steam, until she knew each child was safely inside the vehicle. She then closed the door and locked the negative temperatures out of her house.

Starting with the shredded beef, Helen placed a large rump roast in the crock pot, poured a little water into the bottom of the pot, seasoned the beef with garlic salt and pepper, and added a jar of pepperoncini. The meat would simmer and tenderized all day in its own juices and impart the fabulous aroma of a cooking roast throughout the whole house.

She turned her attention to her famous scones. Using a food processor, she mixed one stick of chilled unsalted butter with the dry ingredients, and then added tart cherries and mini-chocolate chips. Helen whisked sour cream with egg and added almond extract. With a 'light hand', she stirred the mixture into the dry ingredients. One, two, three gentle kneads of the dough, was followed by lightly patting it into an 8-inch circle which would then be cut into wedges. The scones would cook for exactly twelve minutes, and then sit on a rack under a cotton dish towel until they cooled. A half hour before everyone arrived, she would whip the heavy cream into a tight fluff—just a second or two before it turned into butter. Yum!

Paper plates, napkins, and plastic cups were set in place on her counter. Helen cut the bakery buns for the shredded beef, and re-bagged them to keep them fresh. Turning on the dishwasher, she started to tidy up the kitchen. The next line of business was to position the card tables and chairs in the family room and set out the dice, scorecards, and scratch paper.

Helen was right on track when both kids came home from school. They had ushered in a burst of freezing air, wet snow, and a heap of outer clothes. If she could just contain their mess for a few more hours, Ben would be home, and he could take over.

A little frazzled she said, "Ruby, could you help me out by taking Brad downstairs. I've got everything set up for Bunco tonight in the living room, and I don't want it to get messed up."

Ruby, still grateful and cooperative from her makeover, said, "Come on, Nutty Buddy, let's go downstairs and get our homework done before Dad gets home. I bet we can talk him into video games tonight."

Brad pumped the air with his fist, "YES! Hey, Mom, are you and the ladies going to be screaming tonight?"

Chapter 11

Helen was a little worried about how Rosa was going to react tonight. The two women had not talked to each other since the day she had apologized to Ruby for her son's bad behavior. She questioned her own worth as a friend for not being more compassionate toward someone that she truly did care about. It was time to put her claws away and have some empathy for Rosa.

Helen almost gasped after Rosa unwound her scarf and took off her coat. She had to have lost ten, maybe fifteen pounds since Ricky disappeared. She also sported dark, grayish-purple semi-circles under very tired eyes.

Holding up both hands like a preacher, she said to all the women at once, "I know, I know, I look like shit."

The Sarge took one of Rosa's hands between both of her own and rubbed it briskly, as if to massage some warmth and life back into her friend. "My God, Rosa, are you okay?"

"Actually, no. I'm not okay. I'm scared, and miserable, and have no idea what to do about Ricky. I'm living in hell everyday not knowing where he is, or what's happened to him."

"Oh, honey, after giving up my baby I felt the same way." Marge kept rubbing Rosa's hand. "It's like a chunk of your heart has been gashed open, and at the same time a 400 pound weight is on your chest."

"That's exactly how I feel. Sometimes I'm so terrified, I can't even take full breaths."

Marge put an arm around Rosa's shoulder, while still holding onto her hand, and led her to a comfortable chair in the living room. "Helen, could you get some wine for Rosa?"

"I definitely could use some wine. I don't want to seem rude, but I'd really like to not talk about Ricky all night. Terry convinced me that what I needed most was to be with my friends—maybe laugh a little, and *not* think about Ricky for just a few hours. It took a lot for me to come here tonight."

"By all means," Marge said. "I think that's an excellent idea."

Helen handed a glass of wine to Rosa, and held up the bottle to the group. "Anyone?"

There was a chorus of yeses, and you bet, and while Helen poured, she said, "I'll put this on the counter, and just help yourselves if you want more."

Rosa took a slow sip of wine, and inhaling a deep breath, she said, "There are two things I think we all want to do—see Ruby's new hair-do and Helen's long-arm machine."

"Yes, I'm freaking dying to see your quilting studio and machine," Lettie said.

The Sarge suggested that since no one had started eating, it made more sense to go to the quilting studio first. "Then we can come back inside and start dishing up, while we check out the new Ruby. Is that okay with you, Helen?"

Helen wanted to say "Aye aye, Sarge." Instead she said, "Sounds like a good plan. It might be a little crowded out there, but follow me."

Crowded was definitely an understatement. Eight enthusiastic women, and a 14 by 6-foot machine crammed into a space for a car and a half, was more like packed sardines than simply crowded. "Ladies, meet Lily Marie," Helen proudly swept her hand toward the behemoth machine.

"She's beautiful," Beth said, "and so big!"

All eight heads immediately bent over to inspect the large practice piece on which Helen was working. "I love this pattern here," Nancy pointed to a delicate feathered circle.

"And check out this one," Nedra said. "Can you put me on your list for about four quilts, Helen? I want you to use this pattern on one I'm making for my aunt. It'll be perfect."

Nancy raised an index finger, "Put me down for one, maybe two. Okay? I don't have anything finished right now, but by the time you get to me, I'll be ready."

Helen wrote both names in a small ledger with today's date and how many tops each person wanted quilted. She noticed that she only felt a bit apprehensive, and no longer felt like vomiting every time her wait-list grew.

"How about a little demo?" Phree said. "Just something simple."

"Sure, let me fire her up." Helen wanted to keep it short. In about fifteen minutes, all eight women were weaving through the garage back toward the kitchen and food, while talking about the wonders of Lily Marie.

"Man, am I jealous," Lettie said. "I may have to think about getting one for myself. I'd have plenty of room in my barn. The only thing is I really don't want to quilt for other people, so it would kind of be a waste of money."

"Everyone load up your plates, and we'll get Ruby out here to strut her stuff." As usual, Marge was in her zone. "I saw Ruby the other day, and I'm telling all of you that Beth did a fabulous job. While we always knew our Ruby was a beauty, Beth brought out her best for all to see."

"I'll go tell her we want to see her," Helen said, then thought—*And there it is, the dichotomy that is Marge. She annoys, yet is also kind, and she has the ability to hurl both at once.*

All eight women, Helen included, cooed and clucked over Ruby so much that by the time the "Ruby Show" was over, Helen could tell her daughter's confidence had shot through the roof. As she swaggered out of the room flipping her hair to show off the gold threaded highlights, she did an over-the-shoulder wave to the hooting women. When she reached Rosa she bent down to give her a hug, and whispered something in her ear. Helen felt her heart puff in her chest with pride. *She's a good girl, and I'm a damn lucky Mom.*

The women talked of nothing and everything, while they raved over the shredded beef sandwiches, and steadily devoured a counter full of food.

"I don't know what it is about cold weather, but it sure gives you an appetite."

"No kidding," Nancy said, and scooped another ladle of shredded beef onto a bun. "My diet's on hold tonight. Anyone want half?"

Helen watched Rosa closely and noticed that she didn't eat very much. She also didn't add to any conversations, and that was unusual for Rosa. But, on the other hand, she didn't have the same intense sad look she had when she walked in here. No one spoke of Ricky—not one word, and Helen hoped her friend was having the escape she so badly needed.

As always, anticipating the next step, Marge started gathering used plates and utensils. "It's starting to get late, and we don't want to be here all night. Let's move along smartly ladies, and choose where we want to sit."

Helen rolled her eyes at Lettie, and held up a wine bottle, "Any one besides me need a little more wine?" When four women raised their glasses, she walked between the two tables topping off drinks. *Three more hours and they'll all be out of here.*

Players shared bowls of popcorn that were complimented by dark chocolate Raisenettes and Sno-Caps. Someone at the head table rang the bell and play began.

An unusually loud sequence of laughter and shouts brought Brad from his bedroom. He sat on the top step and gawked at the noisy women throwing dice. Ben joined him, and put his arm around his sons shoulder. He let Brad enjoy the wild scene for a few moments, and then escorted him back to bed. "Let's tone it down a notch if we can," Marge said. "Brad and Ruby both have school tomorrow."

There were only five more rounds until they'd be done playing, and then the screaming would be over. With just one more Bunco thrown, Beth and Lettie did their version of the 'Silent Scream' for the sake of Helen's sleeping children.

While Marge shuffled the scorecards into position from highest to lowest, the rest of the women dug money from their purses and pockets for the $5.00 Bunco fee. Helen took the plastic wrap off her baskets of scones and the bowl of clotted cream. She arranged them on a quilted table runner on her dining room table.

"Scones! I love you," Rosa said. "What a perfect night."

Helen was happy to see Rosa perk up and say something other than when she was asked a question. As she carried the teapots to the table, she said, "I made several batches so help yourself to as many as you'd like." She took the cozies off the pots and set them on the antique buffet behind her. "I want to toss out a suggestion about prizes. I know we've all talked about having too many trinkets and knick-knacky stuff… "

"If I get one more candle or Christmas ornament, I could open my own store."

"Amen to that."

"So what's your idea, Helen?"

"Well, you know how Marge keeps track of everything in her little book?" Marge waved the miniature journal for all to see. She had yet to announce what tonight's rankings were. "You also know how she comes up with those charts once a year for us to see who threw the most Buncos, who got the most first places, and stuff like that?"

Phree said, "I always love when we get those charts."

Helen started pouring tea as she talked. "I've been thinking, we could keep all the money we collect for dues in an envelope, and at the end of the year—say the November Bunco or something like that, Marge could tally up the most first places, second places, and so forth, and then we'd all get a nice envelope of cash.

"I love it!" shouted Marge. "For one thing it totally validates my obsession with keeping track of the scores, and with the holiday right around the corner, November would be a perfect time to do it."

"Yeah," Beth stirred sugar into her tea, "who couldn't use a little extra cash that time of year?"

"Then it's settled." Marge drew a thick double line in her little book to show where they were starting. "Since Helen is giving cash for tonight's Bunco, we might as well start the new routine tonight."

"Helen, you're a genius, and Marge you're a…" Beth struggled for the right words, "well, you're a great list maker and record keeper."

Helen took a deep bow. "My bookie and I thank you."

Marge busied herself recording the results from the scorecards, and Phree said, "While we have our calendars out tonight, why don't we come up with two or three possible dates for the Vegas trip?"

"Are you sure you still want to do that?" said Nancy. "I mean, it's really cool, but it's going to be so expensive to pay for eight of us."

"Absolutely. I can't think of anything that would be more fun than all of us in Vegas. And don't worry about the expense, because I'm not. Besides, I'm sure my fourteen-times great grandpa Pastor Brewster would whole-heartedly approve of eight women going on a gambling trip."

"You know, Phree," Nedra warmed up Nancy's mug with some hot tea, and then topped off her own. "He'd probably have you in the public stockade for even thinking about it."

By the time everyone had enjoyed a second, or in some cases a third, scone and as many cups of tea, the next Bunco date was set as well as three possibilities for Vegas.

Lettie pushed her chair away from the table, "My God, Helen, you could go into business selling scones."

"I'll keep that in mind if my venture with Lily Marie goes south."

Since everyone was so uncomfortably bundled up against the weather, no one had bothered to drag along any show-and-tell or hand work. But there were intermittent and on-going discussions about current projects and which books they were all reading.

Beth's voice rose in a rather smarmy tease, "So, Nancy, what's the latest on you and Michael? He sure is a hot one."

Helen noticed Nancy's cheeks immediately blush red. "We spent a lot of time together while he was here."

"And..." Lettie swept her hand toward Nancy, implying 'we want to hear it.'

"We-ell," in a sing-song way she dragged the word into two syllables, "Actually, I'm going out to Colorado for a long weekend next month."

The women simultaneously gasped and shrieked, and Rosa sounded more herself when she asked, "And you didn't think we needed to know this sooner because...?"

Nancy stumbled for words and pulled the collar on her turtleneck sweater as if to let in some cool air, "Anybody else getting warm in here?"

"Give it up, sister," Nedra said. "We aren't leaving until we know everything."

"Honestly, there's not much to tell. We spent a lot of time together, and we just decided last week that I'd head out there for a visit. End of story."

Rosa slapped a hand on the table and pointed to Nancy. "Look at her. I do believe she's smitten."

Nancy smiled and nodded. "I think I am."

"Enough." Sarge stood. "Time to leave Helen to her clean up, so she can get to bed this century."

At this point, Helen was grateful to Marge. She followed the women to where their coats rested on a chair. Some of the ladies beeped their cars to warm up while they enveloped themselves in all forms of outerwear. Phree checked her cell phone. "It says the temperature is -17 right now."

"The only good thing about hosting in January," Helen said, "is you don't have to leave your house." Helen offered the Bunco box of supplies to Beth, who, wrapped snuggly in her coat, scarf, and gloves, reluctantly took it, and headed into the sub-zero night.

Slipping a baggie with four scones into Rosa's gloved hand, a peace offering for their friendship, Helen put a finger to her lips, "Our secret."

Rosa smiled.

FEBRUARY BUNCO – Beth

Sometimes life gets in the way.

Chapter 1

Opening the front door, Beth could tell that everyone in her family was already in bed and had fallen asleep. Shrugging out of her coat she leaned against the door and pulled off her boots. Stepping on a chunk of snow that had fallen off the bottom of her boot chilled her to the bone. Heading straight to the kitchen, Beth flopped her purse and outerwear over the back of a chair that was draped with several other garments belonging to the family. Sadly, the chair doubled as a hall closet. Tim had taped a note to the face of the television set, it was one of the few places in their home that was clutter free. "George checked in at the usual time and is fine. Tim." Since her father's second amputation, he always checked in just before he went to bed around 9:00 p.m. It helped to ease Beth's worries.

Setting the Bunco box on top of one of many teetering piles that filled the family room, she grasped the oak handrail of the stairs and wearily climbed them. Checking in on each of the kids as she went down the hall, she passed a handful of castoff items and small mounds of who-knows-what along the way. While the kid's bedrooms were typically messy for their ages, the preponderance of clutter was confined to the main level and basement of the Stevenson's home. Thankfully the jumble had not yet found its way to the second floor. Beth thought that was possibly due to her strict rule of "Nothing on the stairs" from about a year ago when she had taken a tumble on a pile of debris that had been growing on the fifth step. The laundry she was carrying flew from her arms, as she bumped down several stairs landing squarely on her butt and spraining a wrist. She sat at the bottom of the staircase and cried—not from the injury or pain, but from the frustration at the state of her home and her inability to resolve it. Stepping over one of Katy's stray Barbie's, Beth repeated the silent promise she said every night, "Tomorrow I will take control of this nightmare and change who I am."

Chapter 2

The Stevenson's morning started earlier than Beth had anticipated when, at 5:30 a.m., the phone rang. The calling tree from the twins' middle school had been activated. A water pipe had burst at the school sometime in the middle of the night rendering the boiler unusable. No heat—no school. This bit of news meant that Katherine and Joe would be grousing at home on a too-cold-to-go-anywhere day. Unless a miracle happened and the house had somehow cleaned itself overnight, no friends would be coming to play.

Planning to let the 12-year-old twins sleep-in until Heather left for Whitney High, Beth had her hands full getting her eldest child out the door. Talk about grousing. "It's no fair! Katy and Joey don't have to go to school, I shouldn't either."

"Nice try," Tim said. "There's absolutely no logic to that statement. The furnace in their school is broken, and yours isn't. They stay home—you go to school." Then he added, "Don't forget, they'll have to make up the day at the end of the year when the weather is warm, and no one wants to be inside."

"Nice try, Dad, I'm a senior and graduating on a set date no matter how many snow days we have." She gave her father a scrunch of her nose. "Gotcha."

Tim put both hands up, shoulder high. "Okay, you're right, Miss Smarty-pants. Just go to school and *try* to learn something before your case of Senioritis is completely out of control."

The Stevenson's had gotten used to standing while they wolfed down breakfast. Sadly, all the chairs and tabletops were occupied with clutter, and there was nowhere to sit in the kitchen. "Look on the bright side." Beth splashed orange juice in a glass and handed it to her daughter. "You could stay home and help the twins and me clean house. Or you could go visit Grandpa."

"Yeah, sounds like great options. School's looking better and better every second." Heather unzipped her backpack and handed her mother a form to be filled out for parent/teacher conferences next week. "Since you guys are forcing me to go to school today, can I drive Mom's car? I mean as long as you're staying home to clean…"

"You know I need to check in on Grandpa—probably at least twice today. I also have to get groceries for him, too." Beth already felt overwhelmed, and the day hadn't even started yet. "I'm sorry, sweetie."

Heather's smile turned to compressed lips, and she huffed out a breath. "It's okay, Dad can take us as usual." Heather carpooled with four other girls, and they were each responsible for transportation one day a week. This was Heather's day.

"Let's get going, kiddo," Tim said as he picked up his brief case and car keys. "How about if you drive, and I'm the passenger?"

"Really?" She'd only had her license for about nine months, and Beth and Tim were just beginning to feel more comfortable letting her get behind the wheel. "Cool!" Heather shrieked and ran to get her coat and gloves off a sofa in the family room. Looking over her shoulder she said, "C'mon Dad, let's get going!"

Tim looked at Beth and raised his eyebrows. "Complaining momentarily diverted. Any appointments today?"

"Yeah, I've got four this afternoon, so I'm hoping to get something done this morning." She looked around her and had no idea how or where to start digging out.

"I've got a meeting with the department heads this afternoon, and I should be home about 3:00. I'll get dinner started and help the kids with homework if you're tied up,"

Tim said as he bent over to kiss her, and then tugged on his coat.

"Thanks. My last appointment is a color and highlight job and it might take a little longer to finish." Beth picked up dishes and with the skill of a magician stuffed them into the near-full dishwasher. She told Tim, "I'll think of something for dinner, and make sure we have all the ingredients, and you can take it from there."

Heather walked into the kitchen pulling on her gloves, and then wrapped her scarf into a chic fashion statement. "I'll cook dinner if Dad does the dishes."

"Sounds fair to me," Tim said.

"Let's go, Dad. I don't want to be late."

Tim looked at Beth, and they smiled at each other. "Good luck," Beth said, more to Tim than to Heather.

Chapter 3

At first glance, Beth and Tim Stevenson might come across as an odd match for a couple. Tim had a Ph. D. and headed the History Department at Sauk Trail Community College, and Beth owned a one-woman hair salon. She referred to herself as a 'history buff,' but in reality she was obsessed with history just as much as Tim.

Beth's parents had refused to send her to college to study something as 'useless' as history, and instead were adamant that she be able to support herself if her (future and unknown) husband should ever leave her in "the lurch" as they called it. After a tearful senior year in high school of sparring with her parents, George and Barbara had won, and Beth enrolled in cosmetology school. She did, however, continue reading and studying American History as a hobby.

Three years later, when Tim had an appointment for his first job interview at the local high school, he found himself in need of a haircut. Fate was on their side the day he sat down in Beth's chair at the salon where she worked. When Beth discovered he had just finished his Master's Degree in American History and had plans to follow up with a Ph. D., they struck up a conversation that would have probably bored most people out of their minds. Tim invited Beth to celebrate his new job by joining him on a walking tour of the Frank Lloyd Wright Historic District, and then they spent the next day at the Field Museum of Natural History. When Beth and Tim tell the story of how they met, they always end it by saying, "...and the rest is history!"

Now, after twenty years of marriage and three kids, their home had become swamped with clutter. Beth had always had a problem letting go of her possessions, but in the early years of her marriage she was very organized. Prized collectables were displayed on bookcases, tables, or framed and then hung on the walls. 'Things I might need later' were categorized and placed in labeled plastic bins. Beth didn't know how things had gotten so out of control, but looking back, she felt she could pinpoint exactly when the problem had started. It was about ten years ago, when her mother had become ill and passed away. Barbara Munro had been diagnosed and died very quickly from pancreatic cancer. She left a grieving husband and four children to wonder what in the world had happened to them in such a short time.

Beth's siblings, two brothers and a sister, had long since moved away from the area. They were more than happy to let their little sister be in charge of hard decisions and the day-to-day life of caregiving their parents. Instead of being bitter, Beth chose to be thankful for the opportunity to spend those last six months helping her mother gracefully leave this life. She felt especially grateful for those extremely difficult last few weeks, when she had been blessed with several short but meaningful talks with her mom. At lucid moments when the pain medication was at a minimum, Barbara would thank Beth for being there to help her.

One day with plastic tubing running meds to her withered body, Beth's mother grabbed her hand, and, with large frightened eyes, asked Beth's forgiveness for not allowing her to follow her love of history. She told her youngest child it was one of her biggest regrets. Beth had replied through tears that there was nothing to forgive. She swept her hand over what was left of her mother's wispy hair—all that remained after several rounds of chemo—and told her, "Being a mother is hard work. You did what you thought best, Mom. I know you did it out of love." She took her mother's hand and kissed the back of it. "Besides, I may have never met Tim, and I wouldn't trade that for any history degree."

For the months while her mom was ill and dying, any mail (other than bills) got stacked in a pile, put in a box, and then trotted down to the basement to be out of the way. Six months of junk mail and potentially-useful-items add up to quite a pile. After Barbara's funeral, there was Dad to worry about—not to mention their two-year-old twins and eight-year-old Heather. Tim had just been promoted to department head, and helped at home as much as he could. But the easiest solution to a multitude of junk was to stuff it in a box with the intention of going through it at some future date.

Ten years later, most of the basement had been filled with teetering boxes of magazines, junk mail, kids' school papers, used toys, Tim's professional journals, Beth's bookkeeping for her salon, and just about anything you could imagine. There were boxes and bags of plastic containers from frozen dinners, yogurt, and deli food, next to wobbling towers of drinking cups from every fast food restaurant in the area, and glass jars of all shapes and sizes. They had both tried several times to attack the overwhelming project, but Beth would become paralyzed and quickly find an excuse not to delve into the detritus.

It soon became so daunting, that the only thing they had the energy to do was to turn their back on the problem and shut the basement door. About four years ago Beth found there wasn't much room left in the basement, and that cardboard boxes of various sizes were finding their way into spaces in their main living area. When Bunco rolled around or rare company came to visit, she would shuffle the piles into a spare room and close the door. The room was now filled with clutter, and that was no longer an option.

Their house was full of junk—her junk, and Beth didn't know how or where to start getting rid of it. What really scared her was when her normally patient husband became frustrated and told her he didn't think she *could* get rid of it. "You're choosing this junk over your family," he said when she stopped him from tossing three boxes of empty glass jars with lids into the recycle can. He came just short of using the

"H" word, and while she knew she surely couldn't be a hoarder, she was deeply ashamed.

The thought of what needed to be done to reclaim their home left her panicked, but right now she didn't have time for the luxury of feeling sorry for herself. She needed to check in on her dad, buy groceries for him, get Katy and Joe something for lunch, and finally get them settled into some sort of quiet activity, so she could attend to her four clients this afternoon. She was able to keep her professional life clutter free, and her basement salon remained the only room in the house that gave the appearance of being neat and tidy.

Recently, her friends from the Bunco Club had visited her father occasionally, and it had helped, but she was always too busy playing catch-up to have it be of any major benefit. Beth had seriously thought quitting Bunco would give her a little relief, especially when it was her turn to host. Why had she allowed Lettie to talk her out of it last summer? Now she was faced with the task of trying to make her house look clean and clutter-free in a few short weeks. She loved the Bunco Club and the women who had become her only escape from an overwhelming life, but Beth couldn't see how she was going to be ready to host on time.

Katy shuffled into the kitchen. "Hi, Mom, I'm hungry."

...And we're off to the races.

Chapter 4

"I get to pick."

"Who made you boss?"

"You picked last time. Mom said I could pick this time."

"No way. You always pick some dumb girl thing."

"Why don't you each just go to a different TV?" But Beth knew why.

"No, we want to watch together," said Katy.

"Yeah, it's no fun to watch alone."

It was a twin thing. "Please, just agree on something and settle down. I've got to get to Grandpa's." Beth picked up her shopping list and shoved it into her back pocket. She slid her cell phone into her purse and grabbed her car keys. "I'll be back soon. You guys know the rules—don't open the door for *anyone*, and call Dad or me if you need anything."

The kitchen phone rang, she needed to get going and was reluctant to answer. She checked the caller ID— 'Heritage Manor'. Beth picked up the receiver.

"Beth, it's Ben Delaney. I've got some good news for you."

Sensing what Ben was about to say, Beth lowered herself into the chair with the coats and jackets, causing a pile of objects to sway next to her. She caught an empty Cheerios box before it hit the floor. "Yes?"

"We have an opening ready for George. We'll prepare his suite over the next few days, and he should be able to move in on Monday."

"Oh, that was fast." Even though this had been in the works for months.

"The Manor has a packet of information prepared to help you through this transition period, as well as several medical and personal forms that are necessary to be filled out.

Any papers that need to be notarized can be signed here. We have a notary on the premises." Ben stopped. "Did I catch you at a bad time?"

"Yeah, I mean no. I'm just feeling a little anxious—no, make that guilty. I feel so damn…" she let the sentence trail off because she didn't really know how she felt.

"I understand Beth, and after doing this for many years, I can tell you this is the hardest part. You'll find that once George has settled in, he's going to love it here."

The reassuring words helped to momentarily calm her, "Thanks, Ben. I hope you're right."

"I've seen it over and over. We'll make it a point to involve George in the community, and he'll soon have more of a social life than you do."

That wouldn't be too hard. Beth took a very deep breath and sighed, "I guess it's the best thing for him. At least this is what he claims he wants to do. I admit that knowing you'll be there every day lessens my uncertainties."

"I'll keep a close eye on him, but it won't be long before you see your Dad being very active." Beth thought of her dad's missing legs and wondered just how active he could be. "Do you want to pick up the packets or would it be easier if I dropped them off at your house?"

Good lord, she didn't want him anywhere near her house. "I'm on my way over to Dad's right now, and I'll swing by the Manor to get them."

"If I'm not in my office my secretary will have them, and if you want to see where his rooms will be have her page me, and I'll give you the tour."

"That sounds good. I'll see you soon."

Chapter 5

With an enormous amount of effort, by Sunday night everything had fallen into place for George Munro to be admitted to Heritage Manor the next morning. A manila folder held three thick stacks of paper-clipped Heritage Manor forms that had taken Tim and George hours to fill-out and then locate the appropriate medical and financial information. Beth, near zombie-like, had moved through her old family home gathering items from the checklist that the Manor had provided. Her father would need and want to take personal and necessary items to his new apartment. She boxed and bagged the essential objects and stacked them by the door. Heather was a huge help at the Stevenson's home by supervising the twins, schlepping them to and from various activities throughout the weekend, and making sure they didn't eat candy and junk food the whole time their parents were occupied with Grandpa.

The clock on the microwave read 8:05—*just 20 minutes to get the twins fed and out the door to the bus.* "Joey, find your gym clothes," Beth called up the stairs as she continued to slather peanut butter on slices of bread for Katy and Joe's lunch. *I need to get some lunchmeat sometime today for the rest of the week. I wish I had made the appointment at the Manor for later in the morning. We still need to get Dad and all of his stuff in the car and over there by…* Her train of thought was cut off by her daughter's voice.

"Is Grandpa going to be all right?"

"Of course, pumpkin. Why do you think he wouldn't be?"

"You seem so crabby all the time. I thought there might be something wrong that you're not telling us. Then I thought that maybe if I'd been a better granddaughter—you know, like maybe I could have visited him more, or called him more, he wouldn't want to move away, and you'd be happier."

"Oh, Katy," Beth pulled her scared girl into her arms, "You've been a perfect granddaughter to Grandpa and he loves you. He's so proud of all of you kids." She stroked Katy's hair and lifted her daughter's chin so they could look eye-to-eye. "Grandpa's moving has nothing to do with you, really it doesn't. He doesn't want to live in the house all alone anymore, so he's moving to a new home, that's all. Grandpa wants to be able to make friends with people his own age and have some fun. Do you understand?"

Katy nodded her head and swiped at her nose with the back of her hand, "I really do love Grandpa, and I'll try to be better."

"He knows you love him. We have to be happy for his decision to move. I'm sorry if I've been cranky lately and made you upset." Beth's eyes went to the clock again. "Let's make this a new start for all of us today and be happy about the changes. Now, we've got to get Joey and you out the door and to school on time."

Chapter 6

The cold spell had snapped, and the temperature hovered near a balmy 38-degrees as Tim pulled the car out of the cluttered garage. They could barely fit one of their vehicles into the two-and-a-half car space. On their way to George's house, Beth fussed with the folder of papers, looking them over again as if she might find one that would say, "You've been punked! This really isn't happening!"

George was waiting. And smiling. And excited.

"You look great, Dad," She bent to kiss him and her words worked their way around the lump in her throat. Her father had dressed in his best suit and tie. *He's from a different generation.*

"This is a big day, and I want to look my best."

"Are you ready? Would you like one final spin around the place?"

"No, this hasn't been home to me since your mother died. I've only been biding my time here, until I see her again. I'm anxious to get a new start. I know she'd want me to."

Beth smiled, but it felt like a sad smile as she took hold of the handles of the wheelchair and said, "Allow me to do the honor of pushing you toward your new start." George wiggled his shoulders back and sat straight in his chair, as she wheeled him over the threshold of the home he had shared with his beautiful bride since they were first married so very many years ago.

Things clipped along at a rapid pace as soon as they entered Heritage Manor.

They were brought to the intake area, where Beth noted the carpeted room was more personable and homey than your typical sterile office. A small grouping of a sofa, several wing-backed chairs, and end tables served as a welcoming area for extended family that might join the new resident on move-in day. There was even a toy box to occupy grandchildren or great-grandchildren. Filing cabinets, copy machines, and other workplace paraphernalia were discretely hidden from view. A staff member, Bill, seated the three of them around an oak kitchen-style table and offered beverages in glasses with ice and finger sandwiches on china plates. Another staff member, Amy, asked for the packet of forms, and then she sat at the table with them explaining the procedures, notarizing signatures, and making the transition much less scary than Beth feared it might be. She wondered if Ben's staff took this much time with all the new residents, or if the extra attention was out of courtesy to their friendship. Whichever, Beth couldn't have been more grateful for the consideration the staff was showing her father.

Ben showed up just as Amy was finishing the final form. Either he had ESP, or someone alerted him that George was ready to see his new digs. Tim pushed the wheelchair, while Beth and Ben lead the procession and chatted. As they approached George's room, Beth became aware that several women were sneaking peeks at her father. She even saw two white-haired ladies giggling as he passed by. When they reached his suite, Ben handed George the keys, and said, "We encourage you to lock your doors. We don't really have a theft problem, but with the number of people that come and go from the Manor, it's a good practice. We have the ability to enter at any time if there is an emergency, but we will always respect your privacy. As per your instructions, we'll give Beth a set of keys, too." Ben smiled at him. "Go ahead, George, this is your new home."

Slipping the key into the lock and turning the knob, Beth thought she saw his hand shake ever so slightly. She wasn't sure if he felt excited or scared—possibly a combination of both—just like her. As he wheeled himself from room to room, Beth followed behind. He had a living room with a nice view of the snow-covered golf course, a small but efficient handicapped-accessible kitchenette with an eat-in area, a spacious wheelchair-accessible bathroom, and a good-sized bedroom. A knock sounded at the door, and Beth asked, "Do you want me to get that?"

"Would you, please?"

Beth opened the door to an older woman carrying a pair of bowling shoes. Her hair was white and stylish with a few darker hairs scattered throughout, she wore a pink athletic outfit and said, "Hello, my name is Daisy Canfield. And on behalf of the 'Over-the-Hill-Bowlers,' I'd like to welcome Mr. Munro to the Manor and extend an invitation for him to join our bowling team." Daisy poked her head around Beth to glimpse Mr. Munro and held out her hand to shake.

Beth started to speak, to explain to Daisy that her father was a double amputee, when George nudged her aside. "Why it's my pleasure to meet you, Ms. Canfield…"

"Oh, please, just call me Daisy. We're very informal around here, aren't we, Ben?"

Ben chuckled, "Yes, Daisy, we're like an extended family. May I formally introduce George Munro to you?"

"Hello, George. Would you be interested in joining our bowling team? I want to get a jump on the other teams and get first dibs on the new man-about-the-Manor."

Daisy winked at Ben, and this time he laughed out loud. "Daisy, you are shameless. The rest of the league will be furious when they find out that you've already snared poor George here for your Over-the-Hill team."

"Well," said Daisy, "You know what they say about the early bird. What do you say, George?"

Beth wondered if it was possible that no one in the room noticed her father's legs were missing.

"I would be flattered to join the team. But there might be a small problem. Well, actually, two small problems." He tapped his knees.

"Nonsense," Daisy said. "We have wheelchair-accessible lanes, and I can tell by the size of those muscles that you won't have any trouble handling a bowling ball."

This woman is flirting with my father! But Tim, Ben, and George were all grinning like they were in high school, and the head cheerleader had just said 'Hi' to them.

"Let me give you my room number," Daisy said. "Oh, and my cell number, too. Call me when you get settled, and I'll give you a personal tour of the place."

"Daisy Canfield!" A female voice from the hall called out.

"I should have known you'd be here first," another woman said, as the two walked up to George's door. "I imagine you've already snagged this new fella for your sorry bowling team."

Daisy stood her ground, "Why, yes I have. Charlotte and Thelma, this is George."

George had not had this much female attention since about 1962. The four seniors chatted amiably, while Beth motioned for Ben and Tim to join her in the next room. "My God, Dad's going to need a social secretary."

"They love when someone new comes to the community," Ben said. "It's practically a stampede to see who can get over here fastest." Beth peeked around the corner. Her father was shaking hands with two men—one held a golf putter. "Those two guys are part of the Thursday afternoon poker club. I'm sure they're recruiting George for a little Texas Hold 'em"

"That sounds like fun," Tim said, "and he's actually pretty good at that game."

Ben handed Beth a set of keys for her father's apartment. "My suggestion is for you two to help George unpack and settle in a little, and then leave him to get acquainted with the other residents. We're having an indoor mini-golf tournament this afternoon and the place is buzzing about it. Johnny Meyer has won the championship for the last three months straight. Talk has it that his competition has been practicing for weeks to strip him of the title." Ben smiled at Beth, "I'm sure the social director will be signing George up for a slot in the tournament. The course is also wheelchair friendly."

"Sounds like Dad's in for a wild ride. At this point it appears as though all of my fears were for nothing."

George wheeled into the kitchen where the three of them were standing, and said, "Everyone is coming back in about an hour, and we're going to lunch together."

"I'll leave you to organize your belongings. I'm happy you joined us George, and welcome to Heritage Manor." Ben shook George's hand and left the apartment. Beth heard him teasing Daisy as he closed George's door.

"Wow, Dad, this place is awesome. Can I come and live with you?"

"I have a feeling I'm going to like it here."

Chapter 7

Beth visited her father every day for the rest of the week, but it soon became apparent that she might be overdoing it. George kept busy with activities, and she often had to hunt him down just to tell him she had come to chat. On Friday she took the plunge and told him, "I've got things to do with the kids for the next few days. I won't be able to get back here until maybe Wednesday afternoon."

"No problem, honey. I just signed up for an overnight bust trip to a casino in Wisconsin this weekend. Burt and I are going to room together."

Beth knelt down and hugged him. "Oh, Dad, I'm so proud of you. I'm really happy you're enjoying yourself. You *are* enjoying yourself, aren't you?"

"Beth, I finally know what they mean when they say the 'Golden Years.' "

Driving home, Beth felt a sense of freedom—which immediately led her to feel guilty. "I'm not going to do this to myself. It *does* feel good to have some free time." *Free time…yeah, right.* She now had to clean out her parents' home so she could put it up for sale. The thought almost brought her to tears. Her new found freedom came with some very time-consuming strings attached.

At dinner that night Tim said, "I've come up with a plan for clearing out your parents' house." They were in the living room, Beth, Tim, and Heather seated on a sofa with TV trays, and the twins sitting cross-legged on the floor, plates of food in front of them. They were all aimed at the television.

Beth set her fork down, steepled her hands, and rested her forehead on them. "I think I've reached my breaking point. I don't have a clue what to do."

"You set a date that's convenient for you, and *I'll* call your brothers and sister. They can get their butts back here and help with this." One of Beth's brothers became furious that she had dared to 'throw' their Dad into a home. Her sister had already sent a long list of the items she wanted Beth to pack up and ship to her from their parent's house. "This burden has been your sole responsibility for long enough. You're ready to crack under the stress, and *I* will be happy to inform all of them that if they don't get back here and help—you will *not* be shipping them anything."

Beth had rarely ever seen her husband lose his temper. His raised voice and red face told her he had her back with her siblings. "Make the calls," she told him.

They desperately needed to get out from under this new worry and be able to focus on their own family. Her chat with Katy this morning confirmed that she was being perceived as "crabby all the time" by her twelve-year-old. This craziness *had* to stop, or she would live to regret it. In addition, Heather would graduate from high school in four short months, and if everything went as planned, she would be leaving for college in August.

"But before we deal with George's house, we need to discuss our home. It's *our* turn, Beth. And you need to get to a happy place again."

Beth felt tears pool in her eyes. "I'm so sorry, Tim. I feel like such a failure as a mother and wife and even daughter."

"We've been over this before—you've spread yourself too thin. It's not your fault. Life got in our way, and things got out of control. We did the best we could, but with George at Heritage Manor, we're finally going to have some time to take care of ourselves for a change. We'll start here." He pointed his finger on the sofa and poked it several times for emphasis. "We can begin tomorrow if you want. You decide what's best for you. From now on, I want to see *you* at the top of everyone's list around here." He smiled at his exhausted wife. "After dinner give me two dates that will work for you some time after you host Bunco—four days each, and I'll call the troops. One way or another this job will get done, and you're going to have some help doing it."

Later that evening Tim gave her the results of his phone calls. Two of her siblings would be there to help, but her eldest brother would not. George Junior didn't want anything to do with *ripping* the house out from under Dad after his father had been *forced* into a nursing home by Beth. Tim described to his wife that he was so angry at Junior, he could barely be civil, but he had calmly explained, again, that George Sr. was the one who made the decision to go to a *retirement home*, and he was very happy there. "At that point I immaturely suggested that if he didn't like what my exhausted and overworked wife had done, perhaps he should have moved back here and taken over his father's caregiving. That's when he hung up on me."

"Oh, Tim!"

"He's a self-serving ass, Beth. Always has been and always will be. But the good news is the other two are willing to do whatever needs to be done. They both had high praise for what you've done and even expressed guilt in not helping earlier." Tim held his wife in his arms and suggested they not dwell on her brother. "One thing's for sure, Junior can't be changed. So let's focus on our own life."

"But how do we start?"

"Number one, and this is not up for discussion, you need rest." As Beth started to object, he stopped her, "You have been burning the candle at both ends for too long, and you are almost out of wax. If you don't get caught up with your sleep, you aren't going to be any good to anyone." He pulled her closer into his arms again, and for those few moments she felt sheltered from her problems.

"I know you have Bunco Club here in about two-and-a-half weeks, and I've come up with two plans. I have an idea what to do with a lot of this junk so you can get through Bunco night. When that's behind you, we can start on our house." Tim mapped out his first plan where they would leave their car on the driveway and shove all the junk into the garage. "Plan B: we start right in, tomorrow if you're ready, and see what we can get done by the time the Bunco gals arrive. Anything we can't get to, will then take a trip to the garage for temporary storage."

"I vote for Plan B," Beth said. "Let's see how far we can get."

"Let's face it, most of this stuff hasn't seen the light of day for years, and it's time to throw it out." The thought of a fresh start seemed within reach, and that thought alone made Beth feel better. But the idea of throwing things out caused her internal panic. "It's not going to be done overnight, but if we stick to the plan, we might have a clean house for Heather's graduation party."

"Now that I'm not visiting Dad every day, I could get a little jump on some of the stuff in here." She swept her arm out across the family room. "I could probably get through several boxes and piles in a day."

"And when I get home, I can go through several more."

"We'll make a pile for things we can donate to that thrift shop in town. The proceeds go to the women's shelter. I like the thought that our junk might help someone. I'll have another pile for stuff we're keeping."

"Beth, we're going to need to be aggressive and ruthless and throw most of the stuff away. I know how you struggle with that, but we're at the tipping point where we *have* to do it now, or be forever buried with clutter. I know that's not going to be easy for you, but I'll help."

"I know. I know. I've been trying to figure out how to overcome the fear. I'm very aware it's irrational, but that doesn't make it any easier. I keep going over what you said that time, that I was choosing the junk over the family. Not only is it true, but it opened my eyes to how selfish I've been."

"You are a lot of thing things, Beth Stevenson, and selfish isn't one of them. Let's call it a quirk."

"Okay, so my quirk," she made air quotations with her fingers, "needs to be snuffed out. I *will* do this. I *have* to do this. Every piece of useless crap I pick up I will ask, "Do I want *you* or do I want my family?" "

"Great idea, let's make our motto 'one box at a time.' "

"I'm going to make that my mantra when I feel panic bubbling up inside—one box at a time."

"And when your brother and sister arrive, then your mantra should be, 'they're only here for four days. I can stand anything for four days.' "

As she did every night, Beth went to bed hopeful yet anxious to face her demons.

Chapter 8

Over the next week, Beth visited George only twice at Heritage Manor. They were short visits, because he now had a busy social calendar with 'The Gang' as he called his new group of friends. One night at dinner Beth repeated the phrase to her family, and Joey, her very serious, very literal son said, "Is Grandpa in a gang?"

Beth kept all of her afternoon appointments at the salon without a hitch and had her mornings free for whatever she wanted to do. What she really wanted to do was spend her mornings quilting. But right now, she could almost taste the joy she would soon have by being freed from the junk that imprisoned her. So, she did the one thing she was unable to do for the past ten years. She dug in.

Immediately the terror rose up, and just as quickly she thought to herself, *One box at a time…you or my family*. By the end of the week, Beth was amazed at what she had accomplished. She worked fast as she personally handled over half of the items in the room, regrouped, organized, and stored them in appropriately labeled plastic tubs. One by one she carried the containers downstairs where she shoved, pushed, piled, and restacked them into neat new towers that were "double-parked". The basement looked so neat and spacious she didn't think Tim would realize what she had done. Someday she would attack the problem when her panic was under control.

Early Saturday morning Tim loaded up the van and took the first of many loads to the thrift shop. What he didn't know was that this was the easy part for Beth—if someone could use her old stuff, she could much more easily part with it. He then went to the local Wal-Mart, and picked up a number of plastic bins in various sizes for items that Beth was insisting on keeping. As he carried the containers into the room he said, "If we're getting rid of things, why don't we have more empty bins?"

"Oh, we will when this is all over with, but for now I needed some new ones."

"Hmpf. I don't get it."

"It'll all work out, Hon, we just need to keep moving forward." Beth feared he was catching on to her deceit. "Let's start packing the rest of this stuff into the garage, and we'll have the three most important rooms cleared out for Bunco."

By the time they had slogged through the first week they had a clutter-free first floor. After Tim left for work, but before the trash collector came, Beth had retrieved most of what her husband put out by the curb. *It's just a temporary compromise, I'll get this all figured out someday when I have more time.*

On Monday, with the kids back at school and Tim at work, Beth was looking forward to cleaning and scrubbing her clutter free rooms. She was feeling guilty for being dishonest with her husband, but secure in the knowledge that she had prevented herself untold panic attacks. She'd deal with the consequences later. By the time her afternoon appointments were due to arrive, she had a clean, yes, clean family room. *One box at a time…one room at a time…one deceit at a time.*

Beth yakked to her clients that afternoon, and her mind flip-flopped between guilt and happiness. She had to admit that consolidating the upstairs junk into the bins in the basement and then reorganizing the lot had been a stroke of genius. Not only was the upstairs clutter-free but the basement looked tidy, and she began to think that maybe she could squeeze out a little sewing room somewhere in the house. She realized what a difference a clutter-free home had already made in the family's attitude. The kids seemed happier and were willing to clean up after themselves. So if she had to fudge things a smidgen, so what. This way everyone was happy.

That night, sitting in their freshly cleaned family room, she talked it over with Tim. They planned that once all the useless items and mess had been cleared away, *wink-wink,* they could put up some drywall and construct a room just for Beth and her quilting. Tim told her, "It makes me sad to think we've been so overloaded that you haven't had much quilting time these past few years."

"At least I get to camp every March. You wouldn't believe how much that helps." She smiled at Tim. "And now, with the possibility of having my own sewing room looming on the horizon, I'm feeling even more motivated to get rid of this mess as soon as possible." *I am such a scumbag liar.*

"You know," Tim said, and as soon as Beth heard the hesitation in his voice she stiffened, "you don't *have* to keep the salon going if you don't want to. We can make it fine if you need a break. You might even want to give it a brief shut-down and see how you feel about it."

Beth knew he was trying to be kind by suggesting that she needn't work as hard, "That's an interesting idea, but I really do enjoy my clients. There were times when the salon was the only thing that kept me sane over the past ten years. For me, it's not about the money, it's more about, I don't know, pride? Routine? Stability?" She sighed and her shoulders slumped. "It's hard to explain, but when my whole world seemed to be crumbling around me, I had the reassurance of a schedule, and the personalities of my clients to look forward to. It's just a comfort that I can count on, I guess."

"Oh, I see," Tim teased. "You mean in case your bum of a husband leaves you in the lurch." He put an arm around her and said into her hair, "That will *never* happen, my love."

Chapter 9

The Stevenson household currently had more order than it had had for years, and Beth saw very positive signs in her children. The kids could look forward to having friends over and not be embarrassed. It made her more determined than ever to continue her charade by staying one step ahead of the clutter and keeping it well organized. Bunco was at the forefront of her mind, and for the first time in years, she wasn't dreading it. What she *was* dreading was planning and preparing the food. She had never enjoyed anything culinary, and often wondered where in the world her daughter acquired a love for cooking. Thinking that Heather might be interested in helping her plan the menu or possibly even the food preparation, she developed a scheme that she hoped would open her daughter's eyes to her talents.

That evening, Beth lay out her cookbooks at the kitchen table and started working on the menu. Eventually Heather wandered into the kitchen. "What's up?"

"Oh, I'm just trying to figure out what to serve at Bunco, you know how much I hate doing this. I especially want to make it special, with the clean house and all. I thought I might even pull off some surprises, but I just can't figure anything out." *Now for the hook…* "Any ideas?"

"Hmmm, let me see what you have so far."

And the line… "Thanks, I could really use the help."

After an hour of bonding over food and recipes, they had come up with a knock-out menu. Beth baited the final hook with a small bribe. "I'll pay you to help me get this stuff ready next Wednesday."

"Really?" *Teenagers are such suckers when it comes to money.*

Now for the sinker…"Yeah, and I'll make it worth your time if you help me serve." Beth smiled sweetly at her daughter, like honey dripping from a hive.

"Okay, I'm down with that."

Beth mentally reeled in her catch.

<u>Bunco Menu</u>

Risotto with Scallops

Artichoke Dip* Dill Pickle Dip

*****

Caprese Salad

Oven Roasted Mostaccioli

Italian Sausage Bread

****

Pop & Water

Popcorn - M & M's

chocolate covered raisins - mini Snickers

***

Heather's Tiramisu

Earl Grey DeCaf

*recipe at back of book

To Beth, the menu belonged in a gourmet restaurant and not for a group of chocolate-crazed Bunco players. When Heather pulled this off, she would receive compliments and respect from every woman that night. Hopefully it would boost her confidence, and give her the motivation she needed to follow her dreams toward a career in the culinary arts.

Heather had complained it was a shame that Bunco wasn't on Monday, that way she could have used Sunday for preparations. She made a complete list of the ingredients that would be needed, and asked her mom to have them in the house by the time she got home from school on Tuesday. Heather talked about the 'tablescape' she had in mind, and Beth gave her free-reign to do whatever she thought looked best. "This is so much fun," Heather said as she looked through Beth's fabric stash, pulling out pieces of cloth and draping them on top of others to see how they looked together. A box of miscellaneous candles and candlesticks that had been unearthed in the clean-up was added to her treasures, and she poked around and found three quilts that Beth had made a long time ago and stored for safe-keeping.

"Since this is a quilting group and it's February, I think I'm going to play up the whole Valentine idea. I'm going to use the 'Wedding Ring' quilt as my base, and the rest of the theme will revolve around that. Can you pick up some fresh flowers on Wednesday?" Heather said. "It doesn't matter what they are, as Tim Gunn would say, I'll make it work."

Heather busied herself in the kitchen after school on Tuesday. Beth thought to herself that this had turned out to be the best Bunco she had hosted in years. Her house looked clean and presentable, someone else labored over the food preparation, and the cooking was even being done for her. *It just couldn't get any better.* "What can I do to help, darlin'?"

"I've got it under control. Just keep Katy and Joe out of my hair." *Spoken like a true older sister.*

Beth always cleared her appointments for three or four days prior to Bunco being at her house, so she could shuffle her junk around and get prepared for guests. Not wanting to invade Heather's space, she actually found herself with some time on her hands. "I'll be in the basement if you need me." She decided she could tighten up some of the holes between the stacks of tubs to make it a little more compact...*every little bit helps.* The smell of cake baking for the Tiramisu soon wafted down the stairs. Beth heard the metallic and rhythmic sound of a whisk clinking against a stainless steel bowl, and beaters purring as they whipped some unknown mixture into a froth.

Several hours later, Joe came bounding down the stairs from spending the afternoon at a friend's house, "Hi, Mom. I'm starved, and Heather won't let me in the kitchen."

"Heather's helping me by fixing all the food for Bunco tomorrow night." She straightened up, arched her back, and kneaded the lower portion with her fist. "Dad's picking up Katy from Megan's and is getting pizza from The Depot. So dinner will be here soon."

"Bunco is here? Cool!" Joe said. "Need any help?"

"Well, actually if you could drag those two bags out to the trash, it would be really helpful. They're pretty heavy." She knew the appearance of garbage was important, and there were several items that Beth had labored over tossing. In the end, she decided if her chest grew tight and felt on fire for throwing them out, she could always retrieve them from the trash when no one was looking.

"Sure, I really like when the house is clean." He struggled to pick up both of the overstuffed plastic garbage bags. "I can't wait until all this junk is out of our house. I'll be right back for the other bag."

Beth had made remarkable progress in the two-and-a-half weeks since she started clearing away the clutter. She thought of everything that had been accomplished as a bonus. They hadn't thought they'd be able to start work on their own home until after her father's house had finally landed in the hands of a competent realtor, and here they were—three rooms cleared out and the basement looking great. *I wonder if Tim would notice if I "triple-parked" the bins?*

She thought about a recent visit to Heritage Manor as she had explained, well actually lied, to her dad about how she was cleaning and reorganizing their home. George assured her that he was keeping plenty busy. "I'm anything but lonely, so don't trouble over me at all. We can keep in touch by phone," he told his daughter. "I think I'm going to get one of those smart phones. Everyone has one." Beth had to laugh. Her father sounded like he was fifteen years old, and was trying to keep up with his buddies. She snapped back to the present when she heard Tim and Katy come home with the pizza.

Her husband came down a few steps and said, "Pizza's here. Looks like you've got your own personal caterer."

"Yeah, I'm going to be spoiled real quick if this keeps up," Beth said loud enough for Heather to hear.

"After dinner, I told Heather I'd be on clean-up detail for her."

Beth whispered this time, "That was nice, thanks."

"She's working her butt off, and I'm really impressed," he said. "How are you holding up?"

"Tired, but happy."

"Come on up, and we'll all have some dinner."

Heather leaned against the counter and munched on a slice of pepperoni pizza. Beth could just about see confidence oozing from her daughter, like syrup from a maple tree. Beth looked around at the work her daughter had done and said, "Heather, this is unbelievable, you're such a natural at this—look how beautiful." She gave Heather a big hug, "I'm so impressed with you."

"Honest, this has really been fun, and the kitchen is so nice and clean to work in. I've been thinking, maybe I should go to culinary school like you guys suggested." Beth held her breath as Heather continued, "Maybe after I graduate from there, I could work in a restaurant for a while, and then open my own catering business or something." She looked from Tim to Beth. "What do you think?"

Beth wanted to say, *'It's about time,'* but instead she said, "That sounds like a great plan. What do you think, Dad?"

They talked of Heather's future and decided that the weekend Beth would be busy with her brothers and sister, Tim and Heather would search the Internet for culinary schools and the details for enrollment. Tim said he'd talk to one of the advisors at the community college and see if she had any suggestions. The ball was rolling, and Beth couldn't believe how quickly their out-of-control-life had done a complete turnaround.

And, to top it off, all of her treasures were hidden and safe.

Chapter 10

It was the day of Bunco and after the kids left for school that morning, Beth sat down and read through Heather's instructions. Since her daughter wouldn't get home from school until about 3:00 that afternoon, she had requested some help from her mom to get a few things organized. Beth needed to get cut flowers at the store and do a little prep work in the kitchen. Heather had requested her to find some "pretty" serving dishes.

Most of what Beth owned paled in comparison to the fancy dishes her mother had used and cherished. In the mess of the past ten years, Beth hadn't given them much thought, but she made up her mind to go over to her dad's house and retrieve a few for Heather's debut tonight.

After spending much more than she normally would for fresh-cut flowers, Beth entered her parents' home. It already had a touch of that odd closed-up smell houses get when no one uses them on a daily basis. Beth took her coat off and went directly to the china cabinet. Her feelings surprised her, and she took a moment to let them envelop her. As busy as she'd been with her father since her mom had died, she hadn't let herself think too much about Barbara Munro. Looking at these odd little miss-matched pieces her mother had cherished so much brought fresh tears to her eyes.

She held the 'birthday cake plate' her mom always used on their birthdays and hugged it to her chest. "Oh, Mom, I miss you so much. I wish you were here to see how much Heather looks like you and how she also loves to cook." Beth was swept away by her emotions and memories—funny what one old serving plate could evoke. "I've needed your help and advice so many times."

Standing in front of the hutch, Beth became possessive of these fragile reminders of her mother and grandmother.

Not the type of person who sought revenge, she had long ago squelched any feelings of anger and resentment toward her siblings for leaving her to carry the load by herself. But, by God, they were *not* going to swoop in here and split up Mom's treasure of eclectic china. There were several empty boxes in her car, and Beth went back to retrieve two of them. Looking around, she spotted a few newspapers that were left over from the day she had taken Dad to the Manor.

As she wrapped up and crowded the treasures into a box, she allowed herself the luxury to stop and caress an individual piece that reminded her of some special fleeting moment with her mom. The whole process didn't take long, because there wasn't a tremendous amount to be pilfered. *Pilfered—what the heck am I doing?* She hesitated only a split second and then continued. *No, I've spent the last ten years here, which should count for something. If Heather is truly going to pursue a career in culinary arts, I want to pass these special things on to her.* Beth knew her daughter would appreciate them, and unlike the twins was also old enough to connect some of them to memories of Grandma Barb. One final thing would make its way home with her—her mother's handwritten cookbook. *I hope someday this will be a treasure for Heather.*

Needing to confess to her father, Beth drove straight to Heritage Manor. As she sat in front of him, she felt like a guilty five-year-old and fought the temptation to turn around, go back to his house, and put everything back where she had found it.

"Well," George said, "I'd like to see those other three just *try* to say you don't deserve whatever you want from *my* house. I want you to take those items, and when Heather proves herself as a chef, or whatever it is she's doing, you pass them on to her at the right time. Her Grandma Barb would be happy for her granddaughter to own and cherish them." George had eased her mind, but he started to work up a head of steam. "And when that whiney sister of yours claims she's been waiting for me to die to get her hands on them, tell her *I* gave them to you for Heather." He crossed his arms over his chest, gave Beth a wicked smile, and punctuated his comments by adding, "End of story."

They chatted for a few more minutes over a cup of tea, until someone knocked on the door. "Come on in," George called.

Daisy Canfield opened the door and said, "Oh, excuse me. I can come back later."

"Nonsense," George waved his hand for her to enter. "You remember my daughter, Beth, don't you?"

"Why, of course. How do you do?"

"Have a seat, Daize. We were just talking about the vultures that will soon be coming to empty out my house."

Daize…vultures…?

"Oh, yes, your father told me the other two were coming back home to go through the house, but the oldest son couldn't be bothered."

"Before they get here," George said, "I'd like you to get over to my house and take anything you, Tim, or the kids might like. You get first dibs." Daisy and George shared a hearty laugh.

"Sure, Dad." Grasping at straws she said, "Tim might like some of your tools or fishing equipment."

"Take it. And anything else your family wants before the others get here. Tell them I threw it out years ago, and since they never visited me, they'll never know. Let's face it, they probably won't be back again until my funeral." Again George and Daisy laughed as though he had just said the funniest thing in the world. "Anyway, I've got everything I want right here."

Holy cow! Is this my father talking? On her way out of the Manor she thought again of her dad and said aloud, "More power to him." What a lively old fart he'd turned out to be.

Carefully choosing which would be the best serving dishes to show off Heather's feast tonight, she loaded the dishwasher with the items that were dishwasher-safe and hand-washed and dried the rest. Chuckling to herself, she realized that she had spent the last two weeks allegedly getting rid of stuff, and here she was bringing things into the house. But these were sentimental family heirlooms and they deserved a place of honor in her home. She only hoped that one day some of her quilts would fit that description in her children's hearts. Next, Beth wrapped her mother's cookbook in tissue paper and stored it in a secret spot. *If* Heather went to culinary school, Beth would present this to her on graduation day. The thought made her happy.

At five minutes to three, Heather threw open the door and shouted, "Mooom, I'm hooome!" Beth had made sure she had done everything on Heather's list. "I need to get the mostaccioli noodles marinating in the olive oil. I know the recipe says to do it for only an hour, but I prefer to infuse them a little longer."

Beth handed Heather a glass full of Pepsi with ice and stepped out of her way. "When the twins get home from school, can you keep them out of the kitchen and dining room? I don't want them messing anything up."

"Dad is collecting them and keeping them busy this afternoon. Then he's taking them out to eat somewhere. By the time they get home, they'll go directly to bed."

Heather squealed, "Where did you get these beautiful serving dishes? Are they antiques?"

"I take it you approve? Look carefully. Are they familiar in any way?" She explained the story behind the items to her daughter as they worked together to make this a perfect night. "By the time you take possession of them," Beth told her, "they will have been through four generations. If you pass them on to your son or daughter— that will make five."

"I went to the senior advisor today, and she gave me a list of culinary schools. I might be too late to apply to some of them, but she said to try anyway because sometimes kids end up not going."

"That sounds promising. We'll see what Dad came up with from Sauk Trail."

Heather stopped what she was doing and looked at her mom. She became contrite. "I should have listened to you guys all along. You were right, you know."

"Oh, Heather, it doesn't matter who's right or wrong. We're just happy you have a focus, and," Beth looked around eying the kitchen and nodding approval, "one that you seem to have a natural talent for."

"Thanks, Mom." Heather gave Beth a long and rare hug. "I love you."

"I love you, too, sweetheart."

352

Chapter 11

"You've been busy," Lettie, the first to arrive, said. "It looks wonderful in here." Burning candles perfumed the family room with a cinnamon apple scent, and Beth was actually able to hang Lettie's coat in the hall closet. The other women straggled in and tote bags, which promised a good night of show-and-tell, were deposited on the sofa. One by one everyone complimented Beth on how great her house looked.

"I can't believe how much more time I have now that Dad is at the Manor. He seems so happy, and that's such a relief for me."

Helen said, "Ben tells me he's keeping busy and making lots of new friends."

"That's probably the understatement of the year. Tim and I have been calling him King George since he moved there. I think he might even have a girlfriend or two."

"I'm glad he's getting along so well," Nancy said. "It's got to be a huge burden off your shoulders."

Beth had waited all day for this, "Let's get started with the food while it's still warm. Come into the dining room."

Phree was first to enter when Beth slid open the pocket doors to the dining room, "Did you have Bunco catered tonight? This is gorgeous."

"You might say that." The other seven women nudged and bumped elbows to get into the dining room for a better look. They stood transfixed before a beautifully set table-scape incorporating a double wedding ring quilt with complimentary swatches of fabric. Heather had taken several vases and filled them with fresh cut flowers, then completely engulfed the vases with fabric. It gave the appearance that the flowers were bursting from the cloth. Carefully placed candles contributed a soft glow to everything. The hors d'oeuvres were placed at different heights, with the luscious scallop risotto at the pinnacle. Heather and Beth had decided to use the china tonight instead of the usual paper plates, and candlelight sparked off the translucent porcelain. The results were breathtaking and unexpected.

Heather came through the connecting kitchen doorway with a small bowl of pickle dip and set it next to a chinaware basket of crackers. She said, "Hi, everyone. Please start on the hors d'oeuvres. The main course will be out in about twenty minutes." As Heather turned to leave, Beth saw a huge grin on her daughter's face.

"I dibs her next!" Nedra said.

Marge went into the kitchen and dragged a reluctant Heather back through the doorway. The women burst into applause while Heather turned a bright red. Everyone spoke at once and gave Heather high praise for her exquisite presentation. Rosa said, "I haven't even tasted the food yet, but if it's even half as good as this is lovely—you've got a ton of talent."

Shyly and a little embarrassed, like a third grader standing in front of the class to read, Heather thanked everyone and suggested they start eating. After Heather left the room Phree said, "Tell me she's going to culinary school, or I'm going to cry."

"The good news is, yes, she has agreed to go to culinary school. We just don't know where, yet."

"I don't know about the rest of you, but I'm digging in." Nancy picked up a bread-and-butter sized plate and started with the risotto. "No dieting tonight."

Helen paid close attention to Rosa for signs of her emotional state. She had taken very small portions and hadn't touched half of her food. Her eyes followed the conversation, but she offered nothing—no opinions, no wisecracks—so not Rosa. Marge discussed the after-the-holiday-get-together with Jacob and Niesha, and once again the group baby quilt became a topic.

Lettie shifted the subject to quilt camp. "What's everyone bringing to work on at camp?" While the eight women discussed the details of next month's quilt camp, Heather removed the remainder of the appetizers to a side buffet and started to prepare the table for the main course.

Rosa finally spoke, "I've been thinking I might stay home this time. What if Ricky…"

"Oh, Rosa, no! Please don't do that!"

"You can't cut yourself off from your friends and your life," Lettie said.

"I have no life," Rosa said. "My life is worry and sadness and Googling runaway websites all day."

Helen covered her mouth with both hands. "I'm so sorry, Rosa. Have you heard anything from him? Are these websites helpful?"

"We haven't heard anything except for that one call we got on Christmas day. I'm constantly checking the National Runaway Hotline, where I've left a message for him. So far he hasn't left one for me or responded in any way. I'm afraid he's dead, and that I'll never know what happened to him." With a glassy-eyed stare it was clear Rosa was beyond crying.

The room was silent for a flick of a second and Marge said, "Is there anything we can do to help…anything?"

"Truly, there is nothing that anyone can do. There's nothing even I can do but worry about him and wonder what went wrong with our lives. I know I probably don't act like it, but coming to Bunco is really good for me. Just knowing I'll be seeing all of you helps to keep me sane."

Phree splayed her hands palms up, "Would it help if we visited you? Got you out of the house once in a while? I know it probably sounds awful, but I don't think any of us know what to do. We don't want to make things worse by bugging you, yet we all want to help."

"It's a lose-lose-lose situation," Rosa said. "But I think I might be more comfortable being miserable at home than being miserable at camp. Trying to keep up small talk and pretend all is well with people that I only see once a year would be additional torture. At least with all of you I can break down if I have to." Rosa took a ragged breath, as though her intake of air was bouncing down tiny stairs in her windpipe. "It never leaves my mind."

"Let me just throw this out there," Lettie said. "What if we skip camp this year and have our own little camp at my house? We've all got the time off work already. We could do it in my studio, there's plenty of room, and anyone who wants to sleep at my house is welcome. Or if you'd rather, you could go home to your own bed for the night."

"I like it," Marge said. "It'll work—I'm in. Who else?"

Before Heather served the main course, the Bunco women had all decided they'd have a do-it-yourself quilt camp this year at Lettie's studio, so Rosa could be close to home. That's the point when Rosa cried.

Nedra changed the subject when she asked for an update on Nancy and Michael, "How was that long weekend you had out there? And when the heck is he moving back to Chicago anyway?"

Nancy gave little information about the time spent in Colorado other than to say, "We had a lot of fun, and I got a chance to see his home and studio. Both are quite impressive. I've got a few pictures on my phone. I'll show them to you when we're done eating. As far as the move goes, there's been some progress. Michael just listed his home with a realtor last week, but so far I haven't heard anything. I'm afraid with this recession, it might take a while to sell, but on the other hand, it's in a fairly exclusive and sought after area. So who knows?"

"Wow, you must be excited," Lettie said.

"We all know how I like things to be orderly," Marge said. "So I've been wondering—where do you see this going with him? Have you thought what you'd like to get out of it?"

"A husband," Helen shouted, "she wants to get a husband out of this!"

Nancy blushed and it stained her neck, "Well, I must admit a husband would be nice. But, truthfully, I'm scared to death to think of where this might go—or worse, where it might *not* go."

"Nancy, you're going to have to take a chance at some point and trust him again."

"It's just too scary. There are so many scenarios as to how this could go..."

"Well, actually, there are only two," Nedra said. "You either end up with him, or you don't. Don't allow yourself to get so hung up on the in between minutia. Let it flow, and follow your heart this time."

"That's what got me into trouble before. I was young, foolish, and in love. That's a very bad combination and I made a horrible mistake."

"Nancy, my dear, a mistake is when you wear mismatched socks or lock your keys in your car while it's running," Marge told her. "What happened to you was a life altering experience and something to learn from. It was pivotal, and you never got over it. You never forgave yourself. I speak from experience, PLEASE stop thinking of it as a mistake."

"I suppose you're right, Marge."

"So, you're not young anymore, no offense, and you're certainly not foolish, but you *are* most definitely in love. Enjoy the moment and stop borrowing trouble, for God's sake," Phree said.

Heather walked up to the table and announced, "Dinner is served over at the buffet, ladies."

"I feel like I'm at the Ritz," Nancy said.

During dinner, talk turned to Vegas. Again Rosa said, "I don't know..."

"Whatever works for you is fine," Phree said. "We understand. Let's cross that bridge when we come to it. Ricky could even be home by then."

An April date was the best timing for everyone. Phree had looked into a show for each night, and they discussed the best place to stay—some from hearsay, some from experience. Phree's travel agent had suggested a hotel that was centrally located and within walking distance to most of the strip. Four days and three nights would make a fabulous getaway. The Sarge slid her notebook from her back pocket and started taking notes.

Finishing their wonderful sit-down dinner, Marge, once again, dragged Heather from the kitchen to congratulate her on a fabulous job. "If you can pull this off at eighteen," said Phree, "imagine what you'll be doing at thirty."

"I can't wait to see what we're having for dessert."

"It's a surprise," boasted Beth.

"I've got an idea," said Helen. "Let's just skip Bunco and go straight for the dessert."

"Better yet, let's have the main course settle in our stomachs while we play Bunco, and then we can eat twice as much dessert." Nedra stood.

Marge talked to Heather and gave her several tips on how to organize her recipes. "Make sure you keep copies of all the menus you serve," she suggested. "That way if someone attended a function and wants the same food you served, you won't have to scramble your brains to figure out what you did six months ago." Heather began the process of cleanup while the women got down to the business of playing their beloved dice game.

Just as they finished the last round of Bunco and returned to the dining room, Heather brought out two steaming tea pots covered with cozies. She set them in the middle of the table, which she had arranged with mix-and-match china cups and saucers.

Beth nearly burst with pride when Nancy ran over to Heather, hugged her, and said, "Can I take you home?"

"Just wait until you taste dessert," Beth said, "you're going to kidnap her."

Phree looked at the oversized cake, covered with luscious chocolate curls, sitting on the side buffet. "Is that Tiramisu?"

Again, Beth found herself boasting, "It will be the best you ever tasted. Heather made it herself." Four of the women took a series of photos of the sweet creation with their cell phones as though the Holy Grail had just materialized before them.

Helen grabbed a side chair and set it at the table, demanding that Heather join them for dessert. Phree insisted on getting the recipe, but Marge advised Heather never to give out recipes. "Make 'em pay for it," Marge said waving her empty fork through the air and winking at Phree.

They staged a quick show-and-tell, and Helen surprised Lettie and Rosa each with a top she had quilted for them on her new long-arm machine. They agreed on a date for the next Bunco, and Nancy asked the women if they had remembered the squares of fabric she had asked them to bring.

Lettie teased Nancy, "Sure hope you've got some gossip about that boyfriend of yours by then."

Marge asked Heather if she'd be willing to help plan and cater Niesha's baby shower that she anticipated having for her. "Of course, I'll pay you," Marge added, and Heather bobbed her head.

"I've got an idea," Rosa said, and seven heads spun around to look at her. It was the first time this evening that she'd offered a thought. "Why don't we pay Heather to make our dinners for us while we're at our fake quilt camp? Maybe even our lunches."

"I *love* it!" Nancy said. "I think Whitney High is off school that week for spring break." She looked toward Heather, "Do you have other plans?"

"No, no. I'll do it."

"You can use my kitchen," Lettie said, "that is if you want to. We can work the details out." She turned to Beth, "Is that okay with you, Mom?"

"It's up to the Chef, but I'm fine, if she's interested."

"This just might be our best quilt camp ever," Helen said.

Beth handed the Bunco box to a bundled-up Nancy, "Here ya go and good luck. It'll be over with before you know it."

MARCH BUNCO – Nancy

Never say never.

Chapter 1

She had pulled it off. Even with all the drama surrounding Rosa, she had walked away from Bunco with seven little pieces of fabric. Nancy removed the six-inch square pieces from her tote bag, and laid them out in front of her, like a jeweler displaying gems. She had told the Bunco Club she was making a mystery quilt at camp, and asked each woman to bring a six-inch piece of their favorite fabric to Bunco tonight. She requested they pin or sticky-note their names to it. The miracle was that they all remembered to do it, especially Rosa.

Adding her own swatch of fabric to the others, and sliding them around on her oak table top, she could see the personalities of the women through their color and pattern choices. One piece with a small curly-cue pattern was as tightly wound as Marge, but the pastel colors showed the softer side of her friend that had only recently been exposed to the group. Lettie's choice was bold, geometric, and was contemporary in both design and color. Nancy noted her own block was much different than what she would have contributed in the past. Only a year ago she probably would have chosen a solid, dull color with no pattern or design, something like a frosty gray or gloomy green. The 'new' Nancy had opted for a daring colorful Batik, boasting bright hues with just enough dark to make the square pop.

These pieces of loomed cotton represented eight women who are all friends sharing so much of each other's lives, yet they are all so very different. Stacking the blocks and feeling a little smug about her intentions for them, the corner of her eye caught a blinking light. She had been so preoccupied with her coup, that she hadn't noticed she had voice mail. Frustrated at the thought of a call from her mother—who else could it be since all of her friends were at Bunco with her, she approached the phone as though it was a poisonous snake about to lunge. *Just get it over with. Check the caller ID and make sure it's her. But if you want any kind of sleep tonight, don't even think of listening to that message.*

The phone number was familiar and from Colorado—Michael. Nancy couldn't punch in her four-digit passcode fast enough. "Hi Nan, it's Michael. Hope you're doing well. I've got some good news I want to share with you. Give me a call when you get in, it doesn't matter how late."

He picked up on the second ring. "Hey, Nan. I'm glad you called back." She thought he sounded as though he were smiling.

"I've been at Bunco tonight and just got in."

"How were the gals?"

Nancy settled into a kitchen chair. If she thought sleep would elude her after listening to a message from her mother, she knew after talking to Michael she'd be awake for hours. But it would be worth every tired minute tomorrow. "Oh the usual—loud, fun, hungry—everyone's doing fine except for Rosa. She's really a mess worrying about her son. It's so sad, and it's been so hard on her."

"I can't imagine what she's going through. If that was Nick, I'd be out of my mind by now."

"I know. It's been rough. We're all worried about her. So, you said you had some news?"

"My realtor called me tonight, and someone put a bid on my house. They offered me a decent chunk of money over my asking price in return for being able to take possession earlier than I had planned. The realtor said that's almost unheard of in this economy, but I guess people with money are still willing to pay for a specific location."

"That's wonderful." Nancy tried not to sound too eager *or* too desperate. She rested the phone on her shoulder, filled the tea kettle with water, and set it to boiling on her stove top.

"I decided to come back to Chicago this Friday to start looking for a home for Nick and me. I hoped you might be available to join me?" It came out more as a question than a statement. "That is, if you're not busy."

"No. No…I mean yes!" Nancy laughed. "No, I'm not busy, and yes, I'd love to help in any way that I can."

"Great, I can't wait to see you again. Mom and Dad will pick us up at O'Hare. We'll get in kind of late on Friday, so I'll make sure Nick is settled and comfortable with Grandma and Grandpa. I'm hoping to be down in the south suburbs by about 10:30 on Saturday morning. Does that work for you?"

"That sounds perfect. The mother of one of the kids that I tutor is a realtor—she's pretty sharp. Would you like me to set up an appointment with her?"

"Yeah, I'd really appreciate that, if you don't mind. Otherwise I'd just be throwing a dart at the realtor listings to find someone. Let's say 11:00 in case I get tied up in traffic."

"I'll get in touch with her, and let you know what she says." Nancy scribbled 11:00 on a tablet, and caught herself drawing a little heart next to it. "Do you have any idea of what you're looking for, so I can give her a heads-up?

"I'd like a good-sized house with several acres around it. I'll custom build a studio, unless there's already an existing barn or outbuilding I can modify." Michael's high-end jewelry business had been well established for years, and he could live anywhere he chose as long as he had Internet access. "I plan on accepting the offer, so I'll need to be moved out by

May 31st. That doesn't give me as much time as I had hoped. Nick will be done with school on the 25th, so the timing is good in that respect, but it's still cutting it a little close."

"How is he handling all this?"

"Well, the good news is he's looking forward to being near his grandparents. He thinks it's such a cool adventure being in the big city." Nancy could hear the "but" coming. "Staying here doesn't seem to be helping him face reality. He sees his mom everywhere. It's almost like a fresh wound every day when he wakes up, and realizes again that she's not here."

"Do you think moving to Chicago will change that?"

"I don't know for sure, but I'm hoping it does. I don't want him to ever forget his mom, but to be healthy he needs to move on. I think the love and attention from Grandma and Grandpa sure can't hurt."

"You're probably right about that."

Chapter 2

Time to boogie. *Okay, I really need to update my clichés into this century.* Time to get my ass in gear. Keeping her Saturday morning schedule with her students until 10:00, Nancy cleared her calendar for the rest of day. Flinging her bag onto her shoulder, she locked the door to the clinic, and in ten minutes pulled into her driveway. Michael was waiting with coffee and a bag of warm cinnamon rolls, the perfect fare for a mid-morning nosh. They gave each other a quick peck, and went inside so Nancy could deposit her bag and gather the printouts the realtor had emailed her. There was about half an hour to look over the statistics of the properties and chat.

While the two would-be-lovers had talked extensively about their past, they hadn't discussed much about their future. Driving from house to house, Nancy wondered what her role really was in this process of house hunting. More to the point, she wondered what her role in Michael's future might be. Several times there were little hints and insights. As they strolled through the rooms of the mostly empty homes, Michael said, "Do you need office space in your home? Would this be enough?" and, "I can see us sitting on this deck watching the sun set when we're old and gray." Or, "Do you still love to bake? Would you like this kitchen?"

She answered all his questions, but had a burning one of her own, "And exactly *why* do you want to know these things?"

Since he needed space for a rather large studio, most of the homes they looked at didn't fit Michael's needs. The farther they drove out of the immediate suburbs and into the rural areas, the more promising the properties became. They followed the realtor down a lightly wooded private lane. The trees were bare, and several inches of snow still covered the ground. Michael leaned forward and tucked his head over the steering wheel to look from side to side and then up at the treetops as he drove through the woods, trying to catch glimpses of the home ahead.

"I like what I see so far," Michael said, as they pulled up to a very large log-cabin-style home. "It has that rustic mountain feel that both Nick and I like."

"It's beautiful, but it looks huge."

As they got out of their cars Michael said to the realtor, "I hope the inside's as nice as the outside."

"This property has 3.5 acres—about half is lightly wooded, and the other half is a grassy meadow. It's zoned rural, so you should be able to construct a studio with no problem." She shuffled through some papers, "I can tell you it has been on the market for nearly a year, and the seller is anxious. It is also empty and available immediately."

"So far, so good. I'm eager to see the inside." As soon as the realtor opened the door, Nancy had a feeling this could be just what Michael was looking for. The house was the perfect blend of rustic and elegant, and as they walked between the rooms, their excitement built. Michael pointed out which bedroom could be Nick's, and he thought the spacious dry basement would make a good recreation area for his son.

"The previous owner had a passion for movies," the realtor said as she opened another door. "This theater comfortably seats twelve people."

"Nick's going to love this. Hell, *I'm* going to love this." He turned to Nancy, and she could have peed herself when she saw his excited smile. "What about you, Nan? Would you like this?"

Nancy wanted to ask, "Permanently or occasionally?" But instead she answered him truthfully, "Yes." She would love it here. Who wouldn't? By the time they walked into the kitchen, Nancy thought if Michael didn't buy this house she would. A full bank of windows started just above the kitchen countertop and offered a stunning view overlooking an expansive backyard that was edged with trees and shrubs. An in-ground pool sat empty of water but filled with snow. The woodland appeared to go on forever, where a variety of birds flitted between the trees. The kitchen had a contemporary feel with an extraordinary amount of storage space.

Once again, Michael wanted to know what Nancy thought about the house, and she answered, "It's big. There's a lot to clean."

"I'll hire a cleaning service to come in once a week. Nick's mom and I did that right after he was born. We always thought the family time together was more important than the hours spent cleaning or fighting over it."

"Oh, of course," Nancy felt embarrassed, but didn't know why.

Michael spoke to the realtor. "I really like this, and it's just what I had in mind. If it isn't too inconvenient, would it be possible to show my son tomorrow? Nick's ten-years-old, but I want him to feel as though he's part of the decision making process. I'd also like to go over a few details first with Nancy." He smiled at Nancy, and she immediately went to her 'happy place'.

The realtor agreed to accommodate Michael's needs. For a sale this size in this economy, she'd be more than happy to walk him through again tomorrow. "You name a time that's convenient, and I'll meet you here."

"I'd like it if you could join us," Michael said to Nancy.

"Sure, I'd love to see Nick again." Nancy's stomach let rip with a loud unladylike rumble that could have rivaled the grinding teeth of a too full garbage disposal. The effects from the cinnamon rolls that morning had long ago worn off.

"Why don't we call it a day, and go out for an early dinner? Since I've got a feeling I'll be buying this home tomorrow, I don't care to see anymore properties. We can talk over what we saw, and maybe come up with a solution as to what I should do." It was clear that Michael loved the log house, and he felt certain Nick would like it, too.

Before the waiter of the up-scale restaurant approached their table, Michael sketched with pointed finger on the tablecloth where he thought the best location would be for his studio. "Do you know any good contractors?"

She reminded him that Marge's husband was an electrician, and was probably aware of who the best contractors in the area might be, as well as which ones to avoid. "Good, I prefer to work with people I know." Michael glanced at his cell phone again for any messages from or about Nick, and placed it back on the table.

As they were being served the main course of pan seared salmon, he said, "I'm sorry, Nan, I've done all the talking since we got here. I guess I'm just excited to have found something so fast." Again, his smile made Nancy remember one of the reasons she was so attracted to him. "Tell me what you think. Am I moving too quickly? Did you like the house? Is it possible you'd like to live there with Nick and me?"

She lifted the water glass to her lips to buy some time, and when she had regained composure she said, "I'm not sure what to say. I don't know what you mean by that."

His cheeks puffed out as he set his utensils on the plate and exhaled a long breath. "You have to realize by now that I'm very serious about you. We shared a special bond over twenty years ago, and, unless I'm mistaken, I think we still have it."

Nancy wiped her mouth with the napkin and placed it in her lap. The cloth had felt cool against her lips. "I probably don't have to tell you—I'm scared."

"I've thought about you for a long time. This isn't some overnight thing for me, and we're not kids anymore. I'm not on the rebound from Ellen's death, and I'm not just looking for a good cook, or someone to babysit Nick." He smiled, "Although I *do* remember you were an excellent cook."

"For years I wondered why you never tried to get in touch with me. When Mom told me you were married, honestly, Michael, it shocked and hurt me. Not to mention I was madder than hell at you. Eventually, I realized that I could have made the first move as well. I guess I'd really rather not rehash all this."

"But in order to move forward, I think we need to be at peace with the past." He reached over and covered her hand with his. "Nan, I didn't know what to do, so I did nothing. When I met Ellen, I thought I could leave you and what we shared behind us once and for all. If I'm being honest, I don't think I ever stopped loving you."

"I never forgot you either," Nancy whispered. "One minute I desperately wanted to talk to you, and the next, I never wanted to see you again. If I knew then what I know now..."

"If you could go back with your experience and knowledge of today, what would you change?"

"I try not to think of it, but when I do, I wonder what our lives would have been like had we chosen another restaurant, or had I done something as simple as order a different meal. Do you realize we would have a nineteen-year-old daughter and who-knows how many other children?"

"That's exactly what haunts me the most. I've always wished I could change the past. But then..."

Nancy finished the sentence for him, "But then you wouldn't have Nick."

"He's my joy." Michael studied his hands for an instant and then looked into Nancy's eyes. "Do you think there is any way we can start fresh, or will we always be picking at old wounds?"

"I think I'd like to give it a try."

"Thank God," Michael said. "So can I officially date you—no, make that exclusively date you?"

The waiter broke into their discussion when he stopped at the table to pick up empty plates. "Can I get you some dessert? We have a lovely flourless cake this evening."

Of course, it sounded fabulous to Nancy. She raised her eyebrows and smiled at Michael, who said, "I see we still share the problem of having a sweet tooth." And to the waiter he said, "That sounds great, could you also bring us some coffee, please?" He rose from his seat, "Excuse me, I'll be right back." And he headed toward the men's room.

Nancy took a quick peek at the clock on her phone, and set it next to Michael's. It was only 6:30, and she was hoping he could stop at her condo for a while. She was envisioning the two of them caught up in some hot sex, when her phone rang.

"Hello." Silence. "Hello?"

"Ummm, is Michael Gibson there?"

Nancy was horrified when she realized she'd answered Michael's phone. They had laughed when they found out they both had Androids. Apparently they had also liked the same ring tone, too. But she was more horrified when she realized that another woman was calling him. Was this the reason he'd been checking his phone so much? "Who's calling?"

"Just tell him Monique called, and wants to know if we're still getting together tomorrow while he's in town. He can call or text me any time."

"Sure." Monique? Tomorrow? Call or text any time? One thing about it, the bitch sounded eager.

Chapter 3

Michael approached the table and pulled out his chair to sit, "Anything from Nick?"

"No, nothing from Nick." *But your girlfriend called, you son-of-a-bitch.* Instead she said, "I told the waiter not to bring the cake. I want to go home." He looked hurt...*good.*

"Sure. You feeling okay?"

She glared at him. "Just take me home, please."

The ride to her condo was extremely quiet. Michael had stopped asking her what was wrong, and Nancy stared out her window fighting tears. *How could I have been so stupid? What made me think he was interested in me? I actually thought he wanted to marry me. What an idiot I am!*

He pulled into her driveway. "Can we talk?"

"No. I want to be alone."

"Okay, but I'm walking you to your door."

"My door is right there. You can watch me go inside from here."

"What has gotten into you? I thought we were having a great time—a nice dinner with good conversation. I go to the restroom, and when I get back...you hate me! What gives?"

Nancy got out of the car quickly so he couldn't see her tears, slammed the door, and ran toward her porch. Michael caught up to her and spun her around. "My God, you're crying. Please, tell me what happened? I'm not leaving until we straighten this out."

"Your girlfriend called that's what happened!" Michael pulled back and knit his eyebrows as though he was surprised. *Faker!* "She wants to know if you'll be able to see her while you're here. Oh, and she said you can call or text her anytime."

"Hold on, Nan." His voice was stern and low, "What was her name?"

"I see. You've got so many girlfriends you can't even guess which one it was! I'm an idiot to think you cared about me. I even thought you loved me. That's how stupid and desperate I am for you to want me again."

"Listen to me. I DON'T HAVE ANOTHER GIRLFRIEND. *You* are my girlfriend."

Nancy felt snot running from her nose mixing with her tears. With no tissue in sight, she used the edge of her scarf and spat at him, "Bullshit, Michael!" And then just a smidge calmer and much quieter, she said, "I'm humiliated. Please just go away, and go back to Monique."

"Monique?" he laughed, and that made Nancy even angrier. "Monique is my nephew's wife. You remember my older brother's son Jimmy?"

"He's only eight…" she stopped.

"He's not eight-years-old anymore, Nan. It's been nearly twenty years ago since you saw him. He's married to Monique, and they have two kids with another on the way. We were going to try to get a little reunion going, so Nick could see his cousins."

Oh crap – awkward. "Well, why didn't she tell me that?"

"Because she probably wondered who the hell was answering my cell phone besides me." He put his arm around Nancy, and pointed her toward the door. "And exactly why did you answer my cell phone?"

"I thought it was mine. Their ringtone is the same. Besides, you could be telling me anything. How do I know this mysterious Monique woman is really your nephew's wife?"

"If you let me inside, I'll show you her Facebook page where it clearly has me listed as Uncle Michael."

Nancy unlocked the door to her condo. "You might as well come in. I guess I owe you a chance to clear your name."

After perusing Monique Gibson's Facebook page, complete with an update status of 'Excited Uncle Mike and

Nick are in town. Welcome back to Chicago.' Nancy said, "Looks like I might have overreacted. I guess I owe you an apology."

"That's okay. Now that my name and reputation are clear, a little makeup sex will be fine with me."

"You got it."

Chapter 4

Everything Nancy would need for the next four days at Fake Quilt Camp rested in a huge pile at her front door. It turned out that all of the women would be spending the three nights at Lettie's, except for Rosa. Terry would drop her off in the morning, and pick her up when she was ready to come home. That way Rosa could relax at camp, have a little wine, and not have to drive after drinking.

Nick had loved the log house, and he especially liked the home theatre and in-ground pool. Michael made an offer through the realtor, which the owner immediately accepted. He could take possession on the first of May, and wanted to get things in order so they could move as soon as Nick finished school. He made arrangements for a fresh coat of paint on everything, and asked Bud to go over the electrical wiring and bring everything up to code. Preliminary plans were being drawn up for his studio by a contractor Bud had recommended. Michael told Nancy, "I don't want the two of us to waste any more time than we already have."

In her mind, Nancy went over and over what he said after they both looked at Monique's Facebook page, "I lost you once, and I'm not going to let that happen again." Then he pulled her in for a hug, and said, "Take this as a warning, when I move back here, I plan on being persistent. I'm still in love with you, Nancy Walsh." And then he led her to the bedroom.

Driving down the long farm lane to Lettie's house, Nancy thought how fragile Rosa had seemed when she saw her a few weeks ago at Bunco. She was impressed with the women of the Bunco Club for figuring out a solution that would allow Rosa to escape her troubles with a few days of sewing and being with friends. Rosa's idea of having Heather cook for them was brilliant. They were all chipping in for food and the chef's time, but also planned to give Heather a generous tip.

Nancy pulled into a spot close to the barn and next to Helen's car. It appeared that they were the first quilters to arrive. Opening the door to the fiber studio, the space looked huge enough for three times the amount of campers. All of Lettie's looms had been moved to the outer walls of the structure—thank goodness they were all on wheels. *This is going to be fun.*

"Hey, Girl," Helen said as she popped out a set of legs on a long table that was resting on its side. "Give us a hand with these."

Nancy set down an armload of paraphernalia, and helped with the table setup. "I brought some coffee cakes and a bunch of snack food."

"Great," Lettie said. "I thought we might set up a fifth table for snacks over by the sofa and coffee maker. I call it my 'thoughtful place', just like Winnie the Pooh. "

Nedra and Phree came through the door laughing at something and joined the others with the table and extension cord /power-strip setup. By the time the last woman arrived, Rosa with her husband Terry, the setup was complete. Marge's sewing machine was already purring away as she worked on the first of many projects.

Terry unloaded Rosa's gear from their van, and after a kiss on her cheek, he slipped out the door. "Call me when you're ready to come home." Nancy could tell he was very concerned about his wife.

Before Rosa had arrived, the other seven women discussed the best way to make her feel comfortable under the circumstances. "I think we need to say something about Ricky," Marge said. "We can't ignore him and pretend there's not a problem."

"Agreed," said Phree. "If she wants to talk about it then we talk about it—if she doesn't, we don't. We'll take our cues from her."

"And after that's out in the open, I say we treat her like we always have," Nedra said. "Somewhere in there our Rosa still exists. Let's see if we can't make her emerge a little in the next few days."

After Rosa arranged her sewing supplies at the table, Lettie said, "Anything to report about Ricky? How are you holding up?"

With a less than informative, "Nothing's changed on either front," the subject of Ricky was dropped.

In the awkward quiet that followed, Nancy informed her friends of the recent house hunting with Michael, and the foolish way she handled the Monique incident. The shift in subject was like a balm to the group, and all the women, including Rosa, joined in the Q&A session.

"It sounds serious," Lettie said. "How do you feel about it?"

Nancy exhaled, and set a small stack of pre-cut pieces to the side. She put both of her hands behind her arched neck, and let out a long moan, "Ahhhh! As always, I'm ready to move forward, but petrified at the same time. I have a comfortable routine going, and I like everything about my life except for the horrible loneliness." She asked, and then answered a question out loud, "Is it worth the compromise? I just don't know. And then, of course, there's Nick. At times I'm so scared that I just want to tell Michael I'm not interested and to please go away. But then when I'm actually with him, I don't ever want to lose him again."

"Well, one thing about it, your life will certainly change," Beth told her.

"And that's what I'm not sure about. I think I'd like having a simple relationship right now—him at his house and me at mine. We see each other when we both feel like it, but we have our own privacy when we're done."

"Sounds like dating, and it sounds real boring," Rosa said, and then surprised, no, shocked everyone when the old Rosa materialized. "Any hot sex yet?"

"Well, actually, yeah, there has been. Lots of it and it's great. But I'm not going to let fabulous sex make up my mind for me."

Nedra added kindly, "Maybe just dating is what you need to concentrate on right now. You might be putting the cart before the horse by worrying about anything more serious." Nedra looked over and smiled at her friend. "Date Michael for a while, and if it's right, you'll know it. What scares you now might not even be an issue once the two of you get into your own routine. You'll know when it's right."

"Maybe you need more time to fall in love again," Helen said.

"Oh, I don't need more time to fall in love…I'm already there."

"As far as Nick is concerned, remember one thing," Phree said, "he's not going to stay ten for the rest of your life. Time goes by fast when you mark it in kid years."

"Sooo, here's the elephant in the middle of the room," Marge said. "Do you think he wants to marry you and have another child?"

Nancy blushed beet red, and whispered, "I think so."

"And do you want that?" Again, Marge at the heart of the matter.

"I guess that's where some of the uncertainty is coming from isn't it? I think I'm afraid to be pregnant again."

Chapter 5

Extensive planning had gone into Nancy's mystery quilt, and how she would keep it a secret from her seven friends while she worked on it right in front of them. "It's obviously a sampler," Marge said when she crossed paths with Nancy at the big ironing board. "How many blocks are there?"

"Nine."

"Hmm, where did you get the pattern?"

"I don't remember," Nancy lied. "It's been in my stash for years."

"And you never peeked to the end of the pattern to see what it's going to look like?"

"I guess I've got a weakness for waiting a long time for things to develop." As she stood the iron on end, she said, "It's all yours." Marge picked up the iron to start pressing her fabric, while Nancy gave her an innocent smile and headed back to her station.

The truth was that Nancy had sweat bullets over designing this pattern. Yes, it was a sampler, but it was also much more. She had searched through her patterns, library books, designs on the Internet, and sketched and modified each block until it embodied the spirit of that particular friend. She had just finished pressing the block that represented Nedra—crisp, sharp, exact, detailed. The block had an unusual amount of pieces, and Nancy had precisely cut and sewn Nedra's favorite fabric swatch into the intricate design. This had been the most difficult block yet, but like Nedra herself, it was stunning. Back at her sewing machine, Nancy safely stowed the Nedra design with the other finished pieces. She pulled out a zippered baggie with cut fabric of the final block—Helen, the Mama Bear.

"Starting another?" Beth said. "I can't wait to see the finished top. I know mystery quilts are supposed to be a surprise until the end, but I could never do one because I'd cheat and look ahead before I sewed my first stitch."

"I'll admit it's been tempting."

By this afternoon she should have all nine blocks finished. Eight would represent the women in the Bunco Club, and the final one that she had worked on at home would be the focal point smack in the center. It was a photo transfer of the eight of them posed together. Standing in front of Marge's Christmas tree, arms around each other with laughing smiles and mugging for cameras, as spouses and friends snapped their picture. It was a flawless photo of all of them taken at a happy time (before the discovery of the missing money), and it summarized their friendship perfectly.

A cell phone rang, and while several women reached for their phone, Rosa said, "Hello." She gasped a ragged breath of air into her lungs, then another, and then two more. Her face had gone from gray to ash white, and her eyes were wild and moving rapidly from side to side. Marge jumped to her feet knocking her chair over, and raced to Rosa's side. She gently rubbed her back, and with her other hand grabbed her friend's wrist to check her pulse. Very calmly she said, "Rosa, honey, we have to slow your breathing. Slow down. That a girl, nice and slow."

Helen grabbed a bottle of water, while Phree and Nedra stood ready to catch Rosa if she passed out and fell to the floor.

"I'm sorry. Yes, this is Rosa Mitchell." Three sobs burst from deep in her chest, and Nancy could almost *see* her friend's anguish. Marge lowered her face and kissed Rosa's temple while she squeezed her hand.

"Yes, he's my son. What did he say?"

It was so quiet in the big studio that the distorted sound of a woman talking could be heard coming from Rosa's phone.

"Please tell him it's okay, and that neither of us hates him. We both love him very, very much and would be happy if he came home." Beth passed a box of tissues to Lettie who pulled one out and passed it to the next woman. There were smiles through tears around the work table, as one by one the women realized that Ricky was alive.

"Oh, yes, yes, I'd be happy to do a conference call if you can get him to agree." Rosa shared a big smile with her friends. "Can you tell me where he called from?"

Again the garbled voice.

"That's okay, I understand. Yes, email me anything that you feel might help. I can't thank you enough. I'm so grateful."

She clicked off her phone, and Rosa put her head in her hands and wept, while three of her friends encircled her in a power hug. When she raised her head, her face was red, and her eyes swollen, but Nancy thought it was the biggest smile she had seen on Rosa's face since Ricky had disappeared. "He's alive. My son is alive, and he reached out to me."

It was agreed that Marge would drive Rosa home in case she started to hyperventilate again. Once she was with Terry, the two of them would devise a plan while waiting to hear news of the impending conference call. It was unlikely Rosa would be back at Fake Camp. The call had been from the National Runaway Hotline where Ricky had requested them to forward a message to Rosa. It was only six words. "I'm sorry. Do you hate me?"

The counselor would forward his mother's answer to Ricky, and see if he'd be willing to set up a three-way conference call with a mediator. Rosa, of course, wanted to be near Terry if the call was happening soon. Nancy hoped that after this first excitement settled in, Rosa would be realistic that the call could take days, weeks, or even months if it were to occur at all.

Just as Marge arrived back at the studio, Phree said, "Okay, ladies, it's five o'clock. Put down your projects. Chef Heather awaits us in the farmhouse for dinner."

Chapter 6

Their last night at the studio arrived faster than any of the quilters could believe, and no one wanted to let go of the last precious hours of camp. Rosa had checked in earlier to report there was no word from Ricky, but that Terry and she were still optimistic.

The Bunco friends were all night owls at camp, and they worked and visited well past midnight. The wine flowed, and soon there was more talking getting done than sewing. Four of the women huddled together with handwork in Lettie's 'thoughtful place', while Helen knelt on the floor pinning together a complex quilt top. Marge sat across from Nancy lost in her thoughts, working on a baby quilt she was donating to the women's shelter. Nancy had hopes of getting a second wind.

She had finished all of the mystery quilt blocks, but told her friends there was too much work to assemble the top at camp this late at night. Pulling out another zippered bag, she began work on a table runner. The expansive studio, full of friends, felt toasty and warm. A light snow fell outside.

Thinking of her own family, Nancy remembered how she felt she never really fit in. Her mother had spent her life as an obsessive social butterfly. Adele Walsh sucked up friends and spit them out faster than the normal person could keep track. Nancy called her a friend-a-holic. Her mother remained in a constant frenzy to make more friends, and unfortunately, her younger sister followed in their mother's footsteps. Nancy thought of them as high school girls who desperately needed to be popular. They couldn't understand why Nancy seemed so content to have such a small group of friends. Looking around her at the women talking so easily, she became aware that she belonged here. She was accepted for whom she was, and she knew every last one of them would do anything for her.

While she ached to have a family, Nancy feared she was balancing on the cusp of being too old to have children. Did she want to be one of those 60+ year-old mothers with a child graduating from high school? Nancy thought to herself, "Well, Mick Jagger said it best… 'You can't always get what you want, but if you try, sometimes you get what you need.' " An odd thought struck her—did she want Michael, but need Nick? *Oh great, I* must *be sleep deprived to be taking advice from Mick Jagger.* But the reality of the three of them becoming a family played at the edges of her mind. She sighed out loud, and from the corner of her eye, she noticed Marge studying her.

"You okay?"

Good old Marge noticed everything. "Yeah, just thinking about life, and love, and family." Nancy laughed, "Nothing important."

"Nothing important—like Michael Gibson?"

"Yeah, the one and only Michael Gibson, who was supposed to leave me alone forever." Nancy stopped sewing and rested her head on her sewing machine. Looking at Marge she continued, "Almost twenty years ago, I decided I would go through life single and happy, so I shut out any hope of a husband and family. When Mom and Dad moved to Arizona, I got away from Mom always inviting me to go places with her to meet men."

"She was probably just being a mom."

"You don't know my mom. She thinks husband hunting should be an Olympic sport. Anyway, I pushed all desire of a relationship so far back in my brain, I hoped it'd never see the light of day again."

"Then you get the email…" Marge snipped the trailing thread off a sewed piece and began to press a stack of finished pink flannel blocks.

"Yeah, the email that may well have changed my life—at the very least, completely confused it. And what's the first thing I do? Lose weight for a guy I've been pissed off at for years." Nancy exhaled in exasperation, and made her lips sound like a motorboat. "Oh, Marge, I'm so confused."

"Does he know you're confused?"

"Probably not. When I'm with him, I feel great. I've told him I'm a little scared, but that's a total understatement. He came on kind of strong and talked about us being together forever and stuff like that."

"Nancy, calm down, it's okay to feel scared. Maybe you're so paralyzed with fear that you can't see the bigger picture. For goodness sakes, from what you say the guy never forgot about you. He just went house-hunting with you, and you helped him find a new home to live in with his motherless son. Maybe he got a little carried away, and maybe he's pushing too hard—but if that's the case, you need to give him a clear signal about your feelings."

"But that's the problem, Marge. I don't know what my feelings are. I can't seem to sort them out. And then this whole misunderstanding with Monique happened. I've *never* been so angry at anyone before. I was scary-angry, a hothead, a firecracker. Where did that come from? I've never been a hothead. I don't even know who I am anymore. If this is what happens when you're in love, I'm definitely not interested in going there."

"Of course that's what happens when you're in love. You find emotions you never thought you owned. You're pushed, and you push back. You take, and you give back. Just compare it to your life now. Go ahead and tell me what you felt before Michael entered the picture again."

"Well, nothing I guess. My life was simple and ..."

"Exactly," Marge interrupted. "You felt nothing. Is that really how you want to live the rest of your life—feeling nothing, day in and day out? Take the risk and live, girl.

Enjoy all that life can throw at you, and when a "Monique moment" comes up, do exactly what you did—get angry and throw something back. Have a voice, get mad, forgive, but always keep loving. It makes you strong. It makes you real." As Marge pressed the final item in her pile of pieced blocks a puff of steam escaped the iron.

Nancy studied her friend over the tops of their sewing machines. "How'd you get so fucking smart, Marge?"

There was no hesitation, no thinking it through, no aw-shucks-thanks. She simply replied, "I guess I just love a lot."

When Nancy entered her empty condo the next day, she tried to think what it might be like coming home to the log house with Michael and Nick waiting for her. She had to admit the thought was pleasing. Marge had hit the nail on the head. She wanted to be loved and to love back—to feel again. She unpacked and put most of her quilting equipment away and allowed herself to be proud of what she had accomplished as a single woman. She had paid off her condo, had great credit, and owned a busy learning clinic where she helped both kids and adults with learning disabilities.

Splashing a capful of Tide into the washer, she started a load of laundry, and then checked her work schedule for the next week. She had a full load to make-up from the days off for camp. The following week had some holes, due to one of the local schools having a spring break. It would be some welcome time off because she was hosting Bunco at her house that Wednesday, and wanted to have her mystery quilt top sewn together to show the Bunco Club. She smiled. How could she miss the other women already?

Chapter 7

Nancy fussed for the next week, concentrating on her students, finishing her mystery quilt (which she now thought of as her friendship quilt), and corresponding with Michael via email and texts. After her midnight talk with Marge, she looked forward to hearing from him, and tried to keep her irrational fears under control. She remained focused on the bigger picture, her happiness, and the power of love.

The month of March is always an unstable time for weather in the Chicago area. This past week had been unseasonably warm—one day even reaching 50 degrees. Nancy took advantage of the warmer days, and found herself outside walking off the extra calories she had consumed at camp from Heather's fabulous meals. Each day while she walked, she thought about her Bunco menu, and when she got back to her office she would scribble down another idea or two. She decided to play-up the St. Patrick's Day theme, and by Sunday night her menu was complete.

BUNCO NIGHT

Reuben Dip w/rye bread   Guacamole
Irish Soda Bread w/cream cheese & jam
Pizza Dip w/ chips   Sausage Roll-Ups
Easy Cracker Spread*   Meatballs   Caramel Crispex
Veggies and Dip
*****
Pop Water Wine
Popcorn - M & M's - mini Snickers
chocolate covered raisins
Earl Grey Decaf
Irish Cream Chocolate Cups
Sandy's Citrus Cream Cake

*recipe at back of book

Leaving the clinic around 7:30 on Monday night, she went directly to the grocery store. Nancy often stopped at the market this time of night to pick up two or three items she might need, but shopping for Bunco would be a long haul. Around 9:00 she dragged the grocery bags in her front door and quickly stuffed anything frozen into the freezer. She resisted the temptation to open the chocolate covered raisins or bag of potato chips and have just a few.

It was getting late, and Nancy was dragging. She made sure anything cold was in the fridge and left the rest in their brown paper sacks to be taken care of tomorrow after work. By 10:30 she broke down and made a small bag of low-fat microwave popcorn. She sat in front of her computer, popcorn in hand, hoping for some news from Colorado. There were two messages from Michael, and one from her mom. Nancy hesitated only a minute and opened her mother's first...saving the best for last.

Nancy,

I met a new friend yesterday at the club, and I commented on what a beautiful brooch she was wearing. *(Just like mom to call it a brooch and not a pin.)* Well, we got to talking, and she told me she has all her jewelry done by someone named Michael Gibson. I wonder, is that the same fellow you were so head-over-heels in love with in college? *(Thanks, Mom.)* Maybe you should have tried a little harder to catch him back then. *(Thanks again, Mom.)* She also told me that she just received a postcard from him saying he would be moving to the Chicago area, and be out of commission for several months until his studio was set up again. Isn't that a wonderful coincidence? Why don't you try looking him up. I always liked him. Maybe you can finally get married after all.

Love and kisses, Mom

"Can this woman be for real?" Nancy asked herself out loud.

Her mother couldn't stand Michael when Nancy had dated him. "He has no future. How is an artist," she spat out the word as though she had a mouth full of cod liver oil, "going to support you and a family?" Now she finds her newest and best friend is dripping in Michael Gibson jewelry, and he's suddenly the best thing since sliced bread—well, screw you, Mom.

Nancy pounded out a reply.

> Mom,
>
> Thanks for the update, but Michael and I have been corresponding since last August, and I've been seeing him since December. As a matter of fact, I went house-hunting with him when he came back here to find a home for himself and his son. *(That oughta shake up her bones a little!)* I'll keep you updated.
>
> Nancy

Not "Love, Nancy," just "Nancy." She clicked send and immediately felt guilty. *Tough…get over it.*

After a cleansing breath, she opened Michael's first email to find a short but pleasant, "Hi, I miss you." His second message was much newsier, a lot longer, and filled her in on his moving progress. He had started getting rid of some of their excess stuff and packing items they would need in Chicago. Among the chaos and clutter he felt certain he had made good progress. He told her there were several jewelry orders and one very special piece that he still needed to finish before he could pack up the studio. In spite of having a mild cold Nick remained in good spirits, and looked forward to the move and being near Grandma and Grandpa.

Just hearing from him and reading his email, Nancy's frame of mind had been boosted after her mother's miserable correspondence. She checked the time he had sent it—1:53 this afternoon, Mountain Time. It comforted her greatly to know that while she tutored fourteen-year-old CJ Bader this afternoon, somewhere in the mountains of Colorado the man she had fallen in love with all over again, had been thinking about her.

She wrote back an equally newsy email, updating him on her mystery quilt, Bunco preparations, and confessing that she would be glad to have her hosting duties over with for the next eight months. Michael had enjoyed the holiday Bunco and was impressed by the close friendship Nancy shared with the other women.

Tuesday morning arrived with the last gasp of winter's vengeance. The clouds were heavy with snow, and it came down in big wet flakes. Six inches were already on the ground and another four to six predicted. The good news was that warm temperatures were expected, so the snow that fell wouldn't stay around very long. But the best news was that all of the schools in the area had officially called a snow day, and she was off the hook for going to work today. A snow day at school also translated into a snow day at the clinic. She had established that rule when she first opened to avoid confusion on the parents' part—no phone calls needed to be made, it was understood.

Just like the kids she tutored, Nancy loved an unexpected snow day. She had the whole day free, and the timing couldn't be better. Taking the luxury of sipping a steaming cup of coffee in her pajamas, she went over her Bunco menu making mental notes of what needed to be done.

While preferring to spend a snow day sewing or reading a book on her Kindle, Nancy convinced herself to start the kitchen duties instead. She noticed that the snow was coming down harder, and guessed around ten inches had fallen. The snow plows and salt trucks rumbled as they passed her home. In a short time she had the ingredients chopped and creamed for the Reuben Dip, which she would stow in the fridge until about an hour before the women arrived. It would then be spooned into a hollowed-out rye bread and baked. Yum…hats off to St. Patrick. Nancy knew the Pizza Dip by heart, and she preferred this appetizer served warm in the winter months. Her menu included Guacamole simply for its lush green color.

Nancy fried a pound of Shipshewana bacon. Most of it would be for the Easy Cracker Spread, and with a few left-over slices, she would make herself a BLT for dinner. Caramel Crispex was easy to prepare, and would suffice for a sweet treat. The day's preparations were finished off by washing and slicing celery, carrots, and cucumbers. Tomorrow morning she would make the remaining treats, and the Irish Soda Bread would be prepared just in time to be warm from the oven as everyone arrived.

Cleaning up the kitchen, she started her dishwasher for the second time today, and took her BLT over to the computer. Nancy knew she shouldn't be eating this late (or this much bacon), but she felt ravenous from her long hours in the kitchen. After deleting the junk mail from her mail box, she had one email from Michael, and one from her mom. "This is getting to be a habit," she thought.

Opening Mom's email first, Nancy found what she expected—her mother in a state of shock and disbelief over Michael. Nancy loved her mom as all kids love their mother, but at the same time, it felt downright fabulous to have surprised her with the news about Michael. She knew for sure that her mother had already told half the women at the country club that her daughter and the 'famous' jeweler, Michael Gibson, were seeing each other. A few quick and guarded sentences served as a reply, and Nancy had accomplished her daughterly duty.

Michael proclaimed in his message that he thought about her all the time and wished her luck with her Bunco plans for tomorrow. He expressed how much he looked forward to moving back to Chicago and being able to see her every day. After replying with an equally love-sick note, Nancy checked her Facebook wall, and re-pinned several recipes onto her Pinterest boards. By then her BLT was long gone, and she felt exhausted. Curling up in bed, she didn't even set her alarm.

The first thought that flitted through Nancy's mind the next morning was exhilarating—by tomorrow at this time Bunco will be over. That thought alone gave her motivation to get up and get going.

Food prep went along without a hitch and by 2:00 in the afternoon, she needed only to make the icing and frost the cake. Retrieving the table and chairs from the utility room, she dusted them off before setting them up. Nancy placed the dice, bell, scorecards, and scratch paper in place at each table. Her few special serving dishes reminded her how elegant Heather's tablescape had looked last month. So she rummaged for some candles and threw a clean quilt on the table for a little extra color.

The digital read-out on the microwave said 3:00, and if she played her cards right, she could get about two hours of reading in before she needed to resume her work in the kitchen. When the doorbell rang, she realized she hadn't left the condo in two full days—that had to be some kind of record for her. Opening the door to a FedEx man, he said, "Nancy Walsh? Sign here, please."

Nancy signed the form, wondering what could possibly be in the small box. She knew she hadn't ordered anything, and even if she had, she always gave the clinic's address. Thanking the man as he handed her the box, she saw the return address of Gibson, Ltd. in the upper left-hand corner. Her breath caught in her throat—Michael.

With shaky hands, Nancy eased into a chair at the dining room table. She set the box on the table, and stared at it for a moment, drinking in the excitement of receiving a package from Michael. Then she tore at the tape and brown paper like a five-year-old with a birthday gift. Inside she found a black velvet jewelry box with a note wrapped around it. Nancy unfolded the paper, and, in Michael's handwriting, it read, "I know you've worked hard to prepare for Bunco. Here's a little something to help you have fun. L, M."

Focusing on the box in one quick flip, she snapped it open. First she gasped, and then she laughed out loud. In front of her lay a beautiful and exquisite custom-made pin (or brooch, as her mom would say). It measured about 2 ½ inches square, and appeared to be made out of gold. It read, 'The Bunco Club'. The word 'Bunco' was spelled out in gold, slightly curved downward like an arch, and encrusted with diamonds. Nestled under the arched Bunco was the word 'Club', where three thick squares of platinum dice dangled. One held a diamond in the middle, an emerald centered another, and the final a perfect ruby. Inside the box she discovered another note. This one said, "I know it's a lot on the gaudy side, but after all, what more could a true Bunco Diva want? You already have my heart."

She flipped the pin over and the engraving on the back simply read, 'to Nancy, love forever Michael.'

It took her breath away. Marge was right—it was so much fun falling in love again.

She called Michael, and spent the next hour talking and giggling like a teenager. At one point, she realized she even looked like a teenager. She lie on her bed, phone cradled to her ear, legs crossed, and feet propped on the headboard. Yikes, if she wasn't careful, she'd wake up tomorrow morning with pimples.

Chapter 8

Reluctantly, Nancy hung up from the lengthy phone call with Michael. She spent the better part of the next hour pulling out different colored tops and sweaters to see which one best showed off her new pin. She settled on a bright-red, mock turtle-neck, mohair sweater that Nedra had insisted she purchase. *The girls will die when they see this.*

Nancy almost died herself when she glanced at the clock, 5:00. If everything went on schedule, she could be pulling the Ruben Dip and Irish Soda Bread out of the oven just at 7:00. And that's exactly what was happening when the doorbell rang, and Rosa and Lettie walked in.

"Nancy, it smells wonderful in here." They started to peel off their outerwear, and Nancy walked toward them with her hand at her throat in order to cover the pin with her arm. Nedra, Phree, and Beth were right behind, with Marge and Helen pulling into the driveway.

"Just pile your coats on the chair," Nancy said. "I've got to go get something out of the oven." She turned to head toward the kitchen with a huge smile on her face. *This is going to be so much fun.*

The women congregated at the food table, and Nancy carefully kept her back to them pretending to be busy at the counter. When she knew they were all in the room, she turned to face them. It took a split second, but Helen noticed the pin first and literally shrieked. "Oooooo, *where* did you get that? It's fabulous!"

Nancy had never felt so happy as she said, "Oh, this little thing?" And the louder the seven women shrieked, the happier Nancy became. "Michael made it. I got it this afternoon."

There were murmurings, accompanied by a low whistle, and The Sarge said, "Don't even tell me that's gold and diamonds that I'm looking at."

"Yeppers, it is. It's gold, diamonds, an emerald, and a ruby, along with a touch of platinum."

"Holy Mother of God," Phree shook her head, "Where'd you find this guy?"

Nancy showed them the two notes and the inscription on the back of the pin.

Nedra said, "I never thought we'd be planning a wedding shower for one of us."

"Hold on ladies, it's just a pin, not an engagement ring." Nancy felt a hot blush start in her cheeks and travel down her neck.

"Hell," Phree said, "If you don't marry this guy, I'm gonna dibs him."

One by one the women started filling their plates and sat around the card tables while eating and talking. Every once in a while, someone would re-tell Nancy how beautiful her pin looked. Helen said, "I've got a feeling there's a lot of original, hand-made jewelry in Nancy's future."

With no prodding, Rosa offered an update on Ricky. Nancy noticed her friend didn't have the 'death stare' anymore and actually had a little color blooming in her cheeks. Rosa had not heard another word since the message she received at Fake Camp, but was still hopeful. She reported that she daily checked in with the Runaway Hotline. "These things take time."

When tummies were full to bursting, they agreed it was time to start playing Bunco. Beth said, "The winner tonight gets the pin, right?"

"Not on your life," Nancy said. "But I do have one more thing I want to show you." Nancy went into her sewing room, and came out with a folded quilt top. "Remember my mystery quilt from camp?" Before she revealed the project to the group she said, "It's not really a mystery quilt."

"I *knew* it!" Marge said. "You were holding out on us."

"Well, sort of. It's a friendship quilt I designed to honor the eight of us and how close we've become over the past years." Nancy unfolded the fabric, and held a corner in each hand. When she opened her arms and unveiled the quilt top, there was a rush of squeals and screams of approval. She backed up, laid the quilt on the floor, and then walked around it to join her friends. Several were on their hands and knees examining it closer, and she felt arms slip around her waist from both sides. Just for a fleeting moment, nothing was really clear to Nancy except for the feeling that filled the room and her heart at that instant. This was where she belonged, and where she wanted to be. Surrounded by these seven women, these friends, who were now family, and helped guide her through troubles and share her happiness. She would always—*always* do the same for them.

Clarity came back when Rosa slammed into her and embraced her in a hug. She took Nancy's face in her hands and said, "You are the best. This is perfect. We are all so lucky to have each other, and, and…you *have* to marry Michael."

"You know none of us are leaving here without a copy of this pattern," Lettie said. "As a matter of fact I think we should have a long weekend sew at my studio, and all of us work on our own copies of this beauty."

That night Nancy broke the record for the club's highest Bunco score ever. "Girl, you are on a roll today."

Over Citrus Cream Cake and Irish Cream Chocolate Cups, Nancy served Earl Grey decaf tea, and they discussed next month's Vegas trip. It would be the first week of April, Thursday through Sunday, four days and three nights. Phree said, "I'll have the travel agent email all of us the schedule for the limo pickup."

Nancy served seconds of both desserts, while Phree poured another round of tea. They talked and laughed about kids and family, love, quilting, books, and each other. They set up a date for next month's Bunco and tossed their five dollars into the box. "You know," Marge said, waving five one dollar bills in front of her, "These five dollars are the cheapest and best therapy money can buy."

"You got that right," Rosa said.

Finally, after another half hour, Lettie stretched and said, "Good God, it's nearly midnight. Why does the time go so fast when we're together?"

One by one they started to rise and slip on their coats. "Whose turn is it next?"

Marge, of course, answered, "Lettie's."

"It can't be. Didn't I just have Bunco?"

"Time flies, my dear," Helen said, and patted Lettie's shoulder. "It's been eight long months since you hosted."

"If we don't get together before, I'll see everyone the morning of Vegas," Phree said. "I'll email each of you the itinerary."

"All I can say is it's a good thing we like each other so much."

"No," Rosa said, "Make that 'loves each other so much.' "

"Well put," Marge said, as Lettie clutched the Bunco box under her arm and walked out of Nancy's door.

The Bunco Club Recipes

Lettie – Ice Cream Sandwich Dessert

-Lightly spray the bottom of a glass 9″x13″ pan with oil, so the ice cream bars won't stick to the surface.

-Layer ice cream sandwiches; the number used depends on how large a dessert you want to make. (**NOTE**: the mini-ice cream sandwiches work as well as the regular size, but might be a little more costly. Also, reduced fat can work to cut down on the fats and calories.)

-On top of the ice cream bars, spread Cool Whip and "frost" the sandwiches.

-This is where your imagination comes in! On top of the Cool Whip dribble any combination of Magic Shell chocolate, Smucker's Chocolate Fudge, Heath, etc. You can crunch up Heath Bar or Snickers or Oreos–let your ideas flow. Use caramel syrup and criss-cross with chocolate. HAVE FUN! Then top your creation with crushed nuts for a sundae taste.

-Arrange another layer starting with the ice cream sandwiches, the Cool Whip, syrups, nuts, and crushed candies of choice.

-Freeze for at least 2 hours before serving.

<u>Phree – Tomato Pie</u> / 6-8 servings

4 tomatoes, peeled and sliced
10 fresh basil leaves, chopped; <u>OR</u> 1 tablespoon dried basil
½ cup chopped green onion
1 cup grated mozzarella
1 cup grated cheddar
1 cup mayonnaise
1 tablespoon grated Parmesan or Romano cheese
Salt and pepper

----

1 (9-inch) <u>pre-baked</u> deep-dish pie shell

-Preheat oven to 350°

-Place the tomatoes in a colander or on paper towels in one layer. Sprinkle with salt and allow to drain for 30 minutes.

-Layer tomato slices, basil, and onion in cooled pie shell. Season with salt and pepper.

-Combine grated cheeses and mayonnaise together. Spread mixture on top of the tomatoes and bake for 30 minutes or until lightly browned.

-To serve, cut into slices and serve warm.

Nedra—Green Pepper Soup / 10 servings

2 pounds ground beef (ground turkey works, too)
1 28-oz. can tomato sauce
1 28-oz. can diced tomatoes, un-drained
2 cups cooked rice
2 cups chopped green pepper
2 beef bouillon cubes
1/4 cup packed brown sugar
1 1/2 teaspoon salt
1 teaspoon black pepper

-Cook rice and set aside.

-In a Dutch oven, cook ground beef (or turkey) until browned. Drain off grease.

-Add remaining ingredients and bring to a boil. Reduce heat to low. Cover and simmer until green peppers are tender, about 30-40 minutes.

(Soup thickens as it simmers and sits; if desired, add water to keep it at soup consistency. Otherwise, let it thicken, and call it a stew!)

Rosa – Pizza Dip

8 oz. Can pizza sauce
8 oz. Softened cream cheese
1 - 2 cups shredded mozzarella cheese
1 medium to large size fresh tomato, cubed
1 bunch thinly sliced green onions
Sliced black olives (1 small can, pre-sliced)

Tortilla chips

Spread cream cheese on the bottom of a pie plate.

-Layer with pizza sauce, tomatoes, green onions, mozzarella, and black olives.

-Chill.

-Set out about 30-45 minutes before serving (so chips don't break off when dipping.)

-Serve with tortilla chips.

NOTE: This appetizer can also be heated in the oven and served warm. Heat at 350° for 30 minutes or until mozzarella is melted.

Marge – Meat Balls

2 pounds of frozen/pre-cooked meatballs
1 10 oz. jar apricot preserves
½ cup barbecue sauce

-Put preserves and barbecue sauce in large saucepan. Turn heat on low.

-Add pre-cooked meatballs.

-Follow heating directions on meatball bag.

Variation: Use 14 oz. can of cranberry sauce and 12 oz. jar of chili sauce in place of preserves and bbq sauce).

Helen's Famous Scones

2 cups flour
1/3 cup sugar
1 teaspoon baking powder
¼ teaspoon baking soda
½ teaspoon salt
1 stick cold unsalted butter
½ cup dried tart cherries, or dried blueberries, or dried cranberries, or raisins
¼ cup mini-chocolate chips
----
1 large egg
½ cup sour cream
1 ¼ teaspoon almond extract

Preheat oven to 400° and line a cookie sheet with parchment paper.

I like to use a food processor for the next few steps but you don't have to.

-Add flour, sugar, baking powder, baking soda and salt to food processor and give it a quick pulse. Cut the cold butter into about 12 slices. Add sliced butter to food processor and pulse several times until the mixture resembles coarse meal. (If you chose not to use the food processor cut butter into the dry ingredients using a pastry blender.) Empty the contents of the food processor into a large mixing bowl and mix in your dried fruit of choice.

-In a small bowl whisk sour cream, egg, and almond extract until smooth. Stir mixture into ingredients in large bowl—DO NOT OVERSTIR—it will be lumpy and sticky in places. Using your hands continue to press dough to sides of bowl until the dough comes together. (With scones it is important to use a "light hand" and not over-mix or they will get tough.) Turn out onto parchment paper/cookie sheet and form into an 8″ circle about ¾ inch thick. Tope with a little sugar if desired.

-With a sharp knife cut into 8 wedges and nudge them apart about ½″. Bake 15-17 minutes—they should be lightly golden. I like to cool them on a rack covered with paper towel. Can be served warm, at room temperature, or cold; serve with jam and/or clotted/fresh sugarless whipped cream. Plain is good, too!

Beth & Heather – Artichoke Dip

1 can Artichokes, chopped into small pieces (get can with small size artichokes; 15-16 oz.)
1 cup real Mayo . DO NOT use miracle whip
1 cup grated Mozzarella Cheese
1 cup Parmesan Cheese
3/4 teaspoon garlic powder
1 teaspoon Oregano

-Mix above in bowl and put into pie pan.
-Bake 350° about 30 minutes.
-Serve with toasted onion or wheat crackers.

Nancy – Easy Cracker Spread

8 oz. Cream cheese, softened
½ pound bacon, fried crisp and crumbled
¼ cup apricot preserves

-Combine ingredients and refrigerate.
-Serve with any type of cracker or as a dip for vegetables.

Book Club Questions for *The Bunco Club*

1. How realistic was the characterization? Was there one of the eight women you would most like to meet and why? One you would rather not know and why? Did you have a favorite/least favorite chapter and did that correspond with your favorite/least favorite character?
2. Did you enjoy the point of view changing each month as the Bunco box of supplies changed hands? Why or why not?
3. Did any of the characters or their scenarios surprise you? Which ones?
4. How does the setting figure into the book? Did you feel you were experiencing the seasons and places in which the book was set? Was a particular scene memorable/vivid to you?
5. Did the actions and the situations of the characters seem plausible? Why? Why not?
6. Do you feel/understand Rosa's growing devastation about her son as the book progresses? Will Rosa and Terry's relationship survive the daily agony of a missing child? Were you surprised Ricky was still missing at the end of the book? If Rosa was your friend, what advice/help would you give her?
7. Did Marge annoy you? Was she correct to keep her firstborn a secret from her children and friends? Do you think her children should have felt more betrayed/angrier when they learned of their half-brother, or was their acceptance evidence of Marge being a good mother?
8. What more or what different could Helen have done to protect her daughter from bullying? Is there a point when enough is enough, and you remove

your child from a bullying situation at school, or do you tell them to toughen up and stick it out?

9. Was Phree's discovery of the Mayflower treasures exciting? Believable? Did you learn anything about the pilgrims or the Mayflower that you didn't already know?
10. Should Nedra continue working for *Excel Chicago*, or do you think she is ready to pursue a career as a writer?
11. Did Nancy frustrate you as much as she did the women in the Bunco Club by not being able to commit to a possible relationship with Michael? Nancy's mother was a 'piece of work', do you think she could have added to Nancy's insecurities?
12. Lettie appears to have it 'all together'. Do you think she has a weak spot that she is keeping hidden even from herself? Is she an odd match as best friend to Rosa, or do their personalities complement each other? Do you have a good friend who is your complete opposite?
13. Do you know anyone who exhibits hoarding issues? Are they mild or full blown? Is Beth's situation under control as long as she can stay organized, or does she still have a problem that needs to be addressed? Do you think her husband will figure out what she is doing, and what do you think his reaction will be?
14. Did the book end the way you expected? Were you disappointed, surprised, or happy when you reached the end of the book? Did you want the stories of the women to keep going? Would you read a sequel?
15. Would you recommend this book to other readers?

Karen DeWitt holds an MFA in studio art and has attended several workshops at the Iowa Summer Writing Festival. She is also a member of a Bunco Club that has been together for more than twenty years. Karen lives in the Chicago suburbs with her husband.

If you are interested in communicating with Karen or would like her to visit your book club through Skype, contact her at KarenDeWitt7@gmail.com or by visiting her blog at **KarenDeWittAuthor.blogspot.com.**

45975673R00228

Made in the USA
Lexington, KY
18 October 2015